the
Book of
BLOOD&
SHADOW

The Book of BLOOD & SHADOW

ROBIN WASSERMAN

www.atombooks.net

ATOM

First published in the United States in 2012
First published in Great Britain in 2012 by Atom

Grateful acknowledgment is made to Susan Reynolds for permission to reprint
her previously published translation of the poetry of Elizabeth Jane Weston.

Grateful acknowledgment is made to Indiana University Press for permission
to reprint an excerpt from *Petrarch: The Canzoniere*, translated by Mark Musa,
copyright © 1996 by Mark Musa. All rights reserved.
Reprinted by permission of Indiana University Press.

A CIP catalogue record for this book
is available from the British Library.

ISBN 978-1-907411-44-1

Printed in Great Britain by Clays Ltd, St Ives plc

Papers used by Atom are from well-managed forests
and other responsible sources.

MIX
Paper from
responsible sources
FSC® C104740

Atom
An imprint of
Little, Brown Book Group
100 Victoria Embankment
London EC4Y 0DY

An Hachette UK Company
www.hachette.co.uk

www.atombooks.net

For Susan Curry, and a lost language

All things that move between the quiet poles
Shall be at my command. Emperors and kings
Are but obey'd in their several provinces,
Nor can they raise the wind, or rend the clouds;
But his dominion that exceeds in this
Stretcheth as far as doth the mind of man!
A sound magician is a mighty god.

༄ *The Tragical History of Doctor Faustus*
Christopher Marlowe

PART I

The Blood-Dimmed Tide

*Now I want
Spirits to enforce, art to enchant;
And my ending is despair,
Unless I be relieved by prayer.*

The Tempest
William Shakespeare

1

I should probably start with the blood.

If it bleeds it leads and all that, right? It's all anyone ever wants to know about, anyway. What did it look like? What did it feel like? Why was it all over my hands? And the mystery blood, all those unaccounted-for antibodies, those faceless corkscrews of DNA—who left them behind?

But beginning with that night, with the blood, means that Chris will never be anything more than a corpse, bleeding out all over his mother's travertine marble, Adriane nothing but a dead-eyed head case, rocking and moaning, her clothes soaked in his blood, her face paper white with that slash of red razored into her cheek. If I started there, Max would be nothing but a void. Null space; vacuum and wind.

Maybe that part would be right.

But not the rest of it. Because that wasn't the beginning, any more than it was the end. It was—note the brilliant deductive reasoning at work here—the middle. The center of gravity around which we all spiraled, but none of us could see. The center cannot hold, Max liked to say, back when things were new and quoting poetry seemed a suitably ironic way to declare our love. Things fall apart.

But things don't just fall apart. People break them.

2

In the beginning was the Book.

"Seven hundred years old." The Hoff slammed it down so hard the table rattled. "Imagine that."

Apparently noting our lack of awe, he dropped a liver-spotted fist onto the book with nearly as much force. "Do so now." He swiveled his head to glare at each of us in turn, neck veins bulging with the effort. "Close your eyes. Imagine a scribe in a dark, windowless room. Imagine his quill, scratching across the page, transcribing his secrets—his God, his magic, his power, his blood. Imagine, for just one moment, that *you* will be the one to reach across the ages and make this manuscript yield its treasure." He drew a baby-blue handkerchief from his breast pocket and hocked a thick wad of phlegm into its center. "Imagine what it might be like if your sad, small lives were actually worth something."

I closed my eyes, as ordered. And imagined, in glorious detail, the tortures I would impose on Chris as soon as we escaped from this musty dungeon of mad professors and ancient books.

"Trust me," Chris had said, promising me a genial old man with twinkling grandfather eyes and a Santa laugh. The Hoff was, according to Chris, a bearded marshmallow, hovering on the verge of senility, with little inclination to force his research assistants to show up on time, or, for the most part, show up at all. This was supposed to be my senior-year gift to myself, a thrice-weekly escape from the ever-constricting halls of Chapman Prep into the absentminded bosom of ivy-covered academia, a string of lazy afternoons complete with snacking, lounging, and the occasional nap. Not to mention, Chris had pointed out as my pen hovered over the registration form, "the opportunity to spend quality time with your all-time favorite person, otherwise known as me." Not that this was in short supply, as his freshman dorm was about a hundred yards from my high school locker. The only problem with the dorm was having to put up with the presence of his roommate, who resolutely kept himself on his side of the room while keeping his owlish eyes on us.

And now that same roommate stared at me from across the table, the final member of "our intrepid archival team." Another detail Chris had conveniently neglected to mention. Chris assured me that Max didn't *intend* to be creepy, and was, when no one else was watching, almost normal. But then, Chris liked everyone. And his credibility was slipping by the minute.

The Hoff—Chris had coined the nickname last year, when he'd been the one whiling away his senior year with the get-out-of-jail-free pass commonly known as supervised independent study—passed around the Book. "Decades' worth of experts have tried to crack the code," he said as we flipped through page after page of incomprehensible symbols. More than two hundred pages of them, broken only by elaborate illustrations of flowers and animals and astronomical phenomena that apparently had no counterparts in the real world. "Historians, cryptographers, mathematicians, the NSA's best code breakers gave it all they had, but the Voynich manuscript refused to yield. *Mr. Lewis!*"

We all flinched. The Hoff snarled, revealing a mouthful of jagged teeth, sharp as fangs and—judging from his expression—soon to be applied to a similar purpose. *"That is not how one handles a valuable book."*

Max, who had been rifling through the pages like it was a flip-book, rested his hands flat on the table. Behind his glasses, his eyes were wide. "Sorry," he said quietly. Aside from the soft "Hi" I'd gotten when we were introduced, it was the first time I'd heard him speak.

I cleared my throat. "It's not a valuable book," I told the Hoff.

5

"It's a *copy* of a valuable book. If he ruined it, I'm sure he could scrounge up the twenty bucks to pay you back."

The real thing, with its crumbling seven-hundred-year-old pages and fading seven-hundred-year-old ink, was safely ensconced in a Yale library, eighty miles to the south, where faculty didn't have to settle for high-school-age researchers or cheap facsimiles. The Hoff closed his eyes for a moment, and I suspected he was putting his own imagination to the test, pretending away whatever scandal had stripped him of his Harvard tenure and dumped him here to rot at a third-rate college in a third-rate college town for the rest of his academic life.

Thanks, Max mouthed, an instant before the Hoff opened his eyes and resumed his glare.

"All books are valuable," the professor said. But he didn't press it.

I decided the roommate wasn't so bad when he smiled.

The meeting lasted for another hour, but the Hoff gave up on his dreamlike rambling and instead stuck to logistics, explaining his significant research and our minimal—"but absolutely essential!"—part in it. He'd just weaseled a collection of letters out of some wealthy widow, and was convinced they contained the secret to decoding the Book. (It was always the *Book* when he spoke of it, capital *B* implicit in the hushed voice, and we followed suit, ironically at first, then later out of habit and grudging respect.) Max and Chris would be put to work indexing and translating the bulk of the collection, searching for clues. I, on the other hand, was assigned a "special" project all my own.

"Most of the letters are written by Edward Kelley," the Hoff explained. "Personal alchemist to the Holy Roman emperor. Many believe he authored the Book himself. But I believe his contribution is both lesser and greater. I think he got his hands on it, and

6

solved it. And now we will follow in his footsteps." He pointed at me. "Ms. Kane."

"Nora," I said.

"Ms. Kane, you will deal with the letters written by Kelley's daughter, Elizabeth Weston, which seem to have found their way into the collection by mistake. I doubt they contain anything of use, but nonetheless, we must be thorough."

Unbelievable. I could translate twice as fast and three times as accurately as Chris could, and if the Hoff had even bothered to glance at my Latin teacher's recommendation, he'd know it. "Is this because I'm a woman?"

Chris snorted.

"I can take the Elizabeth letters if Nora doesn't want them," Max said. "It's okay with me."

Thank you, I would have liked to mouth, returning the favor, but the Hoff was watching. And his face was a storm cloud. "*I* mind. This kind of work requires a certain . . . maturity. Elizabeth's letters will give Ms. Kane ample practice in historical translation while the two of you help me with the real search."

Admittedly, if you'd asked me five minutes earlier, I would have said I didn't care whether I was translating important letters, pointless letters, or a sixteenth-century grocery list. But then the Hoff opened his big, fat, sexist, ageist—whatever *-ist* was conscribing me to uselessness—mouth.

"So it's because I'm in high school?" I added. "You know, it's not fair to judge me based on—"

"Do you want to be a member of this team or not, Ms. Kane?"

I could have enlightened him on the difference between *want* and *need*, as in *wanting* to be at Adriane's house mopping up her latest micro-drama, or in Chris's dorm room watching TV (or at least trying to, while pretending not to notice Chris and Adriane making out behind me and Max doing his spook stare from across the room), basically *wanting* to be anywhere else, but *needing* the credits for graduation and the bullet point for my college applications.

"I do, Professor Hoffpauer."

"Good." He stood up and, with stiff, awkward contortions, folded himself into a bulky wool topcoat. "The collection will be waiting here for you tomorrow afternoon. Christopher has a key to the office and will show you proper document-handling protocol."

"The archive's not being housed in the rare-books library?" Max asked.

"As if I'd let that harpy get her hands on these?" the Hoff said. He narrowed his eyes. "Not a word to her about this. Or to anyone, for that matter. I won't have someone taking this away from me. They're everywhere, you know."

"Who?" Max asked. Chris just shook his head, knowing better.

"Young man—" The Hoff lowered his voice and leaned toward Max, casting a shadow across the Book. "You don't want to know."

It was a close call, but we managed to hold our laughter until he was out of the room.

3

It's funny how one thing leads you to another, and another, until you end up in the exact place you're not supposed to be. If it weren't for Chris, I'd never have ended up in the Hoff's lair, facing down the Book; if it weren't for Chapman Prep, there would have been no Chris, or at least no Chris-and-me. And if it weren't for "wild delinquent Andy Kane" getting wasted, stealing a car, and plowing it into a tree with "much-beloved local beauty

8

Catherine Li" and, "in one tragic moment," turning them both into drunken roadkill (reportage courtesy of that bastion of objectivity, the *Chapman Courier*), I'd never have set foot in Chapman Prep. Put another way: If my brother had managed to keep his hands off Catherine Li, Catherine Li's booze, and Catherine Li's father's Mercedes, Chris probably wouldn't be dead.

Funny.

4

Chris is dead.

It's ridiculously easy to forget. Or at least to imagine away. Sometimes, at least.

5

Until the September I turned fifteen—the September I enrolled in Chapman Prep—my life could be divided pretty neatly into two eras. Before Dead Brother; After Dead Brother. BDB, I was the youngest in a family of four, father a Latin professor, mother a part-time bookstore manager, both of them teetering on the edge of divorce but sticking together, in that noble tradition of postboomer bourgeoisie, *for the kids*. ADB, there were still four of us, it was just that one—the only one anyone cared about anymore—happened to be dead.

Not that my parents went crazy. No alcoholism, no untouchable shrines, no unused place settings at the dinner table, no fortunes spent on séances and psychic hotlines, and definitely no elaborate gothic madness of ghostly hallucinations, midnight keening, bumps in the night, or any of that. There was the time, a few months after it happened, that my mother took the pills. But we don't talk about that.

9

No, for the lion's share of ADB, we were a resolutely normal family without even the expected residual dusting of crazy. We visited his grave with appropriate frequency. We repurposed his room within an appropriate number of months. We reminisced with an appropriate level of misty-eyed regret. And we didn't talk about the time with the pills, any more than we talked about my father losing his job because he refused to leave the house or my mother transforming herself into an administrative assistant, the only one in the state of Massachusetts who worked twenty-four hours a day, because apparently even typing up loan applications for an obese bank manager who liked to play secretarial grab-and-seek was preferable to being home. ADB, I got extremely proficient in listening at doorways, which is the only way I learned about the third mortgage they'd taken on the house. It confirmed my suspicions: BDB, they may have been staying together for the sake of the children, but ADB, they were staying together for Andy. More specifically, for the dead Andy who lived in the stucco walls he'd scratched with his sixth-grade bike and the hardwood floors he'd mutilated with his third-grade candle-making kit, and every other scuff, wound, and scar fifteen years of casual destruction had left behind. Imminent bankruptcy and domestic discord or not, neither doting parent would ever leave him behind. I came along with the package.

As much fun as it was at home ADB, school was even better. Under the best of circumstances, middle school is a sixth-circle-of-hell situation, sandwiched somewhere between flaming tombs and flesh-eating harpies. It's the kind of situation that doesn't need gasoline on the fire, especially when said gasoline comes in the form of your older brother murdering the older sister of the third-most popular girl in school. Jenna Li's grief was glamorous. She was a glossy-eyed tragic figure, a damsel in distress with girls fighting over who got to stroke her hair and hold her hand and

10

ply her with comfortingly double-stuffed Oreos. Whereas I didn't cry, I didn't have silky hair, and my brother was a murderer. A drunken idiot of a murderer who wasn't around to blame. It didn't exactly boost me up the social ladder.

Only one constant spanned the chasm between the two eras, and that was Latin. Other five-years-olds practiced piano or took ballet; I memorized declensions and recited mnemonics. Andy rebelled when he was nine and forged our parents' signatures on the permission slip for after-school soccer, but I played the good girl and went along with it, three afternoons a week, *amo, amas, amat*. Whether because I liked the attention, because I was too big a wuss to say no, or because I couldn't resist the opportunity to make my brother look bad, I don't remember. But it certainly wasn't because I liked Latin.

Then Andrew did his thing. And my father stopped leaving the house. Stopped, for the most part, leaving his office, where he hypothetically was burrowed in with nebulous translation projects but was more frequently—we knew but never acknowledged—doing crossword puzzles, ignoring bills, or cradling his head in his hands and staring sightlessly at the family photo on the corner of his desk. He rarely came out and even more rarely let us in, but the door still opened for Latin lessons, and, for that one hour a day, three times a week, the invisible man became visible—or maybe I became invisible, and therefore tolerable. We hunched over the translations, speaking of nothing but a tricky indicative or an ablative that should have been locative, and sometimes, especially when I got good enough to race him to the answer and occasionally win, he rested a hand on my shoulder.

It would have been pathetic if I'd stuck with it just to wring a few drops of parenting from dear old absentee dad, and so I told myself it had nothing to do with him, or us, or Andy, who watched all our lessons from that photo on the corner of the desk,

11

his smugly upturned lip seeming to say that he knew what I was doing, even if I wouldn't admit it. I told myself it was the language that drew me in, the satisfaction of arranging words like mathematical constructs, adding and subtracting until a solution dropped out. Self-delusion or not, it stuck. Latin became my refuge, until the September I turned fifteen, the September I woke up and found myself the same age as my older brother, when it became my salvation.

6

Chapman is still authentically small-town enough to have a right and wrong side of the tracks, although in this case, the tracks are a Walmart. Our house, along with the cheap gas station, the check-cashing depot, and the so-called park, which had more used condoms and broken meth pipes than it did trees, lay on the southern side. Chapman Prep—a palatial stone idyll adjacent to the college campus and in easy walking distance of two Italy-certified gelateria, three high-end stationery stores, four yuppie baby-clothes outposts, and a candle-making shoppe with twice-daily do-it-yourself demonstrations in the back—was comfortably ensconced in the north. And never the twain would have met, were it not for the application I sent for in desperation, the scholarship for local students with excessive need, and Latin placement test scores that—I found out later—had the classics teacher drooling all over his copy of the *Aeneid* and the dean of discipline convinced I'd found a way to scrawl the contents of a Latin-English dictionary on the bottom of my Converse. The acceptance arrived in April, the scholarship money landed in July, and in September my parents pretended to be proud as I headed out for my first day as a Chapman Prep sophomore.

So I was the new girl, at a school where there hadn't been a

12

new girl in two years, and that went about how you'd expect. Fortunately I wasn't in the market for friends. All I'd wanted was a place where no one knew me and no one knew Andy—which might have been why, during the first obligatory small-talk exchange with a girl in my chem class, I said I was an only child.

It just popped out.

I saw my mother hit with it once, not long after it happened. Just some guy in line at the bank, trying to be polite. "How many children do you have?" For a few seconds, my mother did her fish-mouth thing—open shut open—and then the tears started leaking out. The guy felt so guilty he offered my mother a job, and the rest is secretarial history.

I didn't cry. I smiled at the blond girl whose name I couldn't remember and said, "No sisters, no brothers, just me," and then she started complaining about her twin baby sisters and their tendency to drool all over her homework, and that was the end of it. People don't ask questions because they care about the answers. They're only talking to fill up the silence.

I didn't notice the guy sitting at the lab table behind us— which is to say, I noticed him, because even on day one it was clear this was the kind of guy you noticed, but I didn't notice he was listening.

I noticed him again, shadowing me in the hall as I tried to find my way from chemistry to Latin, and then again, passing into the classroom in step with me and grabbing a seat next to mine. Admittedly, the odds were working in my favor on this front, since the loose semicircle contained only five chairs, but the rest were empty, so he could have sat anywhere. It required conscious and vaguely incomprehensible effort to plant himself next to the new girl with cheap jeans, a pancake chest, and hair that defied any description but mousy brown. I told myself I deserved some good luck, overlooking the fact that it would call for substantially

13

more than luck to thrust me into one of those narratives where plain-Jane new girl catches the eye of inexplicably single Prince Charming, because somehow the new school has revealed her wild, irresistible beauty, of which she was never before aware.

Spoiler alert: Chris had a girlfriend. An endless string of them, in fact. Which I guessed from the way he leaned back in his chair, slinging a long arm over the empty one next door, the posture of a guy who's used to having someone to hold on to. So I adjusted the fairy tale to accommodate a damaged Prince Charming who distracted himself from his pain by dating girls unworthy of him, unconsciously reserving himself for his true love and savior— namely, me—and smiled.

"Nora, right?" he said.

I nodded. His eyes were a deep brown, several shades darker than his face, and I suspected they'd be well suited to the purpose of gazing lovingly, if, hypothetically, such a need ever came up.

"Andrew Kane's sister?"

I stopped smiling.

"Chris." He tapped his chest, then waited, as if he'd forgotten his line and was expecting me to fill it in for him. When I didn't, he added, "Chris Moore? JFK Middle? I was in sixth when you were in fifth." He paused again. "Andy helped coach my soccer team."

I made a noise, a *hmm* or an *um*, and wondered how long I could keep from having to respond. I remembered him now, dimly, as one of the many to make out with Jenna Li behind the cafeteria, and it seemed suddenly possible that she'd spread her minions across the globe—or at least the town—with orders to deliver her revenge.

"He was cool," Chris said. Then, "Sorry. About what happened. That must have sucked."

Another *hmm*.

"I moved cross town that year," he said. "That's probably why

14

you don't remember me. Been at Prep ever since. So what do you think of it so far?"

I shrugged.

"Hey. Listen. It's probably none of my business, but . . ."

I steeled myself.

"I heard what you said to Julianne." He must have caught my brow furrow at the name. "In chem class?" he added. "When she asked about brothers or sisters? That's when I recognized you. And you told her . . ." He hesitated, picking at the stiff cuff of his button-down shirt, preppy even for Prep. "Actually, I was right the first time. None of my business." He reached out a hand. "Better idea. New school, new start, right? Meeting again for the first time. Chris Moore."

I took his hand, shaking it firmly. "Nora Kane."

We were still locked together when a ridiculously pretty girl—long black hair, almond-shaped eyes, long legs jutting from a short skirt, the works—danced through the door, dropped to her knees before us, and propped her elbows on Chris's desk. "So, what are we talking about?"

"Filling New Girl in on the highs and lows of life at Prep," Chris said. I realized I'd been holding my breath. But he passed the test. "I warned her there's still time to go back where she came from, but she refuses to listen. You want to tell her?"

The girl laughed. "I think you've just met the low." She gave Chris the kind of light shove you deploy when you're looking for an excuse to touch someone. "Now meet the high."

I'd never understood girls like her—as in, literally couldn't comprehend how they achieved perfection by seven a.m., hair sleek and dry, lip gloss and mascara and foundation and the variety of cosmetics of whose existence I remained unaware masterfully applied, accessories matched to sartorial selection matched to freshly polished nails. Whereas I inevitably showed up to school late, with

15

tangled, wet, and, several months of the year, frozen hair tucked
into a lopsided bun, my socks mismatched, and, on truly special
occasions, some hastily applied drugstore foundation that couldn't
disguise the fact that my nose was slightly too big for my face. My
mother had once thought it would be comforting to explain that
beauty—and the grace and confidence that nurture it—requires
money. She added no maternal assurances about natural beauty,
true beauty, or inner beauty and which, if any, I might possess,
while I elected not to point out that money wasn't the only thing I
didn't have. A mother who bothered to show me how to put on eye
shadow might also have come in handy.

"Adriane Ames," Chris said as the remaining two students filtered into the classroom and grabbed seats. "Feel free to disregard
ninety percent of everything she says."

"And the other ten?" I asked.

"Pure genius. Or so she tells me."

"I also tell him to get a haircut," she said, brushing manicured
fingers across the tight curls that were blossoming into an Afro.
"But does he listen?"

I liked his hair. "Clearly that fell into the ninety percent," I
said. "The odds really aren't in your favor."

She laughed again, a surprisingly abrasive sound for such a
delicate frame. Her voice was musical, but her laugh was pure
noise. "She's cute," Adriane said. "Can we keep her?"

They could; they did.

7

Chris never told anyone about Andy, and neither did I. As if
knowing that he knew meant I could pretend it had never happened, because it wasn't really lying if Chris knew the truth.

He wasn't with Adriane, not then. But he was at the top of her

16

agenda and, as quickly became clear, items on the agenda never lay fallow for long. It turned out he was the reason she'd taken advanced Latin in the first place; I was the reason she passed it. That's where it happened, somewhere in between declensions and Lucretian soliloquies and cheesy "Ancient Romans Go to Market" skits, Chris and I fell in like, and Chris and Adriane—with my Cyranoesque assistance—fell in love. So I had a best friend and soon, by virtue of the transitive property of social addition (girl has best friend plus best friend has new girlfriend equals girl has new best friend, *quod erat demonstrandum*), I had two. Chris and I got Adriane through advanced Latin, Adriane and I got Chris through remedial chem, the two of them got me through the new-girl phase with a minimum of muss and fuss, and for two years we were, if no happier than the average high school student juggling APs and SATs and extracurriculars and defective parents, at least not miserable, and not alone. Then Chris went to college (albeit, via the path of least resistance, down the street), I found Max, we all found the Book, and everything went to hell.

8

E. I. Westonia, Ioanni Francisco Westonio, fratri suo germano S.P.D., the first letter began. *E. J. Weston, to her brother John Francis Weston, greetings.* There were about thirty of them, crumbling parchment pages bound together with fraying twine. They were in random order, some dated, some not, all to the same person. I wondered if he was the one who'd given her the dusty edition of Petrarch's *Il Canzoniere* that had been stored with the letters, rotting in some Boston attic for a century and presumably a European attic for the centuries before that. It was the first time I'd ever seen anything so old, much less been allowed to touch it. The paper was rough under my finger, but delicate, and I realized how easily I could tear it—or crush it or burn it; I could destroy it in any number of ways. I'd felt a similar rush at the Grand Canyon—the first and last time we'd attempted a family vacation in our newly diminished family form—standing at the edge of nothing, knowing what would happen if I took one more step. Not that I was tempted, but there was power in the possibility. It's not often that you get the opportunity to casually destroy something of value. When you're a kid, there's always a new tower of blocks to knock over, another Barbie to microwave. When you grow up, they take away your toys.

It turned out Elizabeth Weston was seventeen years old in 1598, when she'd written most of the letters—already more than halfway through her life. She'd lost her father when she was a baby and gained a new one in Edward Kelley, alchemist, scholar, charlatan, and all-around ne'er-do-well. He dragged her from England to Prague, treated her to a few years of luxury and frolic at the imperial court, then screwed over the wrong person and got himself walled up in a middle-of-nowhere stone tower for the brief rest of his life—and once again, lucky Elizabeth came along for the ride. She whiled away the rest of her childhood in a crappy house near the foot of the prison tower, ferrying messages, gifts, and presumably the occasional filial affection to her imprisoned stepfather.

The whole affair had an appealing air of gothic intrigue, with all the makings of a Shakespearean tragedy or at least—if you threw in a lonely stable boy or trustworthy prison guard—a trashy romance novel. But it didn't change the fact that, as far as the Hoff was concerned, she was a nonentity, which made my translations busywork, leaving me somewhat less than eager to, as he put it, drown myself in history.

But I did what I was there to do. I followed protocol with the letters, touching them as infrequently as possible to preserve them from my skin's oils, careful never to bend or fold or wrinkle, locking them away each night in the Hoff's private safe, six inches of steel protecting them from evil librarians, or whatever other nemeses he imagined lurking beyond his walls. And one *mi frater* and *magnifico Parente* at a time, I translated.

Greetings. I fear my letters of late have been too full of heartache and grievance. But these months have been hard, dearest brother. Harder than I allowed you to know. You will think it strange that I miss such a hostile home, our Father's tower, dark and dank, and its outbuildings, the walls so thin I feared my blood would turn to ice. But even a prison can be a home, when there is food, when there are walls to guard against the night, when there is a father like our Father watching over us. Now he is gone, and with him, our sorry home. Though it may be madness, I miss them both.

That much should have taken me less than an hour, including the twenty minutes needed to transcribe the Latin into my notebook and mark unfamiliar words and confounding verb forms—the dull but soothing warm-up to translation itself, like practicing scales on the piano before moving on to Mozart. But the transcription took two hours, and the single paragraph another two after that. I blamed Chris and his attention deficit disaster, but admittedly, no one forced me to help him cheat at solitaire or plot out a senior-class prank or remember the words to all the theme songs to the Friday-night TV lineup of our youth.

"The thumb wars were *your* idea," he pointed out when I called him a bad influence. "And what about now? I'm sitting here, hard at work, and you're the one distracting *me* with these ridiculous complaints about—"

"Hard at work?" I peered over his hunched shoulders. "You're making paper airplanes."

He shrugged. "It's a dirty job, but someone's got to do it."

19

The Hoff's office was nothing like the beige oversized cubicle my father had once inhabited in the humanities building across the quad. The Hoff's tenure meant the school could never fire him, but they could and did usher him into emeritus status and strip him of luxuries like photocopiers, Wi-Fi connections, and doors. As penance for his encroaching senility, they'd stuck him in a side chapel of the decaying Trinity Cathedral, which had been out of use since the modern and airy egalitarian church was erected on the other side of the main quad. Now Trinity's nave and quire were used for the occasional Phi Beta Kappa induction or faculty tea party, while its ancillary chapels had been divided up into professorial overflow offices. So far, it seemed, the Hoff was the only overflow.

Our work space was a large mahogany table in the center of the room, only a few feet away from the Hoff's usually abandoned desk, stacked high with teetering towers of journals, conference papers, and departmental memos that inevitably went unread. There was no door, just a long, narrow tunnel that led into the main worship area. The Elizabeth and Kelley letters, along with a collection of materials the Hoff had "liberated" from the library and its barbarian overseers, were housed in a large safe in the far corner, to which Chris had somehow charmed him into giving us the combination. Beside the safe was a fraying gray couch with sagging cushions and a faint smell of dog, and this was where the Hoff, when he showed up at all, usually took his seat and then, promptly, his nap. In the Hoff's frequent absence, Chris claimed possession, often paying tribute with a nap of his own.

But that first day, Chris managed to stay awake for the duration, distracting me and drawing occasional disapproving looks from Max, who sat at the end of the table, shoulders bowed, eyes squinted behind the wire-rimmed glasses, index finger tracing line after line of cramped alchemical gibberish. He stopped short of shushing us, but otherwise, the punctilious librarian imitation was complete. I caught a distinct sigh of relief when Adriane showed up to drag Chris away, ostensibly to work on her college essay but presumably to take more interesting advantage of his empty dorm room.

"Pencils down, time up," Chris said, shutting my notebook for me. "You're coming, too."

I shook my head. "Not tonight."

"You have a better offer?"

"Oh, let's see, a glamorous and exotic evening chez Kane, complete with calculus, physics, and some thrilling adventures in Latin translation, because thanks to someone, this afternoon was a complete waste of my time."

"'Someone' sounds dastardly. Point me toward him, I'll beat him up for you."

"He's not so bad," I said.

Chris batted his eyes.

"Though rearranging his face might improve things a bit, so if you think we should give punching a try . . ."

He turned to Adriane. "Do you hear how she talks to me? Can I help it that I'm handsome and charming and irresistible and no girl can say no to me?"

"Nora doesn't seem to have a problem with it," Adriane said. Then kissed him, full on, rising on her toes and kicking up her leg like a black-and-white-movie damsel in desire. "Lucky for me."

"Let's test it out," I said. "*No,* I am not hanging out with you tonight." I paused to take stock. "That wasn't particularly traumatic. Think it was a fluke? No, no, no thank you, no. Easy enough."

Chris grabbed me around the waist, plucking me effortlessly out of the chair and off my feet. He spun me around as I kicked and flailed and shook with laughter. "Help me show this one the error of her ways," he told Adriane.

"Chris, let her be. If she wants to go home . . ."

21

"How could she want to go home when she's got such a better option?" He was still dangling me a few inches above the ground, despite my halfhearted efforts to extricate myself. I was laughing too hard to be of much use. "Come on, you grab her legs, we'll carry her back with us."

Adriane didn't move.

"Now is the time you put me down," I told him, trying to catch my breath.

"As you wish, milady." He deposited me gently back on my feet. "See? Not so hard to say, 'Yes, whatever you want.'"

"So apparently *I'm* irresistible."

"I knew we had something in common," he said.

"You know he won't stop until you give in," Adriane said. "You should come over. We can watch a movie or something."

It was tempting—of course, oral surgery might have been tempting in comparison to what awaited me that night and every night, the empty house, the closed doors, the people unseen and the words unspoken. There was a reason I spent so much time shuttling between Adriane's house and Chris's dorm room. But there was such a thing as too much. He was my best friend; she was my best friend. So maybe I spent too much of my time with them worrying that they were both waiting for me to leave. But sometimes, just in case, I did.

"I really can't," I told him. "Not tonight."

"You work too hard," Chris said, giving me a light shove.

I waved the nearly blank notebook at him. "All evidence to the contrary."

"You sure?" he asked.

I nodded and, as they wove their fingers together and left me behind, tried to look like I'd won something, no matter how much it felt like the opposite.

"That must be weird for you." They were the first words Max

22

had spoken all day. His voice was low and reedy and not altogether unpleasant.

"What?" Mine was hostile. It was one thing for me to feel like an unwanted tagalong—it was another for someone else, a virtual stranger, to confirm the suspicion.

"Nothing." He turned back to his work and didn't look up as I packed my stuff and bundled myself against the chilly October night. Nor did he look up when he said, as if speaking to his ancient pages, "Get home safe."

I always did.

9

Chris was right, I did work too hard, but only because it was an effective way of making the time at home pass with a minimum of musing, remembering, regretting, and a variety of other unappealing activities that the sight of my brother's fading kindergarten paintings, my mother's hastily scrawled notes about missing dinner, again, or my father's closed door was apt to provoke. Even if I hadn't felt at least marginally guilty for slacking off all afternoon, I might have started with the Latin, because translating narrowed the world down to a single page, a line, one word at a time. It was exactly as absorbing as I needed it to be.

I will not tell you of our journey.

We have survived, that is all you need know. We hid when hiding was needed, we ate when we could and starved when we could not. We have arrived tired and penniless, filthy and weak, clothed in the shame of our condition and our need. But we have arrived, dearest brother. We have returned. I had begun to fear Prague was nothing but a dream. Now I know it to be real, and I believe it to be a new beginning.

23

I swear to you now, fear and grief will not win out. Our Mother needs me, and I will neither fail her nor shrink from the burden. There is little need for the regret you express in your letters, as your schooling is paramount. It is for you to uphold the family name and glory, and for me to tend to domestic matters, our property, our home, our Mother. We have secured temporary lodging, and surely it is only a matter of time before I can persuade the Emperor to relinquish our possessions. In times of greatest hopelessness, I have my letters from you to keep me afloat, and I have my poetry. Of course I know it to be little more than a trifle. But you know better than anyone how my soul indulges in its dreams, and I will admit, only to you, that there are nights when I lie awake and imagine myself Ovid reborn. The poems are nothing but words, as your letters are nothing but words, ink on parchment, and yet words continue to save me. I trust you read this in good health, and with full knowledge of my continued love for you.

Farewell.

15 August 1598 Prague.

She didn't blame him for leaving her; she didn't allow herself to blame him, because leaving was a brother's job. I understood more than I wanted of the things going on inside a dead girl's head. A home that felt like a prison, an exile that was simultaneous punishment and relief. The determination, in spite or because of the fact that she had nothing left—a useless mother, an invisible father, an absent brother—to keep moving forward and do what needed to be done.

I allowed myself about three minutes to indulge in that sad little melodrama of identification. There were no extant pictures of a young Elizabeth, so easy enough to imagine my head poking

24

out of some Renaissance dress of rags, mooning around a tower, dragging my mother through mud and river valley, forest and desert and whatever else it was one encountered on the way to Prague. Three minutes, and then I cut it off.

Her prison wasn't a metaphor, it was a stone castle where her disgraced father marked out the last three years of his life. Her money problems couldn't be solved by a scholarship—to a school she no doubt would have been forbidden to attend—and an annual birthday gift certificate to the nearest outlet mall. Her father wasn't invisible, he was dead; her brother wasn't. We weren't the same.

That was the strange thing about translation, speaking someone else's words in a voice that somehow was and wasn't your own. You could fool yourself into believing you understood the meaning behind the words, but—as my father had explained long before I was old enough to get it—words and meaning were inseparable. Language shapes thought; I speak, therefore I think, *therefore* I am. In this case, Elizabeth's letters, written in a language that died centuries before she was born, were already at some remove from her life. Transforming them, word by dictionary-approved word, into modern English meant there would inevitably be a little of me in Elizabeth. It didn't mean there was any of her in me.

10

She was a poet. A reasonably famous one, if not one I or anyone else had ever heard of. And, despite the fact that she was born in England, spent most of her life in Prague, and, just for good measure, spoke fluent German, she wrote exclusively in Latin. Maybe when you were a woman in sixteenth-century Europe hoping to be taken seriously for something beyond whom you slept with and whom you birthed, it helped to cultivate a linguistic superiority complex. Or maybe the language without a people just appealed to the girl without a home.

The more I read of her letters, the more I wanted to know about her, but there wasn't much to find. Famous or not, Elizabeth Weston was a historical shadow, flickering across the officially important lives of Edward Kelley and Emperor Rudolf II, surfacing occasionally in feminist histories or turgid Neo-Latin literature surveys, but she had no biographies of her own, and—judging from the paucity of information on her Wikipedia page—no obsessed amateurs hoarding Westonia trivia and lobbying for the spotlight of scholarship to shine down on her. The only way to know Elizabeth was through her letters.

And so the days settled into a routine. Three times a week, I left school early and joined Max and Chris in the Hoff's musty office. Whether it was Max's stern looks, Chris's laziness overpowering even his tendency to distraction, or my own begrudging curiosity, the paper airplane races and thumb wars tapered off, and often hours slipped by with no more than a few words passed among us, mostly half-articulated requests for this dictionary or that conjugation list, muttered curses, groans of frustration, and the lapping murmurs of unfamiliar passages read softly aloud, searching for the rhythms of the past. More than once when I arrived, Max had a cappuccino waiting, with cinnamon and two sugars, the way I liked it.

"You're actually getting into this, aren't you?" Chris asked once as he walked me out. It was late, and he offered to toss my bike into the car and give me a ride home, but I told him I liked pedaling through the dark.

I never let anyone take me home.

"It'll look good on my college applications," I said.

"Uh-huh."

"Fine. It's interesting. To read something no one's touched in four hundred years? Not the worst way to spend an afternoon."

"Careful," he said. "You're starting to sound like Max."

It no longer seemed the insult it might once have. And when I got home that night, I went straight back to work.

E. J. Weston, to her dearest brother John Fr. Weston, greetings.

The dream is always the same. Our Father leaps from the tower, his white dressing gown billowing behind him like angel wings. He believed the angels would carry him to safety, and always, for an endless moment, I trust his faith. I expect him to fly. But always, he falls. Blood stains his white silk. I wake, and still I hear his voice, screaming my name. In life, he never screamed for me, not once. He dropped to the ground in silence. The guards must have been lying in wait, for they were on him in moments, and dragged him back to his cell. He writhed, he bled, but never once did he call for me.

You tell me I was right to stay in my hiding hole, curled in the hollow base of the tree. You rage against our Father for summoning a helpless young girl to assist with his escape. But I am far from helpless, and I would have gladly given my life to save his. Or so I believed until the moment was on us, and I failed him.

I will not fail him again.

No more of these unhappy musings. You ask for word of Prague, perhaps hoping to relive the memories of our happier youth. The Pražský hrad is as imposing as ever before, its spires scraping the clouds. Many mornings I walk the Stone Bridge at sunrise, watching the Vltava flow beneath. The

linden tree seems taller to me, sturdier than before. I enclose a
leaf with this letter, so that you too can inhale the scent of our
childhood.

There was no leaf: It had probably crumbled away to nothing centuries before. But I understood the impulse. There had been a day, two years before, a perfect March day ten degrees warmer and sunnier than a New England spring had any right to be, a day of lying in the grass with Adriane and Chris, listening to the river burble past, water that was more of a creek than a river and more sludge than water but looked clean and deep in the sunshine, a day of picking out cloud animals, of parades of white elephants and rabbits and dragons marching across the sky, a day when Adriane explained in great detail how to rid my hair of the dreaded frizz and then made a classically Adrianesque segue into discussing the deep-rooted cultural and racial issues embedded in any evaluation of hairstyle and the ways in which our three coifs, respectively half-Jewish, half-Asian, half-black, could chronicle the tale of American race relations for the last two hundred years, all while Chris pretended, loudly, to snore, a day when Chris, drunk on lemonade and freshly cut grass, took both our hands and told us, no laughter in his voice for once, that everything was different now that we had each other, and everything was better. And that day, while they were both sleeping, for real this time, knocked out by the sun, I wandered along the sludgy water and pocketed a smooth gray skipping rock that smelled like the river and that, like the day, I would keep.

It wasn't until the next morning that Chris confided what had happened while I was down at the water, the way first their hands came together and then their lips followed suit, the looks and secret smiles they'd stolen for the rest of the afternoon, behind my back and over my head, knowing what I didn't, luxuriating in the pleasure of anticipation, of what would happen when I was gone. He was so happy, and, later, by my locker, grinning as her fingertip traced out a heart against the rusting steel, so was she, that I was happy for them, and tried not to care that while I'd been having my perfect day, they'd been having an entirely different one, together. I told myself it was a good thing that I hadn't noticed, that everything had seemed the same—that it boded well for the future, and it did.

I still had the rock. But it wasn't the same.

Outside, the night sky was shading into a pearly gray that suggested I should sleep while I still had the chance. But I kept going.

The canons at Strahov have opened their library to me, and many a morning have I lost myself in the words of the masters. In that hushed chamber I feel at home as I do nowhere else in this city, perhaps because I can so easily envision you by my side, racing me through the pages. It seems near impossible you have never known this place, for your spirit inhabits it so fully. If I could wrap myself in its warm quiet for an eternity, drunk on words and ideas and questions I had never before thought to ask, I promise you I would mourn nothing of the life left behind. But the library on a hill is but a temporary refuge. Below, our Mother awaits. The city awaits, its people, I fear, much as you remember them, frothing with tales of courtly betrayals and petty treasons of the heart. Our magnificent Parent remains much in their minds. At the market this morning I overheard two fishwives conferring in hushed voices about the wizard who lived in a tower, cursing those who passed beneath. He communed with the angels, they said, and in his wrath once transformed a squawking infant into a

29

braying ass. I smiled to know of whom they spoke. His power and legend live on in his absence.

The Emperor remains deaf to my pleas, and our worldly possessions are held hostage to his whims. The Court Solicitor, Johannes Leo, has offered himself in our service, and I am inclined to accept his help. Your suspicions of him may be well founded, but your low estimation of my will is unjust. Though less than quick-witted, he has learned the language of the court and, snakelike, has slithered into the Imperial good graces. You need not fear he will slither into mine.

I leave you now, and beg in return some word of your studies. My mind is afire with imaginings of your life at Ingolstadt. To live without a care but the cares of the mind, is there a truer heaven on earth? Send word, and perhaps you may also send your prayers and your strength. If I am to fulfill my Father's final wish, I will need them both.

Farewell.

30 September 1598 Prague.

I liked the fact that she didn't whine. Psychotic father demanding help with some psychotic escape plan; mother who seemed to have abdicated all adult responsibility and, at least in my imagination, spent her days gazing out the window, twirling her hair, twiddling her thumbs, and reminding Elizabeth to marry rich; big brother who was apparently the Little Prince incarnate, too good for the menial labor of family life—she took it all in stride. Less impressive was the fact that she seemed to take it as her due. No feminists in the 1500s, I got that, but did she have to unquestioningly service her father's every whim, even once he was in the ground? He wasn't even her father, not technically, and however much she claimed him as her blood, I couldn't help noticing: She'd kept her own name.

11

I started looking forward to the afternoons in the Hoff's office, to Chris and Max and the hours of quiet. It mattered less than studying for APs or finishing applications, less even than the nights Chris and Adriane and I filled the hours till dawn with movies, midnight drives, urban spelunking investigations of abandoned tunnels and forgotten roofs, even, when we got desperate, the dusty board games in Adriane's basement, anything to avoid talking about the ticking clock and the day, sometime after graduation, when the rest of our lives would separately begin. The letters mattered less than all of that, but because they did, because they were an escape from anything that mattered—or had mattered to anyone in four centuries—they somehow mattered more.

E. J. Weston, to her dearest brother John Fr. Weston, greetings.

You know I would tell you anything, but despite your persistent questioning, I cannot reveal the promise I made to our Father. You cannot understand what he was like in those final days, consumed by that infernal book, determined to finish his greatest work before death stole him away. There were nights when he raved with such fever I feared he might burn before my eyes. I mopped his fiery brow as he raged at the heavens, at the angels, at the Emperor, at me. Forces conspired against him, he alleged, both in this world and beyond. Was he so wrong? There are whispers that his assassin was on a

31

*mission from the Emperor himself. Of course, no loyal subject
could ever suspect the Emperor of such a crime. And no one
can question my loyalty.*

The "infernal book" might have been the Hoff's precious
Voynich manuscript, but even if he'd been around to tell—which
he hadn't in nearly a week—I would have kept it to myself. If Elizabeth was writing about the Book, that meant her letters weren't
so useless after all, and I wasn't about to invite the Hoff to take
them away from me.

*It is loyalty that drives me now. Our Father's last, greatest
work awaits me, and I have finally summoned the courage to
complete it. There is a man whose help I must enlist, whose
name I cannot divulge. I shudder at things they say about him,
the strange mechanical creatures with which he surrounds
himself, their eyes glowing with demonic life. But our Father
trusted him. I can only hope it is a trust this man will not
betray.*

*It pains me to hear of your recent illness, and I urge you
to tend to your health. I know your childish fear of the leeches,
but you must take the advice of your physicians. Only once
was I forced to endure the creatures, but their slime on my
skin, and that exquisite pain as my blood drained into their
engorged bodies, is an experience I will not soon forget. We all
do what we must to survive.*

24 October 1598 Prague.

12

" 'We all do what we must to survive' . . . but there's nothing that explains what she was about to do. What could be so secret that she needs to keep it from the one person she tells all her secrets to?"

"Sex," Adriane said. "It's always sex." She lay flat on the white shag rug, then smoothly rolled herself into a yoga pose, legs stretched over her head, toes touching the floor.

I shook my head. "It's not a guy. It has something to do with their father, and she keeps talking about this *book*, which I'm sure is the same one that—"

"Nora. Seriously. No one cares about your dead-girl letters." Adriane lifted herself into a handstand, legs ruler-straight. "Especially if they're not about sex."

"So what you're looking for is some dead-girl-letter porn? That's what you're telling me?"

"You have to admit it would be more interesting."

"You say that like you were actually listening."

"You didn't tell me I was supposed to *listen*."

"Implied consent," I told her. "You know what Mr. Stewart said, about how every time you set foot into an airport, you give the government your implied consent to search you? Every time you invite me over here, you give me your implied consent to bore you with the details of my mundane little life."

Adriane hand-walked her way over to the wall, then pressed her bare feet against the vintage wallpaper and walked them down to the floor. She held her body in a reverse U, head dangling backward, hair pooling on the rug. "A, it's not *your* life, it's her life. B, maybe your life would be fractionally less mundane if you spent less time obsessing about your homework and more time actually living it. And C, consent rescinded."

"Maybe your advice would seem more incisive if I were upside down, too."

Her body flowed back into an upright position, as if gravity had been temporarily suspended on her side of the room. "And that's another thing," she said. "It wouldn't hurt you to hit the gym once in a while. We're not fifteen anymore, and all those milk shakes—"

"One more word, and I'm reading you another dead-girl letter," I warned her, brandishing the notebook that held my translations. "Word for word. *Slowly*."

"Enough said."

Back when I was still a visitor in the World According to Adriane, rather than a permanent resident, I'd assumed that the constant stretching had been for the benefit of those members of the opposite sex who were frequently in the vicinity when she got one of her sudden urges for half lotus or downward-facing dog. It could and did happen anywhere—waiting in line for a movie, studying for a chem test, decorating for a homecoming rally. You'd turn to say something, and Adriane would be on the ground, skyscraper legs stretched into a split or arcing over her head with calves taut and toes pointed. It took a few months to realize she wasn't doing it for the attention—although she wasn't oblivious to the perk. It was just her body's automatic pilot mode, like complaining about my eating habits and less-than-adventurous social life was her mouth's.

She folded herself gracefully into the large blue beanbag chair shoved into the corner of the room, twisting her legs into a pretzel beneath her. The thick rug at her feet was scattered with discarded books. A natural-born speed-reader possessed of a disgustingly good memory, Adriane was a literary magpie, skimming through the Russians one week and the postmodernists the next, with sporadic breaks for cutting-edge tech journals and the latest Nora

Roberts. She eschewed history and politics—"You know what they say, make love, not treaties"—but anything else was fair game. Fortunately for her attention span, her credit card had a nearly inexhaustible limit that was barely tested by the weekly Amazon binges; fortunately for her treasured social status, she excelled at playing the shallow slacker too cool for anything relating to school. The elementary-school science-fair trophies were kept—both metaphorically and literally—under lock and key.

Classic closet geek. It was the biggest thing she and Chris had in common.

"So we can officially start the countdown," she said—beginning, as usual, *in medias res*.

"To . . . ?"

"Europe. My mom talked to Cammi's mom, who's in the Prep Boosters Club with some guy on the trip-planning committee, and he said Paris is a definite. Can you imagine?"

"Not really."

"Because you've never been there." Her voice was hushed, as if she were speaking of a pilgrimage to a holy land. "The Champs-Elysées, the Bon Marché, the Galeries Lafayette—"

"That's a mall, right?"

"Try cathedral of fashion. And then there's the food, the *pain au chocolat*, the *crêpes Nutella*—"

"You haven't eaten chocolate since the Candy Bar Incident sophomore spring," I reminded her.

"What is your *problem*?"

Adriane had been looking forward to the senior spring-break trip for approximately her entire life. I preferred the delusion that it would never arrive, mostly because my scholarship didn't cover European adventures and the closest to Paris my parents could afford to send me was a breakfast jaunt to Au Bon Pain.

"I'm just trying to figure out what the big deal is," I said.

Adriane and Chris both knew I was at Prep on a scholarship, as they knew that, unlike them, I didn't have my own car, credit card, or trust fund. But they somehow still didn't understand what it meant to never have enough, and I was content leaving them in the dark, because I had no need for their understanding and no use for the pity that would accompany it. "Some of us didn't spend the last three Christmas breaks slurping down *chocolat chaud* on the banks of the Seine," I said, but lightly. "If it was so amazing, why waste half the trip texting me about how you were bored out of your mind?"

"It was only *two* Christmas breaks. And everything's lame when you're stuck with your parents. This time it'll be *us*. Did I mention there's no drinking age in Europe?"

"Only about a hundred and six times."

"Do you have to be such a pessimist all the time?"

"It's not pessimism," I said out of habit. "It's realism. And you know it's your favorite thing about me."

"You know what they say about too much of a good thing." Then she brightened. "Fine. I dare you to be realistically crappy about this: Chris is coming. They always get some college kids to chaperone, and I'm making him sign up."

"So I get to tag along with the two of you on your ultra-romantic Parisian getaway?" I grumbled. "*Magnifique.*"

"Wheelbarrow," she said firmly.

"Yeah, yeah. Wheelbarrow." I sighed, but mostly for effect. The three's-a-crowd complaints were *pro forma* at this point, as I could no longer imagine it any other way. *Wheelbarrow* was Adriane-speak for *stop whining,* because—as she liked to say—the damn thing would be useless without the third wheel.

"Besides, this time we've got one for you, too."

"One what?" I asked, suspicious.

"One wheel," she said. "One *guy*, idiot. Chris is going to get Max to sign up for chaperoning too, and then . . ."

36

"And then . . . ?"

She waggled her eyebrows. "*Parlez-vous la* language of love?"

"Adriane! Not going to happen."

"Tell me you don't think he's cute."

"Ignoring you now."

"Or at least acceptable," she said. "Nice eyes, if you ignore the glasses. And he's got an interesting smile, sort of. Plus, accent. Always a bonus."

"How can you even tell he has an accent? He never talks." Though, of course, that wasn't quite true anymore. Over long afternoons and more than a few evenings holed up in the Hoff's lair—the Hoff himself off napping or drinking or busy with whatever daily ablutions kept him from putting in more than an hour or two of work each week, and Chris taking increasing advantage of the absence to put in quality time with his girlfriend and his PS3—Max had started coming into focus for me. Not as Chris's shy roommate or Adriane's double-date accessory, but as the quiet guy who was always equipped with an extra pencil, an extra Latin dictionary, an extra cappuccino, whatever I needed, often before I thought to ask for it. And she was right about the accent. It was subtle, and impossible to place—a hint of Southern drawl paired with a flat Midwestern twang and an undertone of laid-back California surfer boy. "Why are you so obsessed with this?"

"Is it so wrong to want you to be happy?" she asked sweetly.

I just stared at her.

"I can be altruistic," she said.

"Since when?"

"Fine. So maybe I miss it a little."

"What?"

"You know. The new guy. That moment when he looks at you and you don't know what's going to happen next. But you know *something* will. That first kiss . . ."

"You've been with Chris for two years, not twenty," I reminded her. "You sound like some bored middle-aged housewife dreaming of an affair with the pool boy."

"Do not! Chris is . . . you know. He's Chris."

"And I'm sure he'd be overwhelmed to hear such extravagant praise."

She tossed a throw pillow at my head. "You know what I mean."

I decided not to point out to her that, never having spent years blissfully in love with a perfect guy who worshipped the shag carpeting she hand-walked on, I did not.

"Look, I'm not the one always whining about not having a boyfriend," she said.

"No, you're the one always whining about *me* not having a boyfriend."

"Either way, problem solved."

"Last I checked, Max wasn't throwing pebbles at my bedroom window, begging me to run off into the sunset together."

"Just promise me when he does, you'll say yes."

"Is he showing up with a horse or a convertible in this scenario?" I asked.

"Come on."

"What? Into the sunset's a long ride. I'd want to be comfortable."

"Nora . . ."

"I'd say yes to coffee," I granted her. "Maybe even a movie. *If* he asks. Which he won't."

"But—"

"But if he did, then yes. A movie. As long as it's not a crappy one."

"Fair enough."

13

The Hoff had given me a key to his office, and whenever I wore out my stay in Adriane's house or Chris's dorm, the dungeon of books was always a more tempting refuge than the public library or the nearest Starbucks—both of which were themselves more hospitable than home. Chris still showed up for the nine hours a week he needed to fulfill his history requirement, but most of the time, I found myself alone with Max, both of us scribbling into our notebooks long after the sun had gone down. I had no idea why he spent so much time there, or why, when he had so much work of his own to get through, he kept offering to help with mine. I could hear Adriane's voice in my head, pointing out that *no* guy was that into his homework. On the other hand, historically speaking, no guy had ever been that into me, either.

I turned down Max's offer, every time. Elizabeth's mystery was mine to solve, and I was sure that, although so far she'd done nothing but string her brother along with vague references to her dark and dangerous secret, eventually, she'd have to tell him.

She told him everything.

E. J. Weston, to her brother John Francis Weston, greetings.

There are those who would go to great lengths to learn my secret, and even revealing as little as I do in these letters may prove a mistake. Many a morning I resolve never to speak of it again. But then night comes, and with it, the shadows, and I once again crave your strong hand to lead me through the dark. We are no longer children, and I can no longer flee to you for succor from the beasts that once menaced my sleep. Even if those beasts have now been reborn in waking life. I have enlisted a dangerous ally, as our Father commanded. My very presence seems to enrage him, and I suspect that were it not for the great reward we both seek, my time would be short. This is the man our Father trusted most in this world? This is to be our salvation?

Enough. I will stop this now, with apologies for my distress. I have not forgotten that, as our Father impressed upon us, reason is the last and best weapon of the powerless man. He taught me well the many uses of emotion, the blade that can so easily be turned against its wielder. His lessons are engraved on my soul, so quiet your concerns, and trust that, as always, I can tend to myself.

I will, however, admit, dearest brother, that your suspicions of Johannes Leo were well founded. He has begun to pay me the most absurd of wrongheaded compliments, as if I would believe that my hair smelled of linden leaves or my lips were rubies and my eyes sapphire. If he spoke the truth, I would have jewels enough to outfit our Mother like a queen. He speaks of my beauty as if I were a vase or canvas he coveted for his estate. To my mind, to my words, he gives little thought. He imagines me his Galatea, a mechanical doll with waxen beauty and empty head. Worse, he has begun to speak of the future as if it were a destination we shared. Yesterday he offered a bouquet of lilacs, and the foul scent nearly made me swoon. Weakness, especially my own, repulses me, but for Johannes it is an aphrodisiac. I cannot say, nor imagine, what might have ensued had Thomas not appeared when he did. This is Thomas's power, always appearing when and where he is

most needed, especially when I am the one in need. Johannes,
of course, treated him like a dung beetle, simply because of his
low station at court. Johannes has worked tirelessly on our
family's behalf, interceding with the Emperor when my own
pleas have been ignored, and I am grateful. But on the other
matter, my mind is made up. Despite what our Mother may
believe, the bounds of gratitude go only so far.

I know your time is precious, my most loving brother, and
so I will trouble you no longer with my small concerns. As
always, prayers for your good health are on my lips and in my
heart.

15 November 1598 Prague.

"She's never mentioned this Thomas guy before," I said. "But then, there are a lot of missing letters. I don't understand what she's talking about half the time."

"But she ends up with the other guy?" Max said.

I nodded. She'd married Johannes in 1603 and had seven children with him, dying as the last was on its way out. Any danger posed by the mysterious "dangerous ally" was apparently nothing compared to chasing happily ever after in an era without epidurals, antibiotics, and, more to the point, birth control.

"She did say reason was her best weapon," Max pointed out.

"I know." It was my favorite part. She spent so much time in these letters obsessing about her weakness, but you could tell that, deep down, she knew she was strong.

"Wouldn't be very rational to ditch the wealthy lawyer for the dung beetle," he said.

"I know that, too, but . . ."

He nodded. "But you think it's sad."

Something about the way he said it—not quite patronizing,

but just a little too understanding—made me feel like some cheesy-soap-opera fan craving a Thomas-Elizabeth mash-up. (Thozabeth? Elizamas?) "I get that romantic love is a modern concept and all that, and marriage back then was just a contractual agreement, so obviously it would make sense that she got together with the guy so she wouldn't end up on the street. All I'm saying is that—" I swallowed the rest of it.

"What?"

"Forget it. I'll stop now."

"Stop what?"

"Ranting like a total freak about the love life of some girl who's been dead for four hundred years."

Max offered up a cautious smile. "You're here to satisfy some kind of school requirement, right?"

I nodded.

"And I'm here voluntarily," he said. "On a Friday night, no less. So which of us is the freak?"

"I guess that would be you?"

"You calling me a freak?"

It took me a second to be sure he was joking. And another to decide that I was actually starting to like him. Not in the Adriane kind of way. The speckled green eyes were admittedly nice, and unlike Adriane, I preferred them behind the glasses, which sharpened his blurry features. The hair, brownish blond, and nearly long enough to sweep over his eyes when he lowered his head to avoid attention, was, as she put it, acceptable. But it was also somehow beside the point.

"What were you going to say?" he asked.

"When?"

He tapped the letters. "About Elizabeth."

He said her name like she was someone we knew who'd just stepped out for a slice of pizza but would be back in ten. "It's just

42

strange to read someone's private letters," I said. "It's not like history, like Lincoln or Hitler or something. She's . . ." I couldn't find the words.

"Real?"

"I know, that sounds stupid obvious."

"It's not stupid," he said, with uncharacteristic intensity. "She is real. They all are."

We were quiet. Max rose and opened a window—one of the few that actually opened, as the majority were sealed stained glass, good for a flickering rainbow on a sunny day, less helpful when the ancient, clanking heaters went mad and turned the room into an oven—letting a welcome blast of air into the room. After all this time, it felt almost normal to be working in a church, maybe because the Hoff had so successfully colonized the sacred with the mundane. Giant cardboard boxes filled the empty altar, and leaning shelves crammed with books blocked several of the stained-glass panes, transforming the familiar scenes. Goliath stood tall without a David; Daniel never entered the lion's den. The head of John the Baptist still stared up from its platter, but Salome's pride in her offering was hidden by a shelf of *Studies in Medieval and Renaissance History*, 1987 through 1991.

Max sat down again, straightening his already neat stack of translations.

"You guys having any luck?" I asked. "You know, with the 'real' work?"

"It's all real work."

"Right."

"No luck at all, if it makes you feel better," he said. "Kelley's always talking about the Book, but he's vague. The Hoff's convinced we're onto something. He thinks Kelley's about to lead us to the missing pages—you know there are twelve missing from the Book, right?"

"He may have mentioned that about a thousand times."

Max smiled. I liked the way his eyebrows curled up at the edges whenever his lips did. "And we keep finding these references to something called the *Lumen Dei*. See anything like that from Elizabeth?"

I shook my head, though the phrase sounded oddly familiar. "*Lumen Dei. The light of God?*" I said. "What is it?"

He shrugged. "Could be anything. Kelley was a weird guy. Thought he could raise the dead, turn people into animals. Alchemy. Black magic. Good stuff."

He told me more—how Kelley had tramped around Europe for decades duping people into buying his magic act, how he'd teamed up with the more reputable scholar John Dee and seemingly driven the man insane, how it was said his ears had been chopped off for some long-forgotten trespass, how some believe he was imprisoned only because the Emperor wanted him to yield the secret of the philosopher's stone, and when he refused one too many times, the Emperor had punished his loyal court alchemist with death. At this, Max took off on a tangent about the eccentric emperor and the coterie of artists, philosophers, and mystics he'd assembled in his imperial court—but then broke off abruptly, cheeks pink, perhaps suddenly realizing he'd been monologuing for a good ten minutes. "Sorry."

"No, it's interesting." Listening to him was oddly comforting, like the way my father's lectures about Roman aqueducts had once lulled me to sleep in place of bedtime stories.

His shrug was nearly a shudder. "I highly doubt that."

"It really is. I swear. Substantially more interesting than property liens and marriage proposals." I found myself irritated all over again that I'd been assigned such a total girl job.

"It's all important," he insisted.

44

"Just because I'm in high school doesn't mean I'm an idiot."

"Okay, maybe none of it's important," he allowed. "I've asked around, and most people think the Hoff is a nutcase. You know he used to be the world expert on the post-Hussite era and early Czech Protestantism?"

I decided not to admit I had no idea what he was talking about. "Really? Huh."

"Got obsessed with the Book right after he got here, and hasn't worked on anything else since."

"It doesn't seem like he's working on much at all these days."

"Yeah, he hasn't published for years, not even in the fringe journals. It's like he's just going through the motions now. I think he might have finally given up on ever finding anything. It's sad."

"If you think that, what are you doing here?"

"Well . . ." Max shifted in his seat. "I told him it was because I really admired his work on religious sectarianism in Rudolfine Prague and wanted to learn from the best."

"But really?"

"Really, it's almost impossible to get a good research-assistant position when you're a freshman. So it's either picking a professor no one else would waste their time on . . . or serving slop in the dining hall. And, well . . . want to know a secret?"

"Always."

We leaned across the table, our heads nearly meeting.

"I hate hairnets," he whispered. Then he laughed.

"Am I hallucinating, or did you actually just make a joke?"

"What?" He looked wounded. "I'm funny."

Funny-looking, I might have shot back, if we were actually friends. "Prove it," I challenged him instead.

"Uh . . ."

I tapped a pencil against the table. "Tick tock."

"Don't rush me! Okay. Okay, um. What did the fish do on Friday night?"

"I don't know, what?"

"He went to a movie."

I waited for the punch line, but he just looked at me expectantly. "Well?"

"He went to a *movie*," he said again.

"I don't get it."

"See, he—wait, no, that's it, he went to *see* a movie. Like *s-e-a* a movie. He's a fish. Get it now?"

The snort sputtered out of me before I could stop it.

"See?" he said. "Funny."

"I think maybe that word doesn't mean what you think it means."

"So . . . not funny?"

"Not funny."

He raised his eyebrows. "Let's just say I have other skills to compensate."

The pause was, I suspected, more awkward than either of us had intended.

In the silence, we heard a noise. A rustling sound, just beyond the entryway. Then a soft patter. Footsteps.

"Chris?" I said, but quietly. "Professor Hoffpauer?"

We both watched the dark tunnel that led into the nave, but nothing emerged from it. And its shadows were impenetrable.

"You heard that, right?" I asked in a near whisper. "There shouldn't be anyone in here at night."

Max nodded. "Maybe a janitor? Or some kind of animal?"

We sat very still, waiting for something to confirm or deny his guess. There was nothing.

"We should check it out," I said.

46

"Probably."

We didn't move.

"Could be those shadowy forces the Hoff is always worrying about," Max teased, "come to steal the archive and silence the witnesses."

My laugh rang hollow.

"I know," he said. "Not funny. But like I said, I have other skills." He stood. "This is me being brave."

I stood, too. "Yes, let's bravely go catch ourselves a scary janitor. Watch out for evil mops."

Max gave me an appraising look. "You know, you're not very funny, either."

This time, my laughter was sincere. But it didn't make me any more eager to step into the black.

14

"Did you hear that?" I whispered. The nave was dark, though I was sure I'd turned on the lights when I came in. "What was that?"

"That was my foot."

"Oh. Sorry." I stepped back.

"That's my other foot."

"Right."

We inched forward through rows of pews toward the light switch. As my eyes adjusted, I could make out the stone columns rising into shadow, and the massive cross that loomed over the altar.

We finally made it to the opposite wall. I flicked the switch, but the church stayed dark. "Okay, that's weird."

"Think the power's out?"

"Just here?" At the other end of the tunnel, the office light glowed.

"Maybe a fuse blew."

"Yeah. Maybe."

The church was silent. If there had been a janitor or a stray cat or anything else, it was gone. We were alone. The ceilings receded into the darkness, making it seem almost as if we were standing beneath a starless sky. Dim moonlight filtered in through the stained glass, but all it lit was shadows.

"This is ridiculous," I whispered. Then, through force of will, louder: "We're being ridiculous." I half expected an echo. But my words didn't come back to me. And nothing lunged out of the darkness. It was just an empty church with a blown fuse and, worst-case scenario, a bat's nest in the apse.

"I never figured I'd be spending this much time in a church," I added, just to kill the silence.

"I used to want to be a priest," he said.

"*What?*" It was almost enough to make me forget the dark.

"I said used to," he said. I couldn't see his expression. "They always seemed to have the answers."

"To what?"

He paused. "I don't know. Everything, I guess."

"So . . . you went to church a lot?" Not that there was anything wrong with that, I reminded myself. It just wasn't something I ran into very often. My parents were half-Jewish, half-Methodist, half-Catholic, a few parts Unitarian, and all atheist—though less militant on the subject than their friends, back when they used to have friends, who would occasionally come for dinner and stay for several bottles of wine and drunken discourses on the excesses of evangelical America.

"My parents are . . ." He hesitated. "Believers, let's say. So yeah, we spent a lot of time in a lot of churches."

"*Churches* plural? Are you really supposed to shop around like that?"

"Not shopping," he said. "Moving. Once a year, sometimes twice. Every year a new town, new people, new school—but there was always a church, and it was always pretty much the same, you know?"

"Sometimes you need a constant."

"Yeah."

I did know. "Why'd you move so much?"

"My parents would say it was because of their jobs—but I think they just liked it better that way. They were always so sure that the next city, the next life, that's where they would find what they were looking for."

"What *were* they looking for?"

He shrugged. "What's anyone looking for? Anyway, whatever it is, I'm starting to think it doesn't exist."

I didn't know what to say, and I waited too long to figure it out.

"Let's just check the locks and the front entrance and make sure everything looks okay," he said stiffly. "Then I should get out of here. It's late."

Maybe saying the wrong thing would have been better than saying nothing, but it wasn't the kind of thing you could apologize for. I inched behind him through the darkness, feeling my way toward the large wooden door at the far end of the nave and doing my best not to brush against him. Once, briefly, something feathered across the back of my hand, but if it was his finger, it was clearly an accident, and it didn't happen again.

"Door's still locked," he said, jiggling the knob. "Dead bolt's dropped, too. Maybe we were just imagining things."

"I don't think so." I flipped open my phone to cast a beam of light at the broken pane alongside the door. The glass had given way to a jagged hole just large enough for someone's hand to reach through, raise the dead bolt, and turn the lock. "Someone was here."

I shivered.

"Could have been the wind," Max said.

"Why do people always say that? It's *wind*. How is wind supposed to break glass?"

"Maybe it blew a stick against the window. Or someone threw a rock. I don't know." He was starting to sound irritated.

"It wasn't the wind." I brought the phone closer, shining its light on what I wished I hadn't seen.

The shards of glass were glazed with blood.

15

Someone had been in the church; someone had broken in.

A homeless guy, Max suggested. An idiot bird, Chris guessed later. Adriane concluded it was someone getting an early start in the War on Christmas. The Hoff didn't get a vote, because the Hoff never knew. We were afraid—by which I mean Chris and Max were afraid, and for whatever reason, I let them be—that the spectre of bleeding trespassers would nudge the professor into full-blown paranoia. I think about it, sometimes, what might have happened if we hadn't kept our mouths shut.

But we did.

16

Lumen Dei. Though Max didn't ask about it again, the words stuck in my head. I associated them with that night, with noises in the dark, and bloody glass. But I knew I'd seen them before. Google turned up nothing but a few random references in Renaissance texts I'd never heard of, by people whose names hadn't even made it into Wikipedia, much less my AP Euro textbook. So

I went back to the letters, unsure whether I wanted the answer for purposes of impressing Max or beating him.

It was a cloudy afternoon, the kind of late-fall New England day when heavy gray skies made you start scanning the horizon for winter. Chris and Max were hunched over a copy of *The Renaissance Concordia*, arguing over the provenance of a reference to Machiavelli. The Hoff had actually shown up, but judging from the snores issuing from behind the latest volume of *The Journal of Medieval and Early Modern Studies*, his presence was a technicality.

I paged carefully through the ancient letters, not even sure what I was looking for until I found it, near the bottom of the stack.

E. I. Westonia, Ioanni Francisco Westonio, fratri suo germano S.P.D.

Forsitan hoc dicere blasphemia est, sed Lumen Dei *non est donum divinum.*

My eye must have skimmed over the line when I was indexing the letters. By the time I translated the rest, the gray sky had purpled, and the Hoff had long since retreated to the threadbare couch. "As you were," he'd mumbled, eyes half-closed as he traversed the distance between one napping spot and the next. "Work to be done."

E. J. Weston, to her brother John Francis Weston, greetings.

It may well be blasphemy to say, but the Lumen Dei *is no divine gift. The promise of untold powers, of sacred answers, of godlike abilities and ultimate truth, these are powerful temptations. But surely there is such a thing as too much sacrifice. Those who threw away their lives to stop us, who foresaw the end of the world, now have the cold satisfaction of vindication beyond the grave. For the* Lumen Dei *can indeed end the world. It is a gift, but like the gift of the Greeks, it disguised the enemy within.*

I hate him. Words I never thought I would say I now long to scream into the night. I hate our Father. I hate him for devising it, as I hate the Emperor for stealing him away, as I hate the Lumen Dei *for stealing everything else. Forgive me, brother! My words are true as they are evil, and yet they are incomplete. For I hate no one more than myself.*

The deed is done, the world is broken, and I see no way forward. I cannot, must not, reunite the pages with the book from which they were torn asunder. The mind of God should remain forever beyond the reach of man. Of this, if nothing else, I am now certain. And yet the Lumen Dei *calls to me. The machine is a promise, a devil's pact to divine ends, and I fear my strength is not equal to the temptation.*

This is all that remains of our Father: the machine his genius devised, and the words with which he guided my hands from beyond the grave. I study them often, thinking of him splayed on the floor of his cell, quill flying as he translated the words of God. The angels gave him their names, and he gave them to me, this one meaning water, that one air, this danger, that transgression. Do you ever envy him, dearest brother, and wish that you could hear the angels with such clarity? Envy is weakness, our Father taught us, and yet I know he envied Bacon, though he would never admit it. Our Father spoke to angels, but Bacon spoke to God.

Even in our Father's absence, those pages seem still to

belong to him. All but one. That one details the task assigned to Thomas, and for a time, he carried it with him wherever he went. It still holds the familiar scent of his laboratory, acrid smoke, burnt metals, bitter vapors. This page, Thomas's page, is mine. It is all that remains of a lost future, and will make its home with Petrarch, the one who taught me to know love resting forever with the one who taught me to speak it.

Time grows short, and I have a decision to make. I urge you, as I so often do, not to worry for me, but this time I point not to my strength or my courage but to the mere fact that one can have no cares when one has nothing left to lose. It seems all I have left is you, my loving brother, and so you must save your worries for yourself.

27 April 1599 Prague.

None of it made much sense. There was the reference to "the gift of the Greeks," which I recognized, from years of translating, as the Trojan Horse. The *Lumen Dei*, whatever it was, whatever untold riches had apparently been promised, had brought the opposite. Chaos and disaster, a world in ruins.

I couldn't begin to imagine the nature of a machine that promised "sacred answers" and "ultimate truth"—or rather, when I tried, I couldn't help picturing one of those Guess Your Fortune carnival machines—but I understood all too well what had been left in its wake: grief. That delectable combo of confusion, guilt, self-doubt, what-ifs, regrets about the unchangeable past and paralysis in the face of an unpromising future. She had lost, badly— and in losing, had lost her father all over again. I knew how that worked, too. It was simple physics: Loss attracted loss.

Enough, I told myself, sounding like *her*. The letter wasn't a distress call across the ages from a sixteenth-century maiden in search of a twenty-first-century shrink. It was a clue.

I pulled the Petrarch collection out of the pouch that the archives were stored in, and rifled gently through the yellowed pages. The text was faint, nearly illegible. There were a few poems underlined or circled, with no notes in the margin to indicate why they might have mattered. I didn't speak Italian so couldn't even begin to guess.

> *Trovommi Amor del tutto disarmato*
> *et aperta la via per gli occhi al core,*
> *che di lagrime son fatti uscio et varco.*

Maybe less a clue than a dead end. Feeling vaguely stupid, I closed the book again. As I did, I felt something. The leather binding was incredibly soft, rubbed smooth by age. But my thumb had bumped over a rough spot on the inside front cover. No, not a spot, I realized, taking a closer look. A seam. A slightly discolored square patch of light tan stood out against the dark, with a thin seam running along the edges, an impressive but imperfect repair job, as if to disguise a hole in the binding. Or something else.

There was a bottle opener on my key chain, and on the bottle opener, a sharp enough edge to rip a fraying sixteenth-century stitch. The Hoff was still snoring; Chris and Max were still absorbed in their battle of wits and pedantry. No one was watching.

Not that I would think of defacing a four-hundred-year-old book. That would be insane. Probably not the kind of thing they could arrest you for, but I had no doubt the Hoff would try his best. Obviously the smart thing would be to bring him the book, show him the stitches in the binding and the slightly raised area beneath them, as if something had been slipped inside. But:

This page, Thomas's page, is mine.

The stitches split neatly and swiftly, and the thin leather patch dropped away. I nearly gasped. A tightly folded piece of paper was nestled into the binding. I nudged it gently with one finger, half afraid it would turn to dust if I moved it, much less tried to unfold it. Elizabeth had folded this up and sewn it into a beloved book, where it had rested unseen and untouched for four centuries. She was the last person to hold this, I thought, and now her secret was mine.

Carefully, so carefully, I unfolded the page. It turned out to be two pages, one nested inside the other—and then I really did gasp as I realized what I was looking at. One sheet was crammed with dense Latin, terms I'd never seen before, *acqua fortis, sal ammoniac*, names that sounded like chemicals alongside measurements, some kind of elaborate formula. Beside it was a rough sketch of an odd-looking plant, six pointed leaves framing a seventh rounded one, with a spiraling stalk. But it wasn't the formula or the drawing that caught my eye. It was the other page, which wasn't Latin at all, or any language. It was a page of symbols, incomprehensible but *familiar*, because hadn't I been staring at those symbols every time I passed the massive facsimile of a Voynich manuscript page hanging over the Hoff's desk?

The grouping of the text was the same on both pages, as was the strange drawing. "You guys?" I swallowed hard, trying to knock the frog out of my voice. "I think I may have found something."

17

The Voynich manuscript surfaced in 1912 and has since foiled a century's worth of historians, linguists, and cryptographers, driving at least one of them insane. Its 240 pages are filled with a language of twenty to thirty distinct glyphs, seemingly a random ordering of meaningless ink marks designed to befuddle and humiliate readers, but linguistic analysis strongly suggests that the symbols form a language—possibly one that's yet to be discovered.

Some believe the Voynich manuscript to be a hoax, cooked up in the twentieth century, though carbon dating pushes its origin to the 1400s. The Hoff suspected it was even older than that. He was a traditionalist, as Voynich speculators went, adhering to a theory most had given up for dead. He believed that the demented alchemist Edward Kelley had owned the book but that Roger Bacon, a thirteenth-century friar, philosopher, scholar, and mystic, had written it. The letters were beginning to vindicate him. Kelley referred to a book, written by Bacon in the language of God, and Elizabeth seemed to suggest that—whether thanks to the intercession of his angelic overseers or an epileptic seizure or simply a genius for defrauding gullible acolytes—he had cracked the code and transcribed its holy secrets.

Now we had proof.

18

For a few moments we thought the Hoff might actually pop a coronary, but gradually the red leached out of his face and he stopped ranting about how he would show them all and get out of this hellhole and die at Harvard, where he belonged. When he finally acknowledged our presence, it was only to order us into indentured servitude; naptime was over. "If we work morning, noon, and night, we just *might* be ready with a full translation by the next American Historical Association conference," he told Chris and Max. When they stammered something about classes and homework and, not incidentally, having a life, he made a noise like a deflating tire. "We're talking about the pursuit of *knowledge*," he told them. "This could change the world. This could be your *legacy*. And you're worried about some multiplication tables?"

Chris cleared his throat. "Actually, it's multivariable calculus with—"

"It's useless." The Hoff snorted. "Young man, no one else is going to tell you the truth, so allow me. Your education is a joke. Your classes lack quality and depth, and even if you were learning from the Athenian masters themselves, do you really think the world needs yet another term paper on the themes of protofeminist rage in *Macbeth* or the structural causes of World War I? It's busywork, son. It's a scam to trade your tuition money for a piece of paper that will let you go work at a bank or some *company* for the rest of your life, pretending that because you once read Plato, you can call yourself an educated man." He grazed his fingers along Elizabeth's secret pages, then pointed to the door. "That, out there, is a facsimile of knowledge. *This* is real. The choice is yours, of course. I assume you're not the only student capable of translation work, though in this godforsaken place, one can never be sure."

Chris looked helplessly at Max, who only had eyes for the Hoff. "We'll do what we can," he said, steady.

The Hoff nodded. "And you," he said.

Me.

"You have school, of course, and I suspect I don't need to lecture you about what a waste *that* sand trap of bureaucracy and busywork will turn out to be, but your obligations are your obligations, nonetheless. However, I expect that while you're here—"

"Actually," I said, my voice smaller than I would have liked, "I was thinking that maybe I could stick with the Elizabeth letters. For a while. If that's all right."

His bushy eyebrows nearly receded to his distant hairline. I couldn't blame him. Here was my chance to do something that

57

actually *mattered*, and I was going to pass it up for some wannabe poet's cryptic teen angst?

I was.

The Hoff was nodding. "Yes. Yes, yes. Who knows what else may be hidden in those letters? You follow your instincts, Nora. You're the miracle worker."

I hadn't even been sure he knew my first name.

"You have changed history," he said. "Better, you've *revealed* history. Your Elizabeth translations will no doubt be worthy of publication, perhaps even a small volume of their own. So yes, keep at it."

And then, in awkward slow motion, he opened his arms and lurched toward me. Before I had a chance to back away, he had folded himself around me, his sandpaper skin pressed to my cheek. I held myself stiff, enduring.

"Gratias tibi ago," he said. *Thank you.* "Everything will be different now."

"You're welcome," I mumbled, and waited for it to be over.

19

"Okay, I'm here." Adriane flounced into the church with two pizza boxes and a bottle of vodka. "Now who wants to tell me why? Because giant crosses and creepy statues of the Virgin Mary do not a celebration make."

"They do when it's the scene of our triumph." Chris swung her off her feet and twirled her around, pizza, vodka, and all. "Ever dreamed of kissing a world-famous historian? Pucker up."

Adriane twisted out of his grasp. "As far as world-famous goes, I've got my hopes set on rock star. Or maybe astronaut." She set the celebratory provisions down in an empty pew. "Explanation? Anyone?"

"We made a brilliant discovery," Chris said.

"Nora made a discovery," Max said.

Adriane arched an eyebrow. "Dead-girl porn? I knew it!"

"Ignore her," I said quickly, catching the look on Max's face. "She can't help herself. It's a disease."

"Gutterminditis," Adriane said. "If you want to use the technical Latin term. As I know you do."

The sanctuary, which had seemed foreboding in the pitch black, glowed in the soft light of the overhead candelabras, bright enough to illuminate sculpted stone angels swirling around the pillars and golden candles ringing the altar, dim enough to disguise peeling paint, splintered wood, rust and corrosion and decay. It wasn't the most appropriate spot for a victory party, but when Chris had one of what he termed his brain monsoons, he was nearly impossible to resist. The Hoff was long gone, off to dream of academic glory or librarian torture or whatever enlivened his fantasies—he'd left us to celebrate our triumph with "an exuberance commensurate with your youth."

We scavenged the pizza, downed the vodka—or at least Chris, Adriane, and Max did, while I weathered their mockery and stuck to water, arguing that, as resident "miracle worker," it was probably part of my job description to stay pure—and speculated wildly about the shining futures we might have just ensured for ourselves. Chris foresaw a glowing recommendation for law school three years hence, paving the yellow-brick road all the way to the Supreme Court; I just wanted to make sure I got out of Chapman and into college, useless facsimile of knowledge or not; Adriane, unpersuaded that any of this was a deal big enough for ten-dollar pizza, much less a night of drunken blue-skying, was nonetheless set to write, produce, and costume our inevitable television appearance (albeit presumably on PBS); Max was silent.

"Now can we get out of here and celebrate for real?" Adriane asked once the food and drink were gone.

Chris leapt off his pew and grabbed her hand. "Not until I have my way with you, fair lady."

"Your way isn't exactly churchly," Adriane pointed out. But she held on as he danced her around the nave in a left-footed waltz, whirling with clownish grace.

Max and I watched.

"'I found that ivory image there, dancing with her chosen youth,'" Max said. Then, realizing that I was staring at him, he blushed. "It's a poem. Yeats."

"I know."

He looked surprised. "Really?"

Of course not really—the only poetry I knew by heart was the first and last stanzas of T. S. Eliot's "The Love Song of J. Alfred Prufrock," and that only because we'd been forced to memorize them for sophomore English—but I didn't like that shocked expression, as if it were so out of the question I'd know a random Yeats line off the top of my head. I wondered if he'd been trying to impress me, then dismissed the idea. Max didn't strike me as the type to make the effort.

Then again, neither was I.

"'We have lingered in the chambers of the sea. By sea-girls wreathed with seaweed red and brown,'" I quoted, though it bore no relevance to anything, even in the loosest of poetically metaphorical terms. "Eliot."

"'Till human voices wake us, and we drown.'" It was the next line.

"Are we competing now?" I asked. "Over who knows more poetry by heart? Because if so, this is officially the geekiest conversation of my life."

He tensed, and another red flush crept across his face.

"Joking," I assured him. "Remember, I'm the funny one?"

We fell silent again and watched them dance. Chris lurched about with the best of intentions and a congenital lack of rhythm, but Adriane—physically incapable of an awkward move—twirled and dipped like a Disney princess at the ball, absent only shimmering gown and diamond tiara. "She's beautiful. Don't you think?"

Max shrugged.

"She inspired you to poetry," I pointed out.

"So do spotted toads. And the occasional well-barbecued steak. Beauty's not really a necessary criterion."

"Spotted *toads*? You recite poetry to toads?"

Max stood abruptly and reached out his hand. "Let's take a walk."

I glanced at Chris and Adriane, who had dispensed with the ballroom theatrics and were swaying slowly back and forth, closing in on the very unchurchly inevitable.

"Let's." I grabbed his hand. Wheelbarrow or not, sometimes three was an ugly number.

Without discussion, Max led me up the narrow spiral staircase that rose to the church quire. It was a shallow balcony overlooking the nave, complete with choir risers and a dying pipe organ. "I've never been up here," I said, leaning against the balcony and watching Chris and Adriane sway and spin beneath us. The wooden rail creaked with my weight, sign enough to step back and forget the rituals of seduction playing out below.

"I come a lot," Max said. "I like the way things look from up here. Small."

There was a sudden draft, and I shivered in the blast of frigid air.

"Cold?" Max inched closer, hand on the lapel of his blazer, as if he wanted to offer it but couldn't quite muster the nerve. He almost always wore a blazer, khaki in the early fall, corduroy now in the encroaching cold. It wasn't an unusual uniform amid the New England tweediness of the Chapman quad, but I liked the way Max pulled it off, pairing his jackets with faded vintage T-shirts that looked—as opposed to the crisply colored ironic tees paraded by the occasional out-of-place hipster—genuinely bedraggled, as if they had been plucked from the pile of dirty laundry in his childhood bedroom.

"I like this," I said, pinching the thin cotton of his faded Simpsons T-shirt and tugging it toward me. Then, though I'd never thought of doing anything like it before and didn't technically *think* of it at all, not in any way that constituted conscious thought as opposed to reflexive, unmotivated, utterly irrational action, I kissed him.

He let me. For a few seconds—then he pulled back and adjusted his glasses, looking at me like I was a puppy who'd just performed a particularly complicated dance step, then peed on his leg.

I wanted to die.

"Sorry," I said.

"Why'd you do that?"

Because I'd wanted to kiss someone. Because my two best friends were best friends with each other, a seamless unit who probably spent the majority of their time together waiting for me to go away. Because his eyes were brown in one light and green in another, magnetic in both. Because I'd worked a miracle—or maybe because I'd done so only by imagining I was someone else, someone intrepid and intense and long dead, and I wasn't quite ready to go back to being me. "I don't know."

He laughed. Now I wanted to kill him—*then* die.

"That's a terrible reason," he said.

"Yeah? You've got a better one?"

He leaned forward. He cupped his hands around my face, one warm hand over each cheek. He kissed me.

"Because I wanted to," he said when he let go. "That would have sufficed."

20

We kissed only once more that night, on the steps of the church before he went in one direction and I went in the other. And yes, I lay awake half the night replaying the details in my mind, imagining I could still feel his hands on my face, my neck, the curve of my hip, his fingers entwined in mine, his lips, and the way that, for a few seconds, it felt like we were breathing together. I replayed the goodbye, the awkward moment beneath the streetlight, our breath white puffs disappearing into the night, him not asking me back to his dorm room, me babbling something inane about being able to use my father's car when I asked nicely but sometimes preferring my bike and sometimes not, and then one final, feathery peck on the cheek, the soft touch of my gloved fingers against his. I woke up convinced that if it hadn't been a dream, it had been an aberration, and not only had I guilted him into a pity kiss—*Max*, of all people, a *college* guy, and, more to the point, a college guy who'd never shown any romantic inclinations in my direction—but there was no way I'd be able to return to the Hoff's office. It would be torture, pretending to translate while I wondered whether Max was staring at me, and what kind of pitying, mocking thoughts were running through his head as he did. Or worse, realize that he wasn't staring, because he couldn't care less.

Suffice it to say, I wasn't expecting a happy ending, any more than I was expecting my phone to buzz with an incoming text. From him:

Thinking about you.

21

Max had a half-moon of freckles on his left shoulder.

Max was nearly as bad at getting jokes as he was at making them, but he was ticklish, especially on the bottom of his right foot, and when he laughed, his face turned pink.

Max liked to lie on his stomach and let me trace messages across his bare back as he guessed what I was trying to say. *X marks the spot*, I wrote. *Max and Nora, sitting in a tree*, I wrote. *I love you*, I wrote. He always guessed wrong, and when he did, he twisted beneath me, propped himself up on his elbows, and kissed me, once for each secret message. "Now you guess what that means," he always said.

Max and I barricaded ourselves in his room whenever we knew Adriane and Chris would be out. We locked the door, curled up together on his sagging mattress, and watched movies and ate Oreos and listened to moody indie rock, and a few times, when I told my parents I'd be sleeping over at Adriane's, we stayed there, together, in the dark, until morning.

Max never came to my house. He never met my parents. And he never talked about his, except to say they lived in San Diego, and it was the longest they'd lived anywhere, as if they'd waited until he was out of the house to finally make a home.

Max never knew about my brother.

Max hated Adriane, and the feeling was mutual. She teased him about his glasses and his shaggy hair and the way he gravitated to my side and took my hand as soon as he entered a room,

64

and he blanched every time she described some aspect of her sex life, which she only did to make him squirm. He thought she was dumb and desperate; she thought he was boring. Both were careful never to make me choose.

Max blushed. When he was thinking about kissing me, when I crept up behind him and pressed my lips to the base of his neck, and always when he lied, which he did infrequently and poorly and almost exclusively to spare someone's feelings and never to me. He blushed when, three months after our first kiss, he took off his glasses, blinked owlishly for a few seconds, then told me he loved me. "You tell me that *here*?" I said, shoving him, because we were standing in front of the Walmart, which I would now be obligated to think of as a sacred space, and then I laughed and I kissed him and I said, not for the first time but for the first time like this, "I love you, too."

22

Despite how it felt, we weren't together all day, every day. Life went on. Snow fell, my parents continued to ignore me and each other, Adriane plotted our Parisian adventures while I kept pretending that some fairy godmother would appear to supply the plane ticket I'd never be able to afford but now had to, because going to Paris meant going to Paris with Max. Chris and Max spent more and more time locked up in the Hoff's lair, poring over the Book, laboring to match symbol to word and word to meaning. Using the fragment of the alchemical formula—for that's what the hidden pages had turned out to be—they'd managed to piece together a rough language of glyphs. Applying it to the Book was painstaking, as page after page defied meaningful translation, and then, always, just when they were about to give up, the symbols would yield a line that almost made sense: *Deus in natura se obscurat et celata eius corripimus. God hides in nature, and we plunder his secrets.* Max, not good with frustration, snapped whenever the subject came up, so I stopped asking him about his research and stopped boring him with mine. I'd gone back through the letters that led up to the Petrarch revelation—I just wasn't the kind of person who could skip to the end of a book to find out what happened—and backtracking turned out to be the right call. Because, as even Adriane would have admitted, things were finally getting good.

E. J. Weston, to her full brother John Fr. Weston, greetings.

How you would laugh to see me! Stars sparkle in my eyes, melodies trill in my ears, a soft breeze lifts my steps. Love, which for so long I have thought nothing but a poet's folly, has seized me, and I am transformed. I can no longer deny the truth in Petrarch's words:

> *I bless the place, the time and hour of the day*
> *that my eyes aimed their sights at such a height.*

You will ask what use is a love with no respectable end. You will call Thomas a mere apprentice, but nothing about him could be mere. His touch with the potions is nimble and sure. Despite his lack of schooling, Latin flows from his pen, for so determined was he to penetrate the secrets of the ancients that he schooled himself in their language. To call him ignorant would be ignorance itself. Your Schoolmen have made you forget, dearest brother, that there are many ways of knowing.

Perhaps love has made me frivolous, but there is so much darkness here. Surely you can allow me a few moments of light? This happiness will not last, as nothing does. Our

Father taught us that. The heavens may be immutable, but here
in our earthly sphere, life is constant flux and decay. We can
either watch the world change around us, like our Father before
us, or we can change it to suit our desires.

And thus I have a decision to make. Pray that I choose
wisely.

16 January 1599 Prague.

So Elizabeth was in love.

I wasn't the type to write sappy love letters or moon over
cheesy love songs whose inane lyrics suddenly seemed deep and
true and meant only for me—but I was happy enough for her to
do it for me. *Stars sparkle in my eyes,* I thought, trying to imagine
what Max would do if I laid it out for him like that, complete
with trilling melodies and air-cushioned steps, light banishing
the darkness.

Probably just blush and change the subject.

The next several letters spoke of Elizabeth's attempts to get
her property back from the Emperor, her poetry, her mysterious
ally and the dangers he posed, the decision she faced, and the way
the frozen Vltava glistened in the sun, but more than anything,
they spoke of Thomas.

The laboratory smells like him, a rich mixture of sulfur and
ash. A badge of his low station, he says. But I have glimpsed
the pride that lies beneath his modesty. He has confided his
dreams of discovering the philosopher's stone, not for his own
glory, but for the glory of God.

And though we were both afraid, he took my hand.

One hand in another, nothing more, and yet it was more
than anything I have known.

Shadows flickered in the candlelight. Brother, you never knew how the alchemical chambers terrified me as a child. I would scurry behind our Father's black cloak as it swept through the room, while his men glared at me over their cauldrons, their faces obscured by mushrooms of black smoke. I feared the evils our Father might awaken through his dark conjuring. But Thomas has released me from my fear by revealing the essential truth. Alchemy is not a courting of darkness. It is a quest for light.

I tried to come to the office when I knew Max would be there and Chris wouldn't—and that was strange in itself, wanting to see *less* of Chris for once, wanting to keep Max to myself (an impulse that only made me more certain I'd been right all these years about Chris and Adriane wishing me away so they could be alone). But stranger still was the way it felt to sit at the table beside Max, staring blankly at my notebook, lost in the steady rhythm of his breathing, the smell of his shampoo, the weight of his hand on my leg, the press of his foot against mine, the inches between our shoulders, or the stray hair that he always brushed off his forehead before he leaned in to kiss me. It wasn't conducive to getting much done. I could have written a dissertation on his elbow, or the way his collarbone jutted out from his faded T-shirts, but the actual work went slowly, and never more so than when he bent toward me, touched his cheek to mine, and watched Elizabeth's words flow from my pen.

"You have to stop that," I finally told him.

"What?" He kissed my cheek. "This?" He traced a finger along my jawline, then pressed it to my lips. "Or this?"

I smiled. There were other benefits to coming to the office when Max and I could be alone.

"Watching me work," I said. "It's distracting."

"I don't have to watch. I told you I could help—"

"And I told *you* I'm better at Latin than you are, so I'm not the one who needs help. At least, not with Latin." I leaned in to kiss him, but he pulled away.

"Fine," he said stiffly. "Forget I asked."

"Max—"

"No, you're right. This is a distraction." He scraped his chair down to the other side of the table. "Better?"

"You're being ridiculous."

"I'm just doing what you want."

I swallowed a sigh. "You're right," I said. "I'm being ridiculous." I dragged my chair next to his. "Distract me."

"Just forget it."

I took his pen out of his hand and wove his fingers through mine. "I can be distracting, too," I said, and finally found, in the corner of his lips and the crinkle of his eyes, the hint of a smile. I brushed the hair out of his eyes and I kissed him, and we distracted each other for the rest of the night.

He was oversensitive; he was moody. I could never argue with Adriane's complaints on this front, as I could never tell her the truth, that I didn't mind. And not just because it was one of the things that made him *Max*, but because it was one of the things that made me want him to be mine.

I'd had friends before Adriane and Chris, friends that had fit seamlessly with me because we were the same. We'd worried; we'd obsessed; we'd sought out dark clouds; we'd shared secrets and we'd kept plenty to ourselves. We'd been best friends until my brother's accident, and then we hadn't been friends at all, because after Andy, I couldn't handle any more dark clouds and I didn't want to share any more secrets. After Andy, I wanted easy, and that was Adriane, and that was Chris. They believed in surfaces and taking things as they seemed. They believed life was simple and good—and they willed it to be true. They laughed, they spilled their secrets as if it were nothing, because it was, and they didn't ask questions. They'd been easy when I'd needed easy, and if I couldn't be like them, they'd at least taught me how to pretend.

Max, on the other hand, was hard. Convoluted and cloudy, full of things I wasn't supposed to ask and places I knew better than to go.

With Max, I didn't have to pretend.

Foolish? Selfish? Your words wound, especially as I know you have borrowed them from our Mother. Is it foolish to deny Johannes Leo, when he could do so much for us? Is it selfish to deny our Mother the life at court to which she once grew accustomed, and which our Father's crimes denied her? Perhaps it should little matter that Johannes stinks of the tobacco oil he vainly rubs on his skin, that his hands are clammy as fish scales, and that he cares as little for Cicero or Dante as a rabid dog does for water. But matter it does.

I offer you rational arguments, but my choice goes beyond reason. There is no choice. Thomas belongs to me, and I him. And if our precarious state so concerns our Mother, then perhaps she should dry her tears and contribute to its improvement. It is a daughter's duty to serve her mother, and I have done so with pride. But if our survival is my responsibility, then surely deciding our course also falls to me. I honor our Mother, but I cannot cede my will to hers. Not when the sacrifice is so great.

It was the translation problem again, or maybe its inverse— because we used the same word, everyone used it, no matter the language, *amour, amo, amore, Liebe, love,* but it was impossible to believe that what she felt for Thomas bore any resemblance to what Max and I had together. How could it, considering the centuries that separated us—and not just centuries, but cars, computers, movies, cell phones, safe sex, Oprah, feminism, gay marriage, condoms, free love, revolutions sexual and otherwise. How could *love* have any meaning at all, if it meant the same thing through all of that? Elizabeth's paeans to love were dated a couple years after *Romeo and Juliet* was first published, half a continent away. Say what you want about all the sulking, stalking, and pointless suicides in literature's supposed great love affair, but what could *love* have meant before *Romeo and Juliet*? Not to mention *Pride and Prejudice, Gone with the Wind*? I hated romance novels, romantic comedies, and moony love songs with equal passion—but I wasn't stupid enough to think I could ignore them. I believed in happily ever after as much as anyone, because Jane Austen, Prince Charming, and Hugh Grant promised me it could happen.

But maybe that particular delusion was universal.

E. J. Weston, to her dearest brother John Fr. Weston.

Aristotle teaches us that nature abhors a vacuum. But he discounts the emptiness left in the absence of love. Nothing will fill the hole Thomas has left behind, not air, not aether, not God.

You advised me of what would come if I gave him my heart. Advice which I disregarded, for I am a fool.

There is nothing left now, nothing but the machine, confirming beyond doubt that justice has departed this world. And, though it pains me to say, I am tempted to believe that God has departed as well. Certainly he has abandoned me, and in this, perhaps justice is served.

71

I—

My words have abandoned me as well, it seems.

Farewell.

23 March 1599 Prague.

So Thomas had left her behind, alone. She had given him her heart and, apparently, he'd taken it with him as a parting gift. Abandoning her like her father, like her God, like her hope. And she blamed herself.

Beside me, Max was paging through his dictionary, eyes slit in concentration, shaggy hair wild. I poked his arm, lightly enough to convince me that he was solid and still there.

"What?"

"Nothing." I was tired of this game, comparing myself to a dead girl. I didn't want to think about the meaning behind the words anymore, what it felt like, what was left behind. "Just, hi."

"Hi." Max brushed a strand of hair out of my face and let his hand linger at my temple, just above the skin. His smile was equal parts irritated and bemused. "Can I go back to work now?"

"Go."

I watched him work. Then shuffled my papers, flipped through my notebook, pantomimed productivity, watched him some more.

Elizabeth was silent for weeks. When she did write again, it was only to ask after her brother's health or his studies, everything about his life, nothing about hers. Nothing about Thomas, or about the "machine" and what she was planning to do with it. Nothing until the letter I'd already read, the one that led to the hidden pages in Petrarch. After that, over the course of more than a year, there were only a few scraps of correspondence, colorless descriptions of legal matters and a perfunctory report of what would come next.

*Johannes Leo has promised patience and agreed that the
wedding will be at least two years hence. It defies my
imagination that there can be happiness left in the world,
and yet Johannes Leo's face fills with light in my presence. I
know our Mother will derive great joy from the security of our
union. Perhaps you will as well. As for me, I have learned to
tolerate the scent of lilacs, as I will learn to tolerate the touch of
his hand. I have discovered what fills the vacuum left by love.
It is called necessity, and it will not be denied.*

This time, when I nudged Max, he didn't look up.

23

I saved the final letter until I was alone. It had been a long time since
I'd come to the church by myself at night. Max didn't like me going
without him. He didn't have to say why. We never talked about the
night of the bloody broken window, but neither of us had forgotten it. The protectiveness was sweet, if worth more in theory than
in practice; he couldn't take even a fake punch without wincing.

Fortunately, I could take care of myself.

The lamplight sheathed the office in a soft orange glow, and a
steady hiss of heat issued from the clanking pipes. Though frost
crusted the windows, the office was warm. I'd told myself that I
just wanted to say goodbye to her on my own, a silly sentimental
gesture toward the girl who, in a way, had brought Max and me
together. But the truth was, I'd seen Elizabeth's bio. I knew where
her story ended.

E. J. Weston, to her dearest brother, it began, as they all had.

*You once said you would grant me anything, and now I ask
that you grant your forgiveness for my long silence. In turn,*

I grant you my forgiveness, for yours. The answers you crave await you in Prague, as does the Lumen Dei *itself. It is your birthright, and I wish it to poison my life no longer.*

This is a lie. I wish it a part of me forever. But I must be done with it, if I am to survive. Johannes talks of children, although, dry and empty, I have no more to give. But I cannot deprive him, even if he allowed me to do so. And if there are to be children, I must let this die before they can live.

Three by three is where you'll find me.

I double-checked my translation of the last line, but I hadn't made a mistake—it just made no sense. Neither did the strange stanzas of poetry that followed. Elizabeth had sent her brother examples of her work before, but her poems were rigorous in rhyme and meter, and coherent in content, evoking the poetry of classical Rome, not open-mike night at the local coffeehouse slam. This was different.

Winters know the shadows in that word.
Unless the dark law too should seek the thief
And the good law obtain your city
For those outside the word.

Throughout our epoch, He that is below
Ignorantly deserves an abject prayer
O my guardian spirit
O when the unmixed nectar of the faithless lives with you.

My law is a tepid standard
Thus I surrendered the hound to the dark
Revive your soul at my house
The sun will foretell all things in this way.

Remember the lessons our Father taught us beneath the linden tree, and you will know where to begin.

Then the words broke off, leaving several inches of empty space. When she began again, it was in a darker ink, with a shakier hand.

My dearest brother. My most loving brother. My brother.
I was set to post my letter when yours arrived. Your letter,
unfinished, with the postscript appended by your schoolmaster.

I see now that I lied before, as I cannot forgive your silence,
not when I know its cause.

I write as if you can still hear me, because writing to you
has become my sustenance, and my hand continues along the
page though my soul knows there is no use. You are the only
one who penetrated beyond my words and saw what was real.
Having lost you, I wonder, have I lost what little is left of
myself?

Your health, always so fragile, nonetheless seemed as if it
would hold forever, because it must. We have been connected
all our lives, and now, that connection severed, I float free. I
should float away, and yet I am sinking.

You loved Prague this time of year, the ice on the Vltava,
children stumbling and dancing through the snow, as we
once did. You promised you would return and we would walk
the Stone Bridge together. You have never before broken your
promise.

You are with the Lord now, and He will give you your
reward, our Mother says. That faith protects her. But I have no
reserves of faith to see me through, and no confidence that God
will reward you better in death than He has in life.

I think often of our first journey together, when, barely old
enough to understand, we were torn from our native land and

carried to Bohemia, our new father terrifying with his dark
cloak and forbidding black eyes. You would not remember, as I
will not forget, the night we set camp outside Erfurt, and there
by the fire, you spilled your blood and mine, and swore an oath
to protect me always. Blood hot and sticky between our palms,
you swore you would never leave me.

I can forgive you almost anything, my brother. But I
cannot forgive this.

23 December 1600 Prague.

After what happened to Andy, there'd been a therapist. At
the third appointment, after I'd spent an hour on her patchwork-
quilted couch, box of tissues in my lap, refusing or unable to speak,
she'd given me a homework assignment: Write a letter to my dead
brother. She wanted me to tell Andy I loved him, or hated him, or
that I blamed him for dying, or, for all I know, that I'd borrowed
his Patriots sweatshirt without telling him and accidentally left it
on the bus. I didn't write the letter; I didn't go back.

But sometimes, I talked to him. Lying in bed in the dark, on
his birthday or the anniversary of his death, or sometimes just a
day like any other, while our mother, now just my mother, slept
at her office and my father slept in his and I moved through the
house like a ghost. I talked to him, one ghost to another, and it
made me feel . . . not better, exactly. It made me feel whole. But
not because I thought he could actually hear me. I never fooled
myself into believing that. There was no Andy anymore.

Gone is gone.

Those conversations in the dark were a secret. And if I'd written the letter, that would have been secret, too. Not meant for my
therapist, nor for my parents—not even for him. It would have
been for me. As this letter was for Elizabeth.

Death meant the end of privacy. I knew that. Had understood when my parents tore apart Andy's room, scavenging through drawers and closets he'd locked away from them, reading emails, picking and choosing the pieces of him they wanted to claim, throwing out the rest. They left him with nothing, and maybe he deserved it, because he was nothing, too. But that didn't make it right. And it didn't make Elizabeth's letter public property, no matter how many centuries had passed. I remembered what the Hoff had said about publication, and how Elizabeth's letters were part of a precious historical legacy, an invaluable public record.

You are the only one who penetrated beyond my words and saw what was real.

Maybe those were good reasons to do what I did next, but I came up with them after the fact. When it happened, I didn't rationalize, I didn't justify, and I didn't worry about how much this precious historical legacy was worth or what would happen if anyone realized it was gone.

I just folded it up and slipped it into my notebook. Then I zipped the notebook into my backpack, turned out the lights, and went home.

24

I am a thief.

The drumbeat thudded in my head all night long, and the next day and the one after that. I didn't know how much the letter was worth, but it was four hundred years old, so presumably . . . a lot. If anyone found out I'd taken it, how would I explain myself? What college would let me in with grand larceny on my permanent record? Forget college: Chapman Prep would kick me out, and I'd end up back at the public high school, dodging stink bombs, skirting blood spatter, enjoying the periodic schoolwide drug tests (and concomitant black market for untainted "samples").

But I didn't regret taking it.

And I didn't want to give it back.

I stayed away from the church, from the Hoff, and most of all, from Max, because I was sure he'd take one look and see exactly what I'd done.

He wouldn't understand.

Three days had passed when the phone rang Saturday morning. I almost screened it, like I'd screened his other calls, offering in response only a feeble text that I was getting the flu and had lost my voice. But I couldn't avoid him forever, so I picked up the phone, remembering to cough.

"Where are you?" He sounded frantic.

"Home." I coughed again. "I'm not—"

"You have to get down to the office," he said. There was a high, quavering note in his voice that I'd never heard before.

"What's wrong?"

"I found—I saw—I don't know—" He was hyperventilating.

"Max!"

"Just come," he said. "Please. They're making me hang up, I have to go. . . . I was the one who found him."

Dial tone.

25

Flashing lights.

I spotted them from a block away, lighting the stone church with a rhythmic *red, red, red*. I pedaled faster, dumped my bike in the grass—and that's when I saw the stretcher.

There were cops. There were EMTs. There was the obligatory crowd of gawking students, though only the handful who weren't still in bed sleeping off a hangover. And there was Max, one arm around Adriane's shoulder, the other gesticulating wildly as he explained something to a cop. Max and Adriane, but no Chris.

I could get back on the bike and ride away, I thought. Escape before it—whatever it was—became real.

Instead: "What happened?"

Max dropped his arm and Adriane flinched away from him. They were both pale.

"Someone broke in," Max said. He took my hand, squeezed it. "I came in this morning and found him on the floor. . . ."

The stretcher had disappeared into the ambulance. Sirens blaring, it tore down the street. Sirens were good, I thought. Corpses were never in a hurry.

"Found who?"

Max opened his mouth. Nothing came out.

"The Hoff," Adriane said.

After, I hated myself for it, but in that first moment, all I felt was relief.

Adriane shuddered. "He was just . . . lying there. We thought he was dead, but then he was, like, *twitching*."

The cop cleared his throat. With his thick glasses and the deep worry lines engraved in his forehead, he looked a little like my father, except for the shock of red hair threaded with gray. "You were explaining to me what you were doing here, Mr. Lewis?"

"I'm Professor Hoffpauer's research assistant," Max said. He nodded to me. "We both are."

The cop turned to Adriane. "And you . . . ?"

"I was looking for my boyfriend," she said.

My chest tightened again. "You don't know where he is?"

"He's in our room, asleep," Max said, a note of suspicion

entering his voice. "Why would you come looking for him *here*? You don't belong here."

"Excuse me," Adriane snapped. "He wasn't answering his phone, and I needed to talk to him."

Max glared at her. "About what?"

"It's private."

I put a hand on his shoulder. He stiffened, but didn't shrug me off. "It doesn't matter," I said quietly. "As long as he's safe." As long as we all were. "Is the Hoff—Professor Hoffpauer—going to be okay?"

The cop's frown deepened. "Looks like he had a stroke. That can go either way."

"So he wasn't . . . attacked?"

"Do you have some reason for thinking he would be?"

"I *told* you," Max said, with a flash of anger, "it's missing, all of it."

"What?" I asked.

"The letters. The translations of the Book. The whole archive—everything. Gone."

Now I squeezed his hand.

The cop shook his head. "We'll bring you down to the station to give a statement, and put together a list of everything that's missing, but I don't think you need to worry, not about this, at least. There was no sign of violence at the scene, no sign of a break-in." He flipped his notebook shut and slipped it into his pocket. "My guess? Your prof got a little confused, stuck your papers somewhere, then passed out. I can see why you got spooked, but this is a case for the doctors, not the cops."

"So what do you really think happened?" I asked Max when the cop was gone.

He swallowed hard. "I thought he was dead. When I walked in and saw him like that . . ."

I grabbed him and kissed him, hard. If someone had broken into the office and attacked the Hoff, if Max had gotten there a little earlier— I stopped myself. "Everything's going to be fine."

"The letters are gone," he said, still holding on to me. "Someone got into the safe. It's all gone."

"You're not." I kissed him again, then buried my face in his shoulder.

"I should go," Adriane said. "I don't belong here, right?"

"Adriane—" I started, but she cut me off.

"It's fine."

It clearly wasn't.

"Well, when you find Chris, will you tell him I say—" I paused, because how to phrase the message *For five seconds I thought those sirens were for you, and now I need to hear your voice. I need proof that you're real*? "Just tell him to call me." But when I looked up, she was already gone.

26

I don't do hospitals. It's not the smell, that suffocating stench of cleaning fluid with a hint of the decay it was intended to disguise. It's not the waiting rooms, with their faded, broken furniture and huddled groups of weeping or wailing families alongside dead-eyed survivors with no need to stay and no will to go home. It's not Andy, who never made it that far.

It's the doors. Open doors along dingy white corridors that reveal everything you're not supposed to see. Patients crying, patients moaning, patients vomiting; patients awkwardly mounting bedpans or shuffling barefoot, IV in tow, toward an industrial toilet; bloated patients lying still with tubes running in and out, monitors beeping, machines wheezing and pumping and performing all the functions their bodies have given up.

I didn't have to go alone, but bringing someone with me would have meant admitting I couldn't do it myself.

Also, the Hoff had only asked for me.

The nursing station in the intensive care unit was empty, but eventually a heavy woman in an orderly's uniform noticed me. She was carrying a vial of something that looked suspiciously like urine. "I'm looking for Professor—I mean, Anton Hoffpauer?" I said.

"You Nora?"

I nodded.

"Yeah, he's been asking for you."

"They told me. But . . . are you sure?"

"Took us a while to figure out exactly what he wanted, and how to find you, but yeah, I'm sure."

"I just don't see why he would want—"

"Room seven, honey," she said. "You can go right in."

"How is he?" I asked, stalling.

"In and out. You never know with a stroke. People come back from the damnedest things."

"So he'll be okay?"

She pursed her lips. "Go see him, honey. He'll like that. If you stick around for a while, the doc might come by, and he'll have more answers for you."

But the non-answer was answer enough.

The narrow patient rooms were encased behind thick glass walls, with white curtains draped across for privacy. The door of number seven was open. I desperately didn't want to go inside.

The door creaked when I shut it behind me. Deep breath, I thought, forcing myself to turn around and face him. In and out.

He was pale, with yellowed encrustations around his watery eyes, like a kid who'd cried himself to sleep. The liver spots at his

82

thinning hairline stood out like splotches of ink on a too-white canvas. IV needles threaded into bulging veins. One side of his face drooped noticeably, and when he opened his eyes, only one of them focused on me. It widened.

Why me? I wanted to ask. Why not Max, or Chris, or better yet, a son or granddaughter, someone to take his gnarled hand or stroke his sweaty forehead, to sit beside him and force a smile and not recoil when a rivulet of drool trickled from the corner of his blistered lips.

I lowered myself into the narrow metal chair beside the bed. He was muttering. Nonsense syllables, mostly, the right side of his mouth lagging behind the left.

"Lay da chee," he said, then repeated it, louder. "Lay da chee!"

He curled his left hand into a fist and pounded the bed.

"Shh." I patted the blanket, awkwardly, a few inches from the lump that was his right leg. "It's okay."

His mouth twisted, and he forced out a slurred but understandable word. "Safe!" he shouted. "Not safe!"

"You are," I assured him. And then I took his hand. I had to. "Don't worry."

He pulled away with surprising strength, and jabbed a finger at me. "You."

"Me what?"

"Yortheeun."

I leaned closer, hating myself for noticing the smell, cloyingly sweet and ripe. "I'm sorry. I don't understand."

"You're. The. One." He punctuated each word with a fist against the blanket. "Your blood." And then those nonsense words again that seemed to mean so much. "Lay da chee!"

"Yes," I said, because what else was there? "I know."

That seemed to satisfy him. He closed his eyes. I sat there, listening to his breath rattle in his chest and the monitors play their discordant song, wondering how long I was supposed to stay—and how I could leave him there alone.

The door creaked open. "So how are we doing today, Mr. Hoffpauer?" A young doctor stood in the doorway, his black hair gelled into tiny spikes and a minuscule silver stud in his right ear. The look would have gained a thumbs-up—and likely some gratuitous yoga stretches—from Adriane, but it didn't exactly scream professional competence.

"I think he's sleeping," I said when the Hoff didn't react to his arrival.

"You a relative?"

I shook my head. "I'm his student, I guess. They said he was asking for me."

The doctor brightened. "Oh, you must be Nora? Yes, he was pretty adamant."

"He didn't really seem . . . I mean, he was kind of babbling, like he didn't really know what he was saying."

"That's normal with a neurological event of this severity." The doctor lifted a clipboard from the edge of the bed and began flipping through it, nodding at whatever he saw. "Did he know who you were?"

I nodded. Then, since he was still buried in his clipboard, said yes.

"He was trying to tell me something, but I couldn't understand it. I think I upset him."

"He got angry, right?" the doctor said. "Don't worry, that's normal, too. You can expect some irrational emotional outbursts."

I wanted to point out there was nothing irrational about getting angry when you were stuck in a hospital bed with a ruined body and defective brain. But I also wanted answers. And I suspected I wouldn't get many if I treated him to an irrational emotional outburst of my own.

"So it was definitely a stroke?" I asked.

"Oh, there's no question of that."

"And is it possible . . . I mean, is that the kind of thing someone could *cause*? Like, on purpose?"

He didn't seem surprised by the question. "Certainly excessive stress on the body or nervous system wouldn't help matters. And certain medications can induce—" He frowned, like he'd said more than he'd intended. "We're waiting on the scans, but I suspect he's been having transient ischemic attacks—think of them as mini strokes—for some time now. Has he been acting oddly at all? Doing things, saying things that don't make sense?"

"I really don't know him that well," I admitted, and thought of the open safe, the missing archive. Was it possible that the police were right and he'd hidden the papers somewhere himself?

"It's good of you to sit with him, then," the doctor said. "He's going to need all the support he can get. Does he have any family?"

Again, I had to admit I didn't know. "How serious is this?" I said. "Is he going to get better?"

The doctor finally met my eye. "The stroke affected his speech center. There are mobility issues, especially on his right side, and we don't know yet whether his speaking problems are connected to that, or to a cognitive deficit. There are signs of aphasia, disorganized cognition. . . . It's just too soon to tell."

"You mean you don't know whether he can't talk or can't think."

"We're monitoring the situation. Rehabilitation after a stroke is difficult, but people accomplish amazing things. That said, you should prepare yourself. He might never be the man he was before. You said he was a teacher?"

"Professor," I said, then realized the Hoff's eyes were open, and pinned on me. "He's a very respected professor. Brilliant. World-renowned."

The doctor tugged at his stupid earring. "Well. It's nice to be able to leave a legacy behind, isn't it?"

"He's not dead," I said sharply.

"No, of course not." But we both knew what he meant. The brilliant, world-renowned phase of things was likely over. This is how it happens, I thought as the doctor slid the clipboard back into its holster and escaped. You don't even realize you're living in a before until you wake up one day and find yourself in an after. I smiled down at the Hoff, and the left side of his mouth smiled back. Did he understand what was happening? I suspected he did. But did he understand that this was *it*, that things would never go back to the way they were? That, I doubted. There was a chasm between knowing and believing, and if the Hoff had jumped it, he wouldn't be smiling.

"Don't go," the Hoff croaked, though I hadn't moved.

"I won't," I said. "And when I do, I'll come back. I'll visit."

He lurched upright and grabbed my wrist. His hand was a claw.

"They'll lie," he slurred. "But don't go!"

"Okay," I said, because it had worked the last time. "Okay, I won't go."

"Promise." *Pwomiss,* it came out. Like a little kid.

"I promise."

He let go and sank back into the pillows, a wide, lopsided smile spreading across his face. Such a small thing, to make him so happy. But his whole life had gotten small, I realized. These tubes. These walls. This bed. No more manuscripts to decipher, no more mysteries to penetrate, no more ancient grudges to prosecute. And the only secret language he had to decode was his own.

27

"Please come," I said into the phone, and he did, no questions asked, showed up at the house I'd never let anyone visit, took one look and folded me into a hug that felt like it could last forever if I needed it to.

"Horrible?" Chris asked, still holding on.

"Horrible."

He squeezed tighter. "Maybe you shouldn't have gone."

"I had to."

"At least it's over now."

It didn't feel over.

"I hate hospitals." I pressed my face to his shoulder. It was the only way to wipe away the tears without letting go.

"Because of . . . ?"

"No." It was the closest we'd gotten to mentioning my brother in two years. "This isn't about him."

But maybe it was, as much as anything was. And maybe that was why I'd called Chris, without thinking, without any conscious desire to choose him over Adriane, over Max, because I didn't have to explain myself to him.

"Okay," he said. Then, "Not that my arms are getting tired or anything, but . . . how much longer is the hugging phase going to last?"

"A little longer."

"Okay."

He held on until I was ready to let go.

28

"So this is the inner sanctum." Chris grabbed my desk chair, straddling it backward. I took the bed, my knees pulled up to my chest. It was weird having him here, in my bedroom, playing with the elephant paperweight I'd gotten from a fourth-grade trip to the zoo. "I can see why you've kept it secret all these years."

"Shut up."

"No, truly, it's shocking. Is that"—his eyes widened and his mouth formed a perfect O—"a desk calendar? And a piggy bank? What kind of crazy operation are you running here?"

"Asshole."

He grinned. "You know how compliments embarrass me."

There was nothing shocking, or even memorable, about the bedroom, which hadn't been redecorated in years and so still featured the pink walls and turquoise floor I'd chosen at age nine. The only thing hanging from the cheap cardboard paneling was a Red Sox pennant that I'd confiscated from Andy's room before my parents had a chance to purge it, and a dolphin painting my mother had bought for my sixteenth birthday, because the last time she'd checked, I was a big fan. (The last time she'd checked, I had been eleven.) The furniture was a shiny wood laminate and had been constructed, piece by piece, by my hapless parents a decade before, which meant the bed wobbled, the desk drawers didn't quite close, and both were chipped and scuffed in spots where my mother's hammer—or her frustration—had gone astray. The crawl space beneath the desk, where Chris had dumped his backpack, was the perfect size for a twelve-year-old to curl up in and hide out. I was too big for it now.

I wasn't embarrassed by the small, bare room, or the rest of the house, which could have fit into the east wing of the Moores' mansion. It was the collision of worlds I'd hoped to avoid. Nothing here was untainted with memories of Andy, with guilt and death and grief, with empty spaces no one wanted to fill. And maybe that was another reason it was Chris I'd called, because with Chris the collision had already happened. The danger had passed.

"You want to talk about it?" he asked.

"Not really."

A pause, not an awkward one, but heading in that direction. I realized it had been a long time since Chris and I had hung out alone together. There was a space between us that hadn't been there before, and part of me knew this was Max, and it was as it should be, but most of me was sorry.

He broke the silence. "Excellent. Talking is highly overrated. I suggest video games. Or poker. Funny cat videos?" He paused when he saw I wasn't cracking a smile. "Or we could just sit here and stare at each other really intensely until one of us manages to melt the other one's brain." He narrowed his eyes to slits.

"I didn't ask you to cheer me up."

His brow furrowed in mock concentration.

"I just wanted company."

He held his breath, cheeks blown out like a puffer fish, eyes still lasered at mine.

"This is not going to work."

His nose began twitching, just slightly at first, then wildly, like that of a rabbit on crack, until his head ricocheted back with an explosive sneeze.

I couldn't help myself: I laughed. And if there had been any distance between us, it was gone.

"Admit it," he said. "You can't resist my charms."

I rolled my eyes. "If I admit it, will you stop blowing snot all over my desk? It's called a tissue."

"Ah, she's neat-freaking. Must mean she's feeling better."

"Who are you talking to, nutcase? The hidden camera?"

"Always give the audience what they want," he said. "That's my motto. It's what makes me so lovable."

"Lovable? More like—"

"Ah, ah, ah." He held up a hand to silence me. "Think before you speak. Remember, words can hurt."

"Because you're so sensitive?"

"You know me, I'm like a little girl."

"An insult to little girls everywhere."

"Again with the compliments! See, now I know you're feeling better. Admit it."

"Maybe," I allowed.

"And what do we say when our most brilliant and cherished friend turns our frown upside down?"

I sighed. "We say thank you. Loser." But he knew I meant it.

"Anytime." And I knew he did, too.

He stayed for the rest of the afternoon, but we didn't talk about the Hoff, or the maybe/maybe-not break-in at the church, or anything else that particularly mattered. He regaled me with the adventures we would all have together on our Paris trip in a few weeks, and as usual, I let him believe I'd find a way to be there, stuffing my face and splashing in the Seine alongside everyone else. He whined about the way Adriane kept blowing off their dates for student-council meetings, lacrosse practice, and the various obligations that had accompanied a recent, inexplicable embrace of her heretofore nonexistent responsible side. I complained about Max going into attack mode whenever he got frustrated, snapping angrily at whoever happened to be around, usually me, and then apologizing five seconds later with such limpid puppy-dog eyes it was tempting to pat him on the head and give him a treat.

We still fit together, and that, more than anything, made it all okay. I resolved not to let so much time pass before we did this again. Max wasn't a replacement for Chris; I needed them both.

"You know, if this were a movie," Chris said, "we'd probably decide to ditch those ungrateful fools and start making out."

"And if this were a movie, there would probably be a really awkward moment after you put that out there."

"The air charged with sexual tension."

"Undoubtedly."

"Sparks flying."

"Tongues twisting, lips smacking—"

"Ugh, are you *trying* to make me puke?" he asked, laughing.

I batted my eyelashes at him. "You really know how to flatter a girl, don't you?"

"Like you weren't thinking it."

"I was going to say *vomit*," I said. "It's more ladylike."

"No one says *vomit*. Not even ladies."

"Really? I, a lady, will now use the term in a sentence: The idea of making out with you makes me want to *vomit*. Also to gag, regurgitate, expectorate, and hurl."

He puckered up and blew me a loud kiss, raspberry-style. "Love you, too."

He said it to me all the time, and to Adriane nearly every time they met or parted or hung up the phone. I'd even heard him say it to Max one night, after a few too many beers. They were easy words for him. I almost never said it back.

"I did something I shouldn't have," I said.

"Doubt that. You're not the type."

Instead of arguing with him, I handed him Elizabeth's letter. His eyes widened, for real this time.

"I took it," I said.

"I can see that."

91

"I *stole* it."

"Right."

"So what do I do now?"

He placed the letter on the desk, gently. "You know how much this thing is worth?"

"Do you?"

"I'm guessing a *lot*."

"Tens of thousands, probably," I said. "I did some research."

Chris rarely got serious, and when he did, he was like a different person, stiffer and older. Even his voice got deeper, offering a glimpse of some future Chris, all grown up with a law degree, two kids, and three-piece suits. "Please tell me you didn't steal this with some insane idea that you could sell it."

"Of course not!"

"So then . . . ?"

"It was private," I said.

"You can tell me," he said.

"No, I mean, the letter was private." I knew how it sounded. "It didn't belong to anyone but her."

"She's dead."

"I know that."

We were both silent. I could see him working the problem, trying to find the words to convince me to give it back. He didn't need to bother.

"It's all that's left," I said. "Now that the archive's gone. He needs it." I didn't say that the Hoff probably had no idea the rest were missing, and even if he did, it wouldn't make much difference anymore. That wasn't the point.

"Okay," he said. "So you put it back."

"That's the problem—back *where*? What am I supposed to do, just go to the cops and tell them I found it under a desk somewhere? Or give it to the Hoff? He probably wouldn't even understand—" I swallowed hard and forced myself to deal. "If he was aware enough to know what was going on, he'd want to know why I had it. People might think *I* was the one who stole everything else, and attacked him, and—"

Chris sat down beside me. "Breathe," he said, and with his hand rubbing smooth circles on my back, I could.

"No one attacked him," Chris said. "And no one stole anything."

He sounded so certain. In Chris's world, things like that just didn't happen, and I liked to think the sheer force of his belief in the general benevolence of the universe would, at least in his case, make it true. "He probably took the archive back to his house for some reason. Maybe he thought we were after it. He was paranoid. You *know* that."

"So what am I supposed to do with this?" I said, feeling—irrationally but firmly—that if I'd just left the letter where it was, the Hoff would have been fine.

"Let me take it," Chris said. "I'll turn it in to the history department. Say it got mixed up with some of my stuff or something."

"I don't want you to get in trouble."

"No one's going to get in trouble," he said, again so infuriatingly, wonderfully sure. "It's just an old letter. No big deal. Say it."

"No big deal."

His smile was back. "You scared me there, for a second," he said. "The look on your face, I thought you'd done something *really* bad, like root for the Yankees."

"Never." Now I could smile, too. Everything felt lighter.

No big deal.

"Prepare yourself for a massively brilliant idea," he said before leaving. "Movie night tomorrow. The four of us. Like we used to."

I could have reminded him why we'd stopped movie night in

the first place: Max and Adriane could barely make it through the previews without thrown popcorn, loud cursing, and occasional tears. Adriane may have started out as the biggest proponent of me and Max becoming an official, convenient-for-double-dating, romantically inclined *us*, but her cheerleading days were long gone. Buyer's remorse, she claimed, and chose to ignore me when I pointed out she wasn't the customer.

"My parents are out of town," he said when I didn't answer. "So forget the crappy dorm TV. I'm talking big screen, HD, free food, the works."

"Caramel popcorn?"

He knew he had me. "All you can eat."

"I have to check with Max."

"Tell him it's mandatory." He gave me a quick hug, then tapped the pocket of his backpack that contained Elizabeth's letter. "Now promise me you're not going to worry about this anymore. And that next time I see you, you'll be smiling."

For the second time that day, I promised.

29

"I've never been to your house," Max said on the phone that night, after unenthusiastically agreeing to the double date.

I was lying in bed with the lights out. Some nights we fell asleep that way, listening to each other breathe.

"What was he doing there?"

"I don't know. Hanging out. What's the difference?"

"You tell me," he said.

"He was here, we hung out, end of story. What, are you jealous?"

"No." It wasn't very convincing.

So this was what it meant to have a jealous boyfriend. It didn't feel as flattering as I'd expected. It felt like he was lying on top of me and I couldn't breathe.

It wasn't like him. "What's going on with you?"

His voice was sullen. "Nothing. I've just been sitting around the dorm all day, wondering where you were."

"I was at the hospital," I snapped.

"I know that!" His voice softened. "I'm sorry. I am. I've been worried. And then you were upset, and you called Chris and not me—"

"Who said I was upset?"

"I know you," he said. "Of course you're upset. Seeing him, it must have been . . ." He waited for me to fill in the blank. I didn't. "I'm just worried about you."

I still didn't say anything.

"Nora. I'm sorry. Really."

"Chris is my best friend," I reminded him. "You're not allowed to be jealous of him."

"I'm not. I swear. But something's going on with you. I can hear it in your voice."

There was something comforting about that. The idea that anyone knew me so well—that anyone cared enough to pay attention.

"But I shouldn't have pushed," he added. "It's your business."

So I told him everything. About the visit to the hospital, and about the stolen letter—why I'd taken it, why I needed to give it back. "I should have just told you."

"Yeah. But you didn't. What were you even thinking, stealing it in the first place?"

It wasn't exactly the response I'd hoped for. "I told you, I wasn't thinking."

"Obviously."

"I'm giving it back. It's no big deal."

"It's a huge deal," he said. "And you didn't give it back, you gave it to Chris. Who knows what he'll do with it?"

"What's that supposed to mean?"

"It means you should have come to me," he said.

"So you could yell at me?"

"I'm not yelling." He drew in a deep breath. "What did it say?"

"The letter? What's the difference?"

"Humor me."

I didn't want to tell him the part about her brother. Not when he was being like this. "It was just a bunch of stuff about that machine, and her needing to make a decision. And then there was, like, a poem or something. I don't know."

"What do you mean, you don't know? You don't remember?"

"No, I mean it didn't make any sense. Like it was in code or something. So I don't *know* what it said. Satisfied?"

"You're mad," he said.

"You're observant."

He sighed. "I'm also an ass."

At that, I softened. "It's been a long week," I admitted. "For both of us."

"I'm just worried about you."

"Trust me, I'm not as fragile as you seem to think."

"No, I mean I'm really worried. Someone attacked the Hoff. The idea that you have something they want, whoever they are? It scares me. I wish it scared you."

"Takes a lot to scare me," I said lightly, wishing it were true. "Besides, the Hoff had a stroke. It's sad, but nothing actually *happened*. There is no 'they.'"

"You really believe that?"

"Yes," I said, firm.

"Then so do I."

I laughed. "Now who's lying?"

He was so different from Chris, who didn't acknowledge the existence of darkness. Max understood it. Maybe he was right, I thought, and I should try harder to let him understand me.

"What do you want me to say?" he asked.

"That you know it's not your job to protect me. And even if it were, acting like a jerk isn't really the best way to do it."

"I know that."

"Are you lying now?" I asked.

Silence.

"Are you shaking your head?" I asked, and had to smile.

More silence.

"And now you're nodding?"

"I love that you know me," he said.

"I love that you know me, too."

"Are we okay?"

This time I nodded.

After a moment, he laughed. "I'll take that as a yes." And then, maybe afraid I was going to change my mind, he hung up without saying goodbye.

30

The Moores' sprawling Victorian was the largest house on the block and the only one without any lights blazing, not even the fake antique gas lamps that dotted the lawn and winding driveway. The moon was a sliver, and a dense layer of clouds blocked out the stars. When I switched off my headlights, the night went completely black. It didn't bother me; I'd walked the cobblestone path enough times to do it blindfolded. The door was open, knocking back and forth in the wind.

That bothered me.

"Hello?"

No answer. I was twenty minutes late, and presumably they were all gathered in the soundproofed basement in front of the giant flat screen, having started without me.

The door knocked against the frame again. I stepped inside and pulled it shut behind me. As I sealed myself into the darkness, I heard the breathing, sharp and uneven, like a panicked animal. Close.

A strange metallic scent hung heavy in the air. Familiar.

I was already reaching for the lights when a switch flipped in my head and I recognized the smell. I knew.

I saw the footprints first, red and shimmering under the track lighting, a trail of them heading straight toward me, past me, out the door. Then the drawing, finger-painted in blood, a dot between two curved lines, like an eye, with a lightning bolt speared through its center. There were other prints, not prints at all really, but blurry smears that could have been left by a foot, a hand, a knee, body parts scraped and dragged across the expensive tile.

Mrs. Moore would die when she saw this, I thought, feeling the strange urge to giggle. She was obsessed with keeping her tile clean.

I swallowed the laughter. It tasted like bile.

Chris's house had a long entryway, the Great Hall, Mrs. Moore liked to call it. Opposite the door, a winding mahogany staircase led to the second floor, with its four bedrooms, two bathrooms, and former servants' quarters. A step down on the left led to the kitchen and dining area, which had recently been featured in the *Boston Globe*'s style section under the caption "Country Splendors." On the right lay a living room no one ever used, with its pristine white tiles, white couches, white walls. Chris liked to say it looked like a padded room in a mental institution, "therefore, perfect for my mother," he would add, especially when she was in the room, because she loved his teasing as much as anyone.

He was lying facedown.

His left arm was flung out at an unnatural angle, elbow bent backward and splintered bone poking through the flesh. His right arm was crushed beneath him. He was so still.

And the blood.

Graceful as ever, Adriane perched in the center of it, a child in a puddle. Legs tucked into her chest, arms wrapped around them, face drained of color except for the red slash slicing across her cheek, she rocked back and forth.

Someone was screaming, and I needed it to stop.

I couldn't think.

I didn't want to think.

I closed my eyes. I closed my mouth and held my breath.

The screaming stopped.

But when I opened my eyes, nothing had changed. It doesn't look like he's sleeping, I thought. If he looked like he was sleeping, I could pretend.

"Adriane," I said. The voice sounded far away. Calm. "Adriane, what happened?" Thinking, *This is what you do, you pretend you can handle it, you pretend you're in control, you pretend.*

Thinking, *Don't you dare leave me alone.*

She looked past me, eyes sightless, mouth open, small, weak noises punctuating the panicked breathing. No words, just noise. Like a baby; like an animal.

This is what you do, I thought, and called 911, and told them something had happened, someone was bleeding, someone was dead.

"Get out of the house," the distant voice said. "Stay on the line." And I meant to, but the man kept talking and talking and it was too hard to focus on his words, so I hung up.

I hung up and knelt beside Chris, knelt beside the body. Knelt in the blood, put a hand on his back, then pulled it away, sticky.

I grabbed Adriane, shook her, slapped her, my hand leaving a bloody print on her cheek, screamed again, begged her to wake up, to come back, to *tell me what happened, please, God, just tell me what happened.*

She had something crumpled in her fist. I forced her fingers open, and there it was, like a joke, like a bad penny, like a curse, *E. I. Westonia, Ioanni Francisco Westonio, fratri suo germano*, a stolen letter.

No big deal.

Then the bloody letter was in my pocket and the phone was in my hand again, Max's face grinning from the display, because he'd promised to protect me whether I wanted him to or not, but the phone rang and went to voice mail and I hung up.

He's dead, too, I thought—I knew. Everywhere I looked, Chris's blood. Adriane's empty eyes. "Please, don't leave me here alone. Please." I wasn't sure which one I was talking to, not that it mattered. No one answered, because no one was listening.

Gone is gone.

PART II

The Ceremony of Innocence

Evocat iratos Cæli inclementia ventos;
Imbreque continuo nubila mista madent.
Molda tumet multùm vehemens pluvialibus undis
Prorumpens ripis impetuosa suis.

The sky's inclemency stirs up the angry winds;
the watery clouds are soaking with ceaseless rain.
The turbulent Vltava, swollen with rainy waves,
Bursting, impetuous, breaks through its river-banks.

✌ *"De inundatione Pragæ ex continuis pluviis exorta"*
Elizabeth Jane Weston

1

I have been here before.

2

I have been here before.
   I have done this before.

3

Before.

There were flashing lights, before. Sirens screaming. Someone screaming.

There was blood, before, blood on the road, blood I imagined and blood I saw, blood that shimmered under streetlights as we sped by, tires crunching over broken glass, my father grim and pale behind the wheel, my mother with one hand cupped to her ear, like she was still hearing, or trying not to hear, the call that had summoned us from *before* to now, to *after*. There was blood on the road and there was blood on the torn clothes stuffed into the Ziploc bag, blood on his wallet and his sneakers and the button-down shirt he'd chosen at the last minute because this was supposed to be the kind of party where you were allowed to look, just a little, like you were trying.

There were cops, before, because of the blood. Because of *his* blood, tainted, proving it was his mistake, his fault, his crime.

Or, as he would have said—because he had watched a James Dean movie in English class and then another with Catherine to dupe her into believing he had depth; because he had imbibed, embraced, finally inhabited the legend, living fast and dying young—his beautiful corpse.

The funeral was closed-casket. The blood on the road, the blood on the shoes, that was the last of him I saw.

It was not beautiful.

4

I have done this before.

Waited in waiting rooms—not the carpeted, cheerfully anti-septic, magazine-strewn rooms for waiters who needed to forget where they were, reclining in padded chairs and watching cook-ing shows on the ceiling TV, but rooms that were windowless closets for people whose need for denial had ridden off into the sunset with their hope.

Tried not to look at my parents looking at me. Tried not to shake. Tried to cry. Tried to bargain with a nonexistent God, beg for a reprieve or a miracle or a time machine, anything to go back, to bring *him* back.

I had done this before, so this time, I knew better.

And of course, this time, I had seen the blood seeping out of his body. I had seen his face, too swollen, too pale. This time, in-stead of a Ziploc bag, I had an ancient letter, streaked with dull red brown, as if parchment could rust. Those were the differences.

Everything else was the same.

5

They took me to the hospital because I was covered in blood. They let me stay because Adriane was there, too, her empty gaze unflinching as they stitched up the gash in her cheek, plied her with liquids and gentle tones, shined lights at her pupils, and finally, her parents flanking her eerily still body, ushered her off to "a special wing, better suited to her condition." A special wing, I gathered, for the special kind of people who stared at walls, heard voices, leapt from windows, strung up nooses, sliced deep and bled themselves dry, the people who knew God.

Smart, I thought, though I didn't want to think it. Leave it to Adriane, I tried not to think and failed, to find herself a short-cut, take the convenient off-ramp to crazyville, to leave me alone with the cops, with our friend who had become a corpse and his house that had become a crime scene, with the automated response that now greeted me when I dialed Max's number: *This mailbox is full.*

A scrum of cameras and talking heads pounced as soon as we passed through the sliding hospital doors. My parents shoved me into the car. They shouted at the crowd. The crowd shouted back. Cameras flashed. None of it mattered. I slumped down in the leather seat, squinting against the glint of sun in the lenses. It was only then that I realized it was dawn.

I closed my eyes.

Opened them again.

There were too many things waiting in the dark.

6

There were two of them: the determinedly kind one who'd assured me an absurdly short time ago, at another crime scene, that everything would be all right, and the blond in his early twenties who looked like he'd failed the entrance requirements for gym-teacher college and, while none too pleased to have ended up in his spiffy blue uniform by default, would have to admit that the carefully buffed nine-millimeter tucked into his shoulder holster ameliorated the pain of a dream deferred.

"Tell me what happened," the older one said. The room was white and windowless, the chair too hard. "Go slow. Start at the beginning."

At the beginning, we didn't know what it was, Chris and I. We didn't know if stale pizza and a scratched *Spartacus* DVD—which mercifully froze after the first chariot race, freeing up the rest of the night for botched conjugations and several heated rounds of Egyptian ratscrew—constituted an awkward date, or just a night of shared homework between two people who seemed unlikely to share anything but a cafeteria table, and that only under duress. But even at the beginning, after that first and last painful attempt to satisfy convention—the awkward hand brushing, the mandatory gazing, the aborted attempt at a kiss, halted with his lips somewhere in the proximity of my nose, both of us flinching away at the same moment in simultaneous, horrified laughter—there was something between us: like at first sight.

They didn't want to hear about that.

"We were supposed to watch a movie," I said. "I came late."

They made me run through it from start to bloody finish, and then again, once forward and once backward, wounds stitching themselves together, bodies rising, a horror film played in reverse,

108

and each time I told the story, I let them think it didn't hurt to reach the punch line, to say, again, and again, "He was dead." They asked the same questions in different words, but I had seen *Law & Order* in all its iterations, and I knew liars were always more consistent in their stories than traumatized witnesses telling the unsteady truth. If I had been lying, they wouldn't have caught me. These were the things I thought: How to lie, if I'd wanted to lie. Why there was no two-way mirror. Whether cops really did like donuts, and if so, whether I could get my hands on one, and whether I could eat without throwing up.

Not *why is Chris dead?*

Not *what happened to Adriane?*

Not *where is Max?*

They had taken away my phone.

"I didn't do this," I said.

"Who's saying you did?" That was Cop the Younger.

"If I'd done this, you really think I would have stuck around and called 911?"

"No. We don't." Cop the Elder. "There were signs of a struggle. Blood not belonging to the victim. The perp would have defensive wounds. And someone your size . . ." He shook his head. "But you might know something that could help us. You want to help us, don't you?"

Even without my *Law & Order* expertise, I would have heard what he didn't say: That maybe I knew something because I was a part of it. That maybe I didn't want to help, because I'd stood by and watched someone else get defensive wounds, watched Chris die.

I nodded.

They asked about Chris and Adriane, about their relationship ("totally committed"), how often they fought ("never"), whether they had ever cheated ("*never*"), whether I had been secretly in

109

love with one, or the other, or both ("screw you"). They asked about the symbol painted in Chris's blood, whether I'd seen it before, whether it meant anything to me, whether Chris had been involved in the kind of thing that entailed drawing strange marks in human blood. (I could already imagine the headlines: Sex Triangle Tragedy! Teen Orgy Death Pact! Bloody Pagan Small-Town Sacrifice!)

There were no windows, no clocks. Someone brought me coffee I didn't drink, a wilted sandwich I didn't eat. No donuts.

They asked about Max.

They asked a *lot* about Max.

"He was supposed to be at the house," the older cop said. "You say he never showed up. But he was seen fleeing the area shortly before the body was discovered. His prints are all over the crime scene—"

"It's not the 'crime scene,' it's Chris's *house*. Of course his fingerprints are there. So are mine. So are Adriane's. So are the cable guy's. Maybe *he* did it."

"If he's got nothing to hide, why doesn't he turn himself in?"

Because he can't.

Because he's dead.

I couldn't say it. I couldn't stop thinking it.

"We've attempted to contact his parents using the number the college has on file. It's been disconnected."

"So?"

"Have you met his parents?"

I shook my head.

"Have you met anyone who can confirm for you that Max Lewis is who he claims to be? Are you so sure you can trust him?"

In January, Max had driven me into the foothills, where a still lake mirrored smoky sky and deer tracks carved meridians in the snow. Stripped down and barefoot, we padded toward the water.

110

"'Do I dare?'" he whispered. T. S. Eliot, again, from the poem that had become sacred to the story of us. Did I? "You've lost your mind," I told him, and took his hand. He didn't lead me. We threw ourselves into the water together. It was torture. It was pain like no pain I'd ever felt, like my skin was on fire and my lungs were ice. But no sky had ever been so blue, no water so clear. And after, back in the car with the heater blasting, his wet arms around my shivering body, staticky Elvis on the radio because neither of us wanted to venture out from beneath the wool blanket to search for a new station, reveling in our aggressive weirdness, laughing even as we kissed, my wet hair sticking to his face, his lips tasting of lake, our skin still clammy and our hearts still thudding too fast, it was warm. He never had to tell me to trust him.

"Max is Chris's best friend," I said, knowing they weren't hearing me. "Something happened to him. He needs help."

Or he doesn't anymore, like Chris doesn't anymore.

Stop.

"We want to find him as much as you do," the young cop said. "Trust us."

He had an ugly smile.

"I'm tired," I told them, though that wasn't the right word. There was no word. "I want to go home."

"Just a few more questions."

I stood up. "You can't keep me here if I want to go home." I had no idea whether it was true.

"You say these were your friends," the younger one said.

"I don't 'say' it. It's true."

"Then I know you want to help us help them."

The older cop cleared his throat, shot the younger one a Look. "Just one more," he said. "Then you can go."

I sat down.

"Adriane Ames. Does she use drugs?"

111

"Of course not!"

It didn't seem like a good time to mention the stash of pot she kept hidden—"for emergency situations only"—in a *Wizard of Oz* DVD case.

They exchanged another Look.

"What?" I asked.

"Tox screen turned up drugs in her system. A psychogenic toxin."

"Psychogenic . . . like LSD, or something?"

"Or something, yeah." The older cop put on his kindly mask again. I steeled myself. "The drug affects the frontal lobe; you know what that is?"

"Something in your brain."

"It's the part of the brain that controls personality, mood, and memory," the younger cop said, like he was reading off an index card and inordinately proud of himself for being able to do so.

"I took bio, too," I told him, but it wasn't the textbook diagram of the brain I was thinking of. It was black-and-white horror movies with electroshock and straitjackets, it was that absent look in Adriane's eyes, it was the word *lobe*, too close to the word *lobotomy*.

"Doctors think she took something—"

"She wouldn't."

"—or got dosed with something that would affect her memories. Maybe she knew something she shouldn't have. Saw something."

Something other than her boyfriend getting stabbed six times in the gut and his throat slashed for good measure?

"So that's why she's . . . like that? Because of a drug?" Not because she was weak, or hiding.

I hated myself.

"Is she going to be okay?"

112

He shrugged. "They don't know. But she got lucky."

I wanted to claw out his eyes. "Exactly which part of this qualifies as lucky?"

"Doctors say with this kind of drug, the effects are unpredictable. Say it could have caused a stroke." He watched me carefully.

"You said what happened to Professor Hoffpauer was an accident." I squeezed my hands together so he wouldn't see they were shaking. "You said *not to worry*." I was on my feet again. I was shouting.

"It now seems we may have been wrong."

I laughed.

My legs felt like stilts. Like they didn't belong to me and might shatter if I put my weight on them. But they held me up. "I'm leaving."

"What would you say if I told you we have evidence that your friend Max was in the professor's office at the time of the incident?"

The door was locked. "Let me the hell out of here."

"That doesn't make you think?"

"You said one more question. I answered it. *Let. Me. Out.*"

"You know what's strange?" he said, too casually. "The forensics indicate the victim was stabbed in the entryway of the house, but then dragged himself to the family safe. It was found open, with nothing missing—according to his parents, that is. So I think we can assume he opened the safe once his assailant had fled. Why do you think he would do that, Nora?" Again, he asked so offhandedly, as if the answer couldn't matter less to him, as if he were wondering aloud whether his kid's softball game would be rained out. "Now, I'm lying there, bleeding to death, I go for the phone, or the door. But your friend, he goes for the safe. You got any idea what he thought was in there? Something he would have wasted the last few seconds of his life trying to get?"

I didn't answer. I didn't say anything as they unlocked the

door and handed me off to my parents, and I didn't say anything to them, either, when they loaded me into the car and deposited me at home.

I didn't tell them, or anyone, about the stained letter I had found crumpled in Adriane's hand, the letter whose value had so impressed Chris that, careful and responsible as he was, he could well have locked it up for safekeeping until he decided how to fix my mistake. The letter I'd slipped out of the pocket of my bloody jeans before the cops took them away, and that, as soon as I was safely behind my locked bedroom door, I returned to its hiding spot in the crawl space beneath my desk, like nothing had ever happened and it had never left.

Like Chris hadn't died for it. Hadn't died because of me.

I told myself anything could have been in that safe, and I got into bed, fully dressed, eyes fixed on the ceiling, phone open on the pillow. I lay there, and I listened to Max's phone ring and ring, and I waited for morning.

7

Some simple, logical proofs.

One. Max loved me. Max loved Chris. Max claimed to "find the overabundance of violence in modern American cinema to be bordering on grotesque" but did so only because it was easier than admitting the sight of blood, even on-screen, made him want to puke. Max was *Max*. Therefore he did not do it.

Two. Max loved me. Max would never leave me alone to face Chris's body and Adriane's eyes and the cops and the cameras unless he had no other choice, and not no other choice as in he preferred to stay out of jail and feared sticking around would have the opposite effect, but no other choice as in he needed to stay away to save his own life, or mine. Therefore Max was in trouble.

Or Max was dead.

Three. Max knew I was coming to Chris's house. If Max wanted Chris dead—which he did not—but wanted me alive, he would have chosen a different moment, a different night, one when he and Chris were alone, as they were almost every night, in their dorm room. If Max wanted Chris dead and me dead—which he did not—he would not have murdered Chris and run away. He knew I was coming; he would have waited. Therefore Max did not murder Chris.

Of course Max did not murder Chris.

Four. Max did not murder Chris. Someone else did. The police were looking for Max. Therefore no one was looking for *someone*.

8

A tenable hypothesis.

Someone was looking for me.

9

I didn't go back to school for a week. Most nights I went to bed swearing this would be my last day in hiding, that nothing, not even school, could be worse than those first couple days trapped in the house pretending not to watch my parents pretending not to watch me, and certainly no worse than the long, empty days that followed, when my mother went back to work, my father went back to his office, and I was left alone, feeling each minute of each interminable hour, trying not to see ghosts. I went to bed with the best of halfhearted intentions—and then lay there, wide awake. Running through the now-familiar inventory of items in my room that could be used as weapons—Andy's old bat, the hair dryer with its comfortingly gun-shaped silhouette, the lighter, a bottle of eye-burning wasp repellent, and of course the high-carbon, stainless steel, infomercial-guaranteed slicing-and-dicing knife hidden under my mattress.

At night I was too wired to sleep; by morning, I was too tired to move. School was out of the question. So I stayed in bed, watching the ceiling, my brain fogged, playing dead until I heard the telltale slam of the front door, and then the creak of my father's office door easing shut, confirming that I was, once again, alone.

After the first day, I forced myself to stay away from the TV. I couldn't risk flipping through channels and seeing the shaky cellphone footage of Chris's body being wheeled out of the house that his real-estate-agent neighbor had been kind enough to shoot and, despite the easily foreseeable effect on property values, sell to the highest bidder. And the pictures they showed . . . The most popular was one of the four of us that we posed for on the college green after Chris charmed a bed-and-breakfaster into taking our photo. Chris, in a photogenic display of strength and all-American-boyness, lifts a squealing Adriane aloft in a cradle hold, the camera catching her at the tipping point between annoyance and glee. Max stands behind me, his arms around my shoulders and his lips to my ear, ostensibly whispering sweet nothings but in fact complaining that Adriane had just kicked him in the lower back. I am in the process of deciding whether to pick a fight in defense of my friend or let Max bribe me away from her in ways only Max could devise, but you can't tell from my smile. You can never tell from my smile.

There were other pictures on Chris's hard drive, pictures of Adriane's drunk face, raccoon tracks smeared around her hugely dilated pupils; pictures of Chris posing bashfully with his Han Solo action figure and meticulously assembled to-scale *Millennium Falcon* that no one but me knew he still had; pictures of Max in profile, curled over a book, eyebrows knit together, preemptively angry about some future interruption. There were the pictures I could only assume Chris had erased from his hard drive, since they had yet to surface on CNN, the "artistic" shots Adriane had ensorcelled him into taking one sunny afternoon, the two of them locked in his bedroom with the blinds shut tight and the camera on a carefully positioned tripod, as they—in Adriane's words, after the fact, swearing me to secrecy—"made good use of the time." Adriane, who was now making use of her time staring at the walls of a glorified mental institution, who was unresponsive and unable, who was brushed and bathed and changed like an invalid, like a corpse. Adriane, whom I hadn't been able to force myself to visit, because I couldn't face holding her hand and looking in her eyes and knowing she was no longer there.

I got it. The cable-news morons had a job to do: Score ratings. Spin a cautionary fairy tale. And that picture made for a good one. Two photogenic victims. One assumed killer, and his devilish girlfriend, evil by association. All of them appearing so innocent, so wholesome, so delightfully, painfully *normal*. I had a copy of the photo tacked to the wall by my bed, and I had to leave it there, because it was a piece of him. That's what death did—it turned trash into talismans. A CD he'd burned, a notebook he'd doodled in, a sweatshirt he'd worn: holy relics. I knew how it worked; hadn't I spent the last six years living in a sacred shrine to a dead brother? So I left the picture where it was, but I couldn't look at it anymore. It had been claimed by *them;* it was, somehow, no longer *us*.

Every day was too long, and every day was the same, until one day, for no particular reason, I got out of bed, showered, dressed up in convincing imitation of a normal, well-adjusted member of society, the blameless good girl the cops had officially deemed me to be, and went back to school.

10

I'd prefer not to talk about that.

11

Here's the secret: You don't feel it.

You don't *pretend* not to feel. You don't raise your hand, choke down cafeteria food, ignore the stares just as intently as you ignore the empty locker next to yours that you know has Chris's goofy senior picture taped to the inner door, nestled inside an equally goofy lipstick heart; you don't smile weakly and then sneak off to the nearest bathroom stall to cry every time you overhear someone whispering about your boyfriend, the psycho killer.

You turn it off.

You let yourself go cold and numb, and it's easy, like rolling downhill, like falling out a window, because numbness is all your body really wants, and, given leave, gravity will take its course.

The thing is, no one noticed. I was simultaneously infamous and invisible. Chris and Adriane were the hometown heroes, the golden couple, repository of innumerable yearbook superlatives and hallway-PDA citations. Whereas I, after all this time, was still the new girl, imported under shady circumstances. It had never bothered me. The four of us had been a self-contained unit, with our own stories, our own bad habits—practically, when you considered all the inside jokes and references and things that didn't need to be said, our own language. That was supposed to be enough.

I did my homework. I ate in the library. I flinched at loud noises and sudden movements and kept away from the dark. I shamelessly abused my independent-study privileges, even though there was no study left to be done, given that the files had disappeared and the Hoff had been shipped down to a rehab facility in Texas, and as often as possible, I got the hell out. Some days I went to the movies, letting the flicker of color and light carry me into someone else's story, but there was only one theater in town and only so many times I could sit through *Crap Blows Up: The Sequel*. Mostly I went to campus.

There was a small, round plaza on the western edge of the college green that I'd walked through for years, never paying much attention to the names and dates engraved on the pavement stones. That's where I sat, on one of the stone benches rimming the circle. It emptied during class periods, which guaranteed me regular forty-seven-minute increments of isolation.

The names were students, the years carved next to them either the dates they'd graduated or the dates they'd died—there was no explanatory plaque to make things clear, but the general situation was clear enough from the thick letters engraved at the center of the circle: PRO PATRIA. You learned that one in Latin I, partly because it was remedial, partly because the ancient Romans were so high on dying that way. *Pro patria, for country.* If that hadn't clued me in, the names engraved on the benches would have done the trick. Not people, but battlefields, Normandy, Omaha Beach, Rhine Crossing, Bastogne, Ardennes—apparently whatever wealthy alumni endowed the memorial thought it only fitting that Chapman's brave dead children be stuck in battle for all eternity. *Sic transit gloria.*

The green was green in name only. Where it wasn't a dull, bare brown spotted with a few sad patches of gray snow that had forgotten to melt, it was a sickly yellow, the color of hair sprayed with cheap Sun-In, then doused with chlorine. In summertime, the grove of trees bordering the western edge passed for an overgrown wilderness separating the classroom buildings from the barren athletic fields, but three months of snow and frost had denuded the branches. March wasn't a good look for this corner of New England. Chapman was passable in the dead of winter, as much a snowy wonderland as any of the other carefully picturesque towns dotting the highway, but March was a dead zone of desiccated grass, sagging trees, and melting snowmen. Even the sky gave up for a few weeks, forgoing color for a thick miasma of gray.

It was quiet, quiet enough that I could hear the crunch of leaves beneath a shoe, just behind me. I flinched at the sound of it, imminent invaders of my sanctuary—and the crunching stopped, abruptly. Not, then, the noise of a student who'd overslept, clomping toward class, but of someone who crept, silently and carefully, freezing in place with his noisy misstep, hoping not to be noticed. Someone there to watch.

I told myself that if I pretended it wasn't happening, if I pretended I hadn't heard, if I didn't provoke, then nothing would happen. I'd been the kind of kid who liked to map out contingency plans in case of burglars and kidnappers, who lay in bed practicing fake sleep, under the theory that if I looked harmless enough, the troupe of rampaging killers I imagined climbing into children's windows up and down the East Coast would understand that I was no threat and would, after dumping our nonexistent family silver into their burlap sacks, leave me alone. But I was all grown up now, enough to know that looking harmless only made you easier prey. I turned around.

The tree was too narrow to hide him completely. He peeked out from behind the bark, his face cloaked in shadow.

Max? I swallowed the word, along with the hope. Stood up. Squinted into the woods, looking for the telltale glint of glasses—or a knife. Waited for him, whoever he was, to decide, to move toward me or run away. Fight or flight.

He held his ground, watching me watch him.

"What?" I said sharply. This prey would show no fear.

He knelt, never taking his eyes off me, never moving his face out of the shadow, and played his hand across a patch of gray snow.

Then he ran away.

"Wait!"

But I didn't run after him, because if it had been Max, he would have come to me, and if it wasn't Max . . .

You didn't run after a killer.

Not even if you wanted, more than you'd ever wanted anything, to watch him die.

He'd left something for me, in a smooth patch of mud-streaked snow. It was the size of a hand with its fingers spread. And where the center of the palm would be, he had scraped an eye speared by a lightning bolt. A message for me.

He was watching.

12

I wasn't invited to the funeral. That was in Baltimore, and it was for family. I didn't qualify. Not until Chris's mother emailed me, asking me to go to the campus memorial service on the Moores' behalf and then, afterward, to Chris's dorm room to help the dean pack up his belongings. I was family enough for that.

The chapel was full of kids from the college and Chapman Prep who didn't know Chris any better than the egalitarian minister who prattled on about Chris's achievements—read haltingly off bullet-pointed index cards—and God's plan. "We can't be angry at God," the minister said. God was everywhere in the service, shepherding Chris through a "short but meaningful life," shielding his grieving loved ones in "the bosom of His love," leading Chris to a "lasting peace where someday we will once again be together." His God, under this theory, had planned it all, from start to finish, might as well have wielded the knife. And because of this, because he was in control, because he was watching, we were supposed to be grateful for his interest, no matter its form. We were supposed to say thank you.

"No one knows why Chris was taken from us," the minister said, and I carefully steered my thoughts away from the bloody letter, from the fear that I knew why, that the why was me.

My parents flanked me, both of them in dark-hued work clothes, their hands at their sides. It was the first time the three of us had been in any kind of religious building together since Andy's funeral. That day, at the insistence of my grandparents, we had sat in the front row of Temple Beth El, holding hands and mouthing the words of the kaddish, the traditional Jewish mourning prayer that ignores the dead in favor of paeans to the God who took him away, all of us, my Jewish grandmother, my lapsed Catholic father, my Buddhist-when-and-how-it-suited-her aunt, all of us except for my mother, who pressed her lips together, shut her prayer book, and later, despite the epic fight she'd waged against my father to get Andy a bar mitzvah, let my thirteenth birthday pass unnoticed.

I only had one dress that was dark enough and conservative enough to be appropriate for the campus memorial, and I chose it with regret, because—shallow as it sounds—it was one of my favorites and I knew that after this, I would never wear it again. I didn't cry.

13

The door to the dean's office swung open on my second knock.

"Can I help you?" He was younger than I'd expected, probably in his early thirties, though prematurely balding.

"I'm Nora Kane? I was supposed to, uh—" I stopped, realizing there was someone else in the office, sitting in one of the mahogany armchairs facing the dean's desk. "Sorry. I'll come back."

The dean shook his head. "Please, come in. We've been expecting you."

The other half of "we" stood and faced me. "So you're her."

"This is Eli Kapek," the dean said.

I waited to hear why I should care.

"Eli Kapek," he said again, like it was supposed to mean something. Then, when it obviously didn't, "Christopher's cousin."

Something stretched across Eli's face, something approximating a smile, but not quite getting there. "Forgive me if I'm not particularly pleased to meet you."

I searched his face, wishing, weirdly, that I were blind, as that would give me the social leeway to cross the room and press my fingers to his sharp cheekbones, his narrow chin, his nose that, while crooked and slightly too large for his face, fit the asymmetrical arch in his eyebrows and quirk at his lips, and maybe my fingertips could detect something my eyes couldn't, reveal what I was looking for, which was: Chris.

But it wasn't there. Chris took after his mother's side. His dark skin, his kinky, wild hair, his round, open features, none of it was here in this stranger's sharp, pale face.

I couldn't hate Adriane for whatever had happened to her, for failing to protect Chris and herself and letting a strange toxin take its course; I couldn't hate Max for whatever had happened to him, for trusting me to defend him, maybe somehow save him, when he couldn't do it himself. And I couldn't hate the Moores for leaving town, and leaving me along with it, because any obligation they had to me had died with their son, and you do what you need to do to survive.

I couldn't hate Chris.

But Eli was a stranger, and there was nothing to stop me from hating him on sight, for who he was and what he wasn't, for his failure to be what I needed him to be, and mostly for the fact that he was alive and Chris was not. It would have felt good, having someone to hate, someone other than an imaginary God.

"Can we do this now?" Eli said, not looking at me.

"Nora, Christopher's parents asked me to tell you they would be very grateful if you could help Eli sort through Chris's belongings. He'll take care of the shipping and such." The dean handed him a key.

I already had a key.

The dean ushered us out of his office. "You're not coming?" I asked.

"We find it's best to give close friends and family their privacy in these matters. Unless—?"

"We're fine," Eli said, closing the door on the dean. Then we were alone. "You don't have to come, either."

"Yeah, actually I *do*. The Moores wanted me to."

He shrugged. "Suit yourself."

I could have let myself into the room anytime I wanted; I'd been tempted. I'd spent a whole morning planted in front of the dorm, trying to will myself to go in.

But then I'd gone home.

Maybe I was afraid that once I stepped inside, I would never be able to leave. That I would wrap myself in a blanket that smelled like Max, curl up on the couch scuffed by Chris's sneakers and reeking faintly of dirty socks and stale pizzas past, barricade myself inside in perpetuity, like an Egyptian bride burying herself alive in her pharaoh's tomb. It would be easier with a stranger, I told myself. It would be a simple procedure: Unlock the door. Sort through closets and drawers and shelves full of memories.

124

Dismantle my safe haven sock by sock.

"I didn't see you at the memorial service," I said, trying to keep up as he sped across the quad. I had to take two steps to each one of his.

"I saw you," he said. "You didn't seem too broken up."

"What's your problem?"

He still wouldn't look at me. "My cousin is dead. Maybe you heard."

"You know, Chris never even mentioned you."

"And?"

"And if you want to pretend that you were someone to him, and I was no one, that's your business, but I think it's kind of sad."

"I guess you knew everything about him, and everyone that ever mattered to him?"

"Actually, I did," I said. "You weren't on the list."

"And you were."

I didn't answer.

"So were you, like, secretly in love with him or something? Deep, unrequited passion?"

"I have a boyfriend," I said. I did not say *asshole*. But he got the point.

He muttered something.

"What?"

"Your boyfriend," he said. "You wanted to know my problem. That's my problem."

Of course. Max was everyone's problem. "He didn't do it."

He offered another of his mutant smiles. "I guess I'll just take your word for that. What a relief."

I stopped abruptly, in the shadow of a large stone building, its somber gray face streaked with drying bird crap. "We're here."

14

The room was in ruins.

"Your boyfriend's a slob," Eli said, stopped in the doorway. I pushed past him. The mattresses were on the floor, stuffing oozing from their ripped seams. The drawers had been pulled out of both desks and bureaus; a thick layer of T-shirts, sheets, underwear, books, and notebooks blanketed the dingy linoleum tile.

I couldn't breathe.

"Sit down," Eli said.

"On what?" A strangled laugh. One wooden desk chair lay on its side, the other sat akimbo, one leg missing, its back snapped in two.

Eli took my arm and guided me to Max's bare metal bed frame. We sat.

I swallowed hard. "The cops." My feet were on Max's navy sheets. I'll get mud on them, I thought distantly. Max would hate that. He washed his sheets more often than most college students, or at least more often than Chris—though still not often enough to suit me. It was something we liked to argue about, when we were in the mood, Max politely pointing out that if I wanted his sheets cleaner, I was welcome to clean them, me politely pointing out that he was a sexist pig, him countering that if I really cared about cleanliness, I'd go take a shower and forgo putting all my dirty clothes back on. . . . Now I wished I'd taken him up on it. Just once.

Eli shook his head. "Uncle Paul talked to the cops, to make sure it was okay for me to be here. They said they just looked around and took the laptops. They left everything else the way it was."

"So they lied."

"Or someone else was here. Looking for something."

I thought again of what the cops had told me, about Chris hiding something in his family's safe. I thought again about the letter, and where holding on to it fell on the stupidity scale of one to death wish.

"He's contacted you, hasn't he?" Eli said.

"What? Who?"

"Him. The boyfriend. The cops think he's halfway across the country by now, but maybe you know better. Maybe he's still here until he gets what he came for?"

I stood up. "You think he did this?"

Eli shrugged.

"So he tore up his own room, looking for 'something,' because, what, he couldn't remember where he put it?"

"He tore up Chris's stuff," Eli said. "Then maybe his own, as a decoy."

Chris kept a bunch of flattened cardboard boxes at the back of his closet, a collection he was too conscientious to trash but too lazy to recycle. They were still there. I pulled one out. "Let's just do this," I said. "We don't have to talk."

I picked through the ruins, folding every stray shirt, smoothing out wrinkled history notes, putting scattered paper clips, staples, stamps, and pens neatly back into their containers. Eli didn't question my judgment on which things belonged to Max and which to Chris, nor did he ask why the Moores would want a stack of index cards from a first-semester paper on the Glorious Revolution or a collection of stolen shot glasses, one from each frat. He just took what I handed him and put it into a box. I gave him everything, because if I were Chris's parents, I would have wanted everything.

I wanted everything.

Eventually Chris's side of the room was stripped, bare as it had been on the day we'd moved him in and sprawled out on the empty bed, wondering whether his unknown roommate would mind he'd been summarily assigned the crap bed under the broken window. Max's side was as clean as it was going to get, waiting for his return.

But when I let myself believe in that return, when I tried to imagine it, the screen inside my head went blank. There was no Max without Chris. And I was pretty sure there was no me without either of them.

I would not cry in front of a stranger.

I'd set Max's Voynich notebooks on the side of his desk, and, with my back to Eli, I started leafing through them, anything to distract myself from the rising panic.

They distracted me. Not the scribbled stabs at translation, which I'd seen several times as I hunched over the pages with Max, trying to make sense of the nonsensical, but the bottom notebook: a small, blue, college-lined, spiral-bound notebook with most of the pages ripped out. I'd never seen it before, as I had never seen what lay inside its manila inner pocket: a brown, weathered page of Latin that looked even older than the one I had hidden in my bedroom.

Max didn't even like to make photocopies without express permission from the archival librarian, for fear of damaging the least rare of books. He was mostly oblivious to the demands of the outside world, but when it came to this kind of thing—rare books, manuscripts, letters—he did what he was told. He followed the rules. So if he had something, it was because he was allowed to have it.

Whatever it was.

"You can, you know," Eli said. "If you want to."

Shielding the notebook from him, I pulled out the page and slipped it into my pocket.

"Can what?" I turned around, keeping my face blank.

128

He gave me a strange look. Like maybe he'd seen me. "Take something."

Maybe he had.

"Something that belonged to him," he said. "I can tell you want to."

He held something out to me, a framed picture. I didn't have to get any closer; I recognized the frame. It was the picture of the four of us on the green, the one from the news. "I don't want that."

"Something else, then."

"Is this you trying to be nice?" There had been a roll of packing tape under the pile of crap spilled out of Chris's desk. I started sealing up the boxes.

He didn't say anything for a long time.

"You're right, I didn't know him," he said eventually. He joined me by the box, holding the cardboard down tight as I ran the tape across. "We hung out when we were little, but I don't even think we liked each other that much. Then he moved, and that was pretty much it."

"So why are you here?"

Eli looked up. We watched each other across the sealed box. His eyes were a startling blue. "Truth?"

"Why not?"

"They made me."

"Your aunt and uncle?"

"Them. My parents. Everyone. It was too hard for them, or something. It had to be me, because I didn't know him."

"Because you don't care."

A hint of red flushed his pale cheeks. "Someone murdered my cousin," he said. "I care about that."

Something about the way he was kneeling over the box struck me as too familiar. "Was it you the other day on the green? Watching me?"

"What are you talking about? Someone's following you?"

"Forget it." Wishful thinking, maybe. Creepy cousin beat murdering psychopath any day of the week. "Let's get out of here."

"I can go," he said. "If you want to stay awhile."

"Just to be clear—"

"Yes. This is me trying to be nice."

"I think I liked you better honest." I wanted to stay behind. I wanted to curl into Max's newly made bed and close my eyes, inhale the leftover Max scents, lemony detergent and the cinnamony shampoo that he used under protest because I loved it. There, just maybe, I would finally be able to sleep.

"At least take this." Abruptly, looking like he was thinking better of it even as it was happening, he extended a sheaf of papers to me.

"What is that?"

He shrugged. "I found them in a folder, taped under Chris's desk. While you were in the bathroom."

"And you weren't going to tell me?"

His expression had a hint of something, but it wasn't shame. "I'm telling you now."

I ripped the pages from his hand. They were faded and stiff. Old. Maybe, I thought, forcing myself to tuck them away before I could get a better look, as old as the page I had stolen from the Hoff's collection, old as the page I'd found in Max's notebook, older, far older, than anything Chris should have had in his possession. Taped under his desk, like he was hiding them from Max. From me.

Nothing made sense anymore.

"What makes you think I should take these?" I asked.

"They won't mean anything to Chris's parents."

"And they'll mean something to me?"

"If you don't want them—"

"I want them."

"Suit yourself. Now let's get out of here. I'll send someone for his stuff."

I'd wanted to escape his presence all afternoon, but now I lingered, knowing in all likelihood I would never see him again. One more piece of Chris gone. It occurred to me I would probably never see Chris's parents again, either. Or his house. And thanks to me, his dorm room was officially gone.

I understood, suddenly, why my parents were so determined to keep our house. Sometimes shrines served a purpose.

Eli paused on the steps of the dorm. Maybe I wasn't the only one who wanted to linger. "So let's say, for the sake of argument, your boyfriend didn't do it, and he's hiding out somewhere for perfectly innocent reasons, or he's . . . you know."

"Or he's. Yeah. I know."

"Then who did it?" he asked.

"How the hell should I know?"

"So what are you doing to find out?"

15

I call on you, Max's stolen letter began.

> *I call on all my brothers, to join my struggle.*
>
> *We will reclaim that which has been stolen.*
>
> *That which is ours by right will be ours by blood.*
>
> *We will rout the foreigners who tear down our proud city and rebuild it in their own image. We will topple the Churchmen who proscribe our worship and consign the holiest among us to death. We will reclaim our land by the grace of our Lord. We will destroy the one who seeks to steal our birthright.*

*We seek this power not for evil, but for what is just, and
what is right. Join me, and swear this oath, by our Lord, that
the search will never end until our triumph is at hand.*

It was signed *V.K.*, which meant as little to me as the short
paragraph just above the signature, a language jammed with accents and consonants that could have been Czech, or could have
been Klingon. There was nothing to explain why Max had it, or
whether it meant anything more to him than it did to me.

The letters from Chris's side of the room were unsigned, but
it seemed unlikely their shaky words had been scrawled by V.K.'s
steady hand.

You have no need to worry, read the first one, also in Latin.

*The girl has no suspicion we are watching. And I believe you
are wrong. She has no volition of her own. She once followed
her father's orders. Now she follows Groot. It should be no
trouble to switch her loyalties. The mother is here in Prague.
She pushes the girl to be more practical, to find a household
position, or find a husband. The Emperor has taken all their
possessions. The girl thinks herself a philosopher. Or perhaps
a poet. But these are dreams, and she knows that. She will do
what you need, if you pay.*

15 November 1598.

The girl was Elizabeth. It had to be. But that didn't matter.
Not as much as the look on Chris's face when I'd confessed to
him about my stolen letter . . . while all this time, he'd had a sheaf
of them taped under his desk, like the handiwork of the world's
most wholesomely boring spy.

They were just letters, I told myself. They didn't have to mean
anything.

16

The Whitman Center didn't look like a hospital. Temporary home, over the years, to New England's most famous depressive artists, manic poets, schizophrenic geniuses, and a high percentage of the region's wealthiest worried well, it had long ago embraced the moral therapy reforms that dictated genteel patients with decidedly ungenteel conditions should nonetheless be treated like gentlemen, and as a result, it looked more like a college campus than a mental institution. Building C, a three-story yellow colonial at the top of a hill, sported brightly polished columns along its wide facade, which endowed the place with a certain dignity and made it easy to imagine its patients decked out in their finest nineteenth-century petticoats and top hats, sipping tea while dapper, goateed doctors etiquetted the madness right out of them.

It wasn't until I stepped through the double doors that a new set of images surfaced in my mind's eye, images lodged somewhere in my brain from an old AP Psych slide show, or maybe a late-night horror movie, doctors in white Frankenstein coats looming over gurneys, electrodes dangling from their clawed hands, padded rooms, straitjackets, lobotomized zombies drooling, all hope abandoned.

Building C wasn't a fright show. But it wasn't a tea party, either. Past the reception desk was another set of double doors, which buzzed loudly as the guard ushered me through, then locked again behind me. Yellow walls gave the corridors a sickly tinge. An older woman with thick gray hair knotted into a braid brushed past me, clutching her gown and murmuring something about preparing for a date. I smiled politely, because that's what you do; I smiled but then looked away, because that's who I am. It

133

was impossible to imagine Adriane's parents making their regal way through here, Mr. Ames in his custom-tailored suit, Ms. Kato in one of the silk kimonos she claimed had been handed down through the women in her family for two centuries, though Adriane had once confided that her mother's old-country ancestors were fishermen and fieldworkers, and the silk kimonos, rather than being smuggled over on a 1950s steamer with the young Grandma Kato, came special order courtesy of a Newbury Street "exotic wear" boutique.

It was impossible to imagine Adriane here.

She had a private room and, if you ignored certain problematic elements—the door that locked only from the outside, the metal grate across the window, the call button installed over the bed—it looked like a motel room. A cheap motel, of the kind no one in Adriane's family would ever be caught dead in, but it was better than I'd expected. So was she.

She sat on the edge of a blue armchair, shoulders back and neck erect with that annoyingly perfect dancer's posture. Her sleek black hair was brushed and pinned back with her favorite blue rhinestone barrettes, and despite the tank top and yoga pants—an ensemble Adriane had always been able to pull off with the panache of an undercover starlet caught in the famous-people-are-just-like-us section of some celebrity tabloid—her skin was impeccably powdered, her lashes curled, her lips glossed to a healthy pink and turned up in a faint smile. So it had all been a bad joke, I thought, crossing the room—bad but brilliant, hiding in this place, leaving me alone and afraid. "You suck," I said as my arms went around her. "You suck and I hate you, and why didn't you call?" I squeezed tight, feeling, for the first time since that night, like I could breathe again.

She didn't hug me back.

"Okay, maybe I don't actually hate you."

It's not that she wasn't hugging; it's that she wasn't moving. I let go.

It was the eyes I should have noticed, the eyes beneath the pale silver shadow and delicate liquid liner. They didn't track me as I took one step backward, then another, retreating to the doorway; they barely blinked.

"Oh, aren't you popular, Adriane?" a loud, cheerful voice said behind me. "Three visitors in one day, how nice!"

If Adriane thought it was nice—if Adriane *thought*—she didn't let on.

"You can go on in," the nurse told me. "She doesn't bite."

"Does she . . . Is she . . ." If I couldn't formulate the question, it seemed unlikely I could handle the answer. I changed course. "She looks good."

"Doesn't she?" The nurse beamed. Her round face practically glowed. It was obscene to look so healthy in a place like this. "Her mama comes in every morning to put her together."

That didn't sound like Ms. Kato, who was nobody's "mama."

"Stay as long as you want," she said. "Just try not to upset her."

"So you mean— Can she hear me when she's like this?"

Her meaty hand came down on my shoulder. "She's in there," she said. "It's like I told your friend, all she needs is time to heal."

"My friend?"

"The boy who always brings such beautiful flowers." She pointed to a vase of yellow roses beside Adriane's bed. Adriane hated roses. Though Chris always bought them anyway, unable to comprehend there was any other option. "He told me to say hello to you, if you ever came."

"To me? How did you even know who I am?"

"He showed me a picture," she said. "You're prettier in person, though."

"What was his name?"

135

She hesitated. "Let me think, I'm not sure I—" She grinned. "That's it, Chris. His name is Chris."

It felt like the room temperature had dropped twenty degrees. "What did he look like?"

She waved a hand. "Oh, you know. Good-looking kid. Brown-ish hair. I think."

Once she was gone, I threw out the flowers.

Then I sat on the bed and tried not to think about why some-one was going around calling himself Chris and carrying a picture of me, or whether he was still here, lurking in the parking lot, waiting. I forced myself to smile, and I talked to my only remaining friend.

"This is weird," I said. "Don't you think this is weird?" I felt like an idiot. "The memorial service was crap. But I guess every-thing is. This was supposed to be our year, remember? *L'année mémorable.*" *The year to remember.* I leaned forward. "You want to know a secret? Your French accent sucks ass."

I paused, not sure what was weirder: delivering a monologue, or pretending that we were having a conversation by leaving spaces for her to respond, as if maybe, given the chance, she even-tually would.

"You want to know another secret?" I said. "A real one?"

Another pause.

"I'll take that as a yes. You know how we were going to have this amazing time in Paris, the four of us? Swimming in the Seine, or whatever? It was never going to happen. It was about a million times too expensive. I don't know why that didn't occur to you. Or why I didn't just tell you. I guess I was waiting for the right time. Or, you know, for a miracle." I laughed, sort of. "I'm not sure this counts."

This wasn't right. It wasn't what I should be saying; it wasn't what I needed to say.

"I miss you," I said. "I need you. Please."

But that wasn't right, either. It felt fake, like I was acting for a hidden camera. Reading a horrible script for a horrible TV movie, the kind that starred actors from canceled sitcoms who were one botched audition away from a life of hemorrhoid commercials and dinner theater. It bothered me that I couldn't fill in Adriane's half of the conversation. I knew her well enough. I should have been able to invent her. And not just her—grieving people were supposed to see ghosts, hear voices, hallucinate. Where were my visions? Where was my crazy?

"I'm not going to give you some big speech about how you have to be strong and get through this, or that there are all these people who love you and need you back. Blah blah whatever. But you were *there*, Adriane. You saw what happened. You know who did it."

Maybe it was my imagination. But I thought I saw her pupils skid toward me. I was sure I saw a muscle twitch at the corner of her mouth.

"Do you remember?" I said. I sat on the arm of her chair. I took her hand. "Who hurt Chris, Adriane? What happened to Max? What *happened*?"

She screamed.

She didn't move, she didn't change her expression, she didn't look at me, she just opened her mouth and screamed, like an Adriane-shaped car alarm, and though I stroked her hair and held her hand and apologized, again and again, for saying the thing that should have been left unsaid, she wouldn't stop. It was only when the friendly nurse rushed in, followed by two decidedly less friendly orderlies, and they grabbed her and jabbed a needle in her arm that she turned human again—then passed straight through human to animal, thrashing and bucking against their grip, her screams now mingled with grunts and

137

growls, guttural, embarrassing noises that I didn't want to hear, and finally, a howl that faded to a moan that faded to a sigh as the drugs washed through her veins and she dropped onto the bed, her eyes closed.

"It's not your fault, honey," the nurse told me once the orderlies had strapped Adriane down and gone on their way. It was a kind lie.

"Bye, Adriane. Get better, okay?" I said lamely, leaving her wrecked and helpless, the same way I had left the Hoff last time I'd seen him. Then, I'd gone straight from the Hoff to Chris, because that was home, and that was safe. But that was gone.

When I got back to the house, which had to happen eventually as I had nowhere else to go, my mother was still at work, but my father must have been there, somewhere, because he'd brought in the mail, dumping mine on the kitchen table. Atop the pile of junk was a letter from Chapman Prep, delighted to inform me that, in recognition of my excellent academic record, the scholarship committee had decided to grant my request for funds to cover the upcoming senior-class trip to Europe.

I'd asked for a miracle; I should have been more specific.

17

At night, I translated the letters from Chris's desk, searching for something. Anything.

The formula is difficult, but results are near. The girl does not shy away from difficult work. She may be stronger than you expected. She fears nothing. But her situation grows more dire. The mother is a constant problem, always demanding more. The girl is desperate to get their property back. But the Emperor will never bend. Soon she will need other options.

*I cannot meet you at the normal place tonight. But I can be
there tomorrow, at dawn.*

  14 December 1598.

*Is there no other way? I understand your urgency, but I ask
again that you reconsider. You may need her, but surely you
no longer need me? She still has not guessed she is being
watched. She will be at the gates of the Jewish quarter tonight,
as planned.*

  19 December 1598.

*Make your threats. I have nothing to fear from you. I will tell
you nothing more. I can threaten, too. Approach me again, and
I will see she knows all.*

  19 January 1599.

Whatever I was looking for, I never found it. And Chris, whom
I knew less than ever, was still gone.

18

That was a bad week. It began with Adriane and ended with Dead
Brother's Birthday. My mother had a cache of Xanax hidden in a
tampon box for just such an occasion, and my father stored a fifty-
two-year-old bottle of Glenlivet in his bottom desk drawer, though
maybe the well was running dry, as the year before I'd caught
the unmistakable scent of *eau de* pot seeping out from under his
locked office door, presumably something he'd confiscated from
a student, back when he had any. They each had their own rituals
regarding Andy's grave, my father hitting it somewhere around
midnight, drunk enough to howl at the moon; my mother, whose
good intentions always exceeded her capabilities, would show up

the next day with a tranquilizer hangover and fresh peonies for penance. Which left the whole day clear for me.

I liked the cemetery. A bike path curled around its western edge, and as kids, Andy and I had pedaled furiously past the graves, racing each other out of the danger zone, daring each other, especially in that dusky hour before dinner but after dark, to hop the fence and chase the ghosts. But in the light of day, the Chapman cemetery was the kind of place you had to work hard to be afraid of. It was too sunny and bucolic, too institutional, with its freshly cut grass, its manicured hedges, its perfectly aligned and well-tended graves. I liked it there more than I should have, especially when I had it to myself, and Andy and I could be alone.

If I'd believed in some kind of afterlife, a heaven where lute-plucking angels formed the cheering squad for pickup games with dead Little Leaguers, I could imagine Andy up there bossing Chris around, showing him the ropes. But imagine was all I could do. I'd tried to believe in all of that, after the accident—believe in *something*. I couldn't.

I didn't come to Andy's grave to talk to him. I didn't even bring him flowers.

Someone else had.

There was a fresh bouquet sitting in front of the tombstone, and not my mother's peonies, on time for once, nor yellow roses. These were lilies of the valley, the only flowers I liked—which was something only Max had bothered to know.

Don't hope.

There was a postcard beneath the flowers, facedown against the gray stone. It was Max's handwriting.

I spun around, half expecting to see him standing behind me, his cheeks flushed and his smile apologetic but real. There was no one. But the flowers were fresh. He *had* been there. Maybe he was there still, somewhere, watching me, afraid for some reason to show himself. Max didn't know about Andy. At least, he wasn't supposed to. It seemed inappropriate, not to mention useless, to be angry at Chris for opening his big mouth, as he must have done. But I was angry anyway. Also grateful.

I'd given up calling, but I called him now, and this time the phone didn't even ring. "You have reached a nonworking number," the familiar voice told me. It didn't matter.

Max was alive.

19

CASTOREM NON PVTO DEVM INCVRIA.
NAM SVM EGO ACTVS VEHEMENS AVLA.

I did a quick and dirty translation.

I did not count Castor as a god through my inattention.
For I was violent and was driven from his temple.

It went on like that for several lines. At no point did it say anything that came even close to making sense.

It wasn't signed.

"So what are you trying to tell me?" I said, out loud.

The postcard didn't answer.

On the front was a photograph of a stone statue, a cross-cradling saint on a tripartite pedestal, etched against a backdrop of pure sky blue. The caption was in a language I didn't recognize. It didn't make sense that he would write me a postcard in coded Latin, or that he would leave it on the gravestone of a dead brother whose existence he wasn't supposed to know about, as it didn't make sense that Max was alive and nearby yet hiding from me. There was only one thing about the card that made any sense to me, one thing I recognized, though I didn't want to. That

141

symbol again, the eye with the lightning bolt. Max had drawn it in the lower right-hand corner of the postcard, and beneath it, he'd carefully printed another Latin word, the only one on the postcard whose meaning was clear.

Reus.

The guilty one.

He knew who'd killed Chris—and he was trying to, what? Warn me? Ask me for help, some kind of intercession to save him from a similar fate? For all I knew, he was passing along a recipe for chocolate chip cookies.

What kind of moron writes his SOS in code?

Max wouldn't have sent me a code he didn't know I could decipher. Which meant I had to get home and get to work. I almost ran through the cemetery, eyes fixed on the postcard—not on the frustrating words, but on the familiar curl and swoop of the lettering, the confirmation that he was still in the world, and not just somewhere, but *close*—and that was my mistake, because if I'd gone slower, or stayed at the grave longer, I would never have slammed into Eli Kapek on my way through the front gate, I wouldn't have dropped the postcard, he wouldn't have picked it up and turned it over, slowly, scanning the message that Max had trusted to me.

I snatched it back. Not soon enough.

"What are you doing here?" I said. "Are you following me or something?"

"That's the second time you've asked me that," he said. "So this is the second time I'll ask you: Is someone following you?"

I glared at him. "Apparently."

"Get over yourself."

"So?"

"So?" He echoed my tone exactly. I didn't take the bait.

"So what are you doing here?"

142

"I didn't realize this was your private property."

"It's a cemetery," I said.

"So *that's* why there are all those funny-shaped rocks sticking out of the ground. Want to tell me what *you're* doing here?"

"No."

"Look at that, we have something in common."

"Any chance you're adopted?" I asked.

"What?"

"There's no way you and Chris share the same gene pool."

He froze. Behind his eyes, something shifted. I'd gone too far.

"I'm sorry," I said.

"I doubt that." The teasing tone was gone; his face was a blank. Total system shutdown.

I didn't say anything. I knew better.

"Look, if I told you I just felt like being around dead people for a while, you'd think I was crazy," he said.

But I didn't.

"Have you been to his grave?" I asked.

"Just at the funeral. I had to come here the day after."

"What was it like?"

"It was like a big hole in the ground."

He clearly hadn't expected me to laugh. I wasn't expecting it, either.

"I don't think you're crazy," I said. "I'm here, aren't I?" For my brother, maybe. But not just for him. "I should go."

He shrugged and then, with a studied nonchalance, "So who do you know in Prague?"

"What?" *Just a dead girl named Elizabeth*, I wanted to say. *But I haven't heard from her in about four hundred years.* "No one."

He nodded at the postcard. "Except whoever sent you that."

I looked at it again, careful to keep the message side facing away from him. If the postcard came from Prague—which was

143

too insane to even imagine—how had it found its way to Andy's grave? "What makes you think it's from Prague?"

He had a nice smile. "That statue. It's St. John of Nepomuk on the Karlův most. The Charles Bridge. I'd know it anywhere."

"Because you happen to have some kind of freakish photographic memory for international religious statuary?"

As the smile widened, his eyes slit, crinkling up at the edges. "You know how normal people like to hang up pictures of their family? Or their pets, or Jesus, or whatever? In my house, it's nothing but Prague. Everywhere." He tapped the postcard. "This one's been hanging over the TV since I was seven. St. John of Nepomuk, queen's confessor, arrested in 1393 for refusing to share her confessional secrets with the king. Patron saint of silent suffering. Though I imagine he made some noise when they threw him off the bridge."

"Am I supposed to be impressed?"

He shoved his hands into the pockets of his long black overcoat. He was seriously overdressed for both the weather and the occasion, but somehow it suited him. "Don't strain yourself. My parents used to drill me on the salient details of all famous Czech landmarks, to make sure I learned everything I needed to know on the blessed day we finally returned to the homeland." He stopped smiling. "Mostly I learned I hated famous Czech landmarks."

"I didn't know Chris's family was Czech."

"*They're* not," he said. "Not really, at least not according to my parents. My mother and his father have the same grandfather, and Chris's side of the family skipped out, like, a hundred years ago. We were slow learners."

"You don't have an accent," I said.

"They're Czech. *I'm* American. Born here. Raised here. From here. To their great and eternal sorrow."

"Kind of amazing, isn't it, the unlimited variety of ways parents find to screw you up?" I said.

"Amazing," he said. "I'm guessing you'd prefer I don't ask any follow-up questions on that one?"

"Good guess."

"Okay."

"Okay?"

"Yeah. Okay. Your screwed-up family is your business. Mine is mine. No need to compare notes."

"Okay."

There was a pause, not the awkward kind, but heading in that direction.

"That's the symbol, isn't it?" he asked abruptly. "The one by his body?" He raised a finger, *wait.* "Let me stop you before you go all disingenuous on me—the cops told me there was a symbol, and I know you saw it for yourself, and we *both* saw what's drawn on the back of that postcard."

"I have to go."

He grabbed my wrist. His fingers were long and delicate, but his grip was surprisingly strong. "You say he was your best friend. If you know something—"

"I should tell *you*? I don't even know you."

"He was family," Eli said quietly, still holding on. "I realize that doesn't mean anything to you. Maybe it didn't mean much to me. But he was family, and now he's dead."

"Let go of me."

"That symbol is the key."

"You're crazy." With a forceful wrench, I ripped my hand free. "It's just some scribbles on an old postcard, Eli. Let it go."

"Like you're going to?"

"I'm leaving."

"I can help you," he said.

I wasn't the damsel-in-distress type, so it wasn't the prospect of falling into a waiting prince's arms and letting him slay the dragon that made me hesitate. It was that I was starting to feel a little too close to crazy myself, scouring ancient documents for hidden symbols and imagining secret, sinister connections where none could possibly exist. But I hadn't imagined the postcard.

"I'm not the one who needs help," I said, and I knew Eli would take it as insult, but it was simple truth. Max needed me.

I went home.

20

Not that it did me any good.

CASTOREM NON PVTO DEVM INCVRIA.
NAM SVM EGO ACTVS VEHEMENS AVLA.
DEMVS EI MELA OPPORTUNE. JAM
EMERSVM JAM SIT VINDICI PAEAN EI.
PRIMVM ALIENATVS EST COR MIHI. O CITE
OPE ELISO LICUIT FAS. SIC SINT EXEMPLA
ET SIM EGO IMAGO DESSE. NON CRIMINIS
MEVM OPVS AT IN PAVORE REI SVM.
LACRIMAE SVNT; AD VNDAS MITTE, VBI
AVET FAS.

I did not count Castor as a god through my inattention.
For I was violent and was driven from his temple. Let
us give him songs as we should. Now, already now,
may the hymn for that avenger have risen up! First, my
heart was driven mad. Oh so quickly, once my wealth

*had been shattered, did heaven's will become clear. So
let these be lessons and let me be the image of failure.
My work was not of crime, but still I am in fear of the
matter. There are tears; send them to the waves, where
heaven's will is well.*

Crime, violence, failure, fear.

Vengeance.

A lightning-bolt symbol that marked a killer—that would
lead me to *reus*, the guilty one.

What was I supposed to get from this? What was the secret?

What kind of failure was I that I couldn't figure it out?

And yes, there were moments when I paused to wonder
whether I really wanted to track down the guilty one myself,
given that however much I, in principle, would have loved to
avenge Chris's death, I wasn't much of an avenging angel, lacking
as I did flaming sword, armored wings, and anything with which
to defend myself other than my razor-sharp wit. I wasn't the vig-
ilante type. So I would, under almost any other circumstances,
have been content to let the police handle or mishandle things.
I would have been willing to spend the rest of my life hating a
shadow, even if it meant always waiting for a blade to slash out
of the darkness and finish what it started. But this wasn't about
principles; this was about Max.

Google yielded useless information about a million creepy
symbols, none of them the one I wanted. I had: Max's postcard.
The letters from his room. Elizabeth's letter, stained with Chris's
blood. Dubious connections drawn between an old man's stroke
that might or might not have been a murder attempt, a four-
hundred-year-old book, and a message traced out in blood, snow,
and ink that meant less to me every time I saw it.

I had nothing.

21

Yellow police tape stretched around the perimeter of the old church, but they hadn't bothered posting a guard. I did have one more thing: the key.

The office was as we had left it, stuffy and overheated, stacks of paper and unwashed coffee mugs littering the worktable. Turning on the lights seemed risky, but my inner coward won out over my inner paranoiac—I told myself that I'd never find anything guided by only a flashlight beam, but the truth was I couldn't have made myself sneak into the building if I'd had to do it in the dark.

The safe that had stored the Hoff's archives was empty. A stack of books had been knocked off the desk and lay open on the floor, their pages torn and smashed, their spines slowly snapping, and I knew that must have been the Hoff's last act, committed in a spasm of anger or a desperate attempt to steady himself as the toxin set his neurons on fire, because Professor Anton Hoffpauer would never have left a book in that condition if he'd had any other choice.

That was the first thing I did: pick them up and stack them in a neat if precariously leaning tower the Hoff would have approved of. Then I got started.

It turned out that searching when you didn't know what you were searching for was easier in the movies, when it could be turned into a vaguely boring montage that culminated in cresting harmonies and a triumphant document conveniently snatched out of the first or second file anyone bothered to ransack. It would have taken all week just to page through the first shelf of the Hoff's Renaissance history journals and sort through the stacks of books, categorized by no metric I could determine, unless it was thickness of dust layer. But, remembering what Max had told me about the Hoff being the black sheep of his field, the Voynich manuscript a refuge for crackpots and conspiracy nuts, I narrowed down the search by ignoring everything that had been printed and bound and looked even halfway reputable. Whoever had poisoned the Hoff had—due to lack of time or lack of interest—left behind the tattered notebooks, annotated photocopies, and stacks of loose-leaf covered in the Hoff's cramped and illegible writing that represented a life's work.

I was midway through a report questioning the methodology of the latest Voynich carbon-dating results when, somewhere across the darkness of the main sanctuary, a door slammed. Floorboards creaked. Footsteps approached the narrow tunnel that led to the Hoff's office, and to me.

I turned out the lights.

I ducked under the desk.

I didn't move.

The footsteps drew closer. A narrow beam of light danced across the shadowed shelves and crooked stacks. It glinted off the stained-glass windows, lighting up Jesus's mouth, Mary's hand, Judas's silver, then released them to darkness again.

I'd seen enough horror movies to know how this would end.

I'd seen enough of Chris's body to know how this would end.

If I did nothing, if I stayed perfectly silent and still, there was a chance he would never notice me. He would get what he came for and disappear back into whatever hell had spawned him. Maybe never to be seen again.

Never to be caught.

My cell was wedged into my pocket. As legs strode toward me, then paused a few inches from my face, the whisper of rustling pages just above my head, I flicked it open. With accuracy honed in uncountable classes where under-the-desk texting was the only escape from death by boredom, I pressed a finger over the speaker, then turned off the volume, wincing at the muted beep.

The legs didn't notice.

Calling 911 wouldn't do me any good if I couldn't speak.

I keyed in my mother's number.

From above, a muttered curse, a thump as something slammed against the desk, a cloud of dust.

I will not sneeze, I thought. I will not die a cliché.

The keys were slick with sweat. One letter at a time, careful not to hit the 3 when I meant 6, trying to breathe only when he did, I typed out a message.

In prof h office call police need—

Suddenly he held his breath; I didn't.

Please, I thought. But the office was too quiet; my breath was like the wind. The legs bent. The beam played across my face, and the world blazed white. I lost my grip on the phone, pressed a button that could, if I were a different, luckier person, have been *Send*, closed a fist around it, and prepared myself to smash it into something, an eye, the soft cartilage of a nose, anywhere I could do my damage before he did his, and then the flashlight beam skidded from my face to his.

"That can't be comfortable," Eli said, holding the light just beneath his chin like a Boy Scout about to launch into a truly gory campfire tale. He was grinning.

I considered following through on the cartilage-destruction plan.

"And before you ask, *again*," he said. "Yes. This time I was following you. But in fairness, you're the one who gave me the idea."

"What the hell is wrong with you?" I got out from under the desk, my legs cramped and wobbly from crouching for so long.

150

He put out an arm to steady me but wisely thought better of it before making contact.

"For expediency's sake, I'm going to interpret that as *What are you doing here?*"

"Fine. Let's start with that."

"You first."

I turned the lights back on.

"You seem angry," he said, still smiling. He was dressed in all black again, dark pants and a long-sleeved tee that hugged his surprisingly muscled form. A child's cartoonish idea of a cat burglar's costume that would have been easier to mock if I hadn't been dressed exactly the same way.

"I thought you were going to kill me."

"And you're welcome for not doing that, incidentally. So, what's the problem? Disappointed?"

"Has anyone ever told you how funny you are?"

"I don't actually get that a lot."

"Exactly."

As soon as I said it, I wanted to take it back.

"What?" he said.

"Nothing. *Déjà vu.* Whatever. Why were you following me?"

"Why are you here? No, let me answer that for you, since you're clearly not going to. You know something. About Chris. Maybe about that symbol. And, to further demonstrate my brilliant powers of deduction: All of this has something to do with what you were researching here. Yet for some reason, you've chosen not to share that with the cops. Or with me."

At the mention of the cops, I suddenly realized they might be on the way, and snuck a glance at my phone. I'd managed to delete the message before sending it anywhere.

So much for my survival skills.

"Calling someone?"

"How about the cops, since you think I should be more forth-coming with them," I suggested. "I'm sure they'd love to know you're prowling around a crime scene."

"Right, because that would look far less suspicious than *you*, sole witness, girlfriend of prime suspect, doing the same thing."

"Blackmail?"

"Stalemate."

"So now what?" I asked.

"You find what you came here for," he said. "I help."

22

We stayed across most of the night, picking through the Hoff's unlabeled files, tracing the spiderweb of connections he'd drawn through the Voynich manuscript's shrouded past, from Bacon to Dee to Kelley to Rudolf. Eli didn't ask why I was convinced there might be something useful here, even as the hours passed and it became clear that the scribbled names, dates, and snatches of Latin, French, German, Czech, and ancient Greek would be useful only to the Hoff, and maybe—given that the majority of the pages had been unceremoniously stuffed into the back of desk drawers or files layered in dust an inch thick—not even to him. He did ask how he was supposed to find anything if I didn't tell him what we were looking for, which I admitted was a good question, then went back to the Hoff's scribbles without offering an answer, because I didn't have one.

He was the one who found it.

Just a yellow sticky note, stuck in between a first edition of *The Leviathan* and an old issue of *Renaissance Quarterly*. On the front, the Hoff—or someone—had written *Ivan Glockner, Central Library, Prague, reference dept.* But it was the back of the note that first caught my eye: the word *Hledači*, underlined, with a question mark, and above it, inked with enough pressure to break through the page: the eye, the lightning bolt.

Sometimes, maybe, it was better to be crazy than it was to be right.

"Seekers," Eli said.

"What?"

"*Hledači.* It's Czech. For *seekers*."

So that's why the word looked familiar.

The letters from Max's room were in my bag, along with Elizabeth's. I'd brought them just in case. In case of what, I didn't know. Maybe I'd hoped I would find something that linked them all together. Something that made sense of them.

Maybe I'd hoped I was wrong.

I took out Max's letter and handed it to Eli.

"What is this?" he asked.

"None of your business. There, at the bottom, that's Czech, right? Can you read it?"

"None of my business, but you want me to . . . ?"

"Yes."

"This looks really old," he said.

"Probably is."

"Old like it should be in a library or a museum or somewhere with gloves and alarms and people shushing you."

"Can you or can't you?"

He squinted at the faded text, then read aloud. "'I swear this solemn vow, that I will seek the *Lumen Dei* for the glory of my people, the glory of my land, and the glory of God. I will keep a pure heart and an iron will. If I fail, my sons will continue the search, and their sons, and on and on until the *Lumen Dei* has returned home. Today I am reborn a seeker.'"

"*Hledači*," I said, curling my tongue around the strange sounds. *Lay da chee*, the Hoff's nonsense words, what I'd taken to be infantile babbling. The Hoff's warning.

"'*Přísahám, že budu věrný Hledačům, a zasvěcuji svůj život hledání, dokud neskončí,*'" he continued. "'I swear my allegiance to the seekers, and pledge my life to the search, until our search has ended.'" Eli looked up at me. The letter hid most of his face. "Where did you get this?"

"That's not important."

It couldn't be.

23

You know I submit this report under great duress, began the final letter in Chris's mystery stash. I'd postponed translating it, knowing that this was the last of him, even though there was nothing of him in it.

Someday you will pay for the things you have done.

The journey was uneventful. The astronomer was hesitant. He pretends to care only for advancement at court. But she charmed the truth out of him. He lives to search for answers, and believes this is where he will find them. She has sewn his calculations into the lining of her cloak. I leave this for you at the Golden Bough, and it will be my last until returning to Prague. For the rest of the journey, we will sleep under the stars. If all goes smoothly, we should arrive at the city wall on the Lord's Day.

You have promised not to harm her. I take you at your word. If you break that oath, no threat will stop me from acting.

12 March 1599.

I wondered if Elizabeth had known she was being spied on, and if she could have forgiven it if she'd known the spy was also protecting her. A cowardly weasel of a guardian angel was, I supposed, better than none at all.

24

The Whitman Center seemed dingier this time around, simultaneously less bucolic and less sinister. Adriane's door was closed. I knocked, without thinking, then remembered, and felt like a gut-punched fool—until the knob turned in my grip, and Adriane opened the door.

"Surprise!" She twirled for me, radiant in a strappy yellow dress. Inside the Whitman Center, it was always summer. "You're surprised, right?"

"I'm surprised."

And then there was all the hugging, crying, snot dripping, and tear wiping you'd expect. She didn't want to hear anything about what she'd missed in the last few weeks, nor did she have anything to say about her stay and gradual recovery at the Whitman Center, except that "you can turn any place into a spa if you try hard enough, although I'll admit the food is less than five-star." She'd had no visitors, as far as she knew, aside from her parents, and as soon as she'd snapped out of it enough to be aware of anything, she'd asked them to make sure I stayed away, along with everyone else, until she was completely well. She couldn't stand the idea of anyone seeing her like that; so, in true Adriane form, she explained that from here on in, we would pretend no one had. She didn't ask how I was doing, and she didn't mention any strange visitors pretending to be her dead boyfriend. The incoherent babbling, the wails of "Oh my god, I was so worried" and "Did you see me on the six o'clock news," the derision and subsequent dismissal of all well-meaning messages from well-meaning nonfriends, all of that was easy. When she slid to the floor in an effortless split and pressed her face to her knee with that soft, familiar groan of limb-stretching ecstasy, I almost started crying all over again.

She was back.

"Are you going to ask me?" she said, face against her leg, a curtain of hair shielding her expression.

I didn't want to. Not after what had happened the last time.

"Well?" She looked up.

I shook my head. This all seemed too good to be true. A fantasy, a respite, and so necessarily temporary. I didn't want to do something that might make us both wake up.

"Ask."

She really was back. When Adriane gave an order, it was hard to defy. Especially when it was an order I was so desperate to follow.

"Do you remember anything?" I asked.

She didn't flinch, much less scream. When she raised her head, there was a faint, plastic smile fixed on her face.

"Nothing. One hundred percent blank." The smile hardened. "I guess that makes me the lucky one."

I didn't argue with her, though probably I should have, since she was the one who still had a fading scar on her cheek, the one who would sleep here, with the fluorescent lights, hospital sheets, locked doors, and distant screams, while I went home and curled up in my own bed, the one who'd planned to spend the rest of her life with Chris and, even if the images were buried in some inaccessible corner of her brain, had sat in a pool of his blood and watched him slip away. It was the closest we ever came to acknowledging what I'd gone through while she was sleeping; that I'd gone through anything. For Adriane, that was a lot.

"My turn," she said. "Heard from Max?"

"He sent me a message." It felt strange to say it. I'd almost forgotten what it was like to have someone around who could be trusted. "I think he wants my help, but—"

"Thank god. I knew he wasn't—you know."

"They think he did it," I said, when what I wanted to say was, *Do you think he did it?*

"Obviously. What more would you expect from Chapman's crack law-enforcement team? Competence?"

"So, you don't believe it? You think he's innocent?"

"You even have to ask?"

"I know how you feel about him, and—"

"Nora, come on. He's a mouse. Not a *killer*." Adriane laughed, then broke off abruptly. "Wait, *you* don't think he did it. Do you?"

I had told myself I was completely convinced of his innocence. But if that was true, why was I suddenly so relieved? Adriane had been there. Even if she couldn't remember, some part of her would know. If Max had done something.

Of course he hadn't done something.

She squeezed my hand. "He wouldn't have left unless he had to."

"That's what I've been telling myself. But . . ."

"He's alive," Adriane said. "You're not allowed to feel sorry for yourself. Eventually *he'll* come back."

The unstated corollary hung between us. There was a hard silence.

"How are you doing?" I asked finally. "Really."

"I told you, my sanity's been fully certified by the highest authorities in nutland. They're kicking me out of here in a couple days."

"No, I mean . . . with what happened. Chris."

"We don't have to talk about that."

"But if you want to . . . I mean, you know I'm . . ." Maybe I

157

should have felt sorry for them then, all the parents and teachers and friends who'd ever stuttered through some awkward attempt to fix what couldn't be fixed while I stonewalled, mute and blank, until they ran out of words and walked away, statue-still if they made the mistake of hugging, stroking, squeezing, or otherwise invading my sacrosanct personal space. But instead I just hated myself for being one of them, when I should have known better.

"What do *you* want to talk about, Nora?" There was an edge to her voice. "You want to tell me all about discovering 'the body,' and getting the blood off your hands and what Chris looked like full of holes, whether his eyes were open, whether you screamed, whether I screamed?" Her voice didn't shake; her body was perfectly still. Everything about her was steady, hard—but it was a brittle kind of hard. Like she knew if she tried to bend, even a little, she would break. "Or maybe you want me to talk. You want to hear what it was like to wake up in this place and have some random nurse in orange polyester tell me, 'Good morning, it's Thursday, the sun is shining, your parents brought flowers, my name is Sandra, oh, and by the way, you've been a zombie for three weeks and your boyfriend is dead.'" She raised her hand to tuck her hair behind her ear, and that was the only tell: It was trembling. "Talking won't fix this. So for future reference, the answer to how I'm doing is 'Fine.' If you can't deal with that . . ."

"You're fine," I said, and it wasn't until I did that I realized how much *I'd* wanted to talk—how tired I was of pretending. But I wasn't the one who mattered right now. "I got it."

Adriane had never been much of a crier. But then, until now, she'd never had much to cry about. Perfect boyfriend, perfect life-sized Barbie-style dream house equipped with perfectly competent parental units, perfect GPA paired with a perfectly cultivated pretense of academic slacking, perfect posture, perfect hair, perfect nails, perfect love, perfect life. But it occurred to me now that it was easy to hide tears when you had the perfect smile. Maybe she cried more than I knew.

"So," she said.

"So," I said.

"Gossip update. Never a bad place to start."

I did as she asked. I told her about Holly Chandler's mid-volleyball wardrobe malfunction and Pranti Shah's hookup with Ben Katz, even though he was ostensibly still sleeping with his semi-girlfriend of four years and also, it was said, the new English teacher. We faked our smiles until, gradually, they shaded into real ones. It was easier than it should have been to let ourselves forget.

"Sing it for me," she said after I told her about our history teacher's drunken turn at a local karaoke night, when he had, according to the rumors (and lyrics) flying around school the next day, belted out an improvised love song to his ex-wife.

"Not going to happen."

"I'm in a mental institution," she pointed out. "I'm pretty sure you're supposed to indulge my every whim."

We were both so good at pretending nothing mattered. I wondered if it was possible to be too good. "I promise, if you start believing you're Elvis, I'll buy you a sequined jumpsuit," I told her.

"Please. If I were going to have delusions of grandeur, I'd pick someone with much better fashion sense. Speaking of which, I've taken advantage of my recent leisure time to start putting together an itinerary. And don't you dare complain about the store-to-museum ratio: Trust me, culture goes much better with a side of couture."

"What am I missing? Itinerary for what?"

She rolled her eyes. "Hello? *Bonjour?* Paris? Two weeks from today?"

"Adriane . . ." I glanced at the bars on the windows, the door that didn't lock from the inside.

"I told you, I'm fine, and as of Saturday, I'm home. Plenty of time to shop and pack for *les vacances magnifiques*."

"Are you insane?" I said, without thinking.

"Not anymore." She didn't smile.

"I can't go on that trip," I said. "Neither can you. Not after what happened. The whole point was to go together, and now . . ."

"'And now . . .'? 'What happened'? Since when did you become one of *those* people?" she said, suddenly angry. And behind the anger was something else, something that I knew she would never let me see. Something that could break her. We'd never had so much in common. "Chris is *dead*. Someone *killed him*. That's *what happened*. You think sitting around here crying is going to change that?"

"You think going to another country will? You think you'd have *fun*?"

"It's not about fun," she said. "Not anymore."

"Then what?"

"Look, you're right. This isn't the way we planned it. Obviously. But if I've got a chance to get the hell out of here, even for a week, I'm taking it. Or rather, *ma mère* and *mon père* are taking it for me."

"What?"

"They claim that distance and European air will cure all my ills. Coincidentally, the week they've booked for themselves at some spa in Aruba will do the same for them. No way are they canceling their trip to look after their poor, wounded daughter." She laughed, harshly. "That parent-of-the-year award must have gotten lost in the mail."

"Adriane, I'm sure if you ask them to stay . . ."

"They're going," she said. "Hence, I'm going. Hence, you're going."

"It's not that easy."

"It is if you want it to be."

"Adriane . . ."

"I'll do your calculus homework for you. For the rest of the year."

"I can do my own."

"But I can do it better."

I didn't smile. "I can't go to Paris, Adriane. If you don't want to talk about why, then fine, we won't. But you can't bribe me into it, or joke me into it, and you know it."

"Fine."

"Really?" That was a new one.

"Fine—if you promise you'll think about it."

That was more like it.

"Just promise," she added, "and I won't bug you about it anymore."

"Right."

"Okay, I won't bug you for at least twenty-four hours."

"I missed you," I said.

"I probably missed you, too," she said. "I just don't remember."

25

It should have been a night for celebrating. But Adriane spent it in a glorified mental institution, and I spent it where I spent every night: at my desk, Latin dictionary by my side, postcard in front of me, translation notebook abandoned in disgust, words melting together into useless soup.

There was a soft knock at the bedroom door. "Nora?" My

father. He hadn't been in my room since the night after the murder, when my parents had escorted me from the police station to my bed, tucking me in for possibly the first time ever. Before that, he hadn't been there in years.

I slipped the postcard into the notebook. "Come in."

He perched on the side of the desk. "Hi."

"Hi." I waited.

He tapped the dictionary. It was a heavy, leather-bound Oxford edition, with gilded pages and an extensive list of original sources. He'd given it to me for my eleventh birthday. It would be humiliating to admit exactly how excited I was, but suffice it to say, there'd been squealing. "Glad to see you're keeping up with your translating," he said.

I shrugged. "Homework."

I wondered if he missed those afternoons we'd spent in his office puzzling through that translation of Lucretius we'd never quite finished. At some point three days a week had become two, then one. I don't know what came first: the day his door stopped opening for me or the day I didn't bother to knock because Chris and Adriane had offered me a better option. I wondered whether he was still working on the Lucretius, whether he'd finished without me.

I doubted it.

He smiled. It looked funny on his face, the smile, like it knew it didn't belong and didn't plan on staying long. "Can I see?"

If I said no, he might get suspicious. Also, I was desperate. I gave him the notebook.

He raised his eyebrows. "Homework?"

"It's like a puzzle. We're supposed to figure out what it means."

He ran his finger across my scribbled and crossed-out translations. "Where's the original?"

162

I flipped back to a page where I'd written out the full text of the postcard. He nodded, silently mouthing Max's words.

"Maybe that school's worth the money after all," he said.

"I go there for free," I reminded him.

Ignoring me, he grabbed a pencil and began tapping different letters, counting quietly under his breath. "I wouldn't expect them to be teaching steganography at this level. It's impressive."

"Steganography?" The word sounded familiar, like something the Hoff had once told us about, back when, as general policy, I ignored everything he said.

"Your teacher probably just called them ciphers, or codes, though that's not quite accurate, as generally a code relies on the *meaning* in the message, substituting certain words or phrases for prearranged others, while a cipher will replace each individual letter with another letter or symbol, using some kind of algorithm." He was slipping into teacher mode. His eyes were still fixed on the page. "But steganography depends on disguising the fact that it's a cipher, or indeed that there is even a message at all. The message hides in plain sight, as if written in invisible ink. Which, incidentally, would qualify as a stegotext. Didn't your teacher explain all this to you?"

"It's, like, an extra-credit challenge," I said quickly. "She's not actually teaching this unit until next week."

"Ah, in that case, I don't want to give away the game."

"But what did you mean by plain sight?" Nothing, and certainly not the prospect of encroaching on some random high school teacher's homework rules, could divert my father once he slipped into lecture mode.

The smile returned. "There are a variety of traditional cipher techniques," he explained. "The Caesar Shift, the Atbash—different eras generally had their own favorite forms of spycraft,

163

but given that this appears written in plain text, as opposed to a substitution or transposition cipher, my best guess is you're dealing with a stegotext, probably one where the message is buried amid decoy letters."

"And I would translate that by . . . ?"

"You simply need to know, or guess, the numerical key. If the key were six, then you'd find your message by counting out every sixth letter and disregarding the rest. You understand."

"Right, but how am I supposed to figure out the key?"

"Trial and error," he suggested. "Or the number is sometimes embedded in context clues. Not that you have any here, I suppose." He cleared his throat. "I've got some time, if you want to try to work it through together."

"That would be nice, but . . ." But I couldn't. "I shouldn't. It's homework, you know? I should probably figure it out myself." I pretended not to notice him deflate.

"Of course."

"But thanks. That was really helpful."

"That's what I'm here for," he said. "*Pater ex machina.* Anytime. Well." He cleared his throat again. "I should leave you to it."

"You don't have to," I said. "I mean, I'm done with all my other homework, so . . ."

He was already backing out the door. "No, no. Schoolwork's important, even at a time like this. I'm glad you remember that." Somewhere, a door slammed. Mom was home. "I've got work to do myself," he said quickly. He closed my door behind him, and a few moments later, I heard the telltale thud of him disappearing behind door number three.

Pater ex machina. A cheap trick by which the invisible briefly and inexplicably made itself visible, only to change everything— and then, without warning, vanished all over again. That sounded about right.

Context clues.

One statue. One illegible postmark, one demonic symbol.

One word that meant anything: *reus*.

One word with four letters.

And that was the key.

After weeks of desperate but useless attempts to translate the message, the final step was almost ridiculously easy. I could count to four:

CASTO**R**EM **N**ON P**V**TO DEVM **I**NCV**R**IA.

NA**M** SVM **E**GO A**C**TVS **V**EHE**M**ENS **A**VLA.

DEMV**S** EI **M**ELA O**P**POR**T**UNE. **J**AM

E**M**ERS**V**M JA**M** SIT **V**INDICI P**A**EAN **E**I.

PRI**M**VM **A**LIE**N**ATV**S** EST **C**OR M**I**HI. O **C**ITE

OPE ELISO **L**ICU**I**T FA**S**. SIC **S**INT EXE**M**PLA

ET SIM **E**GO I**M**AGO **D**ESSE. NON **C**RIM**I**NIS

MEVM **O**PVS **A**T IN **P**AVO**R**E RE**I** SVM.

LACRI**M**AE **S**VNT; **A**D VN**D**AS M**I**TTE, **V**BI

AVET FA**S**.

It should never have taken me so long to see it. A truth that appeared only when all the meaningless nonsense was stripped away—it was the only way Max knew how to speak.

CONVENIMECVMADSEPTJMVM VIAE

IANSCICOLLISSEPTEMDECIMOAPRILIS

ADIVVA

I guessed at the spacing; I substituted *I* for *J*, *U* for *V*, and vice versa, as the Latin allowed; I found it.

I found him.

CONVENI MECUM AD SEPTIMUM VIAE
IANSCI COLLIS SEPTEMDECIMO APRILIS
ADIUVA

Meet me Jansky Hill Road seven. Seventeen April.

Google confirmed the impossible. Jansky Hill was Jánský vršek, a street in Prague, only blocks from the palace once home to Rudolf II of Austria, the sixteenth-century Holy Roman emperor.

I called Adriane and told her we were going to Paris. I didn't tell her that we wouldn't be staying—that, instead, we would be risking expulsion by sneaking away from the chaperones, hopping a train to the Czech Republic, and finding our way to a dark corner of a foreign city, where we would wait for something to happen. I'd tell her when we were on the plane, when there'd be minimal time for either of us to have second thoughts, though I knew I was the only one who'd be having second thoughts. I'd convince my parents, if they put up a *pro forma* fight about my going to Paris, that distance would assuage my trauma, and with an ocean between me and that night, maybe I could finally start to forget it. They would know better than to believe me—but they would also know better than to argue.

The Hoff, who had known about the *Hledači* and tried so hard to tell me, had made me promise: *Don't go.* But he was a sick old man with poison in his brain, and he couldn't have known what was about to happen, or what I would have to do.

I had to go. I had to do something; second thoughts or not, I would do this.

Because there was one final Latin word in Max's message, one I didn't need a dictionary to understand.

Adiuva.

Help.

PART III

Master of the Still Stars

O gentle Faustus, leave this damned art
This magic, that will charm thy soul to hell,
And quite bereave thee of salvation.
Though thou hast now offended like a man,
Do not persevere in it like a devil.

∴ *The Tragical History of Doctor Faustus*
Christopher Marlowe

1

The senior class was already drunk. Not on liquor, maybe, although I was pretty sure it wasn't Gatorade that Brett Craig and his "boyz" were chugging with such unbridled glee; Adriane had taught me long ago that all you needed was a little food coloring to turn vodka the appropriate shade of radioactive piss. Nor was it just the frat boys in training. It was the Prep preps, their leather suitcases stuffed with shoes, their wallets with Daddy's credit cards; it was the parking-lot potheads, nervously eyeing the airport security officials and their steel-collared canines; it was the jocks, eager for their binge of food, wine, and sleep, a long-awaited caesura between the last four years of training seasons and the next; and it was even the APers—my ostensible karass—their collegiate fates sealed, their number-two pencils in the trash, their permanent records finally open for besmirching. All of them, high on the fumes of their imagined exploits. The Air France gate and the promise that lay on the far side of our seven-hour flight had managed the miracle no amount of homecoming rallies, unity dances, or spirit weeks ever could: The class, with all its disparate, territorial, and occasionally warring factions, had been fused into a homogeneous, undifferentiated One. And then there was me.

"I'm going to grab some water for the flight."

"You want company?" Adriane asked.

I did not.

I liked the airport; I liked being alone in the airport, anonymous in an anonymous crowd. I liked that it was, at its core, nothing more than a holding area, a No-Place that wasn't a place at all so much as it was a gateway to Not-Here. If you stripped away all the superfluous regional talismans, the Red Sox banners and chowder shacks, it could have been any airport, with the same cell-phone and bank ads lining the walls, the same overpriced convenience stores and salmonella-infested sandwich stands, the same signs detailing what should be done with your explosives, your firearms, and your shampoo bottles, the same plastic chairs, the same blinking monitors, the same desks where, with the right plastic card, you could buy yourself escape. Standing before the ticket desk, I felt like I had when I'd first gotten my driver's license: suddenly, ridiculously free. Untethered. I could forget Paris, forget Max and our shared insanity, even forget Chris; I could, with my emergency credit card, buy a ticket to Peoria or Topeka, somewhere no one would ever find me. I wondered if it would help—if being as alone on the outside as I was on the inside would somehow equalize the pressure, keep me from exploding.

I got an extra water for Adriane—sparkling, the way she liked it—along with two bags of peanut butter cups and a canister of Pringles that would get us through the flight.

I wasn't going to Topeka.

But it was nice to pretend.

2

When I got back to the gate, the flight was about to board, and Adriane was gone.

I suppressed my panic reflex. This was an airport: If she'd gone catatonic again, if the men with knives had come for her, if she'd been carried away by a boy with yellow roses in one hand and a psychogenic toxin in the other, someone would have noticed. So before alerting Homeland Security, I checked the bathroom.

I'd never heard her cry before, but it couldn't have been anyone else. The sobs coming from the stall were as ugly as her laughter, the only ungainly thing about her. The woman washing her hands, the woman changing her baby, the woman dragging her toddler into the opposite stall, they all pretended not to hear.

So did I.

Adriane wouldn't want me to see. That's what I told myself. Adriane would be desperate to avoid the messy, public cliché of ladies' room regret and recrimination, so I backed out and waited for her at the gate, and when she appeared, red-eyed and full of unconvincing complaints about sordid conditions and empty soap dispensers, I went along with it and asked no questions and told myself I was doing her a favor.

3

"You sure you want to leave all this?" Adriane asked, elbows propped on a gargoyle, gaze sweeping across the panorama spread out beneath us. Paris was a postcard, the Seine sluicing through the jumble of pillars and spires that stretched to the horizon, its water the same slate gray as the sky. The Eiffel Tower poked the clouds, dwarfing the dull rectangular office buildings lined up like dominos in the distance. Two hundred feet below us swarmed a mass of photo-snapping tourists, French schoolchildren, and grungy backpackers, all too intent on texting, posing, gelato licking, and avoiding the panhandling troupe of mandolin strummers to bother with the monster that loomed overhead, at least until the bells chimed, reminding the crowd—and the city—that they stood in the shadow of Notre Dame.

"I told you, you don't have to come. I can do this myself."

She snorted. "That I'd like to see."

"Right, because you're the capable, intrepid adventurer. Remind me again, which one of us was hyperventilating on the plane?"

"It's natural to be agitated when you're about to plummet forty thousand feet to the ground. It's inhuman to be sitting there totally calm while pieces are falling off the plane."

"Nothing fell off the plane."

"I know what I saw," she insisted. "And how do you explain all the bumping and shaking? The so-called turbulence?"

"Um, how about turbulence?"

Adriane, who'd perked up as soon as she heard my Prague plan, had spent the bulk of the flight reciting pertinent statistics on meteorites, errant planes, birds with a death wish, anything that might tear through the thin membrane separating us from a wide array—falling, freezing, oxygen deprivation, drowning, crashing, burning—of deaths. Not the first time I'd resented her nearly photographic memory, but fortunately I'd grown expert at tuning her out. I'd been on a plane only twice before, and both times I'd made full use of the barf bags helpfully tucked into the seat back, but this flight was different. We were sealed into a metal can, hurtling forty thousand feet over the ocean, which meant no one could climb through my window, no one could ease open the front door with a stolen key, no one could hover over my sleeping figure with a pillow or a gun or a knife. Yet when I closed my eyes, I still saw Chris; I still saw his blood. So I didn't sleep.

But for the duration of the flight, for the first time, I felt safe.

"You'll believe anything," Adriane said. "That's why you need me along. Someone's got to bring a healthy sense of paranoia to the situation."

"Adriane, this is no joke. I swear, you don't owe me—"

"I'm not laughing." She lowered her voice and leaned over

174

the edge of the railing. Doing my best to ignore the vertiginous drop, I bent toward her. "And I'm not doing this for you," she said quietly. "Or for Max."

She stopped there.

We'd spent a bleary-eyed morning traipsing after our chaperones from one touristic hot spot to the next, and after Notre Dame would have to endure the Pantheon, the Arc de Triomphe, and the Sorbonne before we would be set free for three hours of exploring the Louvre. That was a wide enough window to make it to the train station and hop the 17:40 train to Prague before anyone noticed we were gone. The suitcases had been sent on ahead of us to the hotel, awaiting our check-in, but we had enough clothes and cash in our carry-ons to get us through the next couple days. I'd say it was almost too easy, but I knew better. There was no such thing.

4

The Louvre was practically a city unto itself. Thirty-five thousand works of art, according to the soporific tour guide, the best and brightest of Egyptian, Near Eastern, Greek, Etruscan, and Roman civilizations, not to mention seven centuries of European oil painting, all crammed into fourteen acres of gilded hallway. The café served wine—even to overeager, underage Americans—so, unsurprisingly, the horde went one way. We went the other. In search of something called *Fragments of an Equestrian Statue of Nero*, I told Kyle Chen, the youngest and most apathetic of the chaperones, and because he'd been a Chapman Prep senior recently enough to know me by my Latin-nerd reputation, he waved us off, barely looking at me but sparing poor, soon-to-be-bored-to-death Adriane a glance that shifted from sympathy to appreciation as it descended her body. In fact, it was Adriane who, back before our Paris sojourn had morphed from *Amélie* into *Mission Impossible*, had committed the Louvre's index of unmissable works to memory, mapping out the geometrically optimal route between them—the better to force-feed me the wonders of the civilized world and still finish up in time for chardonnay o'clock.

Now she was in charge of our escape route. It was only a matter of heading into the Denon Wing and waiting out the minutes beneath the impassive gaze of crumbling marble gods before we could risk returning to the central atrium and ascending the escalator that would return us to ground level.

"Someone's watching us," Adriane whispered as we emerged from the giant glass pyramid that marked the entrance to the museum.

"Where?"

"He's just getting off the escalator—our age, gray sweatshirt, black hair. Look."

But when I turned around, ever so casually, there was no one who fit the description, and no one in the horde of tourists who seemed to care about our existence one way or another. They were too busy snapping photos of the glass pyramid and the majesty that surrounded us—to one side, manicured gardens with sculpted hedges watching over drizzling fountains, and to the other, the Louvre itself, once home to centuries of French kings, its baroque pediments now topped by statues of all the dead white men who had tamed civilization on behalf of the French. The austere glass triangle looked like it had been dropped in from outer space, though it was no less out of place than all the digital cameras and miniskirts. I imagined Louis XIV would be less than pleased.

"He's gone," Adriane said.

"Someone from school?"

She shook her head. "Just a guy. But he was definitely staring at us."

"Staring at you, probably," I said. That, as it turned out, was as Parisian as the Eiffel Tower. Even I'd been hit on twice since we arrived, which would have been noteworthy even if it hadn't been nearly two days since I'd showered or changed my clothes. "Either way, let's get out of here."

Adriane successfully navigated the metro and got us to the Gare du Nord without incident, where I broke out my newly memorized sentence, "*Je voudrais acheter deux billets à Prague, s'il vous plaît.*" It got me two tickets and a sour *your accent sucks* look from the narrow, mustachioed man behind the counter.

The Gare du Nord, like pretty much everything in Paris, looked like a palace. At least from the outside. Inside, it felt more like a cavernous shipping warehouse—by way of a Gothic cathedral. Three of the walls climbed up and up forever, while the fourth was missing, leaving in its stead a gaping maw through which the trains could come and go, along with the sun.

"We're actually doing this," Adriane said, watching the trains chug away for parts unknown.

"We're actually doing it."

Her eyes popped. She grabbed my arm, and spoke without moving her lips. "He's here."

"Who?"

"The guy from the museum. He followed us."

"Where?"

She dragged me toward a bathroom alcove. Safely hidden, we peeked around the corner. "He was standing by the café," she said. "Watching us."

"I don't see him."

"I don't see him now, either," she said. "But he was there."

"Are you sure—"

"I'm not imagining this," she said fiercely. "I'm not crazy."

"If you say someone's following us, I believe you," I said. Much as I preferred not to. "Let's just go to the gate. Fast."

The station was teeming with people: sturdy men gripping chic briefcases, businesswomen in impossibly high heels, tourists of every creed, color, and camera model, and a few ragged clumps of children in oversized, mismatched clothing, who Adriane informed me were the gypsy pickpockets our chaperones had warned us about. (They'd made sure to add that *gypsy* was an out-of-date, politically incorrect term referring to a group of people most of whom were perfectly upstanding, law-abiding, oppressed citizens . . . but that nonetheless, we should guard our wallets and beware of children.) We were both rather proud of ourselves for picking our way through the noisy chaos and finding our way to the right platform with a minimum of confusion or disaster . . . until the right platform revealed itself to be deserted and the departure board suddenly informed us that it was awaiting a train to Nice three hours hence. The train to Prague was no longer listed at all. Despite the fact that it was due to leave in the next fifteen minutes.

"There will be an announcement," Adriane said, with a level of confidence she only mustered when she suspected we were screwed.

There was an announcement. In French. At least I assumed it was in French—given the static that garbled every syllable, it could have been in Nepali for all I knew. It could have been in English. It could not have been less helpful.

"*Pardon, Monsieur,*" I said to the first official-looking person we could find.

"*Nous avons un question,*" Adriane said, in the slow, laborious French that had gotten her kicked out of her AP class the third

178

week of school. Just our luck that foreign languages were her Achilles' heel—while mine, on the other hand, was the obscure desire to learn a foreign language that would come in handy only if we built ourselves a time machine.

"Pardon?" the man said.

She enunciated. *"Un question."*

He shook his head.

"Parlez-vous anglais?" I asked, the other French phrase I'd made sure to memorize.

He shook his head again. *"Pardon?"* And then he said something else really fast that I gathered meant we were out of luck.

"Prague," Adriane said, too loud.

The man started speaking again, even faster this time, gesticulating wildly, jabbing his finger first at his SNCF uniform, then at the ceiling, then at us, and all the while, the seconds ticked away, and if we missed this train we'd be trapped in Paris till morning. "What the hell is he saying?" Adriane murmured.

"He's saying that he hates it when rude American girls act like he has any interest whatsoever in their transportation issues, and that the SNCF doesn't pay him to deal with backpacking Eurail trash," said a voice from behind us.

Adriane turned, and the color leached out of her face. "It's him."

The guy standing behind us, smug smile on his smug face, did indeed have a gray sweatshirt and black hair. I wished I hadn't been so quick to dismiss my mother's contribution to the packing list. She'd been right: You never knew when travel-sized Mace could come in handy. "You."

"Me," Eli said. "And I see, as per usual, the fact that it's me and not a crazed serial killer does nothing but disappoint."

179

5

"You *know* this guy?" Adriane said.

"Remember Chris's cousin I told you about?"

She made a face like I'd asked her to taste-test some sour milk. "You said he was cute."

Eli preened.

"No, you asked if he was cute," I reminded her. "I said that wasn't the point."

"Not a no," Eli pointed out.

"What the hell are you doing in Paris?" I asked.

"Following you."

"I told you someone was following us!" Adriane said. "I knew I wasn't crazy."

"Not what I heard," Eli muttered.

"Because you're Chris's cousin, I'm not going to call the cops on you," Adriane said, in a voice pure syrupy poison. "Now we're getting out of here. I know this goes against the whole stalker ethos, but: *Don't follow us.*"

We only made it a couple feet. "I'll tell Prague you say hello," he called.

"Don't give him the satisfaction," I warned her, but it was too late.

"What are you talking about?" she asked.

"Well, those of us headed for Prague are going this way," he said, pointing opposite the direction we'd been walking. "You seem to be heading toward . . . Denmark?"

"Maybe we are," I said.

"Right, and that's why you've been shouting 'Prague!' in that poor guy's face for the last ten minutes. I know where you're going, and I know why you're going, and if we don't go now, we're not going at all, so . . ."

"'We' are not going anywhere."

"Look, let's lay our cards on the table," he said.

"'Cards on the table'?" Adriane laughed. "What are you, my grandfather?"

"You're looking for Max. So am I. We both want the same thing. So why not help each other?"

"Just to be clear," I said. "You're stalking me—*transatlantically*—because you want to help."

"I want answers."

"I don't have them," I said. "And this has nothing to do with Max. We're on spring break."

"No, your school is on spring break. You're on the lam."

"'On the lam'?" Adriane echoed.

"Call me Grandpa," Eli snapped. "I don't care. And keep lying, that's fine. But if you're so sure Max is innocent, you shouldn't care if I come with you. Hell, maybe he is innocent. But he knows something."

"Even if he did, how is it your job to find out?" I asked.

"Who else is going to do it? The idiot local cops? All they care about is not looking stupid on the evening news. And all you care about is helping your poor little lost boyfriend. Someone's got to care about Chris."

"Screw you," Adriane said.

"Come on," I told her. "Let's just go."

"Lead the way," Eli said.

"I wasn't talking to you."

"I'm coming with you," he said.

"That's excellent," Adriane said. "Say it just like that when the cops get here. Nice and creepy."

"You're as bad a liar as she is," Eli said. "You want to call over a cop? Fine. I'm sure they'd be thrilled to reunite you with your chaperones."

"You were right about him," Adriane told me.

"Would this be about my cuteness factor?" Eli asked. "It grows on you, doesn't it."

She turned her back on him, and we started for the gate, ignoring the footsteps behind us. "He must have been adopted."

6

Sometime in the night, somewhere in Germany, moonlit countryside streaking past, blotches in the darkness that might have been cows, trees, houses, or smudges on the window, Eli snoring in his half of the compartment, Adriane curled around her backpack with her knees kissing her forehead, my passport tucked safely into a pouch wrapped around my waist, beneath my jeans—a parent-imposed security measure that had seemed like overkill only until we'd crossed our first national border, and the train conductor, as if rehearsing his lines for some World War II movie, demanded to see our papers—the train rumbling beneath us, its pitch and ferocity unchanged by the shifting terrain, iron tracks stretching through empty fields and unpronounceable small towns, Wuppertal and Bielefeld and Bad Schandau, racing the rising sun, I gave up on sleep.

"Adriane?" I whispered. The two of us were sharing the hard, plastic pallet, our heads only a few inches apart. When we arrived in the compartment, there had been another passenger here, his weathered face peering at us over a wrinkled newspaper, a thin column of smoke drifting up from behind the newsprint despite the DÉFENSE DE FUMER/RAUCHEN VERBOTEN/NO SMOKING signs accompanied by easy-to-understand red graphics. Eli had said

182

something in what he claimed was "rusty high school French," something rapid and annoyed, and within seconds, the old man had folded his newspaper, gathered his bulky duffel, and left us on our own. "I just told him I was afraid we might disturb him with our youthful chatter," Eli explained. "He was grateful for the warning." He hadn't looked grateful; he had looked obedient.

"Adriane?" I whispered again, slightly louder. "You awake?"

Her yes was so soft I thought I might have imagined it.

"What are you thinking about?" she whispered.

But I couldn't answer, because that topic was off-limits.

"Me too," she whispered after a moment.

Some things were easier to talk about in the dark.

"But we'll find him," she added. "He'll be fine."

Not Chris—Max. I felt a stab of guilt. She was right. Max was the one I should be worrying about; Max was the one I could still save.

"You really think you love him?" Adriane whispered. "Do-anything-for-him, happily-ever-after true love?"

It must have been the darkness, or the jet lag. Because we didn't talk like this. Ever.

"You know I do."

"I thought you didn't believe in that. True love. Remember?"

"That was before."

"Mmm-hmm."

Before Max, I had spoken, with the authority of ignorance, of true love as a modern construct, a rationalization to preserve monogamy in a modern society founded on abundance of choice, a sex-and-hormone-fueled illusion, a fairy tale created by fairy tales, all those Grimm stories whose maidens chose their Prince Charmings by bank account and real-estate holdings—and even when Disney took over and set the birds and fish and teakettles to trilling about irrelevancies like true love, the hero was always a wealthy prince, the happy ending a happiness of plenitude and gold. True love is for good wedding toasts and bad movies, I had told Adriane two years before, mostly because I was sick of listening to her nauseating paeans to the many wonders of Chris, the inadequacy of language like *fireworks* and *chemistry* to describe the explosions between them, the detailed elaborations on their future together, her Empire-waist wedding gown, his surprise honeymoon to Bali, their two-point-five children and compromise between his white-picket-fence fantasies and her Malibu beach house, which "don't worry, Nora, will be complete with an old-maid room just for you. Kidding." I had relinquished the down-with-love campaign when I met Max. Adriane had stopped talking about the future.

"What about you?" I asked.

Silence. Eli murmured in his sleep, sounding afraid.

"You still think you would have ended up together?"

"I don't think about that," she said.

"Okay."

After a long moment. "How am I supposed to know?"

"I shouldn't have asked."

But she kept going. "It's not normal to know something like that now. It's not like we were going straight from graduation to the wedding chapel. Even if that's what he wanted."

"That's not what he wanted."

She sat up. "You know this how?"

"I know Chris." Knew Chris.

"Whereas I was just the girlfriend."

"That's not what I meant."

"Yes, it is," she said quietly. "It always is."

Something about the way she said it made me think she'd been stewing on that one for a long time. "Adriane, I never meant to—"

"You don't know everything, Nora. Not even about him."

"So tell me. Tell me anything. Just talk to me."

Adriane lay down again and tucked her knees back to her chest. "Because you're my best friend and you want to be there for me?"

"That sums it up."

"You were his best friend," she whispered. "Not mine."

It wasn't true, not in the way I knew she meant it. But it wasn't enough of a lie that I could argue.

"I'm still here," I told her. "Whenever you need me. I promise."

"You don't owe me anything."

"Then consider it a gift."

There was a long silence, filled only with deep, even breathing and the rumbling of the train, and then an isolated word floating softly in the dark, as if unrelated to anything that came before. "Okay."

We both lay still, and quiet. But I didn't sleep. And I could see her eyes—neither did she. Germany swallowed us up. Eli moaned in his sleep. Adriane watched him; I watched her.

"What do we do about him?" she whispered as the sky was pinking up.

"He's fine." He lay on his side, his back to us, his head like a mess of porcupine needles, black hair jutting out in all directions.

"We can't trust him," she said softly.

"Obviously. But . . ."

"But what?"

"He just wants to find out who did it. Same as we do."

"He wants to use us to find Max. For all you know, the cops sent him. Anyone could have."

"We'll handle it," I whispered.

"Or we grab his wallet and passport and dump him at the next stop."

"Funny."

"Not joking."

"I vote with Nora," Eli murmured, still turned away. "Majority rules. Now shut up so I can sleep."

7

Paris, what little we saw of it, had been less strange than strangely familiar, a postcard landscape of greatest hits. From the Eiffel Tower to the picturesquely quaint *boulangeries;* from the women with chic heels and flowing scarves biking along the river, baguettes in their baskets, to the old men feeding the pigeons beneath Notre Dame; from the beret-clad artists painting riverscapes to the river itself—crisscrossed by bridges, ferrying a parade of sightseeing cruises, lined with used-book stands on one side and hulking white monuments to neoclassical urban planning on the other—the city felt like one big movie set.

Prague was alien.

The language sounded and looked not just foreign but unknowable, consonants jumbled, vowels missing, strange accents— all of them blaring at us in stark Communist-era black and red, *Východ, Kouření zakázáno, Zákaz fotografování, Zavřeno.* The cars were different, squat and stubby, as if the highways had been diverted from the seventies. Even the people looked different, in a way I couldn't have described but knew I wasn't imagining, their faces and clothes all sharing the same basic elements as mine, the same noses and eyebrows and hemlines, but all the same fundamentally *not*.

It shouldn't have surprised me. It was a different country; it was supposed to be different. But I hadn't expected it to be, as I hadn't expected how abruptly the depressing Communist-bloc architecture, with its dingy cement cubes and rusting balconies, would, as the taxi drove us from the train station into the heart of the old city, give way to ornate gray moldings, cobblestone streets, Gothic churches, the watchful gaze of stone saints. Nor had I expected that, as the city swallowed us up, the strange would resolve itself into a place I had seen so vividly in my imagination, in Elizabeth's letters. I hadn't expected that her Prague, that sixteenth-century village teeming with rats and God and plague, was still here.

The cab stopped, and the driver said something I could only have repeated with marbles in my mouth. Eli—whose unexpected usefulness I'd vowed never to admit—responded with *"Děkuji,"* the word for *thank you* I'd memorized in my guidebook but until that moment had no idea how to pronounce, and handed him a wad of the Czech crowns we'd gotten from the currency-exchange booth at the train station.

"Děkuji," I mumbled.

Jánský vršek 7. We were here.

8

Max wasn't. Jánský vršek 7 was a narrow pension sandwiched between an empty tavern and a bluish building with a brass cross on the door and a porcine stone beast jutting out of the lintel. Trapped in the purgatory between motel and hostel, the Zlatý kanec—the Golden Boar, Eli translated—had eleven rooms for rent, all of them vacant, though this was only established once Eli had haggled the stooped owner down from a ridiculously cheap price to an even cheaper one. This despite the fact that the manager—whose thinning cardigan was held together over his belly with an array of mismatched buttons and whose remaining teeth looked like they'd been removed and reattached by a toddler only just learning about square pegs and round holes—could presumably have used the extra cash. Maybe I should have felt grateful to Eli, but instead I felt mute and helpless, like some kid traipsing after his parents, beholden to their dictates and their whims.

"Passports," the manager said, in a thick accent.

I slid my hand beneath the waistband of my jeans to wriggle the passport out of its holder, while Adriane, who despite my warnings kept hers tucked into the inside pocket of a purse that didn't even close at the top, already had hers out—but we were both stopped short by the power of Eli's scorn. Excusing himself to the manager, he dragged us into the corner of what passed for the inn's lobby, a domed space with cobblestone floors indistinguishable from the street and its formerly grand stone walls papered with peeling signs for movies, art exhibits, bands, and—judging from the crudely drawn graphics—plumbers' union protests, almost all having taken place in the previous decade.

"No passports," Eli hissed.

Adriane rolled her eyes. "Somehow I doubt this guy's connected to Interpol."

Eli treated her to an exaggerated eye roll of his own. "It's almost like you've never snuck your way into a foreign country before. Pay in cash, fake names, no IDs, trust me."

I couldn't ask how Max was supposed to find me if he didn't know I was here. And so, after some fast-talking from Eli, a promise that we would, as per the rules, dutifully leave our key with the front desk whenever leaving the building, and an additional 140 crowns changing hands, we got our large brass room keys with nothing more than a scout's-honor promise that the fake names we put on our registration forms were accurate. Eli took the room at one end of the hall that smelled like fish, while Adriane and I took the identical room at the other, dumping our bags on the thin mattresses that bore faint stains of bodily fluids and—I could only imagine—secreted used condoms and colonies of bed-bugs in their dark crevices.

"You take the good one," Adriane said, nodding at the bed with slightly fewer stains. A peace offering. "And about what I said last night, it was late and—"

"We were both exhausted," I cut in before the awkward apologizing could begin. "We were practically talking in our sleep."

"So, you're okay with—"

"Everything's okay," I said. It didn't matter anymore who had known Chris better, who had felt obligated and who had felt like an obligation. It didn't matter, because Chris was gone. "But I think I left something in the lobby."

What mattered was asking the toothless man behind the desk whether there'd been any messages left for a Nora Kane, and deciphering the code on the small note that he handed me, the code that I now understood and that told me where I should go at midnight. What mattered was that Max would be there, too.

9

"What is it?" I asked Eli as he hesitated in the doorway of the inn. We'd decided to start our search (for information, if not—as Eli and Adriane may have thought—for Max) in the most logical place for any dutiful student of the Hoff's: the public library. That was where the Hoff had, based on the note I'd found in his office, met a man named Ivan Glockner, and maybe where he'd first learned of the *Hledači*.

According to our map, the library was a simple walk down the hill and across the river into the heart of Staré Město, or Old Town. We were staying on the left bank of the Vltava, up a steep hill from the river, in Malá Strana, a worm's nest of narrow, twisting cobblestone streets and alleys; dingy storefronts, with crosses or chalices or marionettes hanging in dingy windows; brown-robed monks strolling beside habited nuns, ushered by bells to one church or another; and shadowing it all, the double spires of St. Vitus Cathedral, centerpiece of Hradčany Castle, former home of the Holy Roman emperor, secular emissary of God himself.

Elizabeth Weston walked these streets, I thought, and my hand crept to my abdomen of its own accord, where beneath my shirt, tucked into the pouch with my passport, was the letter Chris had, just maybe, died to protect.

Eli wasn't moving. He took a deep breath.

"What?" I said again.

"You know where the name *Prague* comes from?" he asked.

"No. And don't feel the need to—"

"No one does. Some people think it's from the word *prahy*, which means *eddies in the river*. Or *na praze*, which is basically a dead, empty place with no shade. But you know which explanation I like the best? *Pražiti*. It means *the cleansing of the forest by fire*. Doesn't that sound about right? Cleansing, like the fire is doing everyone a favor. Even though all you end up with when it's done is a dead place with no shade."

I began to wonder whether jet lag could have hallucinogenic effects.

"I told myself I wouldn't do this," he said.

"Slow us down?" Adriane said. "Fail."

He ignored her and wouldn't look at me. "My parents spent my whole life preparing me for this. This place, I mean."

"His parents are Czech," I told Adriane. "They're obsessed with the old country."

"Yeah, I hear life was bliss under the Communists," she said. "Can't imagine why anyone ever left."

"They were kids," Eli said. "Kids don't care about totalitarianism. For my parents, Prague is picnics on Petřín Hill and homemade *knedlíky*. It's home. They didn't notice the tanks in the backyard and the blood in the streets."

Even before she spoke, I could tell Adriane had exhausted her limited ability to feign interest. I'd heard Ms. Kato talk wistfully, endlessly, about the lost wonders of her parents' homeland, a country in which she'd never spent more than two weeks in a row, time that was unfailingly passed in a Ritz-Carlton or a luxury car with tinted windows and a native guide. Adriane didn't have much patience for anything, but when it came to the ambivalences of immigration, she'd exceeded her limit the year she'd wanted to be a pirate for Halloween or, at the very least, a samurai—her mother had instead stuck her in a kimono. "Not to sound like one of those people, but maybe they should just go back where they came from."

"That's supposed to be my job," Eli said. "That's what it was all for. I told them it was a waste of their time. I promised myself I would never come here. But . . . here I am."

"There's a way to fix that," Adriane said.

"Shut up, Adriane."

I didn't know why I said it. And judging from her expression, neither did she.

"Let's go," Eli said, shaking off whatever held him in place. "Guess you can't argue with destiny."

10

The central public library was a depressingly austere block building bracketed by two baroque monstrosities, their elaborate columns, carvings, and pedestals making the "modern" architecture look less forward-thinking than apathetic. We found nothing in the catalog under *Hledači* or *Lumen Dei*, and no record of anyone named Ivan Glockner working in reference in this library or any other in the greater Prague library system. But the young librarian, who looked more like a college student and—with a skunk streak of neon pink in her hair and jagged gold piercings rimming her left ear—not the kind you'd expect to see in a library, directed us into a room in the basement where rare documents were kept, along with an archivist who supposedly knew "everything about everything."

The archivist—in all black, with a spiked collar, the perfect Sid to her Nancy—had never heard of Ivan Glockner either, and he came up empty on the *Hledači* and *Lumen Dei*. But when I asked if they had anything about Elizabeth Weston, he disappeared into the bowels of the stacks and reemerged several minutes later with a red folder, a tattered and faded page nestled carefully inside. "Don't know if this is what you're looking for, but it's indexed to her name," he said, his English accented but fluid. "That's all we've got. Try not to touch it."

He didn't have to tell me; I knew how to handle rare documents.

It was a large room, but the lack of windows and surplus of dark wood and musty bindings had a claustrophobic effect. The air was heavy and still, and smelled faintly of mold. At one of the three wooden tables, a hunchbacked man bent over a newspaper, his finger tracing the tiny print line by line.

Prudens et innatus fuit tua sagacitas. The note was short and simple, easy to translate while Adriane stretched out her calves and Eli peered over my shoulder, eyes fixed on the page.

> *Your instincts were well founded. We have much cause to worry. The daughter, known to us as Elizabeth Weston, has carried her father's work to Prague. Alone she would be of little*

192

risk, but she has aligned herself with a mechanist, a favorite in
the Emperor's court. Rudolf himself is surely bringing all his
demonic power to bear on its behalf.

They are closing in on their dark goal. Weston's house
in Malá Strana is unguarded, and it will be nothing to gain
access. I urge you against leniency on this matter. A mere
warning will be ineffective against a girl raised by Kelley, filled
with such hubris that she believes the Lord should supplicate
Himself to her desires.

Of course, if this be your decision, we will follow without
challenge or hesitation. I have ultimate faith in your wisdom,
and the wisdom of the Church.

Yours in eternal fealty and defense of the faith.

17 January 1599 Prague.

The letter was signed with a symbol rather than a name—not
the lightning-pierced eye, but two dark slashes of ink that looked
more like a sword than a cross.

"We're wasting time." Eli slammed the folder shut. "This is
useless."

The archivist shushed him, his look suggesting he suspected
we'd been handling his precious documents with ketchup-stained
fingers, if not scissors.

Adriane cleared her throat. "I hate to agree with the stalker,
but—"

"Fine." But it didn't feel useless. Maybe it was knowing Max
was so close, that in a few hours I would have him back, that
made me so certain we were in the right place, following the
bread crumbs to wherever they would lead. Hadn't they led me
to Max?

A voice stopped us on our way back to the main reading

room, a hiss from the old man with the newspaper. He crooked his finger at me, bushy gray eyebrows waggling.

"Slyšel jsem vás," he said.

I shook my head. *"Nemluvím česky."* I recited from memory, cringing with each murdered syllable. *I don't speak Czech.* (Obviously.)

There was a gurgle at the base of his throat. Magician-like, he pulled a graying handkerchief from his sleeve and hocked a wad of something viscous and yellow into its center, then folded it neatly and slid it back in place. "I said I heard you. You look for *Hledači*. Search for searchers. Yes?"

"Yes," I said.

His hand was a map of liver spots, but his grip was surprisingly firm. "Ivan Glockner," he said. "You search for me."

"You work here?" Eli asked, looking dubious.

"I am here," the man, who might have been Ivan or might— and I could tell from the look on Adriane's face that she was leaning in this direction—have been a lonely and half-drunk old man with excellent hearing and a proclivity to meddle. "This is enough."

"You know Professor Anton Hoffpauer?" I asked.

"I know many people."

"We're going to be late for that, uh, *thing,*" Adriane said, giving me her best *escape the crazy* eyes. "We should go."

The man hocked another wad of phlegm, then slapped his hand against the edge of the table. So far Prague seemed full of the very young and the very old. I wondered what had happened to everyone in between. "Take my help or leave me be. Your choice."

"We want help," I said quickly. "If you can."

Hair sprouted from his knuckles, significantly blacker than the thin gray tufts curling over his ears and out of his nose. His trembling pen wrote out the letters on the newspaper: *Kostel sv*

Boethia, Betlémské náměstí. "You find Father Hájek. Priest. He tells what you want."

"Thank you," I said as he tore off the corner of the page. The name of the church was written over the black-and-white photo of a young girl, cheerful, vacant eyes staring at the camera, like a face on a milk carton. *"Děkuji."*

"This is not right," the man said, the absence of contractions giving him an oddly prissy air. "You will not thank me." He turned back to his newspaper like we weren't there, wrinkled finger tracing the lines—but his gaze wasn't tracking, was fixed on what remained of the torn photo, the little girl's hand, holding a sagging stuffed rabbit.

"Probably just a lonely old man," Eli said as we left the library. "City's full of them. Wanted someone to talk to, pretended to know something."

"Or he did know something," I said.

The Kostel sv Boethia, Church of St. Boethius, wasn't in my guidebook, but Betlémské náměstí, Bethlehem Square, was. And it was close.

11

The main artery of Staré Město, a diagonal slash across the quarter that efficiently funneled tourists from the Karlův most at one corner to the Powder Tower at the other, had—according to the tour guides we squeezed past, their orange umbrellas held high for the benefit of their obedient herds—once served as a processional path for emperors, kings, and popes, bejeweled eminences of all kinds marching proudly toward the royal palace, dignitaries carried through the streets, sometimes in carriages, sometimes in coffins. It was hard to picture, now that the noble path for heroes and conquerors had become a cobblestone-paved mall.

There were stores selling colored crystal; stores selling knock-off watches, knockoff handbags, knockoff shoes; stores selling presumably bootleg CDs; stores selling matryoshka dolls painted with the faces of presidents, soccer players, movie stars, and, most prevalently, Michael Jackson; stores selling cheap jewelry; stores selling thick Bavarian pretzels and sugared dough roasting on a spit; and most of all, stores selling puppets, their blank wooden faces staring dully through the glass, their limbs contorted by tangled strings, their lips painted into smiles or roars, tears or freckles dotting their apple cheeks—rows and rows of puppet girls and puppet boys, menaced by puppet dragons, wooed by puppet princes, tempted by puppet devils.

Many of these stores were fronted by beggars in ratty clothes, huddled under grimy blankets. Since elementary school I'd been taught to call them, with all due respect, homeless people, but these were undeniably beggars, as if out of a folktale, beggars bent forward on their knees, stretched prone with their faces in the dirt, arms extended and hands clenching a hat containing, in the best of cases, a few loose coins. I didn't want to stare; I didn't want to carefully not stare, like the packs of camera-clutching tourists who kept their gazes averted and stepped past them or over them like they were simply wider-than-usual cracks in the sidewalk.

When the street spit us out into a wide square bordered by an ornate clock tower and a church whose spires made it resemble nothing so much as Disney World's Cinderella Castle, I was glad for the excuse to look up.

Most of the square was filled by an Easter market hawking produce, fried bread, and sausages of various size and color. Having eaten pretty much nothing since Paris but wilted Eurail sandwiches, we sampled all we could. Adriane couldn't get enough of the *rakvičky*, a narrow, nutty-flavored cookie with a crème center, which soured in my mouth when Eli translated the name for us: *little coffins.*

"Don't be so sensitive," Adriane said, mouth full, her no-carb policy apparently on a spring break of its own. She said it again when we paused beneath the clock tower to get our bearings and overheard yet another tour guide—this one in Renaissance drag, though still holding the telltale umbrella—pointing out the twenty-seven white crosses inscribed in the stone pavement, testament to the twenty-seven Protestants who'd been beheaded on a single seventeenth-century afternoon while the Catholic crowds cheered. Presumably they cheered even louder when, according to the perky guide, the executioners started getting creative, slicing off and nailing unfortunate tongues to the gallows, louder still when the severed heads were carried in buckets down the noble Royal Way and impaled on a tower overlooking the Karlův most, where they watched sightlessly over the city for ten years.

Maybe that was why I couldn't shake the feeling that someone was watching us. Maybe it wasn't a shadowy killer with a knife and a mission, but simply the careful scrutiny of a skyline of stone saints and the ghosts of heretics past.

I didn't believe in ghosts.

We ventured into a narrow alley, completely empty and, except for the distant rumble of the abandoned crowd, silent. I kept checking over my shoulder, convinced, still, that someone was there—and if a dark figure was going to attack, what better place for him to strike than this shaded alley, isolated and crumbling around us. But nothing happened, and again, I told myself that what sounded like scuffling footsteps was only branches scraping stone or feral cats tussling for scraps, the flickers of movement only shadows, the prickling sensation on the back of my neck only fear.

Bethlehem Square was only a few turns away. The church

lodged in its northwest corner had no fairy-tale spires or mobs of tourists snapping pictures, just a crumbling Renaissance edifice and a weather-beaten plastic sign announcing times for mass. Inside it was cavelike, dark and cool and damp. Stone walls, stained-glass windows, flickering candles, two beggars asleep beneath a pew, and, emerging from one of the confessional booths, an old priest with the long black robe and stiff white collar I'd only seen in movies and the occasional headline news exposé.

He came to us—to Eli, rather—and started speaking in rapid-fire Czech before we could say anything. Eli interrupted, and for a few moments they talked over each other, the priest's cratered face an angry red, his flabby arms flapping, Eli speaking slowly and firmly, occasionally stumbling over a word, but refusing to give, until finally the priest crossed his arms and nodded, and there was quiet.

"What did he say?" I asked. "What did you tell him?"

"It's fine," Eli said, sounding far from it. "The church isn't open to tourists, and he says you're not dressed appropriately for a holy place."

"Apparently," Adriane said, shooting a look at the homeless guys.

That didn't explain why the argument had gone on for so long, or why the priest had been so angry. "Did you tell him we just want to ask a question? Is this even him?" I turned to the priest. "Are you Father Hájek?"

"It's him," Eli said. "But he won't help us. He says he doesn't know anything."

"Did you even tell him what we're looking for?" I asked. Eli was clearly lying. It was pathetic to just stand there and accept it, like we were blind and he was our guide, assuring us the path was safe and clear when, for all we knew, it ran straight into a dead end. Or off a cliff.

"Ask him about the *Hledači*," I insisted. "Ask him about the *Lumen Dei*."

"I told you, he doesn't want to talk to us," Eli said. "So can we go?"

"Right. We're just going to take your word for it," Adriane said.

I opened my guidebook to the section of simple Czech phrases, determined to find a way to ask my own questions, even if I had to use pictures.

But I didn't.

"*Lumen Dei. Hledači.* Yes. You must hear." The priest's voice seemed scratchier in his halting English. He was even older than the man in the library. The church smelled faintly musty, but the damp scent of mold and decay intensified near him, as if he were its source. "*Hledači,* seekers, yes? You understand this?"

"I guess, but that was four hundred years ago. We need to figure out—"

"Yes, then. But also, now. Many, many generations. They will seek until they find. They are sworn, forever."

"Seek what?"

"You know this. You say it yourself."

"The *Lumen Dei.*"

He nodded.

"But I don't know that," I said. "I don't know anything. Just tell me what it is—what do they want?"

"It is machine," he said. "It is miracle and it is curse. It is bridge from human to divine. It is knowledge and power of God in the hands of man. It is abomination. They are abomination."

"This guy is crazy," Adriane muttered.

"World is crazy," the priest said, glaring at her. "*Hledači,* crazy, yes. Machine is real. And dangerous. You want to live? You choose not to know."

"That's really helpful, thanks," Adriane said. "So now that

199

you've told us everything, we're supposed to forget it or die? Excellent."

The priest ignored her. "This church honors St. Boethius. You know the story of this man?"

We dutifully shook our heads, obedient honor students to the bitter end.

"Brilliant man, Boethius. Philosopher. Scholar. Bright light in a dark age. He finds an ancient masterpiece. Aristotle. Translates it for his people. You know how they thank him for this gift?" This time, he barely paused to confirm our ignorance. His English was improving by the second. "The king wraps cord around his neck. Pulls it tighter, tighter, until his eyes pop out. Then his people beat him to death. You know why? He asks too many questions. They do not like his answers. He pays price."

"Very subtle," Adriane said.

It was remarkable how many creatively gruesome ways of killing people there turned out to be. I wondered, on average, how many corpses needed to pile up before executioners got bored enough to invent new methods. "How do we find this machine?" I said. This wasn't curiosity; it was need. "How do we find the *Hledači*?"

How had they found us?

He didn't answer.

"Are we in danger? Is that what you're saying? From them? From you?"

" '*Est autem fides sperandorum substantia rerum argumentum non parentum.*' "

I translated on the fly. " 'Now faith is the substance of things hoped for, the evidence of things not seen.' "

The priest offered an approving nod. "Hebrews 11:1."

"And is that supposed to mean something?"

He turned away, muttering something in Czech.

"Answer me!"

Without facing us, he spoke. *"Nemluvím anglicky."* Sounding it out slowly and clearly so that even we idiot Americans could understand.

"He said he doesn't speak English," Eli said sourly.

"Got that much, thanks."

The priest hobbled down the central aisle of the church, turning only when he reached the altar. He barked out something short and angry in Czech, then swatted his hand through the air. We were dismissed.

"What did he say that time?" I asked as we stepped out of the church, squinting in the sudden sunlight.

Eli looked faintly sick, like he knew I knew he was about to lie, but there was nothing either of us could do about it. "He wanted to make sure you try *svíčková* before you leave town; he claims it's some kind of once-in-a-lifetime culinary experience." He shoved his clenched fists into his coat pockets. "But I've had it. Tastes like chicken. Trust me."

12

Adriane's take, as we returned to the hostel: This was crazy, this was stupid, this was a waste of our time, if we thought Chris was dead because of some hypothetical ancient machine that was basically a telephone to God and a bunch of four-hundred-year-old nutcases who wanted to hook it up again, then she knew of a nice, cozy mental institution where we could recuperate until common sense and sanity returned, if we believed a crazy priest and some old letter, she had a pile of magic beans for sale and a pouch of pixie dust, surely we now realized that any further inquiries in this direction would be a ridiculous waste of time, as perhaps this entire trip had been a ridiculous waste of time, and by the way, had she mentioned that somewhere out there was a real killer with a real knife, and maybe we should stop chasing shadows and start protecting ourselves?

We crossed the bridge, we pushed our way through the throngs of people, we hiked the Malá Strana hill, and I let Adriane talk, knowing that everything she said made sense—but that none of it explained why a twenty-first-century priest was telling horror stories about a four-hundred-year-old secret kept by a dead girl whose bloody letter I had read and stolen and stolen again. And if Adriane had known about the letter, maybe she would have agreed. But I hadn't told her; I couldn't. It was one thing to hold myself responsible for what had happened to Chris. It would be another to see my guilt reflected in her eyes. That would make it too real.

Eli was silent, too, until we reached the lobby and collected our room keys from the front desk. Then he interrupted her litany to say, quietly, "If a machine like that really existed, people would be willing to kill for it. Lots of people."

"Yeah, and if hot vampires really existed, suicide would be a viable option for wrinkle prevention. Your point?"

"My point is that maybe the *Lumen Dei* is out there somewhere. Real."

Adriane cut her eyes toward me. "You didn't tell me he was a God nut."

"Forget it," Eli said, and headed for his room without another word. We returned to ours. Adriane had the key, so Adriane went through the door first.

So Adriane was the one who screamed.

13

Our suitcases had been torn open, our clothes thrown on the floor, our mattresses stripped. Razor slices split the lining of the bags; the mattresses and pillows oozed stuffing. Every drawer was open, and every pane of glass in the room—mirrors, window, even the TV screen—was smashed.

Whoever had been here, they'd left angry.

Or maybe—it occurred to me, long after it would have done me any good to run—they hadn't left at all.

My survival instincts were constantly letting me down.

Eli was at our side in seconds. Adriane quieted, but she was pale, shaking. We hadn't moved from the doorway.

"My room, too," Eli said. He pushed past us, flinging open the closet and bathroom doors: empty. Whoever they were, they were gone. Which meant, what? We were safe?

I started to laugh.

Eli looked alarmed. "Is she . . . ?"

"She's fine," Adriane said. Her hand met my lower back with gentle but steady pressure, like she would hold me up if I started to fall.

I laughed harder. "Everything's fine," I sputtered, trying to catch my breath, scaring myself now. "Can't you tell?"

Nothing was missing, and there was no clue what they'd been looking for.

"Maybe our passports," Adriane guessed.

Maybe not. I still had the passport pouch strapped around my waist. I still had the letter.

"We have to get out of here," Eli said.

"What gave it away?" I said.

"At least we know he's here," Eli said.

"Who?"

"Who do you think?"

"You think Max did this?" I said.

"Who else knew we were here?"

Thanks to my carelessness, the guy at the front desk and any-one with a few crowns in his pocket who might have bribed him into pointing the way to our rooms, I thought but didn't say, because it occurred to me that he wasn't the only one who knew we were here. "You did," I told Eli.

Eli snorted. "Excellent deduction. While you weren't paying attention, I teleported back here, used my powers of superspeed to ransack the room in under thirty seconds, and then teleported back before you knew I was gone."

"Or you decided to abide by the laws of physics and call in a friend," I said. "For all we know, the guy at the front desk is your long-lost great-uncle."

He shook his head. "Face it. Your boyfriend was looking for something when Chris got in the way. He tore their dorm room apart. And now he's suckered you into coming here—which means whatever he wants, he thinks you have it."

"It makes perfect sense," Adriane said.

"Adriane! You said you believe—"

She held up a hand to quiet me. "Perfect sense if you replace his name with yours," she told Eli.

"Give me a break."

"You followed us to Paris," she said. "You followed us here. You told us you wanted to help us—"

"Because I do."

"But first chance you got, you lied to us."

He shook his head.

"Then tell us what the priest really said."

He pressed his lips together.

"Right. Come on, Nora. We're leaving."

"Nora. You know this wasn't me. Come see my room, it looks exactly the same. You know I didn't do this."

I believed him—and hated myself for it. Trusting him was just more proof that I had to stop trusting myself. I'd made too many mistakes.

"I know it wasn't Max," I said. "Anything else is just wishful thinking."

We stuffed our crap into our bags, then left the Golden Boar with no direction and no idea where we would spend the hours until midnight; we left with nothing but the suspicion that someone was watching us, someone who wanted something and wouldn't leave us alone until he got it; we left determined not to go back. Eli didn't try to stop us; he didn't follow.

"We didn't need him," Adriane said. "We'll figure this out." She put a hand on my shoulder. I didn't shake her off. It was getting dark, and overhead, the castle towers carved dark shadows in the gathering twilight. "We'll find Max on our own."

I had to tell her.

I should have told her already.

And when I did, when I showed her the note and explained his code, when I told her that all we had to do was make it to midnight and he would be waiting for us, she wasn't angry. She twirled on her pointed toes, hugged me, and laughed. "Then that's it," she said. "This time tomorrow, we'll be on a plane home. We'll be with Max. It'll all be okay."

We walked in circles, killing the hours, waiting for her prediction to come true, and I kept looking back, expecting to see Eli shadowing us, darting behind trees and cars or maybe just sauntering behind us, brazen with the knowledge that there was no way to stop him.

But block after block, he still wasn't there. I knew I should have been relieved.

14

The city was different at midnight. Still beautiful—more beautiful, maybe—but uglier, too, with broken glass glinting under streetlights, staticky Madonna blasting from the souvenir stores that apparently never closed, camera flashes from the summit of every tower, a reminder that someone was always watching.

Tourists still choked the main avenues, families given way to drunken stag parties, hooting frat brothers in matching sweatshirts marking them as the Prague Drinking Team, the lucky ones pedaling along on six-seated bikes whose license plates read PARTY ON WHEELS. But the side streets were deserted. Graffiti glowed under the orangey lights: crude, angry slashes the color of blood and rust sprayed across gritty stone walls; words stuffed with too many consonants; arrows and faces and one faint marking that could have been either a cross or a swastika; cryptic symbols of all kinds except the one I was half determined and half afraid to find. Our footsteps echoed against the stone.

"What if he's not there?" I asked as we descended the walkway that led from the Karlův most to the island of Kampa. Below us flowed a still, narrow waterway: Certovka, the Devil's Stream.

"He'll be there," Adriane said.

"And then what?"

She didn't answer.

A slender, solitary figure leaned against the railing, his back to the water, his face in shadow. I didn't let myself believe it until he tilted his head toward us and his glasses glinted in the moonlight.

Max.

He stepped into the pool of light beneath a nearby streetlamp and smiled. He looked thinner than I remembered, and paler, but it could have been the light, which gave his skin a jaundiced glow.

Max.

He held up a hand in greeting but otherwise didn't move, waiting for us to come to him. That was how it always played out in my dreams—except when I got close enough to touch him, he would always jerk out of reach. He would run and I would chase him, but never catch up.

Max.

Here.

Alive.

He was supposed to make everything okay. He was supposed to fix everything that was broken, fix me. He was supposed to hold me when I threw myself into his arms, squeeze me until I felt safe. He was supposed to tell us why Chris was dead and why he had disappeared and why everything had fallen apart, and then he was supposed to know how to put it all back together.

I stopped short of him, a few feet of distance between us. Something was wrong—wrong with me. Because seeing him was supposed to make me feel again, to fill up the empty hole. I did feel: Angry. Relieved. Sad. Grateful. Confused. Scared.

But I didn't feel okay.

I didn't feel safe.

"Max!" It was Adriane who cried out his name, Adriane who ran to him, tears streaming down her face, arms stretched wide. She clung to him, and he let her, and no matter how they felt about each other, there was nothing strange about it. They had both loved Chris; they had both endured, together, whatever had happened that night; they had both survived. Adriane was the normal one, her face buried in the shoulder she had once deemed too narrow and bony, her body shuddering uncontrollably in what she'd once termed Max's "spindly octopus arms." Max watched me, over her shoulder, but he held on and waited for her breathing to slow and her sobs to ebb. When they did, and she finally let go, her face was tearstained but serene.

Something was definitely wrong with me.

He closed the distance between us.

"Where have you been all this time?" I said, not *I love you, I missed you, thank god you're safe.* "Why are we here? What happened that night? Where the hell did you go?" Not *How could you leave me alone?*

He kissed me.

"I'm sorry," he whispered.

Behind me, there was an aborted scream. Then a muffled grunt. I whirled around. Adriane struggled in the grip of a hooded man, his arm pinned across her chest, his hand slapped over her mouth. Then there were more of them; they were everywhere, pouring out of the shadows. Someone punched Max. Someone lunged at me. I flung my fists blindly, waiting for some self-defense mechanism to kick in, trying to remember the hierarchy of pressure points we'd been taught in gym class, aim first for the eyes, the neck, or was it the kidneys? I screamed for Max as two of them wrestled him to the ground. My fist connected with a stomach and my elbow knocked something hard, like a chin or a skull, but that was wrong, I remembered, I was supposed to go for the soft spots, the membranes—and probably I wasn't supposed to be thinking through instructions as rough hands yanked my arms behind my back and bound my wrists. I shouted uselessly, who are you and what are you doing and let go of me and, more than once, help, but no one answered and no one came.

My arms were locked behind my back, and there was nothing to break the fall when the hands forced me to the ground and knocked me onto my back. The man's face was shrouded by his hood, and I could make out nothing but the tip of a nose and the whites of his teeth. He leaned over me, large and terrifying—and stupid, because as he did, I brought up my knee and caught him on the chin, hard, then, in the same motion, gave his balls the kick that had made me a third-grade kickball champ, and with a soft moan, he stumbled backward.

All you did was make him angry, I thought.

But he was already angry. Guess what: So was I.

I scrabbled my feet against the ground and struggled into a sitting position, because now all I had to do was get up before he did, kick him while he was down . . . and find some way to save Adriane and Max, all with my hands tied behind my back.

"*Policie!*" someone shouted behind us. "*Police! Polizia! Policie! Stůjte, nebo budeme střílet!*"

Spooked by the interruption, the hooded men left us in the dirt, and scattered.

"They attacked us!" I cried, climbing off the ground. "We didn't do anything."

Adriane was slouched against the wall, dazed and breathing heavily. "Did that seriously just happen?" she asked the night. "Tell me that didn't just happen."

Max, his arms and legs bound, lay curled in a fetal position against the stone base of the bridge. "I'm okay," he called softly.

I felt the laughter burbling up in me again. Sure, we were all okay.

Czech cops didn't look much like cops. There were two of them, one in jeans and a blue hoodie, one in a gray trench coat, both in their early twenties.

"Thank you," I said, twisting around so they could undo whatever was pinning my wrists together.

The one in the trench coat called out something in Czech— then, without releasing any of us, both cops turned their backs and walked off into the night.

"Wait!" Adriane shouted. "Where are you going? You're cops! You have to help us!"

"I didn't pay them enough for that." Eli stepped out of an alley. "And trust me, you should be glad they're not real cops. That's trouble you don't need."

My jaw actually dropped. "What the hell?"

He shook his head and flipped open a pocketknife, beckoning me toward him with the blade. "Questions later. First—"

I didn't move. He snatched my wrists and before I could pull away, the knife slashed down. I was free.

15

To his credit, Eli cut through everyone's bonds and gave us a chance to ascertain there were no broken bones or gashed wounds before he began to gloat. The first thing—he said, and we all agreed—was to get off the street before the hooded men wised up and came back. "I know a place," Max said, and though he balked at the idea of letting Eli trail along, he could hardly argue with the probability that Eli had saved our lives. That had to be worth something. And whatever lies he may have told or secrets he was keeping, he was still Chris's cousin. That was worth more. Max led us through the narrow streets of Malá Strana until we reached a stone hostel, U Zlatého lva, that looked not all that different from the one we'd left behind that afternoon, except that a stone lion paced the top of the doorframe, instead of a boar. Max held my hand the whole way. It helped.

A little.

Max's room was even smaller than ours had been. A narrow window abutted a wall of stone, and a rusted, leaking sink jutted out beside the bed. We'd passed the communal bathroom on our way down the grimy hallway, a single flickering fluorescent bulb strobing our movements into jerky, stop-motion animation. The door locked behind us, but the ancient hinges looked like something an angry toddler could knock out with one good kick.

"We should be safe here," Max said. "For a while, at least."

"Safe from who?" Adriane asked. "Who the hell were those guys? What is going *on*?"

"Yes, Max, we're all ears," Eli drawled. He was leaning against the door, as if positioning himself for a quick getaway. "Tell us all about what's going on and why absolutely none of it can be blamed on you."

Max pushed his glasses up on his nose. "I'll tell you everything," he told me quietly. "You. Not him." He put an arm around me. It felt strange, after all this time, to be cradled again—to be his.

"Is 'everything' going to include the part where you kill your best friend?" Eli asked.

I squeezed Max's hand. "The police think—"

"I know what they think."

"Is that why . . ." I wasn't sure I wanted this answer. "Is that why you ran?"

He touched my face with the back of his hand, tracing his knuckles along the line of my jaw. "You know I wouldn't have done that."

"Enough." Adriane's voice was harsh, with a ragged edge. She'd pressed herself into the corner with her hands crossed over her chest. It seemed wrong, Adriane on her own, Max and me together. I was supposed to be the odd man out, the cheese standing alone, she must have been thinking. But Chris was dead, and Max was warm and breathing and holding on to me. A display that suddenly felt obscene. "Just tell us what happened that night."

"She doesn't remember," I told him.

Max's eyes narrowed. "None of it?"

She shook her head. "So—please."

He took his arm off my shoulder, and let his hands fall together in his lap. "I didn't kill Chris," he said.

I leaned against him. "We know that." He edged away.

211

"Speak for yourself," Eli said.

"This is going to sound crazy," Max said. "I thought it was crazy, too. But it all has to do with the Book. And this device called the *Lumen Dei*—"

"And the *Hledači*, right," Eli said. "Now tell us something we don't know, like what they'd want with a clueless American college student."

"You know about them?" Max said, his eyes wide.

"You tell us," I said. "Start at the beginning."

"I didn't want to get you involved in this," he said.

I just looked at him, the *too late* implied.

He sighed. "Those men, the *Hledači*. It turns out they've been watching us all along. They watch anyone who's seriously researching the Voynich manuscript. They think it's the key."

"To what?" I asked.

"To putting the device back together. It disappeared four hundred years ago, and for whatever reason, they think the pieces are still out there somewhere, and the Book can help them find it, or help them make a new one."

"Explain this to me like I'm—oh, I don't know, sane," Adriane said. "These people honestly believe there's a four-hundred-year-old machine that will hook them up to God?"

"The device itself actually makes sense," Max said, slipping easily, even under these circumstances, into professor mode. "There was an explosion of scientific and technological advances in the Renaissance—people like da Vinci were practically designing airplanes. And everyone's reason for doing anything was to get closer to God. Alchemy, astronomy, biology—the whole point was to read the Book of Nature like it was a second Bible. Science was just another form of religion—a different way of knowing the world. That was supposed to be a metaphor, but it kind of

212

makes sense that eventually someone would have thought to do it for real. Find God. With a machine."

"I suppose the polite gentlemen in the hooded robes sat you down and gave you a fascinating lecture on all this?" Eli said.

He didn't know Max like I did, and so he couldn't read the tea leaves in Max's face, the pale spots behind his ears and the way his lips moved soundlessly as if his body were rehearsing a rebuttal even before his mind came up with one. Max had a temper, but he didn't yell. Adriane had, early on, classified him as a goat: ornery, but mostly harmless. He didn't look harmless.

"They didn't have to tell me," he said flatly. "I'm a history major. I read."

"You believe this machine really exists?" I asked him.

"It doesn't matter—they believe it." He shuddered. "And whether it exists or not, they're crazy. They attacked the Hoff. They killed Chris. And they . . ."

"What?" Eli said. "They stole your lunch money? They gave you a wedgie? What makes you so special that they just left you alone?"

"They didn't," Max said, so softly that only I could hear him. He dropped his head. "They were waiting for me when I got to Chris's house. Three of them. Chris was already—" He swallowed hard. "Adriane, you were there, too, but . . . blank. You didn't answer me. It was like you didn't even see me. They were arguing with each other, about Chris. They weren't supposed to kill him, at least not before they got what they wanted—someone messed up. And when they saw me . . . I ran."

"You left her there," I said. "Alone and helpless. With a house full of psycho killers."

"I didn't think," he said. "I just ran. But they caught up with me."

213

"Maybe that's why they left me alive," Adriane said slowly. She was pale, but calm. "They might have stuck around and killed me if you hadn't run. Maybe that saved us both."

"That's one way of looking at it," Eli said.

"They knocked me out," Max said. "When I woke up, I was in Prague—not that I knew it. They kept me in a basement." He glared at Eli. "I wasn't special. They needed one of us alive so they could get what they needed."

I put my hand on his back, but he stiffened, and I took it away. "What did they need?" I asked, gently as I could.

"Some kind of map," he said. "The key to where the pieces of the *Lumen Dei* are hidden. They were convinced Chris was hiding it somewhere. I have no idea why. I tried to tell them I didn't know anything, I kept telling them and telling them, but they wouldn't believe me. And then it occurred to me that if they did believe me . . . they wouldn't need me at all anymore."

"Then, let me guess: They miraculously came to their senses and let you go," Eli said.

"I escaped," Max said.

"You." Eli looked him up and down. "Fought off a bunch of zealots with butcher knives."

Max was a couple inches taller than Eli, but what he had in height he lacked in bulk. Never date a guy who can fit into your jeans, Adriane often warned me—failing to mention that it was because I might someday need him to save me from a secret society of murdering Renaissance Faire rejects. Max had always been thin, but he'd never been weak. And though he was now thinner than ever, he had never looked stronger.

"Yeah. Me."

Eli looked away first.

There was something different about Max. Something harder, in his voice, and in his eyes. I wanted to believe it would fade away now that he was safe—now that it was over. But I knew that wasn't how it worked.

And I knew it wasn't over.

I let the boys argue about the logistics of Max's escape: Eli trying to pick holes in the story; Max trying, I could tell by the tension in his facial muscles, not to lunge across the room and knock Eli through the rickety door. It got heated, and then it got petty, and I relished it because when they stopped, there would be no more excuses not to say it, the thing that I had tried so hard not to know.

But eventually my final excuse ran out. So I said it; I made it real. "I think I have the map."

16

Winters know the shadows in that word.
Unless the dark law too should seek the thief
And the good law obtain your city
For those outside the word.

Throughout our epoch, He that is below
Ignorantly deserves an abject prayer
O my guardian spirit
O when the unmixed nectar of the faithless lives with you.

My law is a tepid standard
Thus I surrendered the hound to the dark
Revive your soul at my house
The sun will foretell all things in this way.

It was the part of Elizabeth's letter that had never made any sense, and so I'd ignored it. As I'd ignored the line just above it:

215

Three by three is where you'll find me.

Nonsense words, paired with a number. Like Max's coded postcard—like a stegotext. It would explain why the *Hledači* had come after Chris and the Hoff, why they had taken Max, why they were so convinced we all knew something that none of us knew.

I showed them the letter.

Adriane recoiled. "Is that blood? And you've been carrying that around with you all this time? Tell me that's not Chris's—" But she could see on my face that it was, and backed away.

"You told me you gave this to Chris," Max said. "That he was going to return it for you."

"I did. He was. But when I found him—" I couldn't tell Adriane the truth, that it had been her stiff fingers wrapped around the parchment, that it had been Chris's last bequest to her I'd taken for my own. "He had it in his hand."

"Someone want to fill me in?" Adriane said. "Why would Chris have this? Why would you?"

As I explained, she went very still.

"So you decided to take it?" Adriane said when I reached the night of the murder. "Because stealing it worked so well for you the first time around? Brilliant."

"I imagine she wasn't thinking very clearly," Eli said. "And it doesn't sound like you were much help."

"Leave her alone," I told him. No more excuses. "She's right. This is my fault. What happened to Chris. If I hadn't taken the letter. If I hadn't given it to him. I did this."

"No. *They* did this," Max said quickly.

"You couldn't have known," Eli said.

"This is not your fault," Max said.

"You didn't ask for this," Eli said.

"We don't even know if you're right," Max said.

"You weren't the one holding the knife," Eli said.

Adriane said nothing.

But I could tell from her face. She finally got it. That we weren't crazy. That the past was relevant to our present. That the *Hledači* and the *Lumen Dei* and Chris were all tied together, *somehow*. That it was all because of me.

That I was to blame.

"We can't change what happened," Max said. "But if this is really the map the *Hledači* are looking for, it means we can beat them. If we could find the *Lumen Dei* ourselves, before they do, we'll have leverage—we can force them to clear my name and leave us all alone."

Eli snorted. "Right, or instead of negotiating with potentially imaginary killers, we could get the hell out of the country and go to the cops."

"Like anyone would believe this—especially coming from me," Max said.

Eli smirked. "But it all sounds *so* convincing."

"Eli's right," I said. I didn't look at Max; it felt too much like a betrayal. "This is too big. We came here to find you, Max. And you're here, you're safe—we have to get out before anything else happens."

"You mean like angry guys in hoods trying to slit our throats and throw us into a river?" Adriane said. "I think the anything-else ship has sailed. What's next, ninjas?"

"Not if we leave first," I said.

"You mean if we run away," she said. "From what you started."

"Adriane—"

"If we go to the cops and they don't believe us, they throw Max in jail, what then? What happens when these guys come back for more?"

217

"We can't go back," Max said. "None of us can."

"You don't get to decide that by yourself," I told him. But Chris's killers were still out there. Even if we could go back and somehow be sure they wouldn't follow . . . then what? They washed off the blood and lived happily ever after, while we went home and tried not to fall into the gaping hole they'd left in our lives.

"You don't know everything," Max said. "Not yet."

"Everything" apparently had to be shown instead of told, and he trooped us down to the dusty nineties-era computer in the lobby that offered molasses-speed Internet access to guests. Max typed our names into the search field, and then we all waited an eternity for the page to load.

The top result was a newspaper article.

The top ten results were all newspaper articles.

GIRLS GONE WILD,

GONE MISSING

WHAT'S THE MATTER WITH KIDS TODAY?

KILLER CHICKS FLY COOP

I clicked on the most boring one.

MURDER SUSPECTS FLEE COUNTRY

Chapman, Mass.—Two teenagers wanted for the murder of a close friend have disappeared while on a school trip to Paris. Nora Kane and Adriane Ames, Chapman Preparatory School seniors who police say conspired with Max Lewis to murder 18-year-old Christopher Moore, were last seen on a school trip to Paris. It is believed that within hours of arriving in France, they slipped away from chaperones and crossed the border to Germany.

Local police originally concluded that Lewis (possibly an alias) acted alone in last month's brutal murder, but according to departmental sources, new evidence has come to light that implicates Kane and Ames in the crime. Lewis has not been seen since the night of the murder, and it is now suspected that the three are together. Warrants have been issued for their arrest, and local authorities are coordinating with Interpol to track them down.

Parents of both girls will say only that they are concerned for their daughters' welfare and pray for their safety. On the subject of their daughters' involvement in Moore's death, they had no comment.

I read it over and over again, the sentences losing coherence and melting into a jumble of letters, like a word you keep repeating until it becomes nothing but a string of nonsense syllables.

Warrants have been issued for their arrest. Coordinating with Interpol. Brutal murder.

Words that couldn't mean what they meant, that couldn't possibly pertain to my life.

And yet. New evidence had indeed come to light that implicated me in the crime. I had it in my pocket. Max could reassure me all he wanted, but I knew what I knew.

"I have to talk to my parents," I said.

Max grabbed my wrist and pulled my hand gently away from the keyboard. I let him move for me; I was frozen. "I'm sorry," he said. "It's them. The *Hledači*. They framed you, just like they framed me. They're playing us."

"'No comment'?" Adriane grabbed the mouse and started scanning the other articles. "They couldn't even be bothered to defend me? Probably just bitter I screwed up their vacation. I bet that 'no comment' came from poolside."

"You see why we can't go back," Max said. "They'd pick us up the second we stepped into an airport."

"I have to talk to my parents," I said again.

"We can fix this," Max told me. "Now that we have the map. We have something they want. We can use it."

Eli pressed a cell phone into my hand. "It works in Europe," he said. "But they'll probably try to trace it. Talk fast."

I offered the phone to Adriane, who shook her head. "I've got no comment for them, either." If you didn't know her, hadn't seen her bowing and scraping to her parents—the only people who could make her swallow hard and say yes to anything—if you didn't notice her fingers, clenching and flexing and clenching again, you could almost believe that she didn't care.

I crossed the lobby, nestled myself into a corner with my face nearly pressed to the wall, and dialed the familiar number.

"I'm sorry," I said when my mother picked up the phone.

"Nora? Where are you? What happened?"

"I didn't mean to worry you."

She screamed for my father, then kept asking me where I was, if I was safe, what was going on, too many questions for me to answer. When the line clicked with my father picking up his receiver, she fell silent.

For a moment, we were all silent.

"Are you okay?" he asked.

"I'm okay."

"Where are you?" he asked.

I didn't answer.

"We're your parents," my mother said. "Whatever you've done, we forgive you. We can deal with this. But you have to come home."

I didn't answer.

"I can't do this," she said. "Not again."

There was another click, and then my father and I were alone. I leaned into the wall and touched my forehead to the cool stone.

"*Te diligo*," my father said.

I love you. I couldn't remember the last time he'd said it. There was something about saying things in a language that wasn't your own, something that eased hard words out of your mouth. Because in a way, they didn't seem as real. They didn't count.

And meanwhile, my mother thought I'd done something unforgivable she needed to forgive.

I hung up.

17

In the dark.

In his arms.

The drip of the sink.

The patter of the rain.

The smell of him, fresh and earthy.

The heat of his skin, the whisper of his breathing, the thump of his heart.

His arm thrown over my chest, our fingers twined.

His body molded around mine.

In his bed.

In his shadow.

I slept.

18

I woke up in the dark, confused, for a moment, about where I was and why. The dim red digits of the ancient clock blinked accusingly: 3:47. I was alone in bed.

He was just a silhouette in the dark room, hunched over my bag. The contents rustled as he picked through them.

"Max?"

He turned.

"What are you doing?"

"Nothing," he whispered. "Go back to sleep."

I sat up and flicked on a light, squinting against the sudden brightness. "It's okay," I said. "I'm up. What is it?"

"I was hoping you had some aspirin," he said. "I didn't want to wake you."

"It's okay. But I don't have any."

He came back to bed and turned out the light. My eyes had adjusted to it, and now the night seemed pitch black. "Lie down," he whispered. "Sleep."

I lay down beside him. This time I curled my body around his, and rubbed my hand up and down his arm and back. The rooms were cheap enough that Eli and Adriane had each taken one of their own, leaving us to each other. Adriane hadn't said much before retreating to her room, and she wouldn't meet my eyes. But when I asked if she wanted to go home, she shook her head. "Not without you," she'd said, careful to keep her gaze on Max or the floor, anywhere but on me. "Not until we finish this." I heard: *Not until we finish what you started*.

"Headache?" I asked Max, and kissed the back of his head.

"It doesn't matter," he said softly.

"What doesn't matter?"

"They were good." His voice had dropped to a whisper. "They knew how not to break anything. How not to cause permanent damage, unless they wanted to. They knew exactly what they were doing."

"The *Hledači*?" Saying the strange word aloud, in the dark, felt dangerous, like a summoning spell.

"It's worse when I try to sleep," he said. "Aspirin helps."

I buried my face in his neck. "What did they do to you?"

He rolled away. "It doesn't matter. It's over." He sat up, then climbed out of bed. "I need to get out of here. Take a walk or something."

"I'll come with you."

He shook his head.

"It's four a.m.," I said.

"Which is why you should go back to sleep."

"And you should, too. What if—?" We'd just been attacked by a troupe of masked avengers, and apparently a crazed and murderous secret society was trying to hunt us down—did I really need to spell out the reasons that wandering around, alone, in the middle of the night wasn't the best of ideas?

He pressed his hand to my forehead, like he was checking for fever. "I won't even go outside, okay? I'll go pace the lobby or something. I'm no safer up here than I would be down there—if they know where to find us, it's over no matter what."

"That makes me feel so much better."

He kissed me, lightly, then pulled on a sweatshirt. "I just need to wear myself out a little. Get out of my own head. Then I'll come back to bed."

"Promise?"

"Promise."

So I let him go. But I couldn't sleep without him. Especially not with all the added fuel for my nightmares, images of Max in a basement, hooded figures gathering around him, wielding knives, fists, whatever it was people who knew exactly what they were doing did when they wanted to hurt you without leaving a mark.

No permanent damage.

We'd had a fight, right before we fell asleep. Lying there in his arms, I'd told him everything that had happened to me, starting from that frozen moment in Chris's house, kneeling by Chris's body. But when it came his turn to pick up the story—to go back to that night and everything that came after, he had nothing.

"It's not important," he'd said. "We're together now, that's all that matters."

We both knew it wasn't. But maybe the question was too big, the answer too hard. So I started smaller. I asked him about the letter I'd found in his room, the one that named the enemy. *Hledači.*

I felt him shrug. That wasn't important, either, he said. Just something he'd found, something interesting he was planning to show to the Hoff. Not a big deal; not relevant.

"That's because you don't read Czech," I told him. "Eli translated it for me—"

"You showed it to him?"

"What's the difference? You said it was nothing."

"But you didn't know that," Max said angrily. "It could have been important—private. And he's a stranger. He's nobody."

"I know that, but I was desperate. And *he* was there." There'd been no need to add the obvious corollary.

He took a deep breath and held it, like he was trying to keep in all the things he couldn't or wouldn't say. Then he ran his finger lightly across my back, swirling curves and lines that spelled out a message I would never get.

"I'm sorry. You're right. I'm just worried about you. And

224

you're not desperate anymore, right? I'm here now. You don't need to trust a stranger. You can't risk being naive."

"I'm not being naive."

"Then why is he here?" Max asked. "We could ditch him right now."

"We can't do that," I said.

"Why not?"

"Well . . . for one thing, we need his credit cards." Eli had paid for the rooms, without hesitation. No ancient societies were tracking his credit-card payments, and no Interpol agents were watching for his ATM withdrawals; no one was hunting him.

"So we take them with us."

"Max! We're not stealing his money and leaving him alone in the middle of Prague." It was funny how he and Adriane had had the same impulse. It might have been the first thing they'd ever had in common. No—the second, I reminded myself. The first was that night in Chris's house. They would always share those scars.

"For all you know, he's planning to do the same to us. Or worse."

Maybe it didn't qualify as a fight, not exactly. But it wasn't the way I wanted to spend my first night with Max. It wasn't right. Nothing was.

"I'm sorry," I said, with nothing to apologize for. "He was there when we needed him. I know he's not telling us everything. But I trust him."

"That doesn't seem contradictory to you?"

"I trust him," I said, more firmly, not even sure if it was true. "I want him to stay."

That's when Max finally did let go, and sat up, with his back to me. "Fine. You trust him," he said, voice tight. "What about me?"

"Of course I trust you."

225

"Tell me there's no part of you that believes what they said about me."

"Of course I don't."

He turned and brought his face close enough to mine that I could see his eyes, even in the dark. And he could see mine. "There's no part of you that thinks maybe I'm the one who—"

I pressed a hand to his mouth before he could say the words. "I trust you," I said, my other hand on his, so he could feel that it was steady. "I never had any doubts. Not for a minute. *I trust you*."

He lay down again. He held me again. He kissed me, and closed his eyes, and went to sleep.

Maybe it hadn't always been true. But lying in bed, Max molded around me, our chests rising and falling in sync, his breath misting warm on my bare neck, there was no other truth. *I trusted him*. Those nights alone in the ominous quiet of my house, those nights I'd lain in bed holding a knife, waiting for someone to emerge from the shadows, those nights no longer counted. Those doubts were no longer real. Like all monsters, they disappeared in the morning light. They had disappeared as soon as Max was beside me.

But now he was gone again. Pacing the lobby, nursing secret wounds, hiding from his nightmares or his grief or from me. I sat up and turned on the light. I turned on all the lights.

The Elizabeth letter was folded up inside an empty Band-Aid box, which itself was tucked into a balled-up sock and stuffed into the sleeve of my Red Sox sweatshirt. After what had happened to our last room, I wasn't taking any chances. We'd agreed to decipher Elizabeth's code, if we could, first thing in the morning, but I was awake now, with no intention of closing my eyes until Max returned, safe and intact.

226

Three by three is where you'll find me.

So I smoothed out the letter, found a pen and a fresh page in my notebook, and started to count.

19

SCIVNT BRVMAE VMBRAS IN ISTO VERBO.
NISI PETAT ET ATER PRAEDONEM

JVS EMATQVE VRBAM VESTRAM

EIS BONA EXTRA VERBUM.

INSCITE PER AEVUM, IMVM PROMERUIT
PRECEM INFERUS.
O GENIE
O VBI NECTAR MERVM INFIDELIVM APVD TE
COLVIT.

LEX MEA EST NORMA TEPIDA
SIC CANEM TRADIDI ATRO EGO
RECREA ANIMAM APVD ME
SOL PRAEDICET TOTAS ITA RES.

It didn't take long for Elizabeth's real message to emerge.

SVB MVRIS VBI PATER DEVM QVAEREBAT VBI CERVI MORTEM FUGIVNT MVNDI AD CVLMEN MEDIAM AD TERRAM AD SPECTATE.

> *Beneath the walls where our Father searched for God*
> *where deer run from death look to the top of the world*
> *toward the center of the earth.*

Whatever that meant.

20

"You're the dead-girl-letter expert," Adriane said the next morning as we gathered around the lobby's ancient PC, keeping our voices low in case the clerk got bored enough to eavesdrop. Adriane was acting normal again, whatever normal meant under these circumstances. It wasn't healthy to pretend this well, so I probably shouldn't have been so relieved. "Illuminate us."

I had nothing.

"The search for God," Max said. "That's got to be the *Lumen Dei*. Wherever Kelley built it."

I shook my head. "He didn't build it. She did. And she didn't even start until he was dead." I had filled them in on everything I'd learned from Elizabeth's letters and the anonymous ones from Chris's room. But Adriane was right, I was the expert. And, though I would have felt ridiculous admitting it out loud, I couldn't help feeling like Elizabeth was speaking to me.

"Where was he before that?" Eli asked.

"Prison," I said. "Somewhere in the country, I think."

"That fits with the deer," Max said.

"Doesn't quite fit with my shoes," Adriane put in, with a rueful look at her new suede mules. Then, at the expression on all our faces, "Obviously that's not relevant under the current doomsday situation; I'm just offering an observation. Rule number one of brainstorming, remember? You can't say the wrong thing."

"And yet somehow you always manage to find a way," Max said, but I could tell he was holding back a smile.

It was good to see.

"Who was her father?" Eli asked suddenly, his eyes still fixed on my translation of the letter. "What did he do? Before prison?"

"He was the court alchemist," I said. "Tried to turn lead into gold, that kind of thing."

Adriane sighed. "Of course. A magician. This just keeps getting better."

"Alchemists weren't magicians," Max said. "They were the first chemists, the first pharmacists—even the ones who were trying to make gold weren't doing it to get rich. They thought that by purifying metal, they could purify the soul. They were searching for the connections between the earth and the heavens, the world of man and the world of—"

"God," Eli and I said together, and he was already typing *Prague / history / alchemy / locations* into the search field.

The first, second, and third entries were all for the Mihulka, a fifteenth-century tower that was part of the Hradčany fortifications and had been used as an alchemical laboratory by many of Rudolf II's court alchemists. "Including Edward Kelley," Eli read aloud. Elizabeth's father.

But my eye had already skipped down to the next paragraph, describing the bucolic beauty of the tower, which formed a part of the old castle fortifications and was bounded on one side by the Royal Gardens—and something called the Deer Moat. Which had, during the reign of Rudolf II, been fenced in and used as a hunting ground for deer.

Where our Father searched for God.
Where deer run from death.
We had it.

21

It felt risky to leave the relative safety of the Golden Lion, with its drawn blinds and locked doors—but riskier still to do nothing, and wait for them to find us. So we set out midmorning and—after Eli wove us through an elaborate pattern of concentric circles, sudden turns, and crowd crossings designed, he said, to ensure we wouldn't be followed—joined the flow of tourists streaming toward Hradčany.

"Evasive maneuvers you picked up from a bad spy movie aren't going to help us," Max had said, an un-Max-like sneer twisting his face. "These are pros. There's no middle ground. Either they're nowhere near us, and we're safe—or they spot us, and we're done."

But then he must have seen my expression, or felt my hand tense in his, because he cleared his throat and added, "But maybe this will help."

Whether it did or not, we made it to the castle safely, and in the unseasonably bright sunshine, surrounded by bickering couples and rambunctious field trippers, it seemed unimaginable that there had been any other option, that the sea of sightseers could be hiding men and their knives. I knew it would be dangerous to stop believing in them just because the sun was out. But in my experience, bad things happened in the dark.

Even in early spring, the Deer Moat was so dense with overgrowth that the stone towers of the castle fortifications disappeared almost entirely behind a wall of sallow green. As we plunged deeper into the grounds, the crowds of tourists dropped away—they had come to Prague for history and photo opportunities, not this bald pocket of dirt. By the time we reached the weedy base of the bridge adjacent to the tower, the Prašný most, we were nearly alone, and it was easy to slip off the path and into the trees that dotted the steep slope leading up to the Mihulka.

Max held the compass, which we'd picked up for fifty crowns at a souvenir stand just within the castle gates. It was gilded with fake gold and had a saint on the back.

The top of the world, we'd decided, could only mean true north.

Finding a shovel had proven more challenging, but thanks to Eli's fluent Czech, we'd managed to track down a small gardening store on the outskirts of Malá Strana, where we'd picked up the trowels Adriane had stashed in her bag.

As we found the right spot, the northernmost point on the perimeter of the tower, I kept looking over my shoulder, unsure whom I was more afraid of finding: Czech security officers ready to throw us in tourist jail for digging holes in a national monument; Interpol agents with handcuffs, warrants, and a one-way ticket back to Chapman and the maximum-security prison fifty miles down the road; *Hledači* minions, knives in hand. But no one was there.

We took turns digging. In the centuries since Elizabeth's time, the Mihulka had been used as a gunpowder storehouse, a religious dormitory, and a museum, undergoing various renovations, including one accidental remodeling courtesy of a seventeenth-century gunpowder explosion. There was no guarantee that whatever had been there still was; after an hour, an ever-widening hole, and a growing pile of dirt, there seemed little hope of it.

Then metal clanged against something hard.

I dumped the trowel and pawed furiously at the hard-packed dirt, scooping it out by the fistful, until I'd excavated a small black box. For a moment I forgot why we were there and everything that had happened, all of it washed away in the flood of childlike wonder. Buried treasure!

The box was a dark wood layered with elaborately engraved iron plates, about five inches square, its surface pitted by centuries of dirt and moisture. Someone had melted wax over the hinges to seal them from the elements, protecting whatever lay within. There was a small gold latch on the front. Eli stayed my hand. "Not here," he said. "Not till we get back to the room and lock the door behind us."

"I'll carry it." Max scooped up the box before I could argue and shoved it into his backpack.

I wanted to be the one to carry it. I wanted to run my hands over its surface, this box that had somehow survived four centuries underground, that held a secret worth killing for, a secret that Elizabeth thought could end the world. I wanted to know what was inside.

22

The sperm of Sol is to be cast into the matrix of Mercury, by bodily copulation or conjunction, and joining of them together.

"This is how you build a telephone to God?" Adriane asked. "Looks more like porn for chemistry nerds."

"It's an alchemical formula," Max said. He would know—he'd spent the majority of the year poring over similar gibberish. "The idea is that metals are alive and alchemists are mirroring the divine creation of life, so there's a whole symbolic language of chemical processes as natural, often sexual and generative transformations. 'The sperm of Sol' is probably just sulfur, and 'copulation' is code for combining it with mercury."

Adriane shook her head. "I rest my case."

But she moved in for a closer look. No one but me knew that Adriane had placed second in the regional chemistry olympiad two years running—she'd sworn our chem teacher to secrecy, vowing that if he inflicted public recognition on her, she'd be more than happy to tell the authorities about how he'd "accidentally" given a bunch of sophomores the means to brew their own Ecstasy in the AP lab. She'd kept her secret well enough, but Adriane calling someone a chemistry nerd was the pot calling the kettle Fe_4CSi.

I was sure this alchemical formula was identical to the incomplete one I'd found in Elizabeth's volume of Petrarch, the one we'd celebrated as the key to translating Voynich. The one she'd called Thomas's page, and claimed for her own. It seemed like forever ago. Beneath the formula was a letter, dated October 12, 1600. Two months earlier than the letter stained with Chris's blood, the letter Elizabeth had finished even after learning that her brother was dead.

E. I. Westonia, Ioanni Francisco Westonio, it began, as that one had, but the similarities ended there.

E. J. Weston, to John Francis Weston, the one who remains.

Brother. Dearest brother. I once told you I was fearless before a blank page. This, like so much else, has been proven a lie. The pages taunt me, pleading to be filled with something other than tears. Again and yet again, I fail. Failure has become my most loyal friend.

It is night, and I am alone with the corpse of the city. The candle has burned down. Darkness travels with me now, steady and reliable as Failure, my companions on an endless road. In the darkness, once, I slept. Now I lie awake, listening to the voices of the dead.

Soon the stones will glow in dawn light, dearest brother. Soon the rivers of piss will harden to ice, another winter, another ugly thing costumed in beauty. Too soon. I have waited too long.

I am ready to begin.

"Why don't we just pass it around?" I said, looking up from my translation. My hand was sore from the hours of transcribing, but it was my own fault that I hadn't let anyone help. Eli and Adriane had both pointed out that the work would go faster if

233

we split it up. But: "It should be Nora," Max had said, saving me from having to explain why I wanted to keep the letter to myself, why the work of transcribing Elizabeth's words and turning them into my own was something concrete to hold on to, something sane and normal, why the weight of the pen and the scrape of the ink across the page and even the soreness in my wrist were things I needed to keep going. "This is too long to read out loud."

"Keep reading," Max said. "It's nice, actually. In your voice. Keep going."

I didn't want to. Not for expediency's sake, but because her words cut too close to my truth, and reading them out loud was like sharing a secret I'd never meant to tell. I knew what it was not to sleep, waiting for the dead to rise.

I cleared my throat.

It began in the tower, in the dark and cold. I have told you of our Father losing himself in the magnificent Book. I have yet to confide, because I could not, the secret those pages contained. The secret that our Father gleaned from Bacon's tome. It was a promise, he said. A gift from his avenging angels. It was the Lumen Dei.

The Lumen Dei *was at first nothing to me but a pleasant dream in which our Father could live out his final days. Final days that I believed would never end. I was a child, filled with foolish hope. That child died the night the Emperor murdered our Father.*

I can hear you object, dearest brother. But I have been silent for too long. This letter is our secret, brother, and I ink these words as if I whisper them at your ear.

Rudolf II, Duke of Austria, King of Bohemia, secular leader of the Catholic Church, Holy Roman Emperor,

*slaughtered our Father. Perhaps it was not his hand that
delivered the poison, but it was his dark work. Our fate is his
legacy.*

As our Father knew it would be.

*His final request was simple. I was to take the pages to the
one man who could be trusted to complete his vision. Together,
we would construct the Lumen Dei, and together we would
present it to the Emperor, a gift in the name of Edward Kelley.
I was to relinquish the pages one by one, to ensure this man
would not claim the ultimate prize for himself. He is to be
trusted, our Father told me. But concerning the Lumen Dei,
no one is to be trusted.*

The man was Cornelius Groot.

*You have heard the stories. Whispers of a laboratory in a
hidden corner of Malá Strana, guarded by a stone lion known
to wake in the moonlight, of a chamber of monsters beholden to
his command, of the demons he calls from beneath the earth, of
iron beasts that clang and squeal, their gears forged in the fires
of hell. The stories were no worse than those told of our Father,
and I knew better than to believe them. Yet I hesitated before
the stone lion, a letter from our Father clasped in a trembling
hand. My breath and courage fled. I admit, only to you, my
brother, that I might have turned back, no, would have turned
back, had the door not swung open before me. A hunched man
whose beady eyes glowed yellow in the darkness asked no
questions, only beckoned me inside.*

I watched carefully, but no one flinched at "stone lion"—no
one but me, apparently, foolish enough to read into the coincidence, the stone beast pacing the doorframe a few feet below

our window. Sometimes a lion is just a lion, I told myself. Sometimes . . . but not lately.

Wait here, croaked the stooped servant, who seemed more beast than man, and limped into the shadows from which he had emerged.

I was left alone in Groot's chamber of horrors. Shelves lined the wall nearest me, shelves crammed with jars containing a milky fluid. Within them floated Death. Dead pigs, dead mice, dead hands with perfectly preserved fingernails. At the center of the room, a corpse lay across a marble table, its chest split open, its eye sockets hollow, its lips peeled back in a gruesome smile. A menagerie of clockwork creatures clicked and wheezed inside their cages, watching me with sightless eyes.

—A Kunstkammer of my own, fine as the Emperor's, I like to say. Though not to the Emperor, of course.

Groot's voice was velvet, rich and smooth. He spoke not in German or Czech or his native Dutch, but Latin, as if knowing it would please me. A candle flickered to life and uncloaked his caped figure, on the far side of the laboratory. It was the eyes I saw first. Not his eyes, those narrow pools of darkness I quickly learned to avoid. The eyes that lined the wall behind him, dead eyes floating behind mottled glass, stark white bulbs laced with spiny red veins. Would you believe, dear brother, that no scream escaped me?

—Your Father recognized greatness when it crossed his path.

This, before I could introduce myself.

—The world has suffered a great loss. As have you.

I could not speak.

—You were a beautiful child. But the result is no surprise. Tragedy is never kind to beauty, is it?

As if by magical incantation, this broke the spell. I assure you, brother, it was not vanity that unstuck my tongue. My crooked nose is what it is, my curls do what they will, and the wistfulness in our Mother's voice when she speaks of my younger self as if it were another, golden Elizabeth is more telling than any reflection. I have always known what I am. But to know that Groot had watched me as a child, to imagine that his spindly fingers had stroked my once obedient hair or his voice had crooned rhymes in my ear, that was intolerable.

You know I have never had much affection to spare for the mass of mankind, brother, but never had I met someone so easy to despise on first sight. Yet our Father trusted him. I gave him the letter and watched his long, pale face transform as he read, filling with surprise, wonder, and, finally, desire. When he met my gaze again, his smile matched that of the corpse.

—The end of all true philosophy is to arrive at a knowledge of the Creator through knowledge of the created world.

Bacon, I said, recognizing one of our Father's favorite pieces of wisdom. He nodded. Though I did not understand it at the time, that was the first test.

—Do you understand what I pursue here? My struggle?

His arm swept across the laboratory, its mechanical and organic death. No, I told him, and did not want to.

—We know the world only by acting upon it. We know the Creator only by creating. Paracelsus understands this. Also Agrippa and Porta. Ultimate knowledge derives from ultimate

*creation. The alchemists pursue their philosopher's stone,
purifying the soul as they purify their metal, readying them for
the divine. The astronomers seek our Creator in the heavens;
the mechanists seek Him in the workings of earth. They speak
of reading the Book of Nature. But there are those few of us
who seek to write a new Book. Bacon. Your Father.*

You, I guessed.

—You want to know about the Lumen Dei, *what it
promises us. I want to know your promise. A fair trade, I
believe.*

*Another test. At dawn the following day I returned to his
laboratory, which was shaded in perpetual night. This time, his
hobbled servant spoke.*

*—It is in need of eyes. You are to choose, and then to
supply.*

*Where the corpse had been, a mechanical man lay, an
armless and legless torso with a head of iron. And gaping
cavities where, if I wanted to prove myself, there soon would be
eyes.*

*They watched me from their jars. Brown, blue, green,
black, all with the same dead stare.*

*I chose a pair with large pupils, rimmed with bottomless
black, the pair most closely resembling Groot's inky gaze. I
plunged my hands into the cold water that was not water and
smelled of sickness, and cupped my fingers around two eggs
that were not eggs and felt to be pulsing with life. I once, in the
shadow of Most Castle, held a newly hatched chick in my palm,
its feathers sticky and slick, its heart fluttering warm and
afraid against my flesh. This was the same.*

On his table, the mechanical man waited.

The eyes sank into their holes with wet clicks, the sound of rotting limbs snapping off a corpse. They were only eyes in a cage of metal, but in that moment, I truly believed that my act had brought the man to life, and that the eyes would take their revenge.

From the darkness came applause.

Cornelius Groot stepped into the light.

—I see your Father's blood runs true.

Forgive me, brother, but I nearly spoke the words I have long forsaken. I nearly declared to this man that our Father was not our Father, that our true Father was long dead and Edward Kelley wore his clothes and his wife but could not lay claim to my blood.

I swallowed these words, not for love of our Father, but because I knew them to be a lie. Another man's blood may run through my body, but Edward Kelley's blood runs through my soul. He is my true Father, and Groot saw this, from the start.

—For many years I have labored to create life, as your Father labored to surpass it.

The two of us sat together before the first page of our Father's translation.

—Only God can grant the power to create life. Only God can know a man's soul, as He can know the beginnings and the ends of the universe. Only God can truly understand, and only God can truly destroy. To know God is to know ultimate power. Such would be a miracle. The Lumen Dei *is that miracle. Together, we will build it. Together, we will build a ladder to the divine.*

Blasphemy, I whispered.

This angered him, and when he spoke, there was danger in his voice.

—Blasphemy is a fiction of the Church, which proscribes our questioning and supplies answers of its own.

Our Father had little love for the Church, which bore even less for him, but such talk was unwise. The Church believed the Emperor to be allied with the devil, and I dared not be his opportunity to prove them wrong.

—It is the duty of natural philosophers to question. We seek the unification of man and machine, of material and spiritual, of the heavens and the earth. The Lumen Dei, *too, is a question, one we must prove ourselves worthy enough to ask. The Lord reveals Himself to us in nature, in art, in geometry, you believe this, do you not?*

I could not argue. He had shaped words around the truth at the center of my life.

—Who else but God gave us the desire and the capability to know? We need only muster the will to ask. Will you join me, as your Father wished it?

I joined him, dearest brother. For our Father. But not only for our Father.

So she believed in it. More than that: She *wanted* it. I could understand. She'd lost her father, lost her belongings, her home, her power, and now someone was offering her the control over life and death, over *everything*? Eli had been right: If the *Lumen Dei* was real, of course people would kill for it. Instead, they had died for it—for a comforting fiction. I almost wished it were as easy for me as it was for her. That I lived in a world where God

240

wasn't a choice, wasn't even a necessity, but was simply a fact of existence, obvious and present as the earth and sky. Because at least then they would have died for a reason. Everything would have happened for a reason. Wasn't that the whole point of telling ourselves the nice stories about the old man with the beard and the lightning bolts?

I envied Elizabeth—but I *admired* Groot. Because if you truly believed in the lightning bolts, why not do everything in your power to take them for yourself?

The Lumen Dei *would bring together the four elements:*
earth, air, fire, and water. We would begin where our Father
had, with the liquid of life itself, an elixir to coat and purify
our fantastical device. It was a potion, Groot said, that would
unite the humors of man with that of the heavens, and bring
the microcosm and macrocosm together into one. He selected
for us a young alchemical apprentice who, for a price, could be
trusted to follow our Father's formula and Groot's command.

And so, I found Thomas.

I cannot yet speak of him, except to tell you of our first
meeting, and how his corn-silk hair shined in the candlelight,
and how his blue eyes were kind when they dared meet my
gaze. You know how I have hated my name, but his voice gave
new life to it. Elizabeth, he said, and it was like a song.

If you have found this letter, as I know that you will, you
now have possession of that formula which Thomas prepared.
And with the formula, I leave you a choice. I cannot destroy
the Lumen Dei, *but as I once drew it together, I have now torn*
it asunder, and spread its limbs across this city I used to love.

Follow me now, if you dare, from water to earth, that

element deep in the bones and marrow of life. Groot sent me in pursuit of the sacred earth that had once walked as a soulless man, a pursuit that began and ended with this beast's creator, the holy man who in this way nearly became a god.

If you remember what our Father taught us, about how words do not belong to those who speak them, you can follow me there. But if you love yourself as I love you, beyond measure, you will burn these words and, with them, our Father's dream.

I stopped reading.

"Well?" Max prodded. "Follow her where?"

"That may be a problem," I said, and showed them the chunk of text at the bottom of the page.

ΘΕ ΣΑΚΡΕΔ ΕΑΡΘ ΛΙΕΣ ΒΙ ΘΕ ΓΡΕΑΤΕΣΤ ΡΑΒΒΙΣ
ΓΡΕΑΤΕΣΤ ΚΡΕΑΤΙΟΝ

"Anyone speak ancient Greek?"

Eli sighed, Max grimaced, but Adriane, after furrowing her brow in what I took to be mock concentration, shook her head.

"Problem solved," she said. "That's not Greek."

"I know you suck at languages," I said. "But trust me, that's Greek."

Adriane grinned. "Didn't you tell me once that Elizabeth Weston was born in England?"

"Didn't you tell me, more than once, you weren't listening?"

"Surprise!" she said brightly. "You also told me she considered English her native language and only wrote in Latin because she was an uppity bitch."

"I'm pretty sure those weren't my exact words."

"Words do not belong to those who speak them," she said.

"I can read that part, too. That part's not our problem."

"I'm telling you, there is no problem. Give me the pen."

She wrote:

ΙΜ ΦΥΛΛ ΟΦ ΣΥΡΠΡΙΖΕΖ

"Words do not belong to those who speak them," Adriane said again, tapping the page. "Think about it."

It was like staring at one of those paintings filled with dots—staring and staring until finally, through sheer exhaustion, your gaze relaxes, and the boat or unicorn or tree or whatever you've been trying too hard to see suddenly emerges from the chaos.

ΙΜ ΦΥΛΛ ΟΦ ΣΥΡΠΡΙΖΕΖ

She was right, it wasn't Greek. Chapman Prep taught the Greek alphabet as a novelty act in ninth grade, somewhere between square dancing and the prologue to the *Canterbury Tales*. So it was no trouble to sound the letters out in my head. Iota. Mu. Phi Upsilon Lambda Lambda—*I'm full* . . .

"'I'm full of surprises,'" I read. "Cute."

She smiled. "Try brilliant."

None of us could argue with that.

23

ΘΕ ΣΑΚΡΕΔ ΛΙΕΣ ΒΙ ΘΕ ΓΡΕΑΤΕΣΤ ΡΑΒΒΙΣΧ ΓΡΕΑΤΕΣΤ ΚΡΕΑΤΙΟΝΧ

The sacred earth lies by the greatest rabbi's greatest creation.

Prague, it turned out, had only one "greatest rabbi": Judah Loew ben Bezalel, aka the Maharal of Prague, aka chief rabbi of Prague, born 1520, died 1609, buried beneath the most visited tombstone in Prague's Old Jewish Cemetery, famous the world over, according to the guidebook, for sculpting a living creature from the mud of the Vltava River. A brainless lump of clay clumsily molded into the shape of a man, a divine blessing that allowed a man-made impossibility. Or, as Elizabeth had put it, "sacred earth that had once walked as a soulless man," created by "the holy man who in this way nearly became a god." A creature with no heart, no brain, no breath, no soul; dead matter animated by a spark of impossible life. A golem.

Every week, the rabbi endowed his monstrous creation with the breath of life by inscribing a slip of paper with the *Shem ha-Mephorash*, the true name of God, and slipping it beneath the golem's tongue. Day in and day out the witless creature lumbered obediently through the Jewish ghetto, mopping floors and kneading challah and punishing any drunken goyish thugs who, sodden with liquid courage, decided they were owed a tribute of Jewish wealth or Jewish women. Every Sabbath, the rabbi withdrew the slip of paper from his creature's mouth, and so withdrew the blessing. The breath of life, the *spiritus*, the *nefesh*, whatever animating force divine forbearance had leased to the lump of clay disappeared, and clay was, once again, nothing but clay. Dust returned to dust. Until the Sabbath the rabbi forgot his sacred task, and, deprived of its weekly nap, his Frankenstein monster ran rampant through the ghetto, nearly burning it to the ground. After that, the blessing was withdrawn permanently and the mud retired. There was no doubt this was the sacred earth we'd been charged with retrieving. There was just one problem. The golem was pure legend. Elizabeth had sent us in search of a fairy tale.

Another one.

Josefov, the old Jewish quarter, lay at the heart of the city. Supposedly settled in the tenth century, then settled all over again a century later after a gang of twenty thousand crusaders marched through and killed or converted everyone in the name of God. Inhabited by ten thousand people during its Renaissance golden era, when Emperor Rudolf smiled upon its people and at least mildly discouraged his other subjects from plundering or marauding through the quarter on a regular basis. Razed to the ground in 1895, by which point it had decayed into a slum and only those unfortunates too poor to spread into the rest of the city were still squatting in its urine-spattered streets. Rebuilt shortly after, but even then, despite Prague's one-hundred-thousand-plus Jewish population, there weren't many Jews left in the Jewish part of town; then came the Holocaust, and there weren't many Jews left anywhere.

We had intended to canvass the neighborhood in search of someone who might know more about the golem than we could find in books, hidden knowledge handed down through the generations as myth or bedtime story. But as soon as we crossed Kaprova, the street separating Staré Město from Josefov, our mistake became clear. Maybe this had once been a neighborhood. No more. From what I could tell, it wasn't anything anymore but a holding pen for tourists whose toddlers toted stuffed golems while their parents dragged them from one pristinely preserved synagogue to the next, occasionally pausing to buy a memorial postcard and candlesticks or pop into the Prada store just down the street.

Flyers slapped to the front of every building noted the times for morning prayers and the provisions for mourners needing access to the cemetery for a private kaddish: Somewhere, hiding from the hordes, someone lived here, worked here, prayed here. It was hard to imagine. According to one of the plaques we passed as we wandered in and out of the old temples, trying to get our bearings, the Nazis had razed and plundered Jewish ghettos all over the Continent, but they'd left this one largely intact, not just preserving its treasures but shipping in abandoned and stolen Jewish artifacts from hundreds of miles away. The idea being that, once the Final Solution came to fruition and Europe had been cleansed of its so-called scourge, Prague's Jewish quarter would stand as a museum to the vanished people, the architectural equivalent of a dinosaur skeleton or a wax caveman. It occurred to me that if things had gone according to plan, it probably would have looked a lot like this.

Rabbi Loew—along with every other Prague Jew to have died between the years of 1439 and 1787—was buried in the Old Jewish Cemetery, a small patch of stone and weed that could only be accessed through the Pinkas Synagogue. A sixteenth-century Gothic temple built in tribute to a destroyed German synagogue, it had been rededicated as a shrine to the children of Terezín. The concentration camp on the outskirts of Prague took in more than fifteen thousand children over the course of the war; 132 made it out.

I was only a few steps through the door when a gnarled hand grabbed my shoulder. I froze, choking on a voiceless scream. Nails bit into my arm, digging deep. Next would come the blade, in my back or across my neck, blood staining the ancient floor, a scene the tourists would capture on film to spice up their vacation slide show: Girl stumbles, girl falls, girl bleeds.

I wondered if it would hurt.

"Your friends," a creaking voice said. I finally shook off my paralysis and ripped myself out of his grip. "For their heads."

I spun around. The man who'd grabbed me was old and stooped and, even standing straight, couldn't have been much more than five feet tall. He held a basket of paper head coverings. "Men cannot enter without," he said.

All my breath came rushing back and now, through sheer relief, I almost did scream. But instead I took two of the small white head coverings, shoved them at Max and Eli, and promised myself I wouldn't forget again: Bad things happen in the daylight, too.

We entered the sanctuary on a wave of German teenagers,

their teachers barking orders at them as they pretended to read the inscribed names rather than their text messages. Max and Adriane muscled through the crowd and into the cemetery, where Loew's massive stone tomb was waiting. But I stayed behind for a moment, trapped by the watercolors painted by the young prisoners of Terezín. Some of the children had been talented; most had just been children, drawing lollipop trees and stick-figure people with fat, round heads. There were paintings that could have been hung anywhere—on a kindergarten wall, a refrigerator—seascapes of tropical fish, a giant octopus, a dragon facing off against a golden-haired sorceress, a house in the mountains, all perfectly sweet until you noticed the plaques alongside each picture, inscribed with birth and death dates, nearly all within a decade of each other. Then it was hard not to imagine the squat red and blue house as a distant dream of a safer childhood, the dragon as a Nazi commandant. It was hard not to notice the recurring nightmare captured in one painting after another, the black locomotive puffing smoke into a blacker night, the tracks leading straight to Terezín.

I wondered how many had already lost their parents, and then wondered about the parents who'd lost their children.

I wondered about my own parents, and whether they thought they'd lost me.

And what it would do to them if they did.

"You're shivering," Eli said. I jumped at the sound of his voice; I'd forgotten he was there.

"No I'm not." Yes, I was.

We'd learned about the Holocaust in school, just like we'd learned about the Spanish explorers, the Aztecs, the Emancipation Proclamation, and the Chapman-founding pilgrims. They'd all seemed equally distant—equally unreal. But this building was five hundred years old, on a street whose stones had been laid five hundred years before that, in a city founded in the ninth century.

Seventy years was nothing; seventy years was yesterday. Seventy years ago, this synagogue had been a synagogue, with rabbis and services and bored kids running up and down the aisles, tugging at starchy collars and sneaking outside to get mud on their fancy Shabbat dresses. Kids who were in their eighties now, or who were nowhere. The synagogue was beautiful, all stained glass and vaulted ceilings. You'd have to love God quite a bit to build a place like that just for the privilege of worshipping him. Lot of good it did, I thought. Easier to believe in no God than one incapable of loving you back.

"Let's get out of here," I said. There were a hundred thousand bodies buried in the old cemetery, more than had been symbolically interred in the Pinkas's engraved walls. But cemeteries, at least, I understood.

24

Out in the open air, I could breathe again. The cemetery was bounded by a high stone wall, riven with deep cracks whose elaborate designs looked like they'd been graffitied onto its skin. It was nothing like the cemeteries I was used to, with their neat matrices of polished stones. Here the worn, chipped, dented, tired graves were crammed together, sagging at alarming angles, their inscriptions mostly worn away. A few clusters of three, even four stones leaned on one another, as if the ground beneath them had mercifully shifted to allow for the comfort of contact.

The Germans were still milling about the synagogue, which left us nearly alone with the morning fog settling over the tombs and the moldering bodies piled six deep. We found Max and Adriane near the cemetery's largest tombstone, watching a lumpen older woman who was using a spindly branch to scrape it clean of moss.

"Where have you been?" Adriane whispered.

"We thought she might know something," Max said. "But . . ." He looked at Eli.

"But you realized you need *me*?" Eli said. "The horror."

"You think she does that for free?" I wondered, watching the woman closely. From this distance, in her shapeless flowered tunic and shoes that bore a suspicious resemblance to bedroom slippers, she looked like anyone's grandmother—though admittedly not mine, who shopped exclusively at designer outlet stores and had an allergy to the sartorial category containing concepts like aprons and muumuus.

"Weird hobby," Adriane said, but I wasn't so sure.

"Maybe she's related to him," I said, though I knew it was wishful thinking that any of the long-dead corpses were still remembered, much less mourned, by the living. "And this is some kind of sacred family task handed down through the generations."

"Guess I shouldn't complain so much about having to empty the dishwasher," Adriane said.

Max frowned. "We're wasting time. That's Loew's grave. If she's related, which I doubt, all the more reason to talk to her."

The woman didn't look up as we approached. She just kept at it with her stick, scritch-scratching against the worn stone, one inch of moss at a time.

"*S dovolením,*" Eli said softly. "*Dobrý den.*"

"*Dobrý den,*" the woman muttered, and finally looked up, scowling. "Americans," she said. It wasn't a question.

"You speak English?" I asked, wondering how she'd known. She nodded.

"Can we ask you a question?"

"Find a stick," she said, in a heavy Czech accent.

"Excuse me?"

"You want my time, you give some of your own to the Maharal."

We found sticks.

"We're trying to find out more about the golem." I dug the edge of my branch into a pocket of hard-packed dirt that girded the two-tailed lion on the face of the tomb.

She snorted. "Always, they're looking for the golem. You want to find it? Look in your fairy tales and your Hollywood stories. It lives there. Nowhere else."

"Well, we know the basic story," I said. "The rabbi made the golem and then it went on a rampage—"

"Lies! This is all they know to do!" Her hands tightened on the stick, and she scraped furiously. Silvery wisps of hair had slipped from the pins holding back her tight bun, softening her face. I tried to see the young woman in the older one, but I couldn't find her anywhere in the pinched lips and weathered skin. I couldn't imagine her being anything but what she was. "To say a Jew—the greatest of Jews—helps destroy his people? This way is easier for them. They hide from their guilt."

"They who?"

"Jewish?" she asked.

"Excuse me?"

"You. Americans. Are you Jewish?"

The others mumbled a no. I didn't say anything. I didn't feel Jewish, not here, in the shadow of the temple, with Prague's chief rabbi decomposing beneath my feet.

But Adriane gave me up. "She is."

"Sort of," I said.

"Sort of." The woman echoed me in a broad American accent. In her voice, my words couldn't have sounded more stupid. "*Sort of* pregnant. *Sort of* dead. *Sort of* Jewish. These are impossibles."

"Whatever you say."

"Jewish is not something you decide," she said.

"Right," I said. "So . . . *you* decide?"

"He decides." She didn't have to look up at the gathering storm clouds for me to know which "he" she meant. "He chooses."

"Not for me," I said.

Max cleared his throat. "We don't mean any disrespect," he said, apologizing for me like I was his unruly child. "We're just curious about the rabbi."

She ignored him. "This city was founded by a woman, did you know that?" she asked me.

I shook my head.

"A witch, they say. The prophetess Libuše, wise and powerful. But Libuše is a woman. It is said she cannot rule without a man. And so she marries Přemysl. He rules the new city of Praha and the men are happy. But Libuše's maidens miss the old way. They want their power. So they do what men have always done. They raise an army. Libuše's maidens kill hundreds, thousands, but they cannot win. In the end, they are destroyed. That is Praha, from the very beginning. Prophecy, vengeance, murder, defeat. It was a bloody birth, this city. Its heart is darkness."

"Maybe it's time to think about moving," Adriane said.

"I love Praha," the woman snapped. "This city is in our blood. As our blood runs in its streets, its rivers." She stamped the ground. "Its earth. The story of Praha is the story of tragedy. Again we fight, we rise up, and again, again we fall. And always when we fall, the Jews must pay. The ritual, a virgin in the volcano, a sacrifice for the Lord, you know this, yes?" She didn't wait for an answer. "It is like this, I believe. They throw us into the darkness. Throw Jews out windows. Throw our Torah into a pile of shit. We are *azazel*, you understand?"

"The devil?" Eli said.

"This word you use for *devil*, it means *goat*," she said. "Your

251

village, it lays all its sin onto a goat, then kills the goat and—*pffft*." She whistled through her teeth. "You are cleansed. And the dead goat? After all, it is only a goat."

"Scapegoat," I said.

"We'll pay you a hundred U.S. dollars if you can help us find what we're looking for," Max said abruptly. "Otherwise, we're done here."

The woman rested her stick on the ground beside the tomb, then kissed her palm and pressed it to the stone. "You need to find the golem so bad because?"

"We're students," Eli said. "It's important for our research."

She shrugged.

"*Very* important," Adriane added quickly.

"I do not help liars."

"She doesn't know anything," Max said. "Let's go."

I leaned into him. "You're being rude," I whispered.

"We don't have time for this," he replied, aloud. "Thank you for your help, but we'll go now."

"The golem is a story," the woman said. "It never was. But if what never was, was, you will never find it without my help."

"What do you know?" Max asked.

"I know enough. Tell me a true story, and I will have one for you."

Enough. "Fine," I said. "Truth."

Eli looked alarmed. "Nora, we can't—"

"Someone killed my best friend," I said. "Now they're trying to kill me. Unless I can find a piece of the golem."

"These people, they kill for a handful of dirt out of a story-book?"

"No, it makes way more sense than that," Adriane said. "They kill for a storybook machine—"

"Ignore her," Max cut in.

252

"Even for an American, you are very rude," the woman told him. Eli smothered a laugh. "What machine is this?"

"*Lumen Dei*," Adriane said, drawing out the vowels to give the phrase a ghostly oomph.

The woman stiffened. "Then I cannot help you. But I will take you where you need to go."

25

Her name was Janika, she told us. She was a trustee for Dobrovol-níci Židovského města, she told us, the Jewish Community Volunteers trusted with the keys to the sacred kingdom and all its strictly off-limits domains. Which, she told us, meant she could get us into the attic of the Alt-Neu Shul, the forbidden alcove of Prague's oldest synagogue—where, according to legend, Rabbi Loew had lain the remains of his golem to rest.

She told us all that but would tell us nothing about the *Lumen Dei*. Not where she had heard of it, nor how. Not why mention of it had persuaded her to help us, even though the words, each time we repeated them, turned her face a lighter shade of pale until, with a convoluted set of hand motions to (I assumed) ward off the evil eye, she forbade us to utter them again.

After hours, the Alt-Neu Synagogue was empty, lit only by dim bulbs that mimicked the orange flickering of candlelight. I'd had an art teacher once whose favorite line was that Michelangelo's sculptures were living inside each block of stone; he needed only to let them out. That was how the temple felt, with its curving off-white stone walls and the prayer benches that bloomed from them. As if the building had sprouted from the earth, fully formed. Notre Dame, the Kostel sv Boethia, these had felt old and—even to me—somehow sacred. But they'd also been fearful and imposing, with their elaborate stained glass, gilded statues, towering spires, scowling gargoyles, and impossibly tall stone pillars all working in tandem to make you feel dwarfed, inconsequential, *human*. I could understand how people who lived in squat wooden houses, who pissed in gutters and spent their sixteenth-century days shaping metal or cobbling shoes or begging for scraps, could, confronted by the mountain of glass and stone and gold, have no choice but to believe their lives had been shaped by divine forces, because what else but a divine force could turn stone, glass, and mortar into *that*? The temple felt different. Older, though it wasn't. Old like the desert; old like Jerusalem. Maybe it was the sand-colored walls or the warm glow of false candlelight, or the lack of a gilded altar—here there was only simplicity, an embroidered tapestry covering the ark. It was unsettlingly easy to imagine an earlier time, a bearded man supine before the ark, begging his God for the power to refute death.

Janika ushered us past two security guards—"Golem," she said, and they winked—and up a narrow flight of stairs, into the synagogue's attic, a musty, surprisingly cramped space with sloping walls and eight centuries' worth of accumulated spiritual detritus.

"This is it," she said. "You look, as many have looked before you. There is nothing here."

"Thank you so much," I said.

She coughed, a dry, hacking smoker's cough. "Don't break anything."

We dug through layers of rusted menorahs, moth-eaten linens, dusty tomes in ancient languages. Each of the walls was examined carefully for secret niches, a loose brick or hidden doorway that might relinquish a treasure.

Janika stood in a corner, fingers twitching like they would have been more comfortable holding a cigarette, or at least a stick, watching us carefully and offering the occasional pronouncement on the mildewed curiosities.

A tarnished silver menorah bearing the candle wax of Hanukkahs past: "Menorah belonging to Kafka's great-grandparents. Don't touch."

A slim, rectangular stone box, only slightly wider and longer than my index finger, each end molded into the face of a child. "Mezuzah belonging to the Maharal's daughter. Don't touch."

A squat cup of blackened silver, engraved at its base with Hebrew: "Kiddush cup belonging to the Tosafos Yom Tov. Don't touch."

Looking for something was hard enough when you didn't know what you were looking for; harder still when, deep down, you didn't believe that it existed. I peered out the window, as if the rooftops of Prague would offer an answer. But the slate and stone were silent. Below me, a set of iron rungs marched halfway down the exterior of the church, forming a makeshift ladder. The window was unlocked and, with the gentle pressure of only my index finger, eased itself open. An escape route, I thought.

"Enough," I said. We'd covered every crack and cranny. "There's nothing here."

"We can't give up," Max argued.

I lowered my voice so Janika wouldn't hear. "We don't even know if we're looking for the right thing—maybe we were wrong about what Elizabeth meant."

Max grabbed my arm. "Do you understand what's happening here?" He squeezed. His nails dug into my skin. "This isn't for fun."

"Who's having fun?" Adriane said lightly.

"I know that," I told him.

"But you just want to give up." Max squeezed tighter. "Like you don't care what happens."

"Let go of me." I would not raise my voice.

"It's here, and we can find it. We *need* it."

255

"Max. *Let go*."

He looked down, as if surprised to see himself holding on. He let go, and we both stared at the red marks his fingers had left behind on my skin. No one spoke. I couldn't look at any of them.

"Be careful," Eli said finally. I didn't know which one of us he was talking to.

Max looked ready to spit. "Shut up."

"You know what?" Adriane looped an arm around Max's shoulders. "You and I are going outside, where we will have a deep, meaningful conversation on the merits of stress relief and not turning into a brooding psycho on us, because pop-cultural opinion notwithstanding, that is distinctly not hot. Come."

I braced myself for him to argue, or worse, but instead, he dropped his head, like a nod he couldn't be bothered to finish, and left with her.

"He's not usually like this," I said.

Eli didn't answer.

"He's actually never like this," I added. "He's under a lot of pressure." I was fully aware of how lame it sounded. What had they done to Max in that basement that left him so angry and desperate? And why did I keep saying exactly the wrong thing, when I was supposed to be the one who knew him best? He'd actually left the building to remove himself from my presence, and the worst part: When he had, I'd been relieved.

Eli shrugged.

"Well?" I said.

"Well what?"

"Aren't you going to say something?"

"You don't want me to say something."

"And that suddenly stops you?"

"You're not very good at making excuses," he said. "Which is strange."

"Why is that?" I asked before I realized that the right response would have been to deny that I was making excuses, or that Max needed them.

"Because it seems like you must have had a lot of practice."

"This may be a tough concept for you to grasp, but that's what you do when you love someone."

He sighed. "No, Nora. It's not."

Before I could argue, he turned abruptly to Janika, still in her corner, taking everything in. "*Děkuji*," he said.

"Yes, thank you for taking us up here even though you warned us it was pointless," I told her, keeping a careful distance from Eli. I just wanted to get away from him, and to find Max. "*Děkuji*. I hope you don't get in trouble or anything."

"You run around Praha asking stupid questions about *Lumen Dei*"—she made those convoluted hand gestures again, and I caught a *keyn aynhoreh* murmured under her breath, my grandmother's favorite method for warding off the evil eye—"and you worry about me?" She laughed, but there was no mirth in it. "Trouble will find you. Be sure."

"Why do you say that?" I asked, fed up with all the vague warnings. "If you know something, can't you just tell us?"

"When I am young, every child knows the *Lumen Dei*," she said, looking past us into some middle distance of her past. "My father learns from his father, who learns from his father, and the lesson is passed down."

"What lesson? You mean you know how to build it?" Eli said. "Or what it does?" There was doubt in his voice, but beneath it, something else. Fear?

She shook her head. A few more wiry curls sprung free. "In English, you say that curiosity killed the cat, yes?"

I nodded. "That's not exactly my philosophy, but—"

"Yes," Eli said. "That's what we say."

"Here, we say *kdo je moc zvědavý, bude brzo starý*. You understand this, yes?" She aimed a spindly finger at Eli. "You are Czech, I see that."

"I'm American."

"Do you understand it or not?" I asked.

"'If you're too curious, you'll get old sooner,'" he said. "Too soon. Is that it?"

She gestured to herself with a rueful smile. "I was once *moc zvědava*, you see?"

I smiled back, unsure whether or not this qualified as a joke.

"It is possible to know too much," she said. "*Lumen Dei*, the machine that sees through the eye of God. This is too much."

"We're not planning to *use* it," I said.

"You seek it."

"Not because we're curious."

"You seek it, and so they will find you."

"The *Hledači*? Yeah, we've figured that one out."

She squinted. "*Hledači*? This is what?"

Now I was confused. "They're the ones who . . . Wait, what did *you* mean? Who will find us?"

"*Fidei Defensor*," she said in a hushed voice.

"'Defender of the Faith,'" I translated. "Some kind of church group?"

"They were born of the Church," she said. "But they are not of the Church. They are alone, and they are everywhere."

"So they defend Catholicism or something? Like the Crusades?"

"They defend *faith*," she corrected me. "Man is not meant to know God. We *believe*, we do not *know*. Eve knew this, before the serpent. The *Lumen Dei* is a serpent. An apple. The *Fidei Defensor* protect man from himself."

"Like I said, we're not planning to use the thing," I said.

"Though even if we were, and even if it worked"—and even if there were a God, I added silently, suspecting this wasn't the best audience for that particular train of thought—"why would they care? They love ignorance, so I'm stuck with it, too?"

"Some things are not ours to know," she said harshly. "For the *Fidei Defensor*, it is *kdo je moc zvědavý, bude brzo mrtvý*."

"'Too much curiosity will make you sooner dead,'" Eli said. "Excuse my language, but that's *hovadina*!"

From the way he spit out the word—and the way she flinched—I had a couple good guesses as to its meaning.

"I've heard of the *Fidei Defensor*," he said. "They were a fringe group back in the Renaissance, and they all got slaughtered in the Thirty Years' War. I doubt we'll piss them off enough for them to rise from the grave."

"Now you're an expert on defunct religious sects?" I said.

"Obsessed family, remember?" he said. "So trust me when I say this is one group of nutcases we don't have to worry about."

"*Hovadina? Hovadina!*" Janika was muttering. "*Američani si myslí, že sežrali všecku moudrost světa.*"

"I think you offended her," I whispered.

She opened the attic door. "You leave now, yes?"

"Why did you help us, if you think this is so dangerous?" I asked.

"*Moc zvědava*," she said, shaking her head. "My father tells me this again and again. I am no good at listening. Also . . ." She stretched out a hand, palm up, fingers stretched wide, but didn't continue.

"Also what?" Eli asked finally.

"One hundred American dollars, the rude one said."

I turned to Eli, who looked through his wallet and sighed. "Thirty?" he suggested. "I can't afford any more now, but if you give us your address—"

259

"Thirty," she said firmly, but stopped short of taking the bills. Up close, her eyes were the murky gray-blue of a storm cloud, and I finally saw what I'd been looking for, the evidence that she'd once had a future, rather than a past. "Remember," she said. Her hand reached out, and for a moment I feared she was going to stroke my cheek or cup my chin, but it dropped away without making contact. "There is darkness in this city. And for our people, it will always be worse. When the darkness comes again, they will want your blood."

"Nora has nothing to be afraid of," Eli said, and pressed the money into her hand.

Janika pocketed the bills without taking her eyes off me. "You know he lies."

26

"I'm sorry about today." Max sat on one side of the bed; I sat on the other. There was, in this claustrophobic room, nowhere else to sit. All day, I had waited for this moment, the two of us alone. I had waited for his soft touch and the apology I knew would accompany it; he would be sorry and I would be sorry and, canceling each other out, we would be right again.

I reached across him and switched off the light.

"I'm just scared for you," he said. "We need to finish this. It's the only way we'll ever be safe."

Safe. At least until the next knife flashing in the shadows, or the next car crash, the next botched burglary, the next Ebola outbreak, the next heart attack. There was no safe. Finding this machine, bargaining with the *Hledači*, going home, nothing would change that.

"Please don't be mad," he said.

"I'm not."

"You're a terrible liar." He kissed my neck. "I love that about you."

"I'm not lying. I'm . . ."

"You can tell me. Anything."

"I don't know." How was I supposed to tell him that I wasn't mad about what he'd done, but what he hadn't? Hadn't saved Chris. Hadn't stayed to save me. Hadn't made everything all right again just by putting his arms around me and promising it would be.

"The postcard, on Andy's grave," I said, without intending to. "How did it get there?"

"I told you, we don't have to talk about any of that." He leaned against me, whispering, "'What's past is prologue; what to come, in yours and my discharge.'"

I could feel him smiling. This was our game; it was my turn.

I didn't play. "I want to know."

"Shakespeare," he said. Still trying. *The Tempest.*

And then he gave up. "I set up a dummy account and emailed a guy in the dorm who'll do anything for cash. Sent him the money and the postcard, and I guess he came through."

"You emailed him."

"Yeah."

"Risky."

"I was careful."

"Then you mailed him something."

"Yeah."

"Also risky."

"Worth it, right?"

I wanted to slap him. "You couldn't have just emailed me? Sent me a letter? Told me *something*?"

"I had to do it this way," he said. "I had to be safe. The cops, the *Hledači*—what happened on that night, it could have been worse. A lot worse. I couldn't risk leading them to you."

I knew I should tell him that someone had been watching me, back in Chapman, a figure in the woods who'd left me a message in dirty snow. "Chris told you about Andy?" I said instead. "How come you didn't say anything?"

"How come you never told me yourself?"

I didn't answer.

"Well, that's why," he said. "I figured you didn't want me to know."

"It wasn't just you," I said. "It was everyone."

"Everyone but Chris."

"I didn't have to tell Chris. That was the point."

"But you would have," Max said. "It's okay. I get it."

"I would have told you, too. Eventually."

Now that he knew, I waited for him to ask—not about why I hadn't told him, but about Andy, about what it was like having a dead brother or what it had been like having a live one, and I found I was waiting impatiently, more than ready to finally let him into the locked room where I kept all the stories, the gross-out jokes, the cheesy hip-hop, the smells of sweat socks and hair gel, all the things that reminded me of my brother.

"We should sleep," he said. "Tomorrow we'll have to solve Elizabeth's clue for real or figure out what to do next. Either way . . ."

"Right. Sleep."

I let him fold himself around me and tuck me under his arm. "You know I'd do anything to keep you safe," he murmured after several quiet minutes had passed.

I pretended I was already asleep.

262

27

I dreamed about dead people. Not Andy, not Chris, but Elizabeth, and Rabbi Loew, and the rabbi's dutiful daughter who used a stick to clean out the bright, springy moss which sprouted from his nose and ears at an alarming rate and, in the dream, was named Janika. When I woke up, three hours before dawn, I suddenly understood where to find what we were looking for.

When I woke up, Max was gone.

There was a note on his pillow. *Adriane's upset, can't sleep. Didn't want to wake you—we went for a walk. Back soon. M*

If Adriane had banged on our door in the middle of the night searching for solace, then "upset" had to be a significant understatement, and I couldn't believe Max had let me sleep through it. Nor could I believe he'd been dumb enough to take her rambling through the city in the middle of the night, leaving nothing more than a vague note, leaving me no way to get in touch with them and no idea where they were, leaving me to another sleepless night, with nothing to do but lie awake and wait for them to come back—or wait for them not to.

I don't believe I was trying to punish him when I pulled on my jeans and padded down to the opposite end of the corridor, hesitating only a moment before I knocked. It wasn't supposed to be a lesson: *You disappear, you leave me alone,* again, *don't expect me to be waiting when you come back.* But when Eli appeared, cheeks flushed and hair poking up in spiky cowlicks like an overgrown Dennis the Menace, opening the door wide for me as soon as I spoke the magic words, "I figured it out," I knew whatever happened next would only end up with Max pissed off, again, and found I didn't particularly care.

"The rabbi's 'greatest creation,'" I told Eli, trying not to stare at his surprisingly muscled bare chest and the spiky black cross tattooed over his heart that should have looked trashy but—and maybe this was just the dim light or the lack of sleep or some temporary crisis-induced insanity—added just enough of a punk twist to his sculpted abs to evoke thoughts I most definitely should not have been thinking. I cleared my throat and aimed my gaze at the peeling paint beyond his shoulder. "What if it wasn't the golem?" I asked. The rabbi wasn't so different from Elizabeth's father, I had realized, in that foggy moment between dream and waking. A man who'd spent his life in service to and pursuit of his God. Of course the world thought of the golem as his *pièce de résistance,* as the *Lumen Dei* would have been Edward Kelley's. But for Elizabeth, the fundamental fact about Kelley wasn't his work. It was his fatherhood. "What if it was the rabbi's daughter?"

"What are you doing here?" Eli asked, still blinking away sleep. His boxers—which I also shouldn't have been noticing—were pale blue and studded with Tweety Birds. Oddly, they suited him. "Where's Max?"

"First I thought maybe it was buried with her, which would suck, because most of those graves didn't have names, and even if they did, it's not like we can go dig up the cemetery."

"You know it's the middle of the night, right?"

"But then I remembered the attic—the mezuzah, remember? Janika said it belonged to his daughter, and mezuzahs are hollow. Anything could be inside. It's a long shot, but don't you think it's worth a try?"

"Is something wrong?" Eli asked. "Did Max do something?"

"Are you even listening to me?"

"I'm just not the most likely or logical person for you to come to with your middle-of-the-night brainstorms."

"Look. Adriane was upset, so Max went off with her somewhere. So he's not around to hear my idea, which I think is a good one, and I think the middle of the night is as good a time as any to check it out, since it's not like we can look up Janika No-Last-Name in the phone book. And even if we did, I doubt she'd help us again. So I'm going back to the synagogue. You coming, or not?"

Eli grinned. "I'll get my pants."

28

"*This* is your plan?" Eli said, staring dubiously at the iron rungs climbing up the side of the old temple. They began several feet over our heads, but I was fairly sure he could hoist me up.

"You have a better one?" I asked. "Want to wait until morning and track down another bizarrely willing old lady to let us through the front door—then hope that this one lets us actually *touch* things?"

"It's not the worst idea I ever heard." But he laced his fingers together and opened his palms, ready to cup my foot. "You realize we're about ninety-nine percent guaranteed to get caught, right?"

The street was abandoned. A few streetlights disguised as old-fashioned gas lamps gave the foggy night a warm orange glow. The souvenir stalls were boarded up, and nothing moved but tattered flyers flapping in the frigid breeze. "How do you figure?"

"This is the city's oldest synagogue, a global tourist attraction and holy shrine, in a city where there used to be a hundred thousand Jews and now there are barely any," he said, the *you idiot* implied. "You think they forgot security cameras?"

"Then I guess we should hurry." I stepped into his hands, grabbed his shoulders, and shifted my weight forward, lunging toward the lowest iron rung. My fingers grazed metal, then Eli stumbled under my weight and I almost toppled over. "Watch it!" We tried a second time, and I made contact, grabbing the rung, holding tight, kicking away from Eli, and dangling free. My feet scrabbled against the wall and my arm muscles screamed as I tried to haul myself up, pull-ups never having been my forte. Adriane would have done this in a single, elegant move, I thought, Cirque du Soleil–style, probably cartwheeling or back-handspringing toward the ladder and then scrambling up the side with the ease of a yoga-practicing monkey. She definitely wouldn't have grunted so loudly as she gained one vertical inch after the other, feet finally gaining purchase, the attic window distant but hypothetically in reach.

With my feet finally steady on a rung, I reached down to give Eli a hand up, but he was rolling a trash bin toward the base of the building. He flipped it over, climbed on top, and leapt for the ladder, swinging himself with the grace of a cat burglar, the only hint of effort the straining cords of muscle in his neck.

The climb itself was easy. I should have been terrified, but I wasn't. Maybe it was the moonless night that made the whole thing—clinging to the side of an ancient temple, pushing the window open, climbing silently into the dark attic with Eli's phone screen our only source of light—deeply surreal. Maybe I hadn't fully thrown off my dream.

"Here." I led Eli to where I'd found the mezuzah, inside a large wooden cabinet of curiosities in the back corner of the attic. Spiderwebs brushed my face, and in the dark, it was all too easy to imagine the creatures that had woven them skittering up my leg or dropping down from the ceiling.

"Great. Take it, and let's get out of here."

"I'm not *taking* it. That's stealing."

"Right—when they drag us off to prison, I'll be sure our lawyer notes that's where we draw the line."

"Shut up." Holding the slim stone box delicately between two fingers, I slid off the back panel. There should have been a prayer scroll tucked into the hollow. But when I unspooled the tight roll of parchment, there was Elizabeth's familiar handwriting staring back at me—and something else. A tiny leather pouch, pinched by a drawstring. I shook it, we both heard the soft whisper of loose earth.

"No way," Eli breathed.

Here, in my hand, like a sack of marbles, all that remained of a physical impossibility: the golem.

I had been right.

An alarm sounded. Footsteps pounded up the stairs.

"We have to get out of here!" Eli yanked me to my feet. He hoisted me out the window, then followed close behind, his left foot nearly whacking my nose.

Below us, someone shouted. Flashlight beams danced across the sidewalk.

"Wait!" I hissed. We froze, pressing our bodies to the building, hoping to be camouflaged by stone and night.

The attic lit up. Figures wandered back and forth across the window. Down at the street level, security guards paced the perimeter of the building. I clung to the iron rungs, trying to breathe, willing them not to look up. Frigid gusts of wind walloped me in the face. I tried to tuck my head under my straining arm, and tried doubly hard not to look down.

This had been an insane idea, on the order of swallowing knives or juggling fire. With the wind biting into my bare fingers, already numbed by the cold metal rungs, it looked like it would be a photo finish between jail and death, the latter being the inevitable result if we had to hang on much longer and my body stopped obeying the *don't you dare let go* instructions issued by my increasingly deranged neural command center.

"It'll be okay," Eli said softly from above me.

"Considering our track record, that seems totally likely."

"If you think about it, this is actually very appropriate, given the surroundings."

"'This' being . . . ?"

"Our partial defenestration."

"Our what?"

"Defenestration of Prague? Thirty Years' War? Catholics getting thrown out the window only to survive by landing in a pile of manure? Any of this ringing a bell?"

I appreciated the attempt to distract me; it wasn't working. I craned my neck toward the ground, watching the patrolling guards. Their walkie-talkies crackled, and a moment later, they disappeared inside the building.

"Now!" I hissed, already climbing toward the ground. Swiftly, carefully, and then, three rungs down—my right foot slipped its grip. I shrieked as my left skidded off the rung and, jolted forward, my head hit metal with a tooth-rattling clang. Dazed by the impact, I almost let go of the bar.

"Nora! Hold on!"

Eli's voice was nearly drowned out by the thunder in my head, but I did as it suggested and held on, numb fingers curling tightly around cold metal, legs kicking, kicking, scrabbling against the stone, searching for purchase, arms screaming. *Defenestration*, I thought, dimly, and wondered whether being one-quarter Catholic would qualify me for my own miraculous dung heap.

My feet found their rung. I wasn't going to fall.

It took me a moment to believe it.

"I'm fine," I called faintly. "I'm climbing." I started down again, just as the window swung open above us and a head popped out, shouting something in loud Czech that needed no translation.

"Then go!" Eli shouted, and, though I was still trembling, I scrambled down, willing myself to play monkey for just a little longer, dangled from the bottom rung, dropped with knee-crunching pain to the ground, and stupidly waited for Eli to make it safely down before I began to run.

They chased us through Josefov, up Maiselova, around the corner and down Široká, past the Jewish Town Hall and the Spanish Synagogue and the dark windows of Prada and Louis Vuitton, and into the twisting alleys of Staré Město. We led them in circles, our steps echoing through the empty passageways, our lungs bursting, thick fog and moonless night conspiring to turn our pursuers into nothing but clomping bootsteps and angry voices, the occasional drunks and beggars watching dispassionately as we blew past—and then, somehow, the shouts behind us faded away and we were alone.

Even then, we kept running. Sometimes it was Eli leading the way, sometimes it was me—whenever he fell back, I surged forward, and vice versa, until it almost seemed we were no longer racing the cops but each other, in a silent challenge to see who would give up first.

I did, and nearly collapsed. Eli stopped beside me, not even breathing fast. We both waited, braced for lights and sirens to emerge from the darkness. But they never did—and the pouch of sacred dirt was nestled safely in my pocket. Maybe it was a small victory. But it was the first I'd had in a very long time.

29

"It was my fault," I said.

Eli snorted. "You got that right."

We'd walked in circles for nearly an hour before getting our bearings, thanks to a street-side tourist map whose *You Are Here* was at least a mile from where we wanted to be. All the streets looked alike, faceless stone walls wherever we turned. Prague was silent. Even the drunken frat boys had relinquished the fight and passed out in their puddles of vomit.

"It's not like I *meant* to scream," I said. "I thought I was falling."

"It wasn't your fault because they heard you scream," Eli said. His voice echoed off the stone, and I wanted to shush him, but didn't, because that would have seemed paranoid. Or maybe not—it wasn't paranoia if someone was actually out to get you— but it would have seemed like I was afraid.

And there was a strange comfort in his voice.

"It was your fault because you're the one who dragged us out here in the middle of the night to play Spider-Man," he added.

I reached into my pocket and tightened my fingers around our prize. "You didn't have to come."

"And miss all the fun?" He laughed.

"So this is fun for you?"

"This? Right now? Strolling through a moonlit foreign paradise with a beautiful girl by my side? No. Of course not. Horrific."

"There's no moon." I ignored *beautiful*.

We walked.

We finally navigated our way back to Karlova, and followed it to the bridge. It was surreal to see the broad boulevard empty of its shoulder-to-shoulder tourist hordes. The entrance to the Karlův most was equally bare, watched over only by a bleary-eyed beggar curled up in a tattered black quilt, and by the Old Town Bridge Tower, which, I remembered, had once been festooned with twelve severed heads, their dead heretic eyes scanning the city. The choppy water reflected nothing.

"Why are you here, Eli?" Wind raked across the bridge, and I tried not to shiver, worried about evoking chivalrous gestures. I didn't need his jacket, or his arms.

"Because you gave no indication that you were going to let me go back to sleep?"

270

"No. I mean here, in Prague. You didn't know Chris. You aren't a suspect. No one's after you—not the cops, not the *Hledači*. You don't have to be a part of this. So why are you?"

"It's my job to protect you, remember? From—what did Janika call it? The darkness at the heart of the city. Maybe that's why I'm here."

"You don't even know me," I said. "So that seems unlikely."

"Maybe you make a strong first impression."

I could feel my cheeks getting warm and was grateful for the darkness. "That just proves you *really* don't know me. Try again."

"Another reason?"

"Maybe this time one you don't make up on the spot," I said. "A real reason."

"As you point out, I don't know you. So what makes you think I owe you anything real?"

I couldn't argue. At least under that theory, I owed him nothing in return.

Stone saints lined the bridge, silhouettes of black nothingness against the night. Out of the corner of my eye, a movement, a flutter of black on black. I sucked in my breath.

But it was just a pigeon, startled from its roost.

"Fine," Eli said. "Truth?"

"You tell me."

"You're right." He ran a hand along the stone parapet that kept us from the water, pausing to rest his palm against one of the saints. "Chris was nobody to me. I'd probably be back in my dorm doing a problem set right now if my parents hadn't forced me to come to Chapman. But once I got there . . ."

"What?"

"I know what it's like to get sucked into something you shouldn't be a part of," he said quietly. "When all you want is

271

for them to leave you alone, let you live a normal life, and they *Just. Won't. Stop.* That's all Chris was trying to do. Be normal. And look what happened to him. Now it's happening to you. It's not fair."

I wasn't sure whether to envy him or hate him for being so naive. As if *fair* meant anything. Life did whatever it wanted to, and usually it wanted to crap all over you. But if he didn't already know, let him enjoy the fantasy.

"Your life's not normal?" I said, suddenly realizing how little I knew about him—how little I'd bothered to ask. He was a freshman at some small school in Maryland, he knew three languages and counting, he had whimsical taste in boxer shorts, and . . . and that was about it.

"Parents obsessed with a lost golden age," he reminded me, "doing everything they can to mold me into the embodiment of dead traditions, insisting on speaking Czech, cooking Czech, papering every damn surface of the house with pictures of 'the beloved homeland,' drilling me every night on what to do when—" He stopped abruptly, then laughed. "Well, there's some other stuff. It doesn't matter. Let's just say it's not a recipe for normalcy. Not when I was a kid. And definitely not now."

"I'm sorry."

"I'm not lobbying for a pity vote. You wanted to know, so now you know. Maybe there is no good reason. Maybe I'm just in this because I'm in it. Leave it at that."

I shrugged. The dots didn't quite connect, but he was right: He didn't owe me that.

"I could tell you about him," I said.

"Who?"

"Chris. If you want, I mean."

"Oh." He stopped walking, suddenly, like he couldn't ponder the question and operate his legs at the same time.

272

"Or not." Stupid to even offer, I realized. He'd said it himself: Chris was nobody to him. I leaned over the ledge, peering down at the water, up at the clouds, out at the city and its hulking towers, anywhere but at him.

"That would be good," he said, leaning beside me. Our shoulders touched. "If you want."

I told him about Chris's first basketball championship, and how he'd shown up beneath my window at two a.m., face flushed from hours of liquid celebrating, too drunk to remember that he wasn't supposed to come to my house, that no one was, and challenged me to a game of one-on-one in my driveway, where a rusting hoop had stood unused for the last five years. I told him about Chris and Adriane's first official date, the disastrous movie where she, exhausted from that afternoon's class-council kayak trip, had nearly fallen asleep and he, fighting off the stomach flu that would keep him out of school for the next week, had finally raised the white flag and thrown up on her favorite pair of strappy heels. I relayed, with only a few false starts, Chris's favorite dirty joke, the one about the bartender, the monkeys, and their golf balls. I confessed how, despite Adriane's pestering, it had been Chris who made me and Max possible. After *our* official first date—less disastrous than it was awkward and off-key, full of fumbling and stilted questions and a botched, nose-bruising sequel to our first kiss—it was Chris who promised I had not humiliated myself and I had not made a mistake, Chris who said I deserved better than being alone, and Max was almost good enough to deserve me.

Eli was a stranger, but I told him everything. I couldn't stop talking, not until I made him understand the way that Chris's eyebrows crinkled, asymmetrically, when he waited for the punch line to a joke, and the difference between his smiles, happy, surprised, excited, sorry, in love, because they were each distinct, and each as easily readable as any of the expressions to pass across

273

Chris's open face. Usually, I had to brace myself before even saying his name, but not this time. This was easy. I told Eli how Chris hated fresh broccoli but liked it cooked, and how he thought he could wiggle his ears despite all evidence to the contrary, and we let him believe it. He liked romantic comedies, I told Eli, but only the ones where the gawky girl gets her guy or the jock discovers his inner geek, and only when he was alone with no chance of being caught in the viewing act. He liked the Knicks, the Eagles, the Red Sox, and, on principle, not a single hockey team because he felt that wasn't an acceptable sport.

As long as I kept talking, Chris would be real.

So I described, in vivid detail, the expression on our calculus substitute's face when Chris and Adriane started making out—*after* they had convinced the poor woman (with the help of the entire class) that they were half brother and half sister. But eventually I ran out of words, and he was gone again.

Only when I stopped talking did I realize Eli's hand rested on top of mine.

I pulled mine away.

We started walking again. "So. Incest in calculus," he said. There was a new awkwardness between us. "Impressive."

"I didn't think it would work. Adriane's got *only child* written all over her."

"It's a funny coincidence, don't you think? How you're all only children? You think there's some deep subconscious psychological magnetism going on there, like a post-Jungian quest for familial connection?"

I didn't answer.

"Aren't you going to at least pretend to be impressed by my Psych I psychobabble?" he said.

I don't know why this time, of all times, I said it. "I'm not an only child. I mean. I wasn't." I walked faster, staying a step ahead of him, eyes straight ahead. "Didn't used to be."

A pause. "Brother or sister?"

"Brother. Older." I swallowed. "Andy."

I waited.

Eli didn't say anything.

Finally, impatient, I forced myself to face him. His fists were clenched as tight as his jaw.

"Now is when you traditionally say something like 'I'm sorry.'"

"Your older brother died?" He sounded weird. Freaked out, maybe, but I'd logged my time getting gawked at and whispered about and stared at helplessly by people who couldn't wrap their minds around the capriciousness of the mortal coil. I was an expert in freaked out, and this was something different. Something almost like . . . fear.

"Yeah. Died. A while ago. Forget I said anything."

"No, I mean, I'm sorry—I *am* sorry—you just surprised me. That's all. Do you want to . . . talk about it?"

Not anymore.

"How about we not talk for a while," I said.

He didn't argue, and this time he was the one to speed up, his lanky legs eating up cobblestone so that I nearly had to jog to keep up. Within a few painfully silent minutes, we were back at the Golden Lion.

Max was pacing outside, furious. Adriane was sitting on the ground, slumped against the wall, chin on her chest, sound asleep. "Where the hell have you been? Are you okay?"

"Of course I'm okay." I put my arms around him. He was stiff and tense in the embrace, and after a moment, I let go. "I'm sorry if you were worried."

"'Worried'? '*Worried*'!"

"Don't shout."

"You wander off in the middle of the night—with *him*—no note, no explanation, no way of finding you, and you're sorry if I was 'worried'?"

"You left first," I said.

At those words, Adriane, not asleep after all, raised her head. "I'm glad you're okay," she said, in a thick voice. As soon as the light caught her face, I could tell she'd been crying. Which reminded me of *why* Max had left without me.

I didn't know what it must have taken for Adriane to break. To drop the act and finally admit to whatever was roiling beneath her surface, to feel so alone and broken in the dark that she'd come to me—because I had promised her, on a train through the night, that when she did, I would be waiting.

But I wasn't.

And when I found the note, I hadn't thought of her—or searched for her, or waited for her to return. I'd run off with Eli, as if this whole nightmarish scavenger hunt really *were* a game, a contest between us. Or, more to the point, as if it were *mine*—my problem to fix, my puzzle to solve, my cross, as it were, to bear. Not because I was special, or in any more danger than Max and Adriane—or in any more pain. But because I could translate *a coelo usque ad centrum* the fastest.

This wasn't just mine, I thought, and resolved that this time, I wouldn't forget. Chris had belonged to all of us. And if a person couldn't be split, if a person could only be wholly owned, then, in the end, Chris had belonged to her.

"Are you okay?" I asked Adriane.

She stood up. "I'm going to bed."

"Adriane—"

"Thanks, Max," she said, a softness in her voice I hadn't heard in a long time, then turned away from me and went inside.

"You going to tell me where you went?" Max asked, looking at Eli. "And why you dragged her along?"

"You think *I* dragged *her*? Nora, you want to tell him—"

"Is she really okay?" I said. Eli shook his head, then, disgust plain on his face, left us alone.

"She's fine," Max said, and some of the anger leached out of his voice. "She just needed to talk. So we talked."

"Why didn't you wake me up?"

"I thought you needed the sleep."

"You know me better than that."

Max hesitated. "If you want to know the truth . . ."

I waited.

"She didn't want me to wake you."

"Oh."

"I mean, I think when she got to our room, she panicked. Half of her wanted someone to talk to, but half of her didn't, and you being asleep left her off the hook. She's scared, Nora. More scared than she looks."

"Of talking?"

"Of everything."

"But she talked to you," I said.

"I couldn't stop her from leaving the hostel. But she couldn't stop me from going with her. So I followed her—and I didn't wake you then because there wasn't time."

"She talked to you," I repeated, knowing jealousy was an inappropriate response. Not sure whom I was jealous of.

"Maybe it was easier. I was there, that night. . . ."

It was the thing the two of them would always share, the thing that I would never be a part of—except that I had been there that night, too.

But I had been there alone.

"She's okay now?" I said.

He nodded. "She just needed to talk about Chris, I think. To hear his name. Then she calmed down—until we got back here, and you were gone." The anger surged back into his voice. Apparently our temporary cease-fire was over. "She freaked out all over again. Maybe this is too much for her—for you, too. Maybe I was wrong, and you should both go back."

"Adriane is a grown-up," I said. "And so am I. We can choose for ourselves. We're staying."

"Someone was following us," he said flatly. "Adriane didn't see him, and I didn't want to worry her. But it was one of them, the *Hledači*—I recognized him from before. And I think I saw a knife."

Every muscle in my body clenched. I wanted to touch him, to reassure myself he was whole. I couldn't. But he saw my face and understood.

"Nothing happened," Max said. "I promise. And I managed to lose him—but when we got back, and you weren't here, I thought . . ."

I put my arms around him. His skin was cold. I wondered how long he'd been standing outside, waiting for me to appear. Worrying that I never would.

"I'm so sorry," I said, holding on. "I know—" How it felt, to wait. To wonder. "I'm sorry. I should have left a note."

"You shouldn't have left at all. You should have stayed here, where it's safe."

I don't know who let go first, but we were apart again. "Well, I didn't. And maybe it's a good thing, because"—I drew Elizabeth's letter and the leather pouch out of my pocket; they didn't belong to me, either—"I have something to show you."

30

E. J. Weston, to my foolish brother.

The Jews drink the blood of children. Or so our Mother told us when, as children, we wandered too close to the gates, spying on men who spoke in foreign tongues, draped themselves in foreign clothes, and thirsted for our lifeblood, to be heated in a pot with the foul soups and stews they prepared for their foreign holidays. Our Father promised us we had nothing to fear from these men who worshipped a God that was our God and yet not. Our cousins, he called them, and we pretended to believe it.

Once he got his hands on Elizabeth's latest treasure, Max was a lot more forgiving of our little midnight adventure. He tied a length of cord around the small leather pouch and strung it around his neck, for safekeeping.

I kept the letter.

This translation took me less time than the last—Elizabeth's language was becoming my own, her strange configurations and exotic word choices seeming more familiar with each page I copied into my worn notebook. But it wasn't until past noon the next day that I was ready to share the results.

Our Mother told us of the golem, that soulless creature of night who rambled the quarter and did its master's dark bidding, and that we did believe, and molded our own men from the soft clay of the Vltava banks, urging them to smash, to consume, to destroy. Stories to frighten a child into sleep,

*and yet, when Groot sent me behind the walls in search of the
golem, I believed I would find it. Or it would find me.*

*I confided my destination in Thomas. No, as this is to be
the full record of my transgressions, I will admit here that I
confided all in Thomas, while we stood alone in the laboratory,
our faces illuminated by candlelight. He had labored over
our Father's alchemical formula for two weeks, working from
the first timid light of the moon to the sun's bold return,
and I remained by his side, sleeping only in those brief hours
before the burdens of daylight called me back to life. Our
attentions were directed only to our work, to the delicate
sublimation, dissolution, putrefaction, and distillation, and the
bubbling fluids that resulted, as if by magic, from his tender
ministrations. Until the last night, we spoke of nothing but
the elements and their mixtures, and I stayed silent as Thomas
spun me tales of alchemical greatness, the magi who plundered
the secrets of nature and drew themselves, elixir by elixir,
nearer to God.*

*That last night, I could take it no longer, and confessed to
him the role of this formula we labored over. I confessed to him
that he had, unknowingly, joined us in pursuit of the greatest
glory of all.* Lumen Dei, *the very words were on his lips when
the chemical marriage bore fruit, and our elixir was born, as
if the knowledge of our destination, and his desperate desire to
reach it, had borne us there.*

*Once a secret is told, there is no untelling, brother. There
is no unknowing, a sad truth you will soon understand. And
so Thomas joined me, and I was no longer alone.*

Groot, for reasons he refused to share, was not allowed

within the walls of the Jewish quarter, but he arranged for
my entrance, and offered his servant as accompaniment.
Václav frightened me no less than he had at first sight, and I
would rather have taken the golem. Instead, I took Thomas.
Groot secured us an interview with the great Rabbi, but there
were certain circumstances, he confided, that could not be
avoided.

When the first three stars appeared in the sky, I met
Thomas behind the Church of St. Nicholas. He laughed to see
me. I fear that in response, I blushed.

He shook his head.

—Maybe you should let me go alone, because this will
never succeed.

—Do I look so terrible?

I touched the hat perched precariously on my head, unruly
curls tucked beneath. The breeches were stiff and coarse on my
legs. Father's tunic, too large for me by half, still smelled of him.

—You look beautiful.

And now he blushed in return.

—Too beautiful for this task, I mean. No one with eyes
would believe you were a boy.

—No one with eyes would believe I am beautiful, but I
seem to have you fooled.

She gave herself to him so easily, I thought. A few compliments, a few candlelit conversations, and she was ready to give
everything away. Was she that lonely, I wondered, that desperate
to find someone who would treat her as an equal, listen to her secrets, fill the hole her brother had left behind? Or was she simply,
even without realizing it yet, in love?

Needy or happy? There had to be a difference.

The Rabbi would not speak to a girl, and so I did what needed to be done. We ventured past the gate, shoulder to shoulder, two young men, one sandy-haired with dancing eyes and a crooked smile, one bunched into a large tunic and foolish hat, scrawny of body and delicate of face, and possibly, for the first time since his carefree youth, beautiful.

A song wafted on the air, foreign and intoxicating, and the dark houses watched suspiciously as we passed, as if even the stones knew we did not belong. The temple was low and dark, its earthy walls cool to the touch, nothing like the churches of our childhood, with their golden edges and seas of rainbow glass.

The Rabbi awaited us inside. He stood on the altar at the fore of the chamber and bade us remain in the entranceway. He spoke a smooth German, without the accent of a Jew.

—I have granted this meeting at the behest of a trusted friend. But if I am to grant more, you will have to be persuasive.

I dropped to my knees.

—I come to you in the name of Edward Kelley, the name of Cornelius Groot, and the name of the Emperor. We request a handful of the sacred earth you have endowed with the gift of life.

—Rise, child. Here we kneel only to the Lord.

His voice brushed my face like the softest of feathers. I climbed to my feet.

—Only God can grant the gift of life. I am but a conduit for His grace. Creating brings me closer to the Creator, and

from that union, a miracle emerged. A gift given to my people.
Why should I share it with you?

—Not with me, sir. With the Emperor.

—You speak for the Emperor?

His eyes pierced my disguise, pierced my skin and bones,
and arrowed straight into my soul. I could not lie.

—I speak for the nobility of knowledge and the pursuit of
grace. A pursuit in which the Emperor will be honored to join,
when the time is right.

I did not know from where the words had come.

—The Emperor has done much for my people. You,
however, have done nothing. Yet.

He proposed a trade. In return for what we sought, a
certain golden goblet the Emperor was known to have in his
Kunstkammer, *which was said to have belonged to Joseph,*
of the Twelve Tribes, which was priceless and would result in
certain death for any person caught attempting to spirit it away.

The word *Kunstkammer* was written in German. *Cabinet of*
wonder. Everyone who was anyone had them back then, Max explained, a *Kunstkammer* crammed with paintings and plant samples and unicorn horns. Collecting was in. But apparently this
particular emperor took things to the extreme, his palace a veri-
table hoarder's nest, except in his case the tilting stacks of bottle
caps, magazines, and empty toilet-paper tubes were generally encrusted with rubies.

—Surely you can explain to the Emperor that this will be a
small price to pay.

Again, I felt speared by his gaze, but what was I to tell
him? That the Emperor had murdered my Father and stolen

his land, that while my Father commanded me to offer him this, the greatest gift, I would have preferred a different gift, one that would be his last? Was I to return to Groot a failure, and turn our Father's dream to dust? I could only nod and promise the goblet upon my return.

As Thomas and I crossed the Stone Bridge back to Malá Strana, he despaired.

—There is no way into the Kunstkammer. Even the Emperor's closest counselors have no access without his permission.

—There is a way.

Though the thought of it made me ill.

I did not tell him what I planned to do until the next morning, when the deed was done. I am tempted not to tell you, either, as I know your feelings about Don Giulio, and you know I share them, but believe me when I say there was little choice. And you know Don Giulio has long been willing to do me any favor I like. I will admit my heart once softened for him, but no longer. When he was a child, peeping into ladies' bedchambers, roasting squirrels in the sun, their fur matted with blood from the stick he jabbed into their sides, leaving me gifts of dead birds in gilded boxes, excuses could be made. His mother a servant, his father an Emperor, his identity a truth universally known and yet never to be spoken, it cannot have been an easy life. But he is older now, and though two years my junior, he towers over me. He scares the women of the court with the way he watches them, and there are those who say he does more than watch. His hands are meaty and his breath heavy with onion and fish.

Yet his grandfather still has charge of the **Kunstkammer**.
Help me once more, I asked Don Giulio, like when we were
children. We did not acknowledge the distinction between
now and then, the absence of a brother to protect me from his
roaming hands, but some truths do not need speaking.

Hradčany is different now. Rudolf has made it a city unto
itself, and everywhere are men hoisting stones and carving
sculptures, erecting one monument after another to the
Hapsburg reign. It is well known that the Emperor prefers
to stay indoors whenever possible, and he has constructed
the palace around this mania for hiding, with more secluded
corridors and secret passageways than we could have dreamed
of as children. Don Giulio wrapped a thick, wet hand around
mine as he guided us to the secret heart of the palace, Thomas
following a few steps behind, his presence only barely tolerated
by the mad prince, and only because I had lowered myself to beg.

The **Kunstkammer** *now resides in a long corridor that*
connects the Emperor's living quarters to the Spanish Hall.
Myriad images of Rudolf in vibrant colors of oil peered down
at us from the walls and ceiling. We passed paintings of
Bohemian countrysides and Spanish ports, mountains and
deserts and bowls of fruit, but it is the many faces of the
Emperor that I cannot stop seeing, his sloped eyebrows, his
black beard, the jowls that hang over his ruff, as pink and
fleshy as any pig. His collections have swollen since our
adventures years ago, and Don Giulio swept us past cabinets
that held clocks, leather-bound tomes of Agrippa, Boethius,
Dee, Croll, Paracelsus, Porta, even our disgraced Father, the
jaw of a siren, the horn of a unicorn, statues of the Greek gods

performing their obscene gyrations, crocodile skulls, pitchers
of silver and jasper and gold, coins from the four corners of
the world, bowls of shell, cups of jade, scepters encrusted with
rubies, two-headed fish, a waxen creature with the body of
a horse and the head of a lion, astrolabes, orreries, armillary
spheres, enough musical instruments to deafen the world with
song, two nails of Noah's Ark, and a chest of knives. At this
last, Don Giulio paused, fondling the blades of his father's
collection as if visiting old and dear friends: This one had
killed Caesar; that one had slain a Turkish prince; another,
his favorite, Don Giulio claimed a peasant had swallowed
and carried in his stomach for nine years. This was the knife
he was caressing, blade whispering against his neck, when a
distant door creaked open, and we heard the terrifying footfalls
approach.

   —Here!

   Don Giulio and I squeezed between two cabinets, while
Thomas wedged himself into a similar crevice on the opposite
wall. The Emperor approached. Don Giulio's breath warmed
my neck. A hand clapped over my mouth. Stubby fingers
stole down my back. Our bodies were too close, and with the
Emperor so near, I could hardly scream. Cold metal chilled my
face. It was Don Giulio, who still wielded his knife. I could do
nothing but let him play spider across my tingling flesh, while
I swallowed my bile and the Emperor himself strolled past. I
cannot speak, even to you, of what his hands did with their
dark freedom.

   When the hall grew quiet, we emerged, and before I could
stay my hand, it flew to Don Giulio's cheek, raking thin red

lines across his pitted flesh. Thomas flew at him, but I stopped him with a word: remember. Don Giulio could call the Emperor back, or drag us to his father's feet and name us as thieves, for that we were.

I tell you now, my brother, there are things I would have refused, had the bastard son dared ask, just as I tell myself, in the cradle of night, that I would have refused Don Giulio his desires even if it meant relinquishing the Lumen Dei. But for reasons I cannot fathom, he did not demand, and so I will never know what I might have done.

He gave me the goblet, his fingers brushing mine, his lips twitching like one of his frightened squirrels.

—No one can see us together. These stairs lead to the Bishop's Tower. Wait there, until one bell has passed, then leave. We will meet again, my Elizabeth.

He was gone before I could tell him I belonged to no one, least of all him.

We waited atop the tower past the first bell, and past the second. I willed my hands to stop trembling, but they did so only when Thomas wrapped them in his and told me I was brave. The stars were bright, and I showed him Cassiopeia and Andromeda and told him of the Copernicans, who believed the earth moved beneath our feet. He told me of his mother and sister, who had died together, plague racking one body and then another, less than a week passing from first boil to fresh grave.

I will not tell you where our words went then, or how we passed the seconds of still, cool night, until there was no choice but to descend, or lose ourselves.

With that one goblet, or even a single one of the emeralds that encrusted its golden base, I could have changed our family's destiny. Would there have been any greater sin in stealing the Emperor's riches for myself than in stealing them for a holy man? Perhaps not. But the greatest sin of all would be to deny our Father his final wish, and perhaps, if Groot spoke true, to deny mankind its greatest discovery. And so I tucked my hair into its cap, bound my chest, slipped into my borrowed breeches, and returned to that strange sacred space.

We were, on arrival, commanded to approach the altar, where the Rabbi handled the stolen goblet, a wild gleam in his eyes. Into my waiting hands he dropped a small leather pouch, the very pouch you, my brother, now behold, containing within it a pocket of earth that had been blessed by God, dirt and dust and clay that had once walked as a man.

When the Rabbi turned his gaze to me, I was no longer afraid.

He bared his teeth.

—Next time you visit our quarter, I suggest you wear your lovely hair down. A lady need not cover her head before marriage.

His eyes had seen all. But I found myself unafraid. We were united in our common fate, both thieves, both pilgrims, both servants of what I believe to be the same Lord.

I slept soundly that night, dearest brother, believing the most difficult of hurdles had been overcome. Two days hence, Groot had determined, I was to depart with Thomas on a journey into Austrian lands, where we hoped the astronomer Kepler would supply the final piece of our fiendish puzzle.

We had water and earth, soon we would have fire, and Groot himself was toiling day and night on his own contribution, air, the delicate, whirring machinery that would set the device in wondrous motion. It tempts me to end here, in comfort and hope, as it would be easier than recalling for you what happened that night, in the dark before the dawn, when an apparition appeared before my bed, one that I would prefer to remember as a nightmare but that I know was only too real. As was the blade it held to my throat.

It was a man, and in the shadows he seemed to bear Don Giulio's face, but this was an illusion borne of a dream. It was a stranger, his face hooded by a priestly robe. A man of God, yet what man of God would penetrate the chamber of a lady and hold a knife to her throat?

—To have faith in God is to have faith in the Church. To know God is to know Him through the Church. Your heresy will end. Now.

I know not how I gained the courage to speak, but I was no longer the girl I had been before this journey began, and his was not the first blade to have kissed my throat.

—How is it heresy to seek answers about God?

—Those answers you need have been supplied to you. Your Lord has commanded you to have faith in Him and faith in His Church. You show your strength by ceding your individual concerns to His institution. You show only weakness and avarice by questing for more.

—If the Lord wants to stop me, let Him.

—My child, who do you think sent me?

His voice was almost kind.

—I am giving you an opportunity many feel you should be denied. Turn back. Repent. For if I am forced to return, I will not wake you before I do what needs to be done.

"It must be the warning," Adriane said suddenly. "Remember the letter we found in the library, the one about how they were going to warn Elizabeth to stop whatever she was doing?"

I did—and I remembered that whoever wrote the letter had wanted to do a lot more than warn.

At his command, I closed my eyes. When I opened them again, he was gone. And in the morning, sunshine warming my face and the promise of a journey awaiting me, can I be blamed for dismissing the warning as I would any other imagined creature of the night? Our task was noble, our questions just, and the Church merely clinging to power as changes loomed. The priests had proved themselves terrified by the Lutherans, who insisted on reading their own Bibles in their own vernacular and forging their own relationship with a God who had once been the sole province of the Church's holy men. Was it any wonder that the Lumen Dei *would fill them with fear? What need of the Church and its priesthood had we, when God Himself would soon be whispering in our ears?*

It was curiosity that propelled me, brother, and dedication to our Father. But it was also hubris. Warnings are easier to ignore than follow, as you well know, for by reading this you have ignored so many of mine. And so we continued. And so shall you.

11 November 1600.

31

"The *Fidei Defensor*," I said, pacing the cramped room. "It has to be." I'd worked on the translation straight through till dawn, and past it, while Max lay in bed pretending to sleep. I needed to know what had happened. Why, if she was so in love with Thomas, she had married another man. Who was secretly watching her, and how she had escaped from all the men who came for her with knives. I even, though I would admit it only to myself, wanted to know about the *Lumen Dei*. The machine was a joke, a story, but Elizabeth had believed in it—was terrified and, I suspected, tempted by it—and *something* had happened that convinced her the machine was too dangerous to exist and perhaps too dangerous to destroy. I accused her of trusting too easily, but for whatever reason, I trusted her. I wanted to know if I should.

She had laid this trail for her brother, but I couldn't help feeling that it had also been laid for me.

"We don't know that it was the *Fidei Defensor*," Eli said. "For all we know, the only connections between them and the *Lumen Dei* are a crazy old lady and a dead language."

"But remember how the letter ended?" said Adriane, who remembered everything. "'Yours in eternal fealty and *defense of the faith*.' No way is that a coincidence."

"No, I bet you're right," Max said. We had filled him and Adriane in on Janika's cryptic warnings and the potential existence of a new player in this surreal game. "That's what fundamentalists do, right? Slit your throat as soon as you start asking the wrong questions."

"Fundamentalism has nothing to do with what the *Fidei* were about," Eli said.

"A fundamentalist is someone who wants to substitute what

he believes for what you believe," Max said. "And someone who thinks he knows the will of God better than anyone else. If the cassock fits . . ."

Adriane cleared her throat. "Before you two reenact the Clash of Civilizations, maybe someone can tell me what this means?" She tapped the strange word, written in letters three lines high, at the bottom of the page. Her usually perfect nails were ragged, the manicured red paint scratched and peeled, so on first glance it appeared her cuticles were oozing blood. "It's not Greek."

אתבש

"It's Hebrew." That much I could tell from those long-ago sleepy holiday mornings at my grandmother's synagogue, but no more. Several lines followed the word:

GSV ULIVRTMVI SLOWH GSV PVB.
NZHGVI LU GSV HGZIH, SRH GIRFNKS
DROO GLDVI LEVI GSV VNKRIV.

URMW SRN RM GSV KOZXV GSZG
UVVOH ORPV SLNV.

DSVIV DV SZEV MVEVI YVVM
GLTVGSVI, YFG DSVN R ZN GSVIV, BLF
ZIV DRGS NV.

It had to be another code, and אתבש was the key.

"Atbash," Max said.

"Gesundheit." Adriane smiled.

Max didn't. "Atbash," he said again. "That's what it says."

"*You* read Hebrew?" I asked. "You're a Methodist."

"Episcopalian, actually. But I told you my parents were religious. Hebrew was the first language of God, so . . ."

"So you know Hebrew because of *God*?" Adriane said. I caught her eyeing the exit.

"When you move around a lot, it makes sense that going to church would be the only thing that feels like home," I said quickly. "It's not like he still wants to be a priest or something."

Eli raised his eyebrows. " 'Still'?"

Max didn't have to say anything. I could tell, from his wounded expression, that I'd done wrong. Again.

"No one told me we had a man of God among us," Eli said. "Potential MOG, at least. What changed your mind?"

"Leave him alone," I said.

Max cleared his throat. "You can stop answering for me," he said.

"I was just trying to help—"

"Please, don't." It was the *please* that hurt. So polite, like I was anybody. Nobody. "Nothing changed my mind. I was a kid, and then I grew up. Figured out that the world doesn't need more people to just sit around and pray."

"Ah, so you decided you were going to change the world. *Save* the world." I didn't know why Eli kept pushing.

"So what if I did?"

"Totally explains why you're majoring in . . . history. Am I to assume this world-changing plan of yours includes a time machine?"

"Shut up, Eli," Adriane said. "You're being a dick."

I noticed Max didn't tell *her* to stop helping.

"No, I want to know. What does our resident holy man think of our current endeavor? You don't think your God might have a problem with you tracking down his private number?"

Max had to know Eli was mocking him. I suspected he didn't care. Unlike almost every other guy I knew, he'd never been afraid of his own sincerity, no matter how ridiculous it occasionally made him look.

"I think the *Lumen Dei*, if it existed, would be a miracle," Max said. "War. Hunger. Poverty. You could end them all."

"If God had that kind of power, you'd think he would have gotten around to doing that himself," Adriane said.

"It's not just about the power. It's the *knowledge*. The ultimate answer. Think about it: If you could prove, once and for all, that God existed? If every single person on earth knew exactly where they stood, and what their lives were for? You want to know why I could never be a priest? The real reason?" he said, turning back to Eli. "Faith." He made the word sound pornographic. "If something is true, you shouldn't have to *believe* in it. You should be able to *know*."

There was an odd tension in the room. Adriane laughed nervously. "All I know," she said, "is that if we actually manage to find this thing, or build it, or whatever, we can keep ourselves from going to prison, and, bonus, hopefully stop the crazies from murdering us in our sleep. Not to mention how much we could make off of selling it. It's like *Antiques Roadshow* on steroids."

I gave her a pity laugh. The boys ignored her. "Some might say this is exactly what's wrong with something like the *Lumen Dei*," Eli said. "Because people are idiots."

"She's not an idiot," Max said.

"Chivalrous. But I was referring to *you*. Selling it to the highest bidder is bad enough, but you want to talk disaster? Hand over power like that to some lunatic with a God complex who's determined to create heaven on earth. After all the millions of people who've been killed in the name of God, you want to—"

"Killed because they were *fighting* about God," Max said. "They fight because they have to resort to faith. If there were one truth, one single answer, there'd be no more fighting."

"Some people would call you dangerously naive," Eli said. "And would point out that knowledge can be dangerous."

"So's ignorance," I said. "It's always better to know than not know."

"Pollution," he shot back. "Gunpowder. Nuclear weapons. Knowing isn't all it's cracked up to be. And just because you know how to build something doesn't mean it should be built. Ever heard of the tree of knowledge? The apple? Some people would say the fact that we're too stupid to learn from our mistakes is just proof that we're too stupid not to make another one. And this would be a big one."

"So because we're not perfect, we should all go back to living in caves?" I said, incredulous. "You think that'd be better?"

"We'd be naked," Adriane pointed out. "If you've ever been to a nude beach, you would know it's definitely *not* better."

"You think there wasn't war before there were bombs and guns?" I asked him. "Like cavemen didn't bash each other's heads in with giant rocks."

"Some people might say killing people with rocks is significantly less efficient," Eli pointed out. "It's hard to wipe out a species one head bashing at a time."

"Some people," I said. "Right. What about *you*? What do you think?"

He shrugged. "Who cares what I think?"

"Excellent point," Adriane said, waving the letter and its mysterious cipher at us. "How about we get back to something that actually matters."

"I care," I said. If Max had to expose himself, let Eli do it, too.

He hesitated. "I think you can't argue with history," he said finally. "And I think that if God wanted us to know him, he would show himself. I think faith has an inherent value. There's power in belief—in *choosing* to believe."

Adriane blew a sharp *pfft* through her teeth. "And if God wanted us to fly, he would have given us wings, right? Which makes us all sinners for using airplanes and air conditioners and microwaves and all the other crap God forgot to make himself—oh, and sorry, ugly girls, no makeup, because clearly God doesn't want you to be pretty."

"She has a point," Max said. "For all you know, God *does* want us to know him, but only when we prove we're worthy by figuring out how to do it. Maybe the *Lumen Dei* is that proof."

I snorted.

I didn't mean to, but there it was. Presumably Max thought I was laughing at him, and maybe I was, because I was laughing at all of it, at the machine, at the argument, and most of all at God—at *his* God, he'd made that clear. Maybe I deserved the look he gave me.

"Something to share with the rest of the class?" Eli asked.

I shook my head and rested a hand on Max's shoulder. *I'm sorry*, it meant. It used to be, we understood each other perfectly without talking, and when we did talk, we talked about everything. We understood that, too. Now, it seemed, we didn't talk: We apologized.

"Say it," Max said, rigid beneath my touch.

Fine.

"It's irrelevant, all of this," I said. Though they weren't the ones I needed to convince. "The *Lumen Dei*, even if we manage to track down all the pieces and put it together, is just a very old piece of junk. You can't get definite proof of something that doesn't exist."

"'Something'—that would be God, I take it?" Eli asked.

"That would be God. And you know what? If there *is* a God, and it's that same God who's so eager to have temples built in honor of his greatness, and wars fought over him, and people dropping to their knees telling him what a wonderful, magnificent being he is? If this all-powerful, all-knowing creature for some reason just can't get by without *my* worship? Then let him give me some proof. Or at least get over himself if I decide to go out and get some. You think there's a reason people need faith? Like there's a reason for anything else that happens? Right. Is there a reason Chris needed to die? Or that—" I swallowed it. "Or all the other crap your God pulls? He wants me to worship him, let him explain himself. Let him answer for what he's done. Let him explain to me what's so great about the world and why I should be *so* grateful for my wonderful, magnificent life."

Adriane pulled a wad of tissue out of her pocket and held it out to me.

"What?" I said.

"You're crying."

"No, I'm not." But I wiped my eyes, and they were wet.

I didn't take the tissue.

"Atbash. Hebrew. Great. So how does that help us?" My voice cracked, but they were polite enough to ignore it.

"It's an ancient biblical substitution code," Max said, ignoring it best of all. He scavenged a pen and a blank piece of paper. "You just substitute the first letter for the last letter, and the second for the second to last, et cetera. So *aleph* for *tav*, *bet* for *shin*—in English, you'd sub in *A* for *Z*, *B* for *Y*, you get the idea. Simple."

I hunched over the page, swapping out the letters, piecing together the real message, taking longer than I needed. The silence was a relief.

> GSV ULIVRTMVI SLOWH GSV PVB.
> NZHGVI LU GSV HGZIH, SRH GIRFNKS
> DROO GLDVI LEVI GSV VNKRIV.
>
> URMW SRN RM GSV KOZXV GSZG
> UVVOH ORPV SLNV.
>
> DSVIV DV SZEV MVEVI YVVM
> GLTVGSVI, YFG DSVM R ZN GSVIV, BLF
> ZIV DRGS NV.

Finally, in English once again:
The foreigner holds the key. Master of the stars, his triumph will

*tower over the Empire. Find him in the place that feels like home. Where
we have never been together, but when I am there, you are with me.*

"Poetic," Adriane said.

"And obvious." Max leapt to his feet. "The astronomical clock
on the Old Town Hall tower. The Orloj. You know the little mechanical figures that dance when it chimes the hour? One of them
is a Turk. *The foreigner holds the key*. That *has* to be it."

"I don't know," I said. Something felt off. "She says she and
her brother have never been there together—but they grew up in
Prague. So what are the odds of that?"

"You have a better idea?"

I shook my head.

Eli sighed. "Guess I should put my Spider-Man costume
back on."

"You know what?" said Max. "You two didn't sleep at all last
night—why don't you stay here. Adriane and I can handle this."

She raised her eyebrows. "We can?"

"Yeah. We can. Nora can stay here and rest. With him." He
said it like I should be grateful, but it felt like penance.

"He's fine with that," Eli said.

"This is ridiculous," I said. "We should stay together."

"Why?" Max asked.

So I let them go.

32

They'd been gone an hour when Eli pounded on my door. I ignored it and redoubled my fruitless efforts to sleep.

"I need to show you something!" he shouted.

I let him keep at it for another minute or two before finally
opening the door. "Go away."

"Put your shoes on. I need to show you something."

"Pass."

"So when you show up at my door in the middle of the night, I'm supposed to go with you, no questions asked, but you can't come downstairs with me for five minutes, in the middle of the afternoon?"

In the deserted lobby, he showed me the Wikipedia page for the astronomical clock, highlighting the crucial line: "The Orloj suffered heavy damage on May 7 and especially May 8, 1945. . . . The hall and nearby buildings burned along with the wooden sculptures on the Orloj and the calendar dial face." The clock now hanging in Old Town Square was almost a complete reconstruction of the original.

"So that's the end of it," I said. My stomach was doing strange, fluttery things. Relief, fear, these would have been reasonable reactions, but this wasn't either. I felt like Elizabeth had let us down. Or vice versa. "Whatever she hid there, it's long gone."

"Except you don't think she hid anything there," Eli said. "And neither do I."

"You heard Max. What else could it be?"

"Unlike Max, I also hear *you*," he said. "The clock doesn't fit. And I've been thinking: *master of the stars*. It could be a foreign astronomer, right? And in the last letter she was about to set out on a pilgrimage to see—"

"Kepler!" we said together.

"You see?" he said. "It's perfect."

"Yeah. I see."

"So why aren't we smiling? Tell me this isn't about the rude American boy."

At that, I couldn't help myself, but even the hint of a smile felt like a betrayal. "This isn't about Max," I said. "Explain to me how it's supposed to be good news that she left the next piece with a guy who's been dead for five hundred years. What are we supposed to do, track down his great-great-great-to-the-power-of-infinity-grandson and ask whether he's found anything interesting in his attic?"

"You don't really think she'd have trusted him with this, do you? Think: Is there *anyone* she'd have trusted, other than her brother?"

"Why are you asking me like I'm inside her head?"

Did she trust anyone else? Thomas, of course, but by the time she buried her treasures, Thomas was long gone. There was no one else. Still, something about the clue had been bugging me, something familiar about the phrasing. A place that felt like home, surrounded by people she trusted, where she could imagine her brother by her side. . . .

"Sorry," he said. "You just seem, I don't know. In tune with her, I guess. Did you ever wonder whether— What?"

"What do you mean, what? Did I ever wonder whether . . . ?"

"No. Just now, you thought of something."

"What makes you think that?"

"Same thing that made me sure you wouldn't ditch me on the way to Prague. Your face."

"What's wrong with my face?"

"Let's just say you should stay away from the poker table."

"I get that a lot. And you know what people usually find out?"

"They think they can read you, but they're wrong?" Eli said. The self-satisfied grin was disgusting.

"I'm going back to my room." But I didn't go anywhere. Because he'd guessed right.

"Say it."

"The place that feels like home, where she feels like her brother is with her," I said. "She talked about it in one of her first letters. There was some library at a monastery, up on the hill overlooking the city. Stratton. Strawhill. Something. Her refuge."

300

"Strahov?"

"That's it."

"Then that has to be it!" Eli, suddenly jittery with energy, switched off the computer. "They're famous for their library—you think she hid something in it? In a book? Something by Kepler?"

His excitement was contagious. Especially when I told him about how I'd found Elizabeth's very first hidden message, sewn into the binding of the Petrarch book. This really could be it.

He was already at the door when he noticed I wasn't behind him. "What are you waiting for?"

"*We* are waiting for them to get back." It was the last thing I wanted to do. We were so close; Elizabeth had been waiting for so long.

"Why, just because he threw a little temper tantrum?"

"He was right," I said reluctantly. "I shouldn't have disappeared. We're in this together."

"And that's why he went off with your best friend and left you here with me. You may be miscalculating your *wes.*"

"I don't know what you're talking about." But I did. Max was still mad about the night before; he was punishing me.

Or.

I was trying not to think about the two of them together that night, walking through the moonlight, Adriane sobbing in Max's arms, Max stroking her back, whispering in her ear, telling her she was safe, he was there, everything was going to be okay.

I was trying not to think about the things between them that I wasn't allowed to understand.

"Should I use smaller words? They don't want you around."

Adriane didn't seem to care that I'd broken my promise, that when she'd needed me, I had been gone—gone long enough to reawaken her fear, to make her think she'd lost someone else. She wasn't angry, and she had a right to be. Max, on the other hand, did not.

"We could wait for them," Eli said. "But I don't want to. Do you? Be honest."

"You know everything about every major Czech monument, right? Inhumane parental brainwashing and all?"

"What's your point?" But he looked like he already knew—and that's when I knew I was right.

"The clock is the most famous monument in the city, isn't it?"

"I guess. One of them. So?"

"So you knew about the war damage already, didn't you? And you let them go on a wild-goose chase."

"Does it matter?" Eli said. "He clearly wasn't in the mood to listen. To either of us."

"It matters."

"Fine," he said. "I'll go to Strahov myself—"

"And use your irresistible charm to get them to hand over their rare books to some random stranger with scissors?" Max would hate it if I let Eli go after the clue himself, I thought, knowing I was rationalizing. Knowing what I was going to do.

Max had said it himself: Why stay together? He would forgive me for leaving without him, then I would forgive him for leaving without me. We were getting good at apologies. "Let's go."

"Tell the truth: Was it my inescapable logic or my irresistible charm?"

"Maybe we should try not to talk," I said.

"Ah, your words say you hate me, but your face says . . ." He narrowed his eyes and gave me an exaggerated once-over.

"Yes?"

"You hate me." He shrugged. "At least you're consistent. So, we go?"

I hated to let him think he'd goaded me into it. But there was no reason to wait. "We go."

This time, at least, we left a note.

33

"Sorry we're late," Eli told the old man in the Strahov ticket booth. "I know we were told to arrive fifteen minutes before our appointment, but—"

"Don't apologize to him," I snapped. "It's *his* stupid city that made us late, all these one-way streets and pedestrian zones. What kind of Podunk, backward—"

"It's not his fault, honey," Eli said. He rubbed my back. I glared, and he abruptly withdrew his hand. "Look, sir, as you can see, we're in a hurry, so if you can just direct us to the library, we'll get going."

"The library?" he said, with only the hint of an accent. "But this is off-limits to the public."

I scowled at him, then addressed Eli in a loud stage whisper. "The public? Tell me he did *not* just refer to us as 'the public.'"

"I'm so sorry," Eli said. "She's a little—"

"Don't you *dare* apologize for me."

"Sorry, sweetie."

"Stop apologizing and fix this!"

Eli stared helplessly at the ticket seller.

I rolled my eyes. "Look, Mr. Monk—"

"I'm only a volunteer," the man said.

"Right, whatever. Look, I'm sorry if your library is, like, a state secret or something, but my father made us this appointment and you do *not* want to disappoint my father, okay?"

"Maybe if there's someone we could talk to about this?" Eli said. "Your boss, perhaps?"

I snickered. "God's probably busy, sweetie."

The man looked extremely uncomfortable. "Give me a moment." He disappeared into some back room.

"You're alarmingly good at acting the bitch," Eli whispered. "It suggests practice."

"And you're alarmingly good at acting whipped," I shot back. "Food for thought."

A door at the end of the narrow corridor swung open, and a round man in a long white tunic emerged. His bald head was the same rosy pink as his cheeks; his eyes were cold. *"Dobrý den,"* he said, his accent a weird mixture of Czech and British. "I am told of a problem?"

I forced my hands to remain still at my sides, and tried not to stare too openly at his freshly pressed scapular. It was one thing to lie to a ticket vendor; it was another to lie to a monk.

Good cause, I reminded myself. Presumably even his God would approve.

"We've got an appointment to view some of the items in your rare-book collection," Eli said. "But there seems to have been some kind of miscommunication."

"Your names?"

"Jack Brown and Ella Weston," I said.

Eli curled an arm around me. "Soon to be Ella Brown, right?" He grinned at the monk. "We're engaged."

I shrugged him off. "I told you, I'm keeping my name."

"You said we could talk about it—"

"No, *you* said that. You know Daddy would never stand for it."

"And whatever *Daddy* says goes, right? Never mind that I'm going to be your husband—"

"Not if you keep acting like a child."

"Me?"

The monk cleared his throat. "We have no record of your appointment, and the library holdings are strictly off-limits to the public unless arrangements have been made."

"What is it with you people?" I said. "We are not 'the public.' My father is—"

"They don't need to know who your father is, honey."

"It'll be his name on the check, won't it?"

"I will *handle* this," Eli said firmly.

I gave him a regal nod. "So, handle it."

"Here's the situation," he told the monk. "Ella and I, it was love at first sight—we were taking this astronomy class, and when I saw her . . . it was like, *bam*, I saw stars, you know?"

"He doesn't need to hear this," I said.

"He needs to know why this is so important, honey. So, that was two years ago, and now we're engaged, and to celebrate—"

"This is going to sound totally geektastic," I told the monk.

"It's *romantic*," Eli said. "I'm taking Ella around the world to see the most famous astronomical manuscripts. Because that's how we fell in love."

"Well, technically, Daddy is the one taking us around the world. At least, his credit card is."

Eli sucked in his cheeks. "Her father is helping us out. Which was surprising, considering he hates me—"

"He does not!"

"And he *claims* he made us an appointment to see your first-edition Keplers."

"'Claims'? Are you suggesting Daddy lied?"

"It wouldn't be the first time he'd done something to humiliate me."

"Paranoid much?"

"What about Turkey? And the library in St. Petersburg?"

"You can't blame him for that disaster in Turkey. And

St. Petersburg admitted it was their mistake, and so Daddy says construction on the Ella Weston Wing will go forward as planned."

"That's how he gets people to do what he wants," Eli explained to the monk. "He throws money at them. I told him Church officials couldn't be bribed, but . . ."

"Daddy says anyone will do anything if the price is right," I said.

"You want to tell him when he said that most recently?" Eli said.

"Daddy *apologized* for that."

"He tried to pay me off," Eli said. "Ten thousand dollars if I'd break up with his daughter. It was disgusting."

"It was a *test*, sweetie. Don't worry, you passed." I turned to the monk. "He just wants what's best for me."

"He wants you to marry someone from a more appropriate dynasty," Eli spit out. "He wants to pimp you out like you're some broodmare horny for a stud—excuse me, Brother."

The monk, whose bald head had gone from pink to a deep rose red, looked excruciatingly uncomfortable. "Perhaps the young lady could have her father call the abbot," he suggested.

"I guess that's what we'll have to do," I said. "I didn't want to see the stupid books anyway. This whole trip is his idea, you know. I'm just going along with it to be nice."

"You said you wanted to!"

"That's called nice. Come on, we'll call Daddy from the hotel, and—"

"No!" Eli rifled through my bag and pulled out the phrasebook, flipping through it furiously. Then he grabbed the monk's shoulders and, in halting, mispronounced Czech, said, *"Posílá mě otec Hájek. Hrajte dál."*

The monk raised his eyebrows. "Your Czech is terrible," he said. "But your words are convincing. Come."

He marched us down the corridor and up a narrow staircase. We fell a few steps behind. "What did you say to him?" I whispered. The Czech hadn't been part of the plan.

"'Please, in the name of love, help me to be a man,'" Eli said.

"You're joking."

"It worked, didn't it?" Then, raising his voice for the monk to hear, "I told you I would handle it. Aren't you going to thank me?"

"Thank you."

"I was thinking a kiss."

The monk turned back to us with an encouraging smile, as if eager to witness young love in action, although it was hard to believe our little show had evoked anything in him but a recommitment to celibacy.

"We're in a monastery," I told Eli, with all the Ella Weston ice I could muster. "Have some respect for the Lord."

34

To reach the library, we had to pass through a vaulted entry hall lined with glass cabinets, their shelves holding an array of seashells; impaled insects arranged by species, two by two by two; polished arrowheads; dead butterflies; rag dolls playing miniature violins; taxidermied eels and sharks and lobsters; a giant turtle with the face of a pterodactyl; a chain-mail shirt draped over a large wooden cross. There was also—its 2007 label suggesting that someone in the monastery had missed the memo on developing nations, political correctness, and the fact that living in a desert shouldn't automatically qualify a person or his possessions for membership in a tastefully arranged freak show—a donkey whip from modern-day Kabul.

"*Kunstkammer*," I murmured, and the monk looked back in surprise. He nodded.

"We collect," he said. "We have always."

The stuffed sea creatures were staring at me, the insects were all too easy to imagine back to life, and the rag dolls were no less beady-eyed or more trustworthy than the rest of their kind. But it was the whip that chilled me the most.

"Come." The monk drew us into a long, narrow hall, its gilded wood paneling glowing in the warm light. The walls were lined with books, the curved ceiling layered with frescoes of the ancient Greek philosophers—everything about it screamed cathedral, but whatever was worshipped here, in this room, beneath the wild stares of Pythagoras, Aristotle, and Socrates, it wasn't God. Or at least not the same God worshipped in the cathedral two stories below, with its barbed crosses and stained-glass Jesus. Not God alone.

The monk settled us in velvet chairs pulled up to a sturdy wooden table, and, with a short, angry burst of Czech that apparently brooked no argument, sent a minion off in search of the first editions. They were delivered to us one by one—aging, mildewed volumes placed delicately on low wooden reading platforms, their covers a worn leather, their pages crammed with dense Latin text and complex astronomical engravings, planets dancing on geometrical orbits, mathematical equations littered with stars. The minion disappeared nearly as soon as he'd arrived, but the monk watched closely as we leafed through the pages, pretending to ooh and aah at regular intervals and, occasionally, reminiscing about the kooky dead astronomer who had first brought us together. He didn't notice how carefully we ran our fingers over the binding, searching for bumps and bulges, telltale irregular stitching, any kind of sign that Elizabeth had been there before us.

Johannes Kepler was, among other things, the imperial astronomer of Prague, the legendary natural philosopher who deciphered the laws of planetary orbits and transformed the Copernican system from an aesthetically pleasant diagram into a physical model of the universe, the author of the world's first science-fiction novel, and the devout acolyte who dreamed of understanding God's grand design and whose theories on the harmonies of the planetary spheres launched a thousand astrological crackpots. But in 1599, when Elizabeth and Thomas were running around Prague searching for sacred chalices and blessed dirt, he was an impoverished and henpecked nobody, toiling away in the hinterland, dreaming of a better life. He had, by that time, written one book, the *Mysterium Cosmographicum*, in which only the savviest minds of Europe saw what was to come. Strahov had three first editions in its collection, and in the third, I found a seam in the binding, just like the one in the Petrarch. To assuage any doubt, nine small letters were inscribed at the bottom of the second page:

$$E\,I\,W$$

$$I\,F\,W$$

$$f\,s\,g$$

It wasn't a code. It was a greeting—the one she could never help herself from making. *E. I. Westonia, Ioanni Francisco Westonio, fratri suo germano*. That's how sure she was that her brother would live long enough, and know her well enough, to retrieve what she had left behind. Because how could her *fratri suo germano* do anything less?

Eli saw me see it. So he was ready.

"I have to pee," I said loudly. The monk flinched.

Eli hunched over his copy of the book. "So pee," he said.

The monk cleared his throat. "Toilets are one flight down, second door on the left."

I tugged at Eli's arm. "Well?"

"*I* don't have to go."

"But *I* do."

"Right. So go."

"By *myself*?"

"You're potty-trained."

"There's, like, a *crypt* down there," I said.

"Like, seven floors down. I don't think you need to worry."

"It's *dark*. And I'll get *lost*. Just come with me."

He looked up from the book, mouth set in a firm line, a boy who'd decided to wage his first fight as a man. "Sweetheart?"

"Yes?"

"Grow up."

I slapped the table. The monk jumped, hands twitching as if eager to snatch away the rare texts before I could seize one to throw across the room. "Why do you have to be so selfish?"

Eli's eyebrows nearly met his hairline. "*Me?*"

"It's always about what you want, what you need."

"Do I look like a mirror to you?"

"What about last night?" I said, watching the monk. His bald pate was on fire.

"What happened last night?"

"How about what *didn't* happen last night?" I said, voice rising. "There are *two* people in that bed, you know. And just because *you're* satisfied doesn't mean that I don't need you to—"

"I can escort you," the monk said hastily.

"Really? You'd do that?"

He cleared his throat. "Of course."

"See, now that's a gentleman," I told Eli.

He shrugged. "So marry him."

I hooked my arm through the monk's and let him guide me out of the library, past the miniature *Kunstkammer*, and down the stairs to the bathroom, where I stalled inside for as long as I dared.

When we returned, I could tell from the smile on Eli's face that it had been long enough.

35

"I'm sorry about yesterday," Eli said as we descended toward Malá Strana, Elizabeth's letter folded into his pocket. Strahov stood on a hill with the entire city stretched out beneath it. Several twisting paths cut through the grass, crisscrossing on their way back to civilization. We chose the steepest, away from the picnicking families and old men with grandchildren perched on their shoulders. "About getting you in trouble with Max. And being an ass about your brother."

"I'm not in trouble with Max." We weren't going to talk about my brother. "That's not how we work."

"Right."

"And just for the record, there's nothing nefarious going on with him and Adriane."

"I'm not worried about your little high school soap opera. He's capable of worse."

"You can't still think he had anything to do with Chris. After everything?"

He didn't answer.

"If you really thought he was guilty, you'd call the cops," I said. "You wouldn't just be sitting around chatting with the guy who murdered your cousin."

"That's very logical," he said.

"Which is why I don't get why you treat him like that."

"Like what?"

"Like you hate him. You barely know him."

"I barely know you, too."

"Right, but you don't act like you hate me," I pointed out. "Most of the time, at least."

"No, I don't. So, Logic Girl, maybe you're asking the wrong question."

"So now I'm supposed to ask what the right question is. And let me guess, you tell me that's for you to know and me to find out? Sorry, I'm not playing this game."

"You're not playing any game," he said. "That's what's going to get you in trouble."

"Trouble with what?"

"Forget it." He walked faster, kicking off small avalanches of gravel with each heavy step. I hurried to catch up, scuttling down the hill in mincing baby steps, feeling the potential for a disastrous skid every time my foot touched the ground.

"I'm already in trouble. In case you haven't noticed."

"I said forget it."

"Why are you like this?"

"All I wanted to say was sorry," he said. "About Andy. I get it now."

"What?"

"Why you can't let yourself believe in all this. Why you need the *Lumen Dei* not to be real."

"I thought I was pretty clear I can't believe in it because it's ridiculous and because there's no such thing as—"

"God. You were clear," he said. "Because if there were a God, he took your brother away. He took Chris away. What would you want with a God like that? But if there were a machine—a miracle—that could prove you were wrong, you'd be stuck with him. And you'd have to ask why he took them."

"You think that scares me?"

"I think you're afraid to believe there's something out there that wants to take everything you love away from you. And maybe . . . afraid to hope that with the *Lumen Dei*, with the power it's supposed to confer, maybe you could bring them back."

36

When we got to the hostel, they were waiting.

I was waiting, too, for the accusations to start, and was prepared to defend myself against the charge of wandering off recklessly—to say I was sorry again, for yet another thing I didn't regret—but as soon as I saw them together, standing side by side, a matched pair with arms identically crossed and heads tilted toward each other, my urge to apologize evaporated. In its wake was fury—and something else. All those months I'd begged them to give each other a chance, to stop bitching and whining long enough to have an actual conversation—but maybe I'd been better off with the cold war. Adriane had always made it clear: She could have anything and anyone she wanted. I'd taken it for granted that she hadn't wanted him.

It was insane to even imagine.

But it would be naive not to. And Max was the one who'd said we couldn't afford that.

"You found it, didn't you?" Max lifted me off my feet, kissed me. "I can tell."

I suppressed the urge to ask why he wasn't mad, since that would be implying he had something to be mad about. "What happened with the clock?" I asked instead.

"Nothing. But you already knew that." He kissed me again. "Good thing I fell for someone smarter than I am."

"So you finally figured that out."

"I'm slow," he said. "That's my point."

Sometimes it astonished me how soft his hands were. Like he'd worn gloves all his life, touching nothing, until me. He tilted his forehead to mine, a brain kiss, he'd called it once. He whispered, "I'm sorry. For everything."

I didn't answer. I didn't ask what he was apologizing for.

"So? Show us what you found," Max said. "This should lead us to the last piece. This could all be over soon."

"We found it," Eli said, handing Max the sheaf of wrinkled pages. "But we weren't the first."

There was a page of astronomical calculations, and another long letter, four pages in Elizabeth's careful hand—or, more precisely, three and a half. The final page had been torn clean through.

Adriane closed her eyes. "Shit."

I watched Max's face. He held it almost perfectly still.

"We won't know what's gone until we know what's there," he said finally. He wrapped his fingers around mine. "Maybe it'll be enough."

"Look who's suddenly glass-half-full, letter-half-intact," Eli said. "Looks like Adriane's anger-management classes are working out for you after all."

Max leaned into me again, forehead to forehead, eyes calm, like Eli had never spoken. Fixed on me, like we were alone, and all that mattered. "'All our knowledge brings us nearer to our ignorance.' Eliot. As per usual."

I didn't want to say it like this, like I was trying to convince him or convince myself, but I did, in a whisper, not even that, my lips brushing his, the words slipping straight from my mouth to his. "'I love you.' Nora Kane."

37

E. J. Weston, to the persistent John Fr. Weston.

It comes to me I have told you little of Groot, whose shadow fell over my days. You have, I doubt not, heard tales of his mechanical creatures and the strange devices he imagines into being, machines to carry a man beneath the sea or turn winter to summer. Prague has no shortage of wizards, but I will always believe that Groot numbered among their greatest.

He could be cruel. Václav bore the brunt of his rages. The strange servant descends from an old Czech family, once powerful members of the Bohemian Estates, who lost much of their number and all of their influence in the aftermath of the Hussite uprising. Much of his family now labors at court, but to judge from his mutterings, Václav would sooner drown in a sea of piss than serve the Emperor.

I know you deem such sentiments unbefitting a lady, but these are his words, not mine.

I had no understanding for the ties that bound Groot and Václav, but bound they were, for near twenty years, and for all Groot's fits at his servant's clumsiness and close resemblance to a boar, for all Václav's scowling sulks and the delicate mechanisms he was always dashing on the floor, Groot claimed him indispensable.

Groot labored many years to fulfill a secret desire, the unification of nature and artifice, the endowment of his machines with the spark of life. Creation, he often told me, is the closest we can come to divinity. Failure was his loyal and constant friend. I lacked sympathy for this, once, but I now feel the burden he carried, and understand why he carried it with such little grace.

You will wonder that I say nothing here of my other life in these sleepless days, the arguments with our Mother and the fruitless struggle to regain our property from the Emperor and, in the endless meantime, keep a roof above us with food beneath it. I say nothing here of the continued ministrations of Johannes Leo, the man you will soon know as a brother, and I, impossible though it seems, as a husband. I say nothing, even, of my poems, which now again seem the only light and truth in a dark life.

This life continued, as life does, but it daily lost color and meaning. I bore a duty to our Mother and to our family, and an opposing one to our lost Father, and every day it grew more difficult to reconcile the two. It was as if I were two selves in one body, and as one swelled, the other shrank away, until our Mother, our poverty, even you, dearest brother, ashamed as I am to admit it, receded into the distance. Life narrowed to the Lumen Dei, *and so, with no thought of propriety or fear, I saddled a horse and, riding beside a man who was neither my husband nor my blood relation, set off into the wild.*

It was a ten-day ride to Graz. Most nights found us beneath the stars, our horses tethered to a tree, our hands linked, our thoughts lost in each other. You disapprove, I know. But I have promised you truth. There was only one truth for me in that lonely countryside, and it is the lie we told all who passed, the lie we told ourselves, the lie that became true, in spirit if not on earth, the lie of Thomas and Elizabeth, husband and wife.

316

Does it surprise you to know that while you were penning me letters that sang of Johannes Kepler's wild exploits of imagination, the beauty you found in the Mysterium Cosmographicum *and its vision of the universe with its heavenly spheres, that while you rhapsodized about another star joining Copernicus and Ptolemy in the firmament, I was dismounting before a small and crooked house in the small and crooked town of Graz, watching your bright new star sweat as he drew water from a well, not nearly fast enough to suit his carping crone of a wife? The great man, little older than you, welcomed us when we presented the letter by Groot's hand, a parchment page assuring Kepler that only he had the skill to read our fate in the stars, and determine the most auspicious astronomical moment for operating our machine. The* Lumen Dei *exists both in this world and beyond. It unites the* spiritus *and the bodily realm, but can do so only when heavens are in their proper alignment. For this, we needed Kepler.*

—Astrology, most astrology, is, of course, so much foolishness and blasphemy; you must know this.

Kepler's dark hair was curlier than mine, his face cratered as the moon, and as he spoke to us, his wife fluttered about, demanding this pot or that shoe, demanding most of all his attention, though why she would want it was mysterious, as the river of hate that flowed between them was unmistakable. Married nearly a year, he confided in us, his voice a discordant harmony of unspoken regrets. I promised myself, silently, that Thomas and I would never come to this, and in Thomas's eyes I saw the same vow.

—I slight the astrologers, not their enterprise. From that crawling, festering pile of maggots and dung, a sure hand may withdraw a pearl.

The hand, he had no need to explain, belonged to him.

He explained nonetheless, at length, the ways in which his studies of the stars far exceeded those of his rivals, a truth that soon would be universally acknowledged across the Continent, and yet what could easily have become an insufferable bout of boasting transformed itself, before our ears, into an anxious plea for us to carry word of his studies back to Prague. Had we the ear of the Emperor, he wanted to know, or the ear of Groot or Hájek, anyone who could rescue him from the hell that was Graz: the Archduke's campaign against the Lutherans, his wife's misery, his own ill health, their imminent poverty. As if we were not strangers but his bosom friends, he confessed that all would soon be lost, by his own weakness and mistakes, if he could not convince someone of the worth of his ideas. And here he shifted paths yet again and returned to singing the praises of his own work, towering, as it did, above the heads of all who had come before.

Finally, Kepler seated us before a bowl of warm broth and retreated to his small study, where, he told us, he would happily plunge into the muck and seize a pearl. He emerged shortly before nightfall, his hair wild as his gaze, cheeks flushed, fingers stained with ink and clutching a sheath of pages, one of which he handed to me.

—You have read my book?

I allowed that I had.

—Then you understand.

There was no need to ask what it was I was presumed to understand, for he continued.

—They ask how the universe is arranged, philosophers, mathematicians, and they draw pretty pictures, impossibilities on the page. They save the phenomena by telling one ugly lie after another, epicycles upon epicycles, and the fools care not. It is not enough, I tell you, to ask how the cosmos is designed. We must ask why. For to understand His design, the why of it, is to know the mind of God. My work, your Lumen Dei, they seek the same end, do they not? Illumination of the grand design and its reasons for being. His reasons. You will tell the Emperor of my contribution, will you not? You will explain what I can provide for Prague and the Empire, if he can provide for me?

I assured him that I would, and had it been possible, I would indeed have done so. Kepler, for all his rambling ambitions, spoke as if with my own voice. Even now, I believe that to know how is useless if we do not know why. And there are too many who forbid us to ask.

Our final task had been completed with ease; the universe had bent to our united will. This was the unspoken hubris between us as we galloped back to Prague, a page of astronomical calculations sewn into the lining of my cloak. We believed we would soon bring the Lumen Dei into this world and ourselves to glory, and then as the natural course of events, as simple as water falling from high ground to low, we would be married.

How it pains me to remember the ease with which we forgot ourselves. Both of us near impoverished; my

319

Mother depending on me to restore the family to its rightful position; marriage an unthinkable step at this stage of his apprenticeship; an alchemical apprentice an unthinkable match for marriage, at least in the eyes of our Mother. On looking at Thomas, she could see only our Father, and for me, a life of misery and destitution, of empty stomachs and cold prisons. She would, I knew, forbid our union. We could dream of our future, but God had failed to give us the tools with which to build it. These, dearest brother, were the truths we happily ignored on that journey back to Prague, and as we approached the banks of the Vrchlice, only a day's ride from home, our smiles were wide as the river.

That is where they found us.

The first arrow whistled past my ear, but the second found its mark and sank deep into my stallion's flank. A third and fourth arrow flew, one piercing his eye, the next his long black neck. I was thrown from the horse, thankfully landing a safe distance away from the thrashing beast, and could do nothing but watch his dance of pain and his eventual surrender. Thomas's horse fell just as swiftly, and I waited to bear the consequences of an ignored warning, waited to die at Thomas's side, knowing with my final breath that I had stolen his life.

But no blade was drawn. We were bound and blindfolded, bundled into a ragged carriage and released into a pungent room. Despite the care our captors had taken to ensure our ignorance of the place, I knew it by smell alone. Our Father brought me to Sedlec only once, but the earthy scent of aging skulls is one not quickly forgotten.

Their efforts gave me hope. Had they brought us here to kill us, I thought, surely they would not have bothered to disguise our path.

My blindfold was removed, though the binds were not. Thomas slumped in a corner, only the slight movement of his chest reassuring me that his life had been spared. Thus far. Our three captors wore masks.

—We know what you were doing in Graz. We know what you do with Groot. We want the Lumen Dei. *And we will pay handsomely.*

There is no Lumen Dei, *I told them.*

At this, the second man spoke.

—Not yet. But there will be, and it cannot fall to the Hapsburgs. It would be a crime against the Czech people, and all the peoples of the world who have yet to fall under their blade.

—A crime against the Lord. The Emperor, despite his denials, will always be a friend to the Church. Their hands will mold a miracle into a transgression.

If you know of the Lumen Dei, *and you know of Groot, what need do you have of us? I asked. Take it from him.*

I looked at the third man as I spoke, the one who had stayed silent. Another wasted subterfuge. I knew him even without his low, croaking Czech. I knew his hunched back, as I knew his clomping limp. Václav. Groot's loyal servant, the only man trusted with Groot's secrets. If anyone could steal from Groot without my help, it was he. And yet I held my tongue. Václav could not know I had recognized him, or I would never leave his sight alive.

321

—It must be you.

—It will be you.

—More florins than you could spend in a lifetime.

—You will deliver it to us by sundown two days hence.

—Or we will find you, and that will be the end of you.

I did not ask how they knew the **Lumen Dei** *would be ready within two days, for if anyone knew Groot's progress, it was Václav, and even at that moment, brother, can you believe I felt a thrill of anticipation at the thought of the device come to fruition?*

—You need not answer us now.

—You will answer with your actions.

—Or you will answer for them.

They blindfolded us again. The carriage carved an eternal path through the countryside. And then a boot to my gut toppled me to hard ground, and I heard the horses retreat into the distance. They left us there, blind and bound in a darkness that stank of cattle dung. Rubbing my head against Thomas's shoulder, I was able to remove my blindfold, and, our fingers working together, we managed to set ourselves free. We found ourselves in a crumbling alley. A snuffling cow watched us with blank eyes. The air carried voices to us, eager haggling over the price of cattle and beef. We could be no more than a few blocks from Wenceslas Square. We were not simply alive. We were home.

Thomas held me. He was shaking. I had done this to him. I had drawn him into this. I had nearly destroyed him.

I must tell you something, I confessed.

—And I you. But not here.

He brought me to the crypt of the Church of St. Boethius,
where, he said, he had been baptized and had for many years
served the priests in their most menial tasks, stoking fires and
patching holes. The priests would protect us, he said. He lit
a candle and held me as I told him about the man who had
appeared in my bedchamber, the man with the priest's robe and
the knife, who had warned me to turn back.

I believed the priest now, as I had not before. I would die
if I helped the Lumen Dei *come to life. And, at the hands of*
Václav and his fellows, I would likely die if I did not.

I could bear this. The choice, at least, would still be mine.
My fate, for the first time in my life, was something I could
take upon myself.

But I could not bear bringing that same fate upon Thomas.

I held him, in the lowest depths of that dark church, and
told him why this had to be our end. He did not argue.

—There are things you need to know.

He had brought us to the church so I could hear his
confession, and so I did. And as he spoke, I thought of the
arrows that had laid down our horses, and I longed to return to
that bloody riverbank, to throw myself in the path of the final
arrow, to die ignorant, and so, in love. Better to be killed by an
arrow than by the words of the one I most trusted.

Better to be betrayed by my body than by my heart.

The rest of the letter was torn away.

"It was him," Adriane said. "The letters you found in Chris's room. Thomas was the spy."

"You don't know that. He could have confessed anything," I said. "A secret wife. A third nipple."

323

"She has sewn his calculations into the lining of her cloak, remember? Thomas is the only one who would have known where she hid the formula," she said, always remembering too much. "It was him. You know that."

I did. He had brought her to the Church of St. Boethius to confess his betrayal. The same church we had visited on our first day in Prague, the church where an angry priest had given us our first frustrating non-answers about the *Hledači.* It couldn't be a coincidence. But how could it be anything else? "He loved her," I said stupidly.

Adriane shrugged.

"It doesn't matter," I said before anyone could say it for me. "I know. We have a bigger problem."

She had been so sure he loved her.

"I guess Strahov wasn't the home away from home she thought it was," Eli said. "The monks betrayed her."

"Or someone found it since then," Max said. "Someone recently."

"And left the whole thing except for the last piece, then sewed it back up in the binding again?" Eli said. "That seems equal parts elaborate and useless."

"Crazy people do crazy things."

"It doesn't matter who did it," Adriane said. "It's done. We're screwed."

"Maybe not," I said. "We have most of what the *Hledači* want, right? We have three out of four pieces—they've got nothing. So they should be willing to bargain with us." If we could find a way to contact them without getting ourselves killed; if we could give them everything they wanted, betray Elizabeth, and reward Chris's murder, just to save ourselves; if this whole thing hadn't been a game of make-believe, the pleasant delusion that we could actually win.

"Or they take what they want, kill us, and go on their merry way," Eli said.

"So then we go to the cops," Adriane said. "We go *home*. We've got evidence now. And we're telling the truth. They have to believe us eventually."

"No, they don't," I said. "And even if they do, then what? Whoever killed Chris is still out there. Nothing happens to them?"

"The *cops* happen to them," she said. "What were we really going to do, even if we could get them to trade the killer for the machine? Kill him? Torture him? Ask him for takebacks?"

"It's so easy for you? To give up?"

She bared her teeth. "I'm not the one who's forgetting why we're here in the first place. This isn't about your precious Elizabeth and her stupid machine. It was supposed to be about saving Max. And finding out what happened to Chris. That's what matters. To me, at least."

My chest tightened.

Adriane smoothed back her hair. Amazing how, bereft of her myriad beauty products and alternating between the same three or four pieces of clothing every day, she still managed to look date-night-ready. Whereas I'd reached the point where I was avoiding mirrors for their own safety. "We played a good game," she said, in a softer voice. "But it's over. It was always going to end here, one way or another."

Max put his hand over mine. "She's right."

That was when I knew it was over. If Max was ready to give up—Max, who had been more adamant about this fight than any of us, and who had the most to lose—then there really was nothing left.

We had failed.

I looked at Eli. He raised his hands as if in protest. "Party crasher, remember? You don't need my vote."

"I want to know what you think."

"The cops don't think *he* did anything," Adriane pointed out.

"They don't think you did, either," Max said quietly. "Not really. They're using you to get to me."

"Maybe," I said. "Or maybe the *Hledači* set us all up—"

"And maybe we can get the cops to believe that," Max said. "Or we could try making some kind of bargain, like you said, but it'd be safer to do once we're back home. If I'm behind bars, at least the *Hledači* can't get to me."

I couldn't think about that.

"You really want to give up?" I said. "We'll be arrested as soon as we walk into an airport."

"But at least you'll be safe." Max folded the torn letter, running his fingers along its crease. "I did this all wrong," he said. "Everything. You shouldn't be here. None of you."

"You shouldn't, either."

"You're right."

"So we go home?" Eli said.

"We?" I asked. "I thought you weren't part of this discussion."

"You go, I go," he said. "You tell the cops a story like this, you're going to need all the witnesses you can get."

"Then we go home," Max said.

"Home," Adriane echoed, and I wondered if the word sounded as strange to the rest of them as it did to me.

38

And then we were alone together.

Max. Me. And everything unnamable that had come between us.

"You're tense," he said, kneading my shoulders.

I let him touch me, but I didn't respond.

326

"Adriane seems like she's doing a little better," he said.

I went rigid.

"Why do you care so much all of a sudden?" I didn't like the way my voice sounded; I didn't like how his hands went still on my shoulders, and how the room went so suddenly quiet, like we had both heard a crack and were just waiting for the tree to fall.

"I have to tell you something," he said, and there was fear in his voice.

I wanted to take it back. Or at least to tell him to stop, to swallow the confession before it was too late.

"So tell me."

"Turn around," he said.

"Just say it." I shouldn't have to look at him when he did.

"Please," he said.

I faced him. Max. With his flopping hair and wire-rimmed glasses and unexpected smile. Max, who was supposed to love me.

"I never wanted you to know," he said. "But Adriane—"

"Just say it." I could barely force the words out.

He swallowed hard. His face was milky white, like a sick child's. "I'm glad it was her."

I didn't get it.

"That night," he said. "With Chris. I'm glad it was her, and not you. Do you know what she told me, that night she was so upset?"

"No," I said, now completely confused about where this was going. "You said it was private."

"She told me how horrible it was not to remember. How she couldn't stand having this huge hole in her memory—that *anything* could have happened. That she already feels empty because Chris is gone, but this, it's like a piece of her is gone, too. She's telling me all this, and she's crying, and I was trying to

327

comfort her, telling her everything will be okay—but *she'll* never be okay again. Not really. And all I could feel? Was relieved. I'm *glad* it happened to her. Because"—he swallowed again, his eyes wide behind the thick glass—"I couldn't stand it. If that happened to you."

"That's it?" I said softly. "That's what you needed to tell me?"

"Chris was my best friend," he said. "You have to understand that. But—"

"But you're relieved it wasn't you. Of course you are. That's normal."

"I can't think about you losing me, the way Adriane lost Chris. Or if something happened to you, and I was the one who—" He shook his head. "I can't. So I'm glad. I'm *happy* it's them and not us. That's how twisted I am. Every time I look at her, I think: Thank god. She's ruined, and I'm *grateful*. Because you and me, we're still whole. We're untouched."

"Max . . ." I folded myself around him. "It's okay."

"It's not," he said, muffled, his face pressed to my shoulder. "I shouldn't."

"I promise," I said, and tipped his head toward mine, and I kissed him, the way I had kissed him the first time, in the quire of the church, our lips tentative, our fingers clasped, our hearts pounding, and I let it all go, doubt, anger, jealousy, fear. I kissed him and I pulled him down on the bed beside me and we tangled ourselves together and forgot, for a moment, everything but warm skin and hot breath and soft lips and love, and need.

And for that one moment it was as if we really had been left whole.

39

Dinner was Max's idea. Later, that seemed to matter. But none of us had argued with him, so maybe it didn't. There would be no flight until morning, no need to hoard what remained of our cash, no doubt it would be our last chance for a long time to spend a night together pretending life was good, we were happy, the future was clear, no excuse not to eat. He was different, now that he'd finally let everything out. There was a new lightness about him, and it was infectious. Not that we were skipping down cobblestone lanes or singing in the misty rain. But it was the first time we'd ventured into the city with neither aim or fear, the first time we'd walked its streets without peering *through* them, as if, squinting hard enough, we could bring its ghosts into sharp relief. For one night, Prague was no longer a repository of secrets. Nothing had happened to us, we told ourselves, so maybe nothing would happen. We made up something to believe in: That we had escaped. That, for a night, we were invisible.

It was reckless, but maybe no more so than anything else we'd done, and we were allowed to be reckless, because it was the last night, and in the morning, everything would end. The cops would find us, and likely the *Hledači* would soon after. Then whatever happened would happen. I wasn't going to spend my last night in hiding. The city was lit up, brimming with tourists and drunkards and lovers, Cinderella castles twinkling overhead. Its shadows remained; we ignored them. What could happen in the Magic Kingdom?

It was Max who selected the restaurant, a bistro along the water. It was tucked away from the street, across an empty piazza and then down a narrow alleyway, with only small, hand-painted arrows promising us that an outpost of civilization lay ahead.

We ate on the terrace, beneath sparking heat lamps and flickering candlelight, the perfumed wax, smelling vaguely of hotel shampoo, overpowering the fishy scent of the river. A low stone wall separated us from the lapping water, and across the river, a glowing skyline of churches threw golden shadows on the water. The Charles Bridge was so close we could have pelted dinner rolls at the dark figures crossing its span. There were white tablecloths, linen napkins, suited waiters who brought wine without asking questions and took our order with a congratulatory wink.

The sky was huge.

We ate quietly, at first. The restaurant was nearly empty, and there were few sounds to drown out the elevator music pumped softly from tinny, unobtrusive speakers. Only the clatter of silverware on plates, wine trickling into glasses, chairs scraping stone, distant traffic that whispered like the ocean, the unexpected splash and quack of a school of ducks bobbing beneath us, diving for food. But eventually, we began to talk, nimbly hopping from one safe stepping-stone to the next, avoiding the treacherous waters—the past, the future, the present—that flowed between. A movie that Adriane and I both loved, in defiance of reason and taste. Eli and Max's shared loathing for organized sports. Parents and their belief that progeny were lumps of clay to be sculpted into whatever ugly pot or vase or teacup shape they so chose, a discussion that occupied Adriane and Eli while Max took my hand under the table and stroked his thumb across my open palm. I watched the bridge. Its stone guardians were saint-shaped holes of pure nothing in the sky, gaps in reality. I imagined getting too close, being sucked into the void. The spaces between.

40

The bridge. That was Max's idea, too. Just once, a postprandial stroll, he called it, smiling, bemused, as usual, by his own pretension. Across and back again, to hear the street violinists and watch the lip-locked couples and gaze at moonlit Prague from the most famous point on its map. A final goodbye to the city that had, in an unexpected act of leniency, let us live.

Maybe we'd had too much wine, or just too much, because the night had left us fearless, and so we agreed.

We'd stayed late at the restaurant, late enough to watch the waiters sweep beneath the tables while getting drunk off stolen swigs of pilsner, and with a few exceptions, the bridge's couples and musicians had already gone off to sleep. Stragglers groped in the dark niches between the saints, and a lone violinist played Pachelbel's "Canon" on an endless loop. Mounds of dirty wool blankets marked territory up and down the bridge span. The mist had condensed into a chill rain. Clouds blocked out the stars. Beggars formed supine flesh statues beneath the stone martyrs, oblivious to the fact that their paved beds were turning into puddles.

Though probably not oblivious, I supposed. Just resigned.

We stopped midway across the bridge, leaned against the ledge, watched the water below and the castle above. St. John of Nepomuk watched over us, expression cheerier than you'd expect from someone who'd been tossed overboard just for doing his job. The statue had looked cleaner on Max's postcard. Airbrushing: It would be nice if they could develop a technique for applying it to life.

"Imagine never going back," Adriane said, low enough that only I could hear.

"Stay here forever?"

"Feels like here is all there is."

I knew what she meant. Chapman, with its tiny buildings, tiny population, tiny aspirations, seemed like something I'd read about once and hadn't quite believed in. The only piece of home that seemed real anymore was Chris's body, Chris's blood. That was home, now. That was waiting for me.

"You think you're different?" Adriane asked suddenly, under her breath. The boys were absorbed in the view or their own midnight wonderings.

"Than what?"

"Than before."

"I don't know. I guess."

She didn't ask how. I wouldn't have known what to say. More frightened? Angrier? Braver?

Alone.

"I should be different," she said.

I didn't ask her how, either.

"Better," she said. "But I'm not."

I shivered.

"Is chivalry dead?" Adriane asked, rousing the boys from their stupor. "Someone give this girl a coat."

Eli had already thrust his into my hands before Max finished fumbling with his buttons. I took it with a weak thank-you.

"Milady," Max said, offering his to Adriane instead, with a shallow bow.

It was all too awkward. I looked away. Down, at the rain-slicked stones. And saw the black heap of blankets rise up.

Not blankets, not beggars, but robed men, rising around us, like monsters awoken from slumber, closing in from all sides, their glinting blades warning us not to scream.

Hledači.

332

One of them pointed at me. "You come quiet," he said, in a gravelly voice, "and your friends live."

It was framed as a choice, but then a robe was flung over my head and their hands were all over me, holding me in place. An arm curled around my throat. It squeezed, tight. I thrashed my head, tried to whipsaw at the waist, tried to punch, to kick, anything, but the arm was a vise. Pins and needles tingled up my arms and legs, legs made of twigs, of Jell-O, useless and weak and then numb and then gone. All of it gone but the pressure at my throat and the stars behind my lids and the tiny gasps of a losing struggle to breathe. Floating away. I screamed soundlessly into the black.

Somewhere, far away, voices, please no and we have what you want and don't fight them and I'm sorry and just let go and this is your fault, this is what you get, this is where it ends, but that was Chris's voice and Chris was dead and I was on the ground and why was this taking so long I just wanted it to stop I wanted to sleep and Chris was waiting.

"What the hell?" That was Adriane's voice, sharp and real, cutting through the fog, and suddenly air was rushing down my throat, into my lungs, the pressure blessedly gone. I gasped, sucking it in with abandon, blissed out on oxygen. And then there was a scream, and then there was a splash, and then there was a silence. Someone pulled the thick wool away from my face. It was Eli, and Eli's arms around me, dragging me to my feet.

"Go!" he shouted. "We have to go!"

The robes whipped in the wind as the men inexplicably backed away from us, and in the distance, sirens, and the one with gravel in his voice pointed at me again, calling out, "Destiny will find you. You are *vyvolená*!"

Adriane put an arm around my waist, slung my arm around

her shoulder, but my legs were working again and I allowed myself to be pulled away, running along the slippery stones, across the bridge, into the alleyways of Malá Strana, into the safety of the dark, and it wasn't until we were huddled under a cold, damp archway, shivering, Adriane and I pressed to each other, Eli sheathing a knife I hadn't known he had and wiping a smear of blood from his neck, the night too quiet, our breath too loud, that I let myself ask the question, not wanting to hear the answer, not needing to hear it.

"Where is he?"

I already knew. I knew when I opened my eyes to the suddenly bright night, and saw Adriane's pale, terrified face, saw Eli's wild rage, saw the cowards hidden behind their robes and hoods, saw what was no longer there.

I knew when I heard his scream. And the splash.

And after it, the nothing.

PART IV

Twilights of Dew and Fire

Menschen, die über dunkle Brücken gehn
vorüber an Heiligen
mit matten Lichtlein.
Wolken, die über grauen Himmel ziehn
vorüber an Kirchen
mit verdämmernden Türmen.
Einer, der an der Quaderbrüstung lehnt
und in das Abendwasser schaut,
die Hände auf alten Steinen.

People who walk across dark bridges,
past saints,
with dim, small lights.
Clouds which move across gray skies
past churches
with towers darkened in the dusk.
One who leans against the granite railing
gazing into the evening waters,
His hands resting on old stones.

⤳ Franz Kafka

1

What we didn't do:
  Call the cops.
  Find Max.
  Go home.

2

"Are you okay?"

Adriane kept asking.

"Yes," I said sometimes. And it could have been true. I was breathing. I was walking and talking, still processing one reality after the next, whether or not I wished otherwise.

"I don't know," I said sometimes. It felt like the arm had never left my throat. Like I was still floating.

"I will be," I said sometimes.

"Stop asking me that," I said sometimes.

Eventually, she did.

3

We slept curled up together. And that was strange: We slept.

Not Eli.

We had returned to the Golden Lion because there was nowhere else to go and because, he said, if they'd known where to find us, we'd be dead already. Our doors were still locked, our belongings intact. We shut ourselves into a room together, bolted the door. Eli took position beside it, listening, waiting, his fingers curled around his knife, guardian of our sleep. He was still there when I woke up.

We looked for Max. Of course we did. I made them go back, after we hid for hours, in the cold dark, swapping panicked whispers about what had happened and what would happen next.

What had happened. "It was Eli," Adriane said. Not *Eli stopped them* or *Eli saved us*, because he hadn't. Hadn't stopped them quickly enough; hadn't saved us all. "Turns out he's some kind of crazy ninja or something."

"I thought we were dead. All of us," she said. "But then I turn around and suddenly he's doing flips and he has some kind of knife that he's using like a sword and he fought them all off."

"Six of them," she said. "One of him."

"Max was trying to protect you," she said. "That's how it happened. They were fighting him off, and he went over."

"It happened so fast," she said.

"He was just there. Then he was gone," she said.

I didn't ask questions.

Eli paced, ready for a fight. When none arrived, I forced him back to the bridge, then to the river beneath it. Otherwise I would go on my own, I said, and neither of them argued. Adriane couldn't stop touching me, a hand on my back, a shoulder to my shoulder, an arm threaded through mine. And I let her, because it was good to know she was there. Because it was hard not to think: And then there were two.

No body washed up on the shores of the Vltava; no cops trolled its waters. No sirens blared, no lights flashed; no tourists bent over the ledge, scanning the river. No one attacked us. The bridge was just another after-hours tourist attraction, lovely and littered. Max wasn't there waiting for us. Max was gone.

I called all the hospitals anyway. But I already knew what they would say.

4

So.

Chris was gone.

Max was gone.

The *Hledači* were coming for us—coming for me.

And then there was the small matter of my supposed destiny.

"Talk to me," Adriane said. Eli stood guard outside the door. Whether to keep them out or keep us in, I didn't know. Adriane had wanted to walk, just the two of us—too dangerous, Eli said. Not without him. Adriane argued; I couldn't be bothered. I didn't want to walk. The door was bolted; the pillow smelled like Max. I wanted to stay.

So she threw Eli out.

"Please," she said. "Say something."

Something, I thought. But couldn't make the effort. Thumbprint-shaped bruises had bloomed on my neck in the night. I'd been marked.

She stroked my hair. "I'm sorry," she said. "I'm so sorry."

I was on a tightrope, and I couldn't let her knock me off. I couldn't fall.

"I shouldn't have let you come," she said. "We could be home right now. Everything could be normal."

She meant that this was my fault. I'd handed death to Chris along with a letter. Then I'd brought it to Max. She probably thought she was next.

She hugged me, wrapped her slender arms around my stiff body. I could sit here forever, I thought. Go catatonic; disappear. See how she liked it.

Adriane started to cry.

"Please don't," I said.

I couldn't.

The tears came harder. She turned her face from me, crossed her arms over her chest. "He's not dead."

"Yes. He is."

"Nora, I know it sounds crazy, but—"

"No."

"You don't know what happened."

"We both know what happened," I said. "We can't—I can't—" This time, I hugged her. She shuddered in my arms, struggling to catch her breath. "I can't pretend it's not true. Don't make me do that."

"Okay." I could feel her draw in one deep breath, and the next, and then she pulled away, eyes dry. "Okay. If that's what you want. Okay."

She gave me a long, appraising look. "You need a haircut."

I almost laughed. "I need a shower."

"Seconded."

"Though not as much as you do."

"That, my friend, is a stunningly accurate insight."

"You go first," I said. "It's okay."

"You sure?"

I nodded.

"I don't want to leave you here. . . ."

"The bathroom's right down the hall. And even you can't shower for more than half an hour."

She grinned weakly. "Watch me." She gathered fresh clothes and a towel, but stopped with her hand on the door. "It's not okay," she said. "I get that. You *know* I get that. But it will be. You will be."

"Promise?"

She nodded.

"As I recall, someone once told me to disregard ninety percent of everything you say," I told her.

The smile faded. "He should have listened to his own advice."

5

Bury it. Somewhere hidden, somewhere deep: deep enough to silence the scream. That was all. The simple recipe for sanity, for one foot in front of the other. The only way to hold on. To keep going.

If I wanted to keep going.

6

"Get in here," I told Eli, and he did.

"Sit down," I told him, and he did that, too, perching stiffly on the old radiator beneath the window.

I sat on the bed, trying not to inhale Max. Adriane wouldn't be gone for long. I needed to focus.

Here I was, in a foreign country, with this person I'd known for less than a month. This stranger. I knew he spoke Czech; I knew he hated his parents, or thought he did; I knew he had sea-colored eyes that slit when he was deciding whether to laugh. But nothing else: not how old he was, not what his life was like, not what he really wanted. I knew nothing that mattered, except that he had lied to me. I had let him.

"So. Crazy ninja skills," I said.

"It's a hobby."

"Six men. With knives. Versus you."

He shrugged.

"But apparently you also have a knife. And I guess, crazy knife-fighting skills?"

"Always be prepared." He held up three fingers in the Boy Scout salute.

"You were ready for them."

He hesitated. "I was ready for something."

"They were waiting for us on that bridge, like they knew we were coming," I said, and waited.

The words sat between us.

Finally. "There are some things you need to know."

"About you."

"About Max."

I hadn't expected that. Nor had I expected him to produce a manila folder and hold it out to me. "Or should we wait for Adriane?" he asked.

I took the folder. "Adriane won't listen to anything you say. She doesn't trust you."

"But you do?"

"I don't find that a useful question anymore," I said. I sounded cold; I felt cold. "I want to know what you know. If I can use it, fine."

"And if you can use me—"

"Also fine."

"You may feel differently when you open that folder."

"About you?"

"About everything."

"I'll risk it." I opened the folder.

It took a while to leaf through the stack of photos and emails, to understand what I was seeing, in print, in pixels, in full color and black and white, in brutal, time-stamped detail. It took a while—and then the bottom dropped out.

"Who are you?" I said when I could speak.

"Eliás Kapek. Eli. Just like I told you."

"And everything else you've told me?"

He held his gaze steady, giving nothing away. "I've been as truthful as I could."

I closed the folder, forcing myself not to fidget with its edges. Nor would I crush it, tear it, set fire to its remains.

"You're not Chris's cousin," I said.

"The Moores are perfectly safe, I promise."

"I didn't ask you that." Although I should have. It should have been my first concern, because if Eli wasn't Chris's cousin, then someone had forged the Moores' email claiming he was. For all I knew, someone had conveniently gotten them out of town, incommunicado. Or worse. My brain had gone foggy. "Everything I know about you is a lie. But you're expecting me to believe what's in this folder. That you've chosen now to tell me the truth."

"Believe it. Don't believe it. But it's all true."

The truth, according to Eli and his assembled evidence, made elegant sense. The dossier told a simple story.

> **Item:** One birth certificate for a Max Lewis.
>
> **Item:** Faded newsprint testifying to the death of Max Lewis in 1996, at age three.
>
> **Item:** One photocopied sheet of IDs, each with Max's photo, each with a different name, Max Schwarz, Max Black, Max Voják.
>
> **Item:** Email, addressed to anon34, detailing the successful effort to acquire Chris as a roommate and use him to monitor Professor Anton Hoffpauer's research program.
>
> **Item:** Email, to same, with updates on research protocol and progress made.

Item: Email, to same again, describing the recent discoveries of a certain Nora Kane, who might be *vyvolená*.

Item: Email, to Max, from anon34, advising that he go forward immediately, dated the night of Chris's death.

Item: One photograph of Max and two strange men on the steps of a church, all three in black robes.

Those were the highlights.

"He was one of them," Eli said. "I'm sorry. But there it is."

I shook my head. That felt too feeble. "No."

"He told you himself—the *Hledači* monitor everyone working on the Voynich manuscript. Max was sent to Chapman. He was assigned to Chris. And to you."

"No."

"The police couldn't find any record of his parents, of his past. It's because he doesn't have one. It was all a lie."

It couldn't all have been a lie.

I longed to return to that bloody riverbank, to throw myself in the path of the final arrow, Elizabeth had written, *to die ignorant, and so, in love. Better to be killed by an arrow than by the words of the one I most trusted.*

"That letter you found in his room, it's like the original membership recruiting brochure. *Hledači* carry them when they're on important missions. It's some kind of badge of honor. He must have gotten in some serious trouble for leaving it behind."

"What about the other letters? The ones under Chris's desk. They weren't his, were they?"

He hesitated, then shrugged. "They don't matter."

"They do to me." I needed to know if Chris had been a part of this.

346

"They weren't his," Eli said. "You needed incentive to get involved."

"*You?* You planted them."

He didn't respond.

"So the other letter, you planted that one, too."

"No. I didn't even know he had it until you showed it to me."

I snorted. "I'll just take your word for it, then."

"That letter belonged to Max. Think about it. He brought you to Prague—you and Elizabeth's letter. Or did you think that conveniently timed scholarship money was just the universe's way of saying thank you for being a friend?"

"How did you know about that?"

"And it doesn't seem strange to you that the *Hledači* conveniently left us alone to track down the pieces of the *Lumen Dei*, then struck at the very moment there was nothing left for us to find?"

"It's almost like they had a man on the inside," I said pointedly, but he was on a roll.

"And last night. Dinner was his idea. The bridge was his idea, and like you said, they were waiting for us. He delivered us right into their hands. Us and every piece of the *Lumen Dei* that we managed to track down—because *he* insisted on being the one to carry them."

"So why would they kill him?"

"They must have double-crossed him. Maybe it was punishment for the mess he made."

"The mess. You mean Chris."

He nodded.

"Where's the knife?" I asked.

"Nora, I swear, I'm not here to hurt you. I—"

"Then you won't mind me holding the knife. While we talk."

It was longer than I'd expected, and heavier. I felt better with it in my hand.

"I would tell you more if I could," he said. "Believe me. But the less you know, the safer you are." He tapped the folder. "You weren't ever supposed to see this."

"So why show it to me?"

"You needed to know."

"Who are you?" I said again, though I told myself the answer no longer mattered. He was a liar, a good one. A liar and a forger, who delighted in pain.

Or he wasn't.

"We're going to tell Adriane that I'm a PI hired by Chris's parents to find his killer," he said.

"But that's not true, is it."

"No."

"You want me to lie to her."

"Yes."

Because lies were nothing to him.

"Why would I do that?" I asked.

Max was a terrible liar, I reminded myself. He blushed; he fidgeted. He told truths no one wanted to hear.

He told me he loved me.

People lied for a reason. They lied to fill a need—for gain, for escape. But I'd had nothing he needed.

He said he needed me.

"I can protect you," Eli said. "That's why I'm here."

Another lie, and this one I could read on his face. "I don't want your protection," I said. "I want your help."

"Semantics."

"Help to go after them. The *Hledači*. To destroy them."

I saw his answer before he voiced it, in the taut muscles of his neck, the narrowing of his eyes, beneath his lies, a truth: "That's all I want."

"Why?"

348

"I can't tell you that."

"What can you tell me?" I said.

"What do you want to know?"

I wanted to un-know, un-see. To hand the folder back without opening it. To leave the postcard on my brother's grave, to stay in Chapman wondering whether I would ever see Max again, believing he would save me. I wanted not to question him when he could no longer answer. I wanted not to doubt. I did not want to know.

I wanted to believe.

"What did the priest say to you, on that first day? The one you fought with in the Church of St. Boethius."

I could tell I had surprised him.

"I can't tell you that, either," he said. "I'm sorry."

"Okay—then tell me what the *Hledači* meant on the bridge, about my destiny." The word that they had called me, the word that had appeared in Max's email. What was supposedly Max's email. "What's *vyvolená*?"

"*Chosen,*" he said. "*The chosen one.* You."

The single bark of laughter came unbidden. He didn't crack a smile.

"The *Hledači* believe that *ta, která ho najde, bude jako ta, která ho ukryla.*" he said. "'She who discovered it will be as she who disguised it.'"

"No one's discovered it yet," I said. "Isn't that their main problem?"

"You found the map," he said. "They've been searching for it for centuries. They believe God guided your hand, that you must be Elizabeth Weston's spiritual heir. *Lumen Dei má v krvi, její krev je v Lumen Dei.* 'The *Lumen Dei* is in her blood, as her blood is in the *Lumen Dei.*' Her blood. Your blood."

"Trust me, I am not related to Elizabeth Weston."

349

"You're thinking literally," he said. "They're thinking spiritually."

"So they don't literally want my blood."

"Well . . ."

"Great."

"It's why Max got close to you," he said. "And why he convinced you to come to Prague—why he pretended to help you track down the pieces. Because they needed the *vyvolená* to be the one to find the *Lumen Dei*."

The Hoff had known, I realized. *You're the one,* he had said. *They'll lie. But don't go!* Could he have meant that *Max* would lie, would kill, would do anything to get me to Prague to fulfill my supposed destiny?

Max, I remembered, was the one who found him.

"That doesn't explain why you pretended to help," I said. "Or how you know any of this."

"I knew some from the beginning. I know more now. And I told you. I'm here to protect you—"

"Because I'm *vyvolená*. Right. So you're crazy, too."

"Because if they think you're the *vyvolená*, you're in danger. They'll want to use you, just like Max did."

"Max loved me."

"That doesn't mean he wasn't using you."

"And you? What have you been doing all this time? Pretending to care about Chris? About—any of it?"

"Using you," he said.

I felt no satisfaction from the admission. I suspected it would be a long time before I felt anything again. "And are you sorry?"

"I . . . regret the need."

"That's not the same thing."

"I know."

"Are you one of them?" I asked.

350

"No."

"Are you lying?"

"No."

"You want me to believe that everything about Max was a lie. Everything he said, everything he did. Everything between us.All lies. That he was a murderer. And all those months with him, I just never noticed."

"He was good," Eli said.

"So how good are you?"

"If their agenda was my agenda, we wouldn't be here right now," he said. "I would just give them what they want the most."

"Me."

"You."

"With your crazy ninja skills."

"They come in handy."

"When you want them to," I said. If Max was *Hledači*, and Eli had known, he'd likely wasted little effort trying to save Max from his own, the men who'd pushed him to the edge of the bridge, and over it. If Max was *Hledači*, if everything unthinkable was true, then maybe I should have felt grateful.

I still felt cold. "Get out now. Please."

"What are you going to do?" he asked.

"Oh, so sorry, but I'm afraid I can't tell you that. I'm sure you understand."

"I'm trying to help you."

"Right now you need to do it from somewhere else."

"Nora—"

I threw the folder. Incriminating evidence fluttered and flapped, drifting gently to the ground. "*Go.*"

Once I was alone, I collected the pages from where they had fallen and stuffed them into my backpack. Then I returned to the bed, picked at loose threads in the stained floral spread, imagined the weight of him on the mattress, on me, the creak of the bed-springs beneath us, the flutter of moths and the scuttle of rodents in shadowed corners, the things he whispered to me in the dark.

The best lies, the most believable lies, are mostly truth. I read that once, somewhere.

In a world without absolutes, the truth is whatever you choose to believe. I read that, too. But I never understood how you choose. Or choose not to.

Adriane came back from the shower damp and radiant. "Your turn," she said. Then, "You okay?"

I stood up. "Eli's not who he said he was."

"Then who is he?"

I could admit I didn't know, and didn't know if it mattered. Or I could lie.

7

"Seriously, what kind of PI doesn't carry a gun?" Adriane complained. She pulled on her hood, casting her face in shadow.

"If everything goes smoothly, we won't need a gun," Eli said. It was strange to see the black robes billowing around them, stranger still to feel the scratchy wool of my own robe brush against my ankles, to peer out from beneath the hood that cut off all periphery vision. So this was how the world looked to the *Hledači:* narrow and rimmed with darkness.

"Well, in that case, I'm sure we'll be fine," Adriane said. "Things have been going so smoothly for us up till now."

Eli stopped. The Letohrádek Hvězda, the Star Summer House, was in our sights, a glowing, six-pointed oasis in the dark field. It was a moonless night, and our path was lit only by the light of his phone screen. "If you don't want to do this, you can wait here. But decide now."

Adriane raised her hands, palms up, balancing the options. "Hmm. Sneak into the hornet's nest, or wait here, alone and defenseless, for hornets to come to me."

I let their bickering wash over me. They were both afraid, and this was how they hid it. But not me. I'd buried my fear along with my grief. It was too big—too dangerous. Feeling anything would mean feeling too much.

"Let's go," she said, then, as we padded through the grass toward the *Hledači* hive, added, "but just in case circumstances prevent me from saying it later, let me add a preemptive 'I told you so.'"

I'd given her a choice. Not the real one, of course. But a choice nonetheless. Eli, the private investigator, wanted to handle this himself, I'd told her. Go to the authorities about Max's death, the *Hledači*, all of it. The all of it that she knew, at least. I couldn't tell her about the folder. Too humiliating, if she believed the evidence, if she looked up from the emails and photos with eyes full of pity for the pathetic loser who'd been so easily deceived. And if she didn't believe it, if she believed in Max . . . what would that say about me, and whatever weakness made me so eager to doubt?

Eli would take care of things, I offered, and we would go home.

"They can come after us there just as easily as they can here," she'd said. "Look at Chris. That's not going to be me."

"So what do you want to do?"

"We go after them," she said. "We take it all back."

The clues, the stolen pieces of the *Lumen Dei*.

Our lives.

I didn't ask which.

The Letohrádek Hvězda, a daytime tourist attraction, was locked down at night, but Eli, the fake PI without a real weapon, had a knife and a paper clip, and within minutes, we were inside.

I couldn't imagine what it would have looked like in the benevolent daylight, but at night, with its unsettling angles and bas-relief stone gods watching us from every surface, it was too easy to understand why a sect of religious fanatics had chosen the Star Summer House as their home base. Rudolf's grandfather had built it as a hunting lodge-cum-sacred site, perfect for whatever weird mystical rituals he—and apparently five subsequent centuries of gullibles and nutcases—chose to attempt. The building foundation was set in the shape of the Star of Solomon, the better to connect with the powerful forces of the macrocosm, and everything—the number of levels, the floor colors, the painted walls and stucco-carved ceilings depicting heroic Greek gods—was dedicated to aligning with the four elements and thus turning the building into some kind of magical lightning rod for divinely approved conjurers. The *Hledači*—as apparently everyone who was anyone in the secret-society crowd knew—had bought it hook, line, and sinker. According to Eli, that is. Another thing I didn't tell Adriane: the not-insignificant possibility that Eli was still lying, and we were walking into an ambush.

I believed that Eli hated them—that, for motives of his own that had nothing to do with helping us, he was nonetheless helping us.

But it had become clear that my beliefs were no longer to be trusted.

The robes had been easy to acquire. The plan was simple: We would descend into the bowels of the Star Summer House, the secret chambers supposedly dug out beneath its basement, and, costumed as rank-and-file *Hledači*, we would float past the guard posted by the hidden doorway, infiltrate the nest of murderously busy bees, then seek out incriminating evidence we could photograph, record, or steal.

The backup plan was simpler: We would run.

8

We didn't have to run. The robes proved the only password we needed, and we were waved into a warren of cavelike chambers and corridors lit only by dim gas lanterns and flickering candles. *Hledači* scuttled past us with urgency, and we kept our heads down, our bodies turned inward, as if engaged in intense conversation not to be disturbed, and hugged the shadows as we followed behind.

We had delivered ourselves into the hands of our would-be murderers, and still, I was not afraid.

Adriane held the phone, its camera activated, her finger on the shutter. And we joined the flow of *Hledači* into a dark chamber, round as the building above us was sharp. Atop a golden altar stood a man whose robe was white and whose eyes, from where we hovered at the back of the crowd, seemed bottomless and black. The stone behind him was inscribed with a familiar symbol: an eye speared by a lightning bolt, painted in dark red, twenty feet high.

I hadn't expected a crowd.

I'd pictured the *Hledači* as a ragtag collection of eccentrics, the crumbling remains of what had once been a fanatical army, now dwindled to ten or fifteen at the most. Eli had apprised me of my mistake, but seeing it was different. Now I believed: The *Hledači* was still an army, hundreds strong. A cult, a people, all draped in the same heavy black, their voices raised in a unifying chant, their words echoing off the curved stone, swelling to fill the chamber, until they fell into abrupt silence at the sight of their leader's raised fist. He shouted in Czech, and the crowd thundered.

Adriane hid the phone beneath her robe, its recording function taking in the leader's voice as it rose and fell with mesmerizing rhythm and Eli whispered the only translation we needed: "He says he's called them together because the *Lumen Dei* is closer than it has ever been before, and they need only one more piece to meet their destiny. That nothing will stop them."

And then the man stopped, and his masses filled in the quiet left in his wake with a new chant, which needed no translation, for mixed into the alien words was one I recognized, one that was repeated, an angry drumbeat driving them to a fever pitch.

Vyvolená!

Vyvolená!

VYVOLENÁ!

The fear had come back. And every time they said that word, it grew.

"Maybe we should get out of here," Adriane whispered.

This time there was no bickering.

With the *Hledači* absorbed by their bloodlust rally, the other chambers were largely empty, giving us free rein to wander, searching for anything we might use as leverage with the cops or the *Hledači* themselves. We found it behind a wooden door carved with a woman mounting a centaur. The room, its walls lined with fraying, leather-bound books, may have begun life as a library but now clearly functioned less as a storehouse for ancient wisdom than it did a repository of information on the search for the *Lumen Dei*, beginning in the sixteenth century, ending with us.

This was what we hadn't dared hope for; it could save our lives.

Adriane snapped photo after photo while Eli and I leafed through stacks and files of personnel dossiers, crumbling newspapers, journal articles about the Voynich manuscript, paintings and photographs of those who studied it, potential *vyvolenás* from nineteenth-century London, Nazi Germany, imperial Japan, all of them discarded without care or organization, like trash, in favor

356

of the documents and photos that papered the back wall. It was the wall of crazy found in every Hollywood serial killer's lair: Surveillance photos of Chris and Adriane and me. Our birth certificates, our report cards. Photocopies of the Voynich symbols. Arrowed diagrams connecting us to each other and to the Hoff and his book. Crowd shots with blood-red circles marking my face. Intimate pictures capturing the faces we saved for when we were alone.

There were no pictures of Max.

We had dropped our hoods to paw through the treasure trove, so when the door swung open, the man with slender hands and white-blond brows—who looked like he was only a few years older than us and, in another life, could have been a real librarian, in charge of a book collection rather than a murder plot—knew us for exactly what we were. The enemy.

He snapped something in rapid Czech and, because Adriane was the closest, grabbed her wrist, swung her into his arms, and braced one hand on her head and the other on her shoulder. "Tell me what you do here," he said in halting English when the Czech drew no response, "or I break her neck."

Adriane went pale.

Eli, who had been on the other side of the room when the *Hledači* burst in, crept slowly along the wall, out of sight, toward us, but still too far away to stop the angry wrenching of muscle and snapping of bones, if it came to that. He drew his knife.

The *Hledači* snatched the phone from Adriane's hand and flung it against the stone floor, grinding his heel into the cheap plastic casing until it split. It didn't seem to matter much. Evidence wouldn't help us if we never lived to use it.

"Let her go," I said. Not pleading, but ordering.

When I spoke, his eyes met mine and widened. "*Vyvolená*," he whispered.

"That's right. *Let her go.*" I couldn't believe the imperious voice coming out of my mouth.

"And this is the other," he said, turning to Adriane, who was still immobilized by his grip, "the friend of the chosen one." He pressed his lips to her ear and whispered something—and whatever it was made her draw in a sharp breath and go even paler than before. "I will not harm the *vyvolená* or her people," he said aloud, and let her go.

Adriane flew toward me, and in the same moment, moving so fast it seemed like he wasn't moving at all, Eli was across the room. He seized the *Hledači* from behind and raised the knife to his throat. "No screaming, understand?"

"*Ano,*" the man said. "Yes." His eyes were still locked on my face.

"Adriane, get the door. Nora, find something to tie him up with."

We used his shoelaces. While Eli held the knife steady at the man's throat, I yanked his wrists behind his back, looped the laces around once, twice, focusing on the small hairs sprouting from the knuckles and the grubby, broken nails. These hands might have held down Chris, I thought. Trapped him in place as the knife slipped in.

These hands might have forced Max over the side, into the water.

I pulled the knot tight, tight as I could. The laces bit into his flesh. Good.

"What did he say to you?" Eli asked Adriane.

She shook her head. "I don't know," she whispered, like she couldn't draw enough breath to speak. "It was Czech."

"What did you say to her?" Eli asked the *Hledači*.

The *Hledači* said nothing.

"Not feeling chatty? Good. Because now we're all going to

358

walk out of here nice and quietly, and if you make a sound, or do anything to alert any of your friends, I'm going to shove this knife straight into your kidneys. *Oddělám tě na ulici a vykuchám tě jako rybu.* Got that?"

The man nodded.

"You want to take him *with* us?" I said.

"We can't stay here. Too risky. But we need information, and we need evidence, and our new friend broke the camera. So grab as many files as you can stuff under your robes. I'll grab *him.*"

Adriane's face was still emptied of color. But she didn't argue, and neither did I.

"You walk in front," Eli said. "I'll follow behind. With the knife. And just to make sure our friend doesn't get any bright ideas—"

The knife flashed. A narrow slash of red streaked across *Hledači* scalp. Eli's hand slapped over his mouth just in time to muffle the scream.

"What did you *do*?" Adriane said in a choked voice as a curtain of blood streamed from the gash. The man blinked wildly and flung his head back and forth as rivulets of red flowed into his eyes.

"It's shallow, but it should keep him blind and docile at least until we get him out of here," he said.

"You know this because?"

"Saw it in a movie. Trust me."

Adriane looked away. But I watched the blood cloud his eyes and, again, wondered if those eyes had watched Chris's blood pool from his body, watched and then turned away and let him die.

"You shouldn't have done that," I said. But as the *Hledači* gasped with pain, I felt it growing inside of me: a smile.

9

The room we found was five flights up, rented by the hour. I'd seen enough *Law & Order* episodes to imagine what it was usually used for, but if I hadn't, its multicolored stains and moist, overripe perfume would have given it away. It stank of sweat and sex. The three of us had easily managed to half walk, half drag the *Hledači* out of the Star Summer House, down two empty blocks, and up the decrepit staircase. The man sleeping on the stairs didn't even stir when we stepped over him.

A tattered gray shade blocked the only window. A single bare ceiling bulb cast more shadows than it did light. Bound to a chair, the *Hledači* was gagged by a pillowcase Eli had stuffed into his mouth. It seemed like overkill. The room delivered its message from every inch of peeling paint and rotting floorboards: Even if anyone could hear you scream, it was a sure thing no one would care.

Eli paced, holding the knife he'd promised not to use again. He spoke in Czech, firing rapid questions, then pulled out the gag.

The man pressed his lips together.

"*Mluv!*" Eli shouted.

"I speak to the *vyvolená*," he said, in halting English. "Not to you."

"*Nemusíš se rozhodnout,*" Eli snapped.

I stepped forward. "The *vyvolená*, that's me, right? So here I am. Speak."

"They will come."

"No one's coming for you," Eli said.

"Not for me. For *vyvolená*. You will not stop them."

"Actually, we will," I said. "And you're going to help."

"I respect the *vyvolená*," he said. "You will lead us to the light."

360

"How am I supposed to do that?" I asked. "What are they planning to do once they come for me?"

"You will lead us to the light," he repeated.

"Let's say I'm not interested in doing that. What's it going to take to get you to leave us alone?"

"We can pay," Adriane said. "A lot."

"We need only *vyvolená*," he said.

"And the rest of the *Lumen Dei*," I said. "There's not going to be any light without that, right? So if it stays hidden, you're screwed, and you don't need me."

"We will all always need you."

"We brought you here to help us," Eli said. "If you can't do that, we've got no use for you." He fingered the knife, running a thumb along the blade. "Think your friends will be jealous when you get to meet God face to face? You don't need a machine. Only this." He raised the knife.

"You will not harm me," the *Hledači* said.

"So where'd you get that nasty cut?"

"You stand so far away," the *Hledači* said. "Do you fear me?"

Eli crossed the room in three swift steps. His blade slashed down, stopping just short of piercing the man's flesh. "Do you fear me?"

The man threw his weight forward, tipping the chair onto its front legs, and snatched a handful of Eli's shirt, yanking it down so hard it exposed the dark tattoo over his heart. Eli twisted out of his grip.

The *Hledači* spit in his face.

"You are a child," he said. "But you are still scum. You will never stop us."

"Nora. Adriane. You should leave now," Eli said, circling the *Hledači*. "You don't want to see this."

Maybe I had known it would end here. I was probably

supposed to care. "We agreed...." But the objection died on my lips.

"He knows things," Eli said. "He's going to tell us what they are."

"Oh yes, I know many things. I know what you are. *Kolik toho vědí? Co když jim řeknu všechno?*"

"What's he saying now?" I asked.

"Trust me," Eli said. "Leave."

"Stay," the *Hledači* jeered. "I have many gifts for you."

"We're leaving," Adriane said, pulling me out the door, and I let her, because closing the door behind us meant we weren't a part of it, whatever it would be. Our hands were clean.

10

No one screamed.

Muffled voices, thuds, scratches, breaking glass.

A dark stain blotted out most of the hallway ceiling, bloody against the rust-colored walls. Just water, I told myself.

"How long do we wait?" Adriane said.

I shrugged.

"What do you think he's doing in there?" she said.

"Do you care?"

"No."

11

Eventually.

"Eli?"

I knocked harder. "Eli?" No answer.

No sounds at all from behind the door.

I turned to Adriane. "What do you think?"

"I think I'm still wishing we had a gun."

"I'm going in," I said.

She spread her arms wide: *Be my guest.* Then she pulled out a car key that fit a Mercedes parked four thousand miles away, gripping the jagged silver like it was the world's smallest knife.

"Seriously?"

"Told you that self-defense class would come in handy one day."

"Actually, you told me the only hard part was pretending to pay attention while you drooled over Coach Gorgeous."

"You know I've always been good at role-play." She raised the key. "Just remember: Aim for the soft tissue. Or the balls." She sang tunelessly, "'Eyes, throat, nose, groin, that's the way you make 'em scream.' Coach Gorgeous wasn't great with rhymes."

I opened the door.

The chair was empty. The window was broken. Eli lay on his stomach, face turned toward us, eyes closed. Forehead bloody.

I couldn't breathe.

Adriane dropped to his side, and a beat later, I followed her, lips forming the word *please* even as I hated myself for thinking it, because if wishes or prayers or whatever hadn't saved Max, or Chris, or Andy, I didn't want them saving him. And yet: *Please.*

"Pulse," Adriane said, fingers at his throat.

We turned him over, watching his chest rise and fall. Adriane called out his name, then slapped him.

"Adriane! Don't."

She slapped him again. Nothing. "You want to carry him out? Or leave him here? Or maybe just hang around until our new friend shows up with reinforcements?"

"Eli!" I shouted. "Wake up!"

His lids fluttered, dropping shut again for a moment, then opening to reveal dazed saucer eyes. He blinked slowly, twice, and groaned. "He got away."

"He hasn't lost his grasp on the obvious," Adriane said. "That's got to be a good sign."

"Can you stand?" I took his arm. He let me help him into a sitting position.

"He hit me with something." Eli rubbed the drying blood on his forehead. "I'm okay. Just"—he tried climbing to his feet, then thought better of it—"give me a minute."

"We may not have a minute," I said. "They know we're here—"

"How did he get free?" Adriane asked.

"I don't . . . He just did," Eli said.

"Uh-huh."

"Let him rest for a second," I told her.

"It doesn't seem a little strange to you?" she said. "The guy's about to spill his guts, Eli kicks us out of the room, and next thing you know, he's gone?"

"Right. I untied him, threw him out the window, then whacked myself in the head. Does that sound about right?"

"For all I know, you sliced and diced him and stuffed him in the closet."

Eli looked around pointedly at the four bare walls and distinct lack of hiding places.

"Or, fine. Under the bed. Out the window. Wherever. Makes as much sense as him magically untying himself."

Eli stood. "I'm okay now. Let's get out of here."

Adriane didn't argue. In fact, she didn't say anything as we raced down to the street and wound a convoluted route through Prague, returning to the hostel only after we were sure no one had followed us.

"We're going to our room now," Adriane told him when we

made it back to what now passed for home. "And we're locking ourselves in until we figure out what to do next. Don't call us, we'll call you, and all that. Come on, Nora."

"I'm on your side," he said. "You know that. Nora, you know that."

"We made a mistake," I said. "It was a stupid plan."

"So we make another one."

"No, *we* make another one," Adriane said. "When we need you, we'll let you know." She turned and started for the dingy staircase, apparently assuming I would follow her.

"Nora—" With the black eye and dented forehead, he looked sweetly pathetic, like a cartoon puppy with a torn ear. I hesitated. Adriane didn't know everything.

But then, neither did I. And whose fault was that?

"You should rest," I told him. "Then we'll talk."

"Just take this," he said, and pulled a creased page out of his pocket. "I found it in the library. Before the guy showed up."

"What is it?"

"Proof I'm trying to help you," he said.

I accepted the offering but didn't bother to look at it. "Anything else you want to tell me?"

"About what?"

"What happened in that room. Or anything . . . about anything. About you. You want to prove something to me, try starting with some answers."

His back straightened. "You're right. I should get some rest."

"Right."

"I am trying," he said.

"Try harder."

12

Don't think about Max.

  Don't think about Max.

  Don't think about Max.

  I was trying, too.

13

Latin had always made sense when nothing else did. That was the point of it, for me. Language as mathematical equation, slotting one word in for another, shifting positions, adding, subtracting, substituting, applying one rigorous rule after another, until eventually, from the jumble of letters, a single, true meaning emerged. One meaning, hidden beneath all the mistakes and wrong turns. One puzzle, one solution. Latin was a question that supplied its own answer.

"Why are you even bothering?" Adriane asked, flopped on the bed, eyes closed against a rising sun.

"Because it could help."

She sighed.

"They wanted it; we have it. That's got to matter."

"No, Nora. It doesn't."

I ignored her and turned back to the page Eli had given me, the end of Elizabeth's story, its jagged edge a perfect fit with the torn page we'd found at Strahov.

The torn page Eli had found, or claimed he had. But if he'd stolen the rest himself, why? And why give it back to me now? If he was only pretending to help us, why wasn't he doing a better job of it?

I stopped thinking about that and focused on the words. *Mihi dixit se fecisse pecuniae causa.*

It was the money, he told me. It allowed him to imagine a future, before he had anyone with whom to imagine it.

But it was not just the money.

It was no accident, he said, that Václav had come to him. Václav had known Thomas as a child, not well, but well enough. Václav had seen Thomas's family consigned to poverty because his ancestors had been foolish enough to stand against the Empire, and against the Church. Like Václav, Thomas came from a once-distinguished line that had nearly been extinguished at the hands of the Hapsburgs, only because they longed for a closer relationship with their Lord, closer than the Church could allow.

Václav asked him to consider what would happen if the Hapsburg Emperor, secular leader of the Church, gained the full powers of divinity. Ruled with the power of God, rather than only His divine imprimatur.

—He asked me to save my people, and save myself.

And he paid you, I said.

—And he paid me.

All Thomas needed do was report on my actions, a simple request before he knew me. Once he did know me, once we became something to each other, he could do nothing. Václav was dangerous, not just to Thomas, but to me.

So he continued to spy.

—I knew no other way. If I had told you the truth . . .

He had been afraid, I knew, but not of Václav. He feared

me, and what I would do, if he confessed. What we would both lose.

Did you know what was going to happen tonight, I asked him, what they would demand of me?

—I know Václav believes he needs you. He believes that the Lumen Dei *must be handed over willingly. By you.*

Thomas grasped my hands and promised to save me, to finish this, to redeem himself.

—No.

They had given me a choice, these cowards who hid their faces. I would not turn from that. I would destroy the Lumen Dei, *or I would join Groot in presenting it to the Emperor, or I would spirit it away and deliver it to Václav, reaping my own reward. None of these choices could guarantee my life, but any of them would be mine. Ours, Thomas corrected me, swearing he would stand by me.*

—No. Mine.

I left him there, in the dark of the church, penitent. I left him behind, and when I saw him again, it was too late.

For two days, I was tortured by the choice that lay before me and the betrayal that lay behind. Dearest brother, how many times I wished you could guide my hand. But the choice was mine alone and, however poorly, I made it.

Groot rejoiced at the arrival of Kepler's calculations, and he proudly showed me the device he had constructed in my absence. The Lumen Dei *was as glorious as promised, and with Kepler's work in hand, Groot and the Emperor could easily align it with the heavens and entreat the Lord.*

I dared not go home, lest the angry priest return. I dared

not venture into the city, lest Václav's men grow impatient.
I dared not face Thomas. I stayed in Groot's laboratory, and
there I slept, on a bed of straw and feathers, pretending, when
I crossed paths with Václav, that I did not know his secret,
nor he mine. I dared only ask God for guidance, but, as ever,
received only silence in return.

Perhaps this is why I chose as I did. Perhaps I had grown
impatient waiting for Him to answer. The **Lumen Dei** *needed*
to be given willingly, Thomas had said, and that was how I gave
it. It was neither for silver nor to spare my life that I brought
the **Lumen Dei** *to the edge of the city that night and gave our*
Father's legacy away. If left with Groot, the device was destined
for the Emperor, and forgive me, but I could not grant such a
gift to our Father's murderer. I could not give Rudolf and his
heir power over this world and the next, any more than I could
consign the Continent to a millennium of Hapsburg rule.

I believed I was doing right. I could not know what was to
happen.

This is what I tell myself, in those sleepless hours before
dawn. I could not have known.

But I know this. Of all my regrets—and if measured by
tears, there are enough of these to flood the river—I regret
most that I left Thomas behind that day without telling him the
truth. I regret that the last words I would ever say to him were
harsh, and he will never know that I forgave him as soon as
the confession escaped his lips. That I had no other choice.

She had forgiven him. Inexplicably, impossibly, she had
forgiven him. I was disgusted. And maybe, against my better
judgment and two decades of feminist rearing, a little ashamed,

because I couldn't have done it. She loved him enough to forgive him, no matter what he had done. And then lost him anyway.

She was probably better off.

I could steal from Groot, my brother, but I cannot steal from you. This is the only reason I have not dashed the Lumen Dei *to pieces, but dismantled it with care, and led you down this dangerous path. You now hold Kepler's calculations, and all that is left for you is to build the spine of the device, the brass and wood guts of the machine that can do no more harm to me but untold amounts to you and your world. We both know how easy it is to ignore a warning. I have learned that it is also foolish. But perhaps it is foolish to issue so many, while at the same time giving you all you need to go forward.*

So few things in this world are eternal, but it appears my foolishness numbers among them.

Your path ends here—

The rest was in English.

> *BE IT BUT GREEN EVIL, THE MYTH TRODS.*
> *LURE A RARE SKY.*
> *HOW, FATHER? VISIT. WIN.*
> *MOUTH WELT, BE THORN.*

I knew Elizabeth well enough by now to know her poetry was never just poetry. Especially when it was about as poetical as a kindergartner's crayoned Mother's Day card. I played with the meaningless words, trying out different substitution algorithms, searching the rest of the letter for a number, a clue, something to yield the answer. There was nothing.

We were so close. One more piece, that was all the *Hledači* needed to fulfill four centuries of dreaming, and this was the key to stopping them. Elizabeth hadn't convinced me that the *Lumen Dei* was worth killing for, or that it would be any more dangerous in the hands of the *Hledači* than it would be in a landfill, so maybe there was no reason to care. But I did. It was nearly the only thing I cared about anymore—it was the only thing left. They'd taken Chris away from me; they'd taken Max. They would *not* take Elizabeth, or her legacy. Whether the *Lumen Dei* was worth the world or just worthless, they would not have it.

Not after what they'd done.

I flipped through the letter again. But maybe the answer wasn't there. Maybe it was in the nonsense words themselves. Maybe it was just that simple.

An anagram, a child's game. My father had liked to play with them, back when he played. Every sentence is a liar, he used to say. At least anagrams are up front about it.

> *BE IT BUT GREEN EVIL, THE MYTH TRODS.*
> *LURE A RARE SKY.*
> *HOW, FATHER? VISIT. WIN.*
> *MOUTH WELT, BE THORN.*

There were enough letters for an eternity of false starts. *Ebbed Eighteen Thirty Volt Strum . . . A Leakier Sun Worry . . . A Vise Forthwith . . . Trouble Tenth Whom.*

Every line had a ridiculous number of permutations. But I had endless patience and an emptiness to fill, and every once in a while, I hit on a word that sounded right. It sounded like Elizabeth.

Birthright. Knew. Love. I let instinct guide me. It shouldn't have worked. But:

> *YOUR BIRTHRIGHT SLUMBERS BENEATH THE*
> *DOVE,*
> *WHERE I FIRST KNEW TRULY WHAT IT MEANT*
> *TO LOVE.*

Their first kiss, I thought. On a stone tower that had fallen centuries ago.

Or their first fade to black, in a grassy field somewhere in the empty map between Prague and Graz.

The first place he took her hand, the first place she looked into his eyes, the first place he held her and tilted his forehead to hers, his gaze fixed on her lips, and whispered, because it was only for them, "I love you."

Max.

Adriane had scrunched up his jacket, the one he'd draped over her shoulders on that last night, and tucked it under her head. His jacket, under her head, like it was a pillow, like it was nothing. I didn't say anything. It probably smelled like her now, anyway.

She deserved to know.

"Adriane . . ."

Her eyes were closed, but she was awake. We'd shared too many sleepovers for me not to know the tells.

"It's naptime," she said, without opening her eyes, a tinge of sleep in her voice.

"I need to—"

"What?"

Tell you something.

"Ask you something."

I stopped. We both waited. Finally, "What?"

"When did you know you were in love?" I asked.

She stretched, catlike, angling her body toward the dim sunlight. A faint smile crept across her face. Maybe she had been asleep after all, because when she spoke, it sounded almost like she was describing a dream. "It was at the Spot," she said. It was the name we'd given to the narrow spit of land that stretched toward the center of the Chapman Reservoir. Shaded by sugar maples, bordered by gently lapping blue, reachable only by a twenty-minute hike from the road and discovered only by mistake, it was the perfect spot for summer swimming, fall picnics, and breezy nights beneath a blanket, under the stars. The kind of spot that makes you feel like you're in an impossibly boring movie about impossibly true love. It was our spot, the four of us, though Max and I had often snuck off there on our own. Apparently we weren't the only ones. "We weren't even doing anything. Just lying there. He'd made this cheesy crown for me out of weeds, and I was afraid I had bugs in my hair, but other than that, it was perfect. That's when I knew."

"Really? Not until senior year?" We hadn't found the Spot until a few weeks before school started—almost two years after she and Chris had started dating.

She opened her eyes and sat up. "No, of course not. Way before that."

"But then how was it at the Spot?"

"Oh. Right." She paused. "I hate to tell you this, but . . . I've known about that place forever."

I shook my head. "We found it together. That day when we were lost—"

"That's what you wanted to think, because it made a good story. So we let you."

"What? Why would you lie about that?"

She shrugged. "Why would I lie about this?"

"Fine. You lied. Everyone does, right? Forget it."

"Come on, don't be mad." It was her whiny, kidlike voice, the *who, me?* of sloughed-off responsibilities and evaded blame. "You have to forgive me; I'm your best friend." When it was convenient. "It's in the rule book."

"I forgive you," I said mechanically, my mind somewhere else. I'd read Elizabeth's bloodstained letter so many times I almost had it memorized, especially the last line: *I can forgive you almost anything, my brother. But I cannot forgive this.*

She couldn't forgive him leaving her behind; you could never love anyone enough for that. But anything else, she could forgive, because she loved him—as she had loved Thomas, no matter what.

I forgave him as soon as the confession escaped his lips.

When she knew truly what it meant to love?

That couldn't be right. Some things had to be unforgivable, no matter what. Some things, when broken, stayed that way.

But it didn't matter what I thought. This was Elizabeth's game. And Elizabeth had believed in forgiveness.

I stood up. "I know where it is."

"What?"

"The *Lumen Dei*. The final pieces. Are you coming?"

"Why bother?" she asked. "You heard the *Hledači* guy. Even if you find something, it can't help us."

"What happened to 'We go after them and take it all back'?"

"We went after them," she said flatly. "It didn't work."

"That doesn't mean—"

"We have the files we grabbed. We can give them to the cops."

"And then what? Cross our fingers and hope that's the end of it? Wait for them to come?"

Adriane stretched again, sighing as she spread her arms to the corners of the mattress, as if what we were discussing had no consequence and was keeping her from a pressing nap. "You want to know what that guy whispered in my ear?"

"You told Eli he was speaking in Czech."

"And now I'm telling *you* the truth. He said, 'Go home and forget this, and we will not follow. We have what we want.' It means we get our lives back, Nora. It means if we drop this, and just go quietly, maybe we can leave here with something left."

I didn't ask her what it was we had left, because the only answer was: each other. I didn't know if it was enough.

374

"And you believe them?" I said. "What about all the 'chosen one' stuff?"

"Isn't that more reason to get the hell out? We can't fight them, Nora. I thought we could, but once I saw them all together—" She shook her head. "There's too many of them, and they're too crazy. I'm done. You go do what you need to do, but I'm staying."

"I'm not leaving you here by yourself. It's not safe."

"And it's going to be safe with *you*? The 'chosen one,' out poking the bear that's already pretty eager to eat you? I think I'll take my chances with the cockroaches and the guy at the front desk."

"Are you sure this isn't about something else? Because nothing has changed, except that we're so close."

"Nora, you know how you don't want to talk about what happened, and I'm respecting that and giving you your weird distance, just like I always do?"

"My weird distance?"

"How about you give me some? You finish your scavenger hunt. Then we'll go home."

"I can stay with you."

"No, you can't." She didn't sound angry, just decided. "So you might as well go find your treasure. Maybe you're even right. Maybe it'll help."

"Okay, I get it," I said, and tried to.

"I hope you find it, Nora," she said as I was almost out the door.

"Why do you even care?"

"Because you do."

"I thought we both did," I said—then, without asking, reached behind her and took Max's jacket.

"It's not that cold out."

"Cold enough."

14

Eli was waiting in the lobby, sprawled across the one ratty couch, his eyes half-closed, doing an excellent job of pretending not to watch the door. He jumped up as I passed.

"Where are we going?" he said.

"'We'?"

"I'm obviously not letting you out that door by yourself. It's not safe."

"And you are?"

"There was another clue, wasn't there?" he said. "And you figured it out. It's the only reason you'd risk leaving."

"Maybe I'm out of conditioner. It's a mistake to overlook the value of moisturizing."

"You know either we go together, or I follow you."

"Under other circumstances, screw you."

"But . . ."

"But in this particular case, you might be useful."

"So what I'm hearing is: *Please, Eli, would you be so kind as to lend your assistance, because I desperately need you.*"

"Trust me, you're still hearing *screw you,*" I said.

"Good enough. So do we wait for Adriane?"

"No. We do not."

15

"And what makes you think I can get us down to the crypt?" Eli asked, staring up at the gray exterior of the church. The Kostel sv Boethia, where a priest had woven us our first *Hledači* tale. The Kostel sv Boethia, where Thomas had confessed the worst of himself to the woman he loved; where Elizabeth had loved him enough to forgive.

Sometimes a coincidence was just a coincidence. Sometimes not.

"Maybe if you ask nicely, your priest friend will give us permission," I said.

"We're talking about a sacred crypt where they've buried the bones of their martyrs. I don't think a *pretty please* is going to do it," Eli said.

"And he's not your friend," I said. "You forgot that part."

He didn't rise to it. "We should try the back."

Behind the church: an empty street, a long stone wall with two half-empty plastic cups of beer, a locked door.

"Not a problem." Eli scouted several feet of gutter and returned with a bent piece of metal wire, which slipped easily into the lock and twisted beneath his sure fingers. Something clicked.

"That easy?"

The door slipped open. "That easy."

We tiptoed inside and down a narrow flight of stairs, burrowing into the earth. A dim bulb, like a holy night-light, cast a glow on the rust-colored walls and low, arched ceiling. There were unlit candelabras, stone faces howling from pillars, mysterious stains spreading from tombs set into the floor. All the makings of a low-budget horror movie, complete with idiot teens blundering around in the dark, hunting and hunted.

And, carved in bas-relief at the apex of a stone arch, a dove, with an olive branch dangling from its beak.

I pointed at the stone bird. "This is the place."

"It's a Catholic symbol of the Holy Spirit. Finding a dove in a crypt is like finding a beer in a baseball stadium. Not to mention you don't even know if you solved the code correctly."

"Yes. I do." I wedged my fingers into the darkness between

the stones directly below the dove. Something shifted. "It's loose," I said. "This has to be it."

Eli stayed my hand. "You sure about this?"

I stared at him. "The dove. The church—the same church. How much more do you need?"

"No, I mean . . ." He looked away. "This is hallowed ground. We can't just rip up the floorboards like it's your parents' basement."

"That's not what we're doing."

"You would never have dug up the cemetery. You said that."

"Okay, but—"

"There are people buried here, too."

I was trying very hard not to think about that. "I'm not digging them up."

He looked unconvinced.

"Look, you insisted on coming with me. If you want to go, go. But I'm doing this."

"I just—" He closed his eyes and lowered his head, moving his lips soundlessly. Only for a moment, and then he faced me again. "Okay. Let's do it."

I didn't ask if he had been praying, or to whom, for what. Nor did I allow myself to ask for forgiveness of my own as I pried the stones loose from their hallowed home. It's not like God had ever asked forgiveness from me.

A dark layer of earth and grime lay beneath the stones. Nestled in it, coffinlike, was a wood and iron box, three times the size of the one we'd excavated beneath the Mihulka. I had known I was right; it wasn't until I wrapped my hands around the box that I actually believed it. This was it, the blood and guts of the *Lumen Dei*—not just a handful of earth or a promise of alchemical transmutation, but the actual building blocks of the machine, the iron or wood or gold that would give it a shape and form.

378

Silence blanketed us.

Eli nodded. *Go ahead.*

Four hundred years ago, Elizabeth had sealed her birthright inside this box. She had turned her back on the wealth and power the *Lumen Dei* promised to deliver—even if it was nothing but useless gears and sticks, she could have traded it for a home, a future, a life independent of a man she didn't love. And if it was the golden ticket they all believed it to be, if it could illuminate men's minds with a divine light, deliver on its promise, grant omniscience, omnipotence, the ultimate answer . . . she had turned from that as well. Left it behind, for the one person she trusted, for a brother who'd committed a single, final, unforgivable betrayal, for a ghost.

Or maybe for me.

I opened the box.

16

Václav Kysely, to the sorceress Elizabeth Weston.

What did you think? That you could have your wealthy court dog throw me in debtors' prison and I would rot there? That you could bury your secrets in the dirt and no one would ever dig them up?

I followed you, as you should have known I would. I watched you dig your hole and bury your stolen treasure, and I waited until the time was right. Now I have the most important piece of the device, and soon I will discover where you have hidden the others. I will succeed where my master failed. And when I do, I will rid the earth of its scourge of usurpers. I will begin with you.

This is your warning, Westonia, as you please to call yourself, putting on airs as if no one will know the mud you crawled out of, no one will smell the stench of shit that still clings to you. I know. I remember.

I will revive the Lumen Dei, *and I will escape my master's mistakes. He believed the* Lumen Dei *to be a part of you, and thus insisted it be surrendered willingly. But I have long believed it was not the device that need be surrendered. It was your blood. And your blood I shall have.*

Be sure of this, little girl, as you can be sure that I will make whole what you have torn asunder. Someday, you will hear the call of the machine, and you will return to this dark coward's hole in search of it, and you will find only my words filling the emptiness.

Hear my words now, and hear them in the dark, night after night. I am coming for your machine. And when I find it, I am coming for you.

The symbol inscribed beneath the signature was the color of rust, and all too familiar. The *Hledači*—the first *Hledači*—had gotten here first. Aside from the letter, the box was empty; the *Lumen Dei* was gone.

"They've had it all this time?" I said, unwilling to believe it. "We went chasing after astronomical calculations and *dirt*, and all this time they've had it practically built and ready to go? And we basically gave them everything else they needed."

We had failed—failed before we even began. And not just failed, but helped *them* succeed. Whether Max had given them the other components willingly, or whether they'd taken them by force, that didn't change the fact that we'd probably delivered the whole *Lumen Dei* into the *Hledači's* open arms. I'd expected Elizabeth to somehow save me from beyond the grave—instead, I had managed, four hundred years after her death, to help the people who'd ruined her life. I'd helped the people who murdered Chris. They took him from me, they took Max from me—and in return, I gave them everything.

"Not everything." The heavily accented voice came from behind us. "Not you."

When I turned, the image was so incongruous it took me a moment to process what was happening. A priest. Holding a gun.

"On your knees," he said, raising the weapon. "Both of you."

"I thought you didn't speak English," I said. In the dark of the crypt Father Hájek looked older than he had before. Ancient. But the gun was a shiny piece of modern technology, and his hand didn't tremble.

His crinkled smile didn't reach his eyes. "I make do. When convenient."

Eli said something in Czech.

The priest shook his head and gestured with the gun. "Down. I'm waiting."

I lowered myself to my knees. A breath later, Eli followed suit. The empty box sat between us.

"No," Eli murmured, answering the question I hadn't bothered to ask. "I didn't. I swear."

But it didn't matter anymore, did it, whether Eli had led us into ambush or not. Here we were. Lost.

"Like I told your friends, I can't help you. I'm not your *vyvolená*. I'm nobody. So you might as well just go ahead and shoot." I couldn't believe how easy it was to say. Maybe because none of this could possibly be real. Somehow, after all this time, I was still waiting to wake up.

"Nora—"

"What? I'm tired of running, and I'm tired of waiting. Chris is dead because of me. Max is dead. Because they wanted me. Now they've got me. I'm just speeding us to the logical conclusion."

The priest's smile widened. "You have not told her."

"Nora." Eli swallowed. "He's not part of the *Hledači.*"

The thick gold chain hanging around the priest's neck had probably been there the first time I met him, but of course that day I'd had no reason to notice the spiked golden cross that dangled from it, a cross that looked more like a sword. And when I'd seen that cross painted across Eli's heart, I hadn't made the connection. Maybe I hadn't wanted to.

"Fidei Defensor," I said, my eyes fixed on Eli's face. I saw something there I'd never seen before: the bare truth.

I'm sorry. His lips formed the words. No sound came out.

Nothing more useless than a prayer for forgiveness.

"If she knows this much, she knows too much," the priest said.

I couldn't help it: I laughed. "Seriously?"

Father Hájek tilted his head, confused.

"The murderous psychopaths, the God phone, the *vyvolená*—fine. Crazy, but I'm in. I accept it. This? You're a priest. With a gun. Talking like you're in a Mob movie."

"Nora, don't."

"Or what, he'll fit me for some cement shoes? Schedule me for a meeting with the fishes?" The laughter bubbled out, and some small voice in the back of my head was timidly suggesting that hysteria was probably a less-than-helpful survival reflex, but as it had no more useful suggestions, I told it to shut up. "Why not ask your friend up there to strike me with lightning—less muss and fuss."

"You didn't tell me about the mouth," the priest said.

No wonder Eli had worked so hard to convince me that Max was playing the part of Thomas the betrayer in our little Renaissance revival. So what did it say about me that I'd so readily believed him? "You tore the letter yourself, didn't you?" I asked. "Why? You just wanted more time to watch me squirm before you delivered me to him?"

"I told you, I swear I didn't—"

"The Kostel sv Boethia marks the end of the path for those who seek the *Lumen Dei*," Father Hájek said. "And so we wait here, and we watch, and they deliver themselves into our hands. As have you."

Eli asked a question in Czech.

The priest shook his head. "English, please. You must forgive his rudeness, *vyvolená*. He is young."

Eli cleared his throat. "I said, 'What's with the gun?'"

"I warned you that this would end as necessary. You chose not to listen. She is a danger."

"You think I know too much? Trust me, I know nothing," I said. "And definitely nothing about you. Or any of this. I'm happy to keep it that way."

"It is what you know. It is also what you are."

"The *vyvolená*."

He nodded. "You are an innocent, and for what I must do I beg His forgiveness—"

"Feel free to beg mine, too."

"—but it must be done."

"We get her out of the country," Eli said. "You know you can pull some strings, hide her where they can never find her."

"Until the day she goes to them. *Kdo je moc zvědavý, bude brzo starý.*"

"Curiosity will kill you," I murmured.

"You see? You know much." The priest sighed. "Lie down, please. You may wish to close your eyes."

Do something.

383

Do anything.

"Assist her," the priest said.

Eli put his hands on my shoulders. The grip was gentle, the pressure firm. I let him push me to the stone floor. Stretch my arms out to the sides, press my cheek into the cold grime. The priest wore mud-spattered sneakers under his cassock. Beneath a sculptured saint, a spider skittered across its web. The stones butted each other with jagged edges, sharp and rough as the day they'd been laid—no foot traffic to smooth them down over the centuries. No visitors to this crypt, except the few who came to worship, the few who came to hide, the few who came to die.

I would not close my eyes.

"Please," I said. "I hate the *Hledači*. I hate the *Lumen Dei*. I don't believe in any of this—I don't have any curiosity. You let me go, I will leave and never, ever, ever come back."

"There is always a chance. And this we cannot risk."

"Because it would be so wrong for us to finally know?" Eli asked. "We've been throwing away our lives for centuries, for what? Because we're so afraid what would happen if someone finally asked the question and got an answer? Aren't you ever curious? Don't you ever wonder if we might be wrong?"

"She has corrupted you."

"It's not her," Eli said angrily. His hands tightened on my shoulders. "It's me, it's this, all of this."

"God demands faith, son. Some knowledge is not yours to pursue. God wills us to preserve his sanctity."

"Then she's right. Let God kill her," Eli said. "It's not our job."

"You are young, and there are allowances to be made," the priest said. Then his voice went cold. "But you will remember your oath. Hold her down."

Father Hájek knelt before me and drew a small vial from beneath his vestments. He poured a clear liquid into his hand, then brushed two wet fingers against my forehead. *"Per istam sanctan unctionem et suam piissimam misericordiam, indulgeat tibi Dominus quidquid per visum."*

Through this holy unction and His own most tender mercy may the Lord pardon thee whatever sins or faults thou hast committed by sight.

He pressed his oil-slick fingers to my ear. *"Per istam sanctan unctionem et suam piissimam misericordiam, indulgeat tibi Dominus quidquid per audtiotum."*

Through this holy unction and His own most tender mercy may the Lord pardon thee whatever sins or faults thou hast committed by hearing.

The last rites.

Eli leaned his head to mine. I bucked against him, struggling in his grip. If this was going to happen, it wouldn't be while I lay helplessly on the ground and tolerated his pathetic apologies. He squeezed tighter. The priest chanted.

"Per istam sanctan unctionem et suam piissimam misericordiam, indulgeat tibi Dominus quidquid per odorátum. Per istam sanctan unctionem et suam piissimam misericordiam, indulgeat tibi Dominus quidquid per gustum."

I was actually going to die.

"Get ready," Eli whispered.

I would not lie still; I would not close my eyes.

Please. My mouth formed the word, but I didn't speak it. I would not beg.

The sacrament drew to its inevitable end.

"Now," Eli whispered.

I held my breath, and he let go.

And lunged at the priest.

And tackled him to the ground.

And a gunshot cracked.

And I was on my feet, and running, up the stairs, out the door, down the alley, away, unbloodied, alive, free.

And the shot echoed in my ears, and I wondered.

I didn't look back.

17

I had to go back to the hostel.

I couldn't go back to the hostel.

I had to warn Adriane.

I couldn't lead them to Adriane.

I warred with myself—but all the while, I was running, and when I stopped, I found myself in front of the Golden Lion, because there was no other choice.

The room was empty.

I should have stayed with her, I thought. For a million reasons, I should have stayed.

I shouldn't have acted like I was alone.

Because now I was.

18

"That other girl left this for you," said the mulleted guy at the front desk, twisting his nose ring with one hand and holding out a torn slip of paper in the other. "She said I shouldn't give it to anyone but you."

She'd taken her chances with him after all.

She was safe.

> *They came looking for you. I hid. Meet you @ 9*
> *the last place we were us. Ditch Eli. Stay safe. A*

The last place we were us: It was in a different country, a different life. But I knew what she meant, and she knew I was the only one who would. The restaurant where we'd had our last dinner, where we'd had our last night with Max, and maybe she'd chosen it because it was convenient and easily alluded to and at the forefront of her mind, but maybe she needed to go back—to remember, one last time, being us, or to vanquish the ghosts—before we fled to the airport and never looked back. Maybe we both did.

But nine p.m. was hours away, and I couldn't stay where they could find me. They could find me anywhere.

So I got lost.

19

The sky was bleached of color. Fog shrouded the city; spires bled into smoky sky. Cobblestones shimmered, slick with rain. I walked aimlessly, my shoes skidding on wet stone. Fat drops splattered on saints and clocks and hunched shoulders and crumpled wrappers and spits of meat. Still, from the tip of every tower, bright flashes, cameras like lightning bugs, tourists watching the rain fall and the city skitter.

Always, in Prague, someone watching.

My father had taught me about palimpsests, age-stained manuscripts that had been written over again and again, one layer of meaning peeking out from beneath another, and another beneath that. Nothing is ever erased, he had told me once, not long before Andy was. There are always traces; there are always signs.

That was Prague: a palimpsest. Dead eras like onion skins, one atop another, post-Communist on Communist on art nouveau on baroque on Renaissance on late medieval on early medieval

387

and on back to the original settlement, the angry Bohemians and their warrior queen. Graffiti sprayed on Gothic churches, cubist facades on Renaissance palazzi, Lady Gaga tracks spurting from tiny speakers at the base of a baroque storefront housing a selection of nineteenth-century-style marionettes probably manufactured in China. It was a Picasso version of a city, all noses and elbows and foreheads jutting out at impossible angles, oil layered over newsprint layered over canvas, beautiful and terrifying at once.

It wasn't just the buildings; it was the people. History moved too fast here, washing over the city like a high tide that receded, day after day, each wave leaving its own distinctive detritus behind: the Nazis, the Soviets, the West. Imagine going to sleep in one city and waking up in another, still in the same bed, still in the same house, but with new laws, new uniforms, a new day outside your window. The old men who hoisted their grandchildren on their shoulders, the stooped women who collected tickets, they had been children in a city that spied on itself, that hid from secret police, that lost its jobs for speaking up or poached its jobs for telling tales, that was interrogated, that was locked away, that hid in dark rooms scanning for illegal radio broadcasts, that danced in the street as tanks rolled past, that spoke Russian and hated the taste of it on their tongues, that expected every day to be like the next . . . until one day, it wasn't. These men, these women, did they envy the generation of willful amnesiacs who had been born into capitalism and freedom and plenty and preferred to believe life had always been this way? It was easy to imagine, because it was what I would have wished for myself. The capacity to forget. To wash in, fresh and smooth, with every new tide, no yesterday, no tomorrow. You couldn't erase the layers; you could only hope to ignore them.

I shoved my hands into my coat against the cold, and my fingers closed against a scrap of paper in the pocket, in Max's pocket.

Wait for me, it read, inexplicably, in Max's hand. I dropped it in the gutter and watched his words dissolve in the rain.

Time passed, rain fell, I walked. There was nowhere to be but lost. Without meaning to, I found my way to the cemetery.

The cemetery was closed, safe from the twilight behind its stone walls, but there was some comfort in knowing it was there, the weathered gravestones and sighing trees a few feet from where I sat on wet ground, legs crossed, back pressed to stone, straining to hear a faint chant or melody or prayer leaking from the nearby evening worship but hearing only bells, distant churches chiming yet another hour. I listened and breathed and assured myself that I was still alive, and I sat there watching the sky darken, without knowing why. Maybe I was waiting for him.

And eventually that was where he found me.

20

"You wanted to know if I was sorry," Eli said.

I didn't know why I hadn't run. Instead, I let him lower himself beside me. I didn't want to look at him, but I spared a sideways glance. He'd wrapped a bandage around his left hand, and he winced as he shifted his weight onto his right leg. I didn't see any bullet holes.

"I am sorry."

"So you followed me. Again."

He shook his head. "I figured you'd be here. You have a thing for cemeteries."

It was the worst thing he could have said. Like he was inside my head, worming his way into the places I'd thought were secure.

"Don't," he said. "It's like the sixth or seventh place I looked. It was luck."

I wondered what he'd read on my face, that he knew.

"Is this where you warn me not to scream?" I said.

"You've got nothing to fear from me."

I forced a laugh.

"Did you miss the part where I saved your life?"

I ignored him. With the synagogue museums locked down for the night, Josefov had cleared out. The rain had tapered off, but a gloom hung over the empty street. It couldn't have been more than five or six, but it felt like the dead of night.

"I'm sorry," he said again. "I didn't mean to—" He stopped, and lowered his head to his hands. They were trembling. But when he raised his head again, his face betrayed nothing. "Will you listen to me? No more secrets. I'll answer anything. Just hear me out first."

"The truth," I said, the word a joke.

"The truth," he said, like he meant it.

More likely more lies, I thought, and I'd had enough of those. But what if they weren't?

"So talk."

"It wasn't all a lie," he said. "Everything I told you about my family, the way I was raised, that's true. My parents are Czech— but they're also *Fidei*. Like their parents, and their parents before that. Et cetera. We're born to the oath and the sword—that's what they believe, and that's what they taught me. Absolute faith, absolute obedience. The Church disavowed the *Fidei* centuries ago. It's only survived by enforcing an insane level of discipline. You do what you're told. You don't ask questions. Like my parents didn't ask questions when the *Fidei* sent them to America."

"Just following orders," I muttered.

"It's not like that. The *Fidei Defensor* have pledged their lives to protecting the soul of the world. They truly believe the *Lumen Dei* could destroy us all. Whether by bringing down the wrath of

God for trespassing our human bounds—or by blowing us all up when people like the *Hledači* get their hands on the fuse. They'll do anything to stop it."

"Including shoot random American teenagers."

He stiffened. "I told you I understood, about wanting a normal life. My parents were just pretending to be normal, to fit in. But I wanted it. You don't know how much. College, a life, everything. And this year I finally talked them into it. I got out. Met people who didn't have their destinies prescribed for them in the 1600s. People who'd been watching TV and getting drunk while I was memorizing the pressure points that would incapacitate enemies of the faith. I was going to do it. Tell my father I wanted out for good, that it was all crazy."

"And then what?"

"What do you mean?"

"You wanted out—to do what? Who would you be, if you weren't Eli Kapek, demented warrior of the faith?"

He looked blank. "I . . ." He laughed sourly. "I have no idea. Pathetic, isn't it? I like Stephen King. I like kickboxing. I like doing my laundry. Not exactly a recipe for a full and happy life. There's no dream deferred, Nora. There's nothing but what my parents gave me, which was no choice. About anything. From day one. I was done. And I was finally going to tell them. That's when we got the call."

"About me?"

"About Chris. The *Hledači* watch Voynich scholars. We watch the *Hledači*. Your professor's attack was a warning sign. The murder was confirmation. And because the only people who knew anything were a bunch of teenagers . . ."

"They sent you."

"It was supposed to be an honor," he said bitterly. "I was supposed to thank them for it. Screw that."

"But you did what you were told."

"Yeah. Like a good little soldier of the faith."

"And you used Chris's memory to get me to trust you. Which is disgusting."

"I did lose a cousin I barely knew to the *Hledači*. That was true."

"But it wasn't Chris."

"No. It wasn't Chris."

All the things I'd told him, the stories of us—and the things I'd told him about Andy, about me. Things I didn't tell anyone. For a moment, I wanted him dead. Not out of anger, or revenge, but because it was the only way to erase what he knew. To turn secrets back into secrets.

"And Chris's parents?"

"They're safe, like I told you. They think we're the FBI, and they're hiding out from the Mob."

"So you were there to find the *Hledači* or something? That's why you have all those files on Max?"

"Sort of."

"What does "sort of" mean?"

"By the time I got there, Max was long gone. We knew that. They didn't send me to Chapman for him." He stopped.

"They sent you for me."

"Yes."

"Because of this *vyvolená* crap."

"Because they knew the *Hledači* would be back for you, and that would draw them out."

"So I was bait." I waited for fury to overtake me, but either I couldn't be bothered to make the effort or some part of me knew I didn't have much right to feel surprised, much less betrayed, as if he had owed me anything, much less truth. I'd been very clear that he couldn't be trusted, and eventually, clear that he wasn't who he said he was. If I'd failed to reach the final conclusion, it wasn't because he hadn't left enough bread crumbs.

"I told them we should get you out of the country once we had Max. That it was enough."

"Apparently you don't carry much weight with the *Fidei Defensor* high command."

"You didn't want to leave," he reminded me. "You wanted to win. So I tried—"

"The torn letter. That was you."

He nodded.

"You stole the other half, to stop us from finding anything, and then—what? Changed your mind?"

"I went against the oath. And then . . . what I did today."

I realized it wasn't just his hands that were shaking. Faint tremors ran along his jawline, as if every muscle was straining to suppress some explosion from within. His skin, pale on the best of days, had turned a sickly paper white. His hands had receded into his cuffs, fingertips poking out like he was a kid who'd stolen his older brother's sweatshirt, and his expression matched the crime, guilty and watchful. It was the face of a boy waiting to be punished.

"Father Hájek, he was, like, your boss or something?"

"You could say that."

"And I'm guessing today isn't going to get you employee of the month."

His lips trembled more when he tried to smile. He didn't volunteer any details about what condition he'd left the priest in.

He swallowed hard. "So that's the story. Questions?"

"Why?" I asked. "Why help me?"

"What was I supposed to do, let him shoot you?"

393

"No, not today. I mean, yes, today. But when you changed your mind about hiding the last letter. And even before that. That first day in the church when you were arguing with Father Hájek. You were trying to help, weren't you? Get them to lay off?"

"I didn't say that."

"No, you didn't."

"Maybe I don't believe everything I'm supposed to believe," he said. "Maybe I haven't in a long time."

"So do you believe I'm the *vyvolená*?"

"I didn't," he said. "Not at first."

I groaned. "Come on."

"It was when you told me about your brother."

"That's why you weirded out," I said.

"It's a coincidence. Your brother; Elizabeth's brother. But it's more the connection between the two of you. I can feel it. I know you do."

"I never said—"

"You didn't have to. It's the way you talk about her. The way you treat the letters. The way you won't give up on her. How sure you were in the crypt."

"I came here for Max," I said. "I kept going for Chris. And to save myself. It's got nothing to do with Elizabeth Weston, or some imaginary connection between the two of us."

"You don't feel any connection to her at all?"

I didn't want to feel it; I didn't want to feel anything anymore. So I forced myself to laugh, then held up my hand. "God is not guiding this. I think I'd know."

"If you say so." He stood up, brushing off the grime and, at the same time, any indication of vulnerability. "We have to get you out of here. Out of the country. Tonight. They're not going to stop coming after you, and neither are the *Hledači*. And I am not going to let them hurt you."

I got to my feet. "Adriane's waiting for me. I have to make sure she's safe."

"Oh. Adriane."

"What 'oh'?"

"We have to talk about that, too."

"Careful, Eli."

"She told you to meet her somewhere, didn't she?"

"Because your crazy friends came after her. What else was she supposed to do?"

"I bet she told you not to bring me along."

"She doesn't trust you," I said. "Shocking, I know."

I couldn't have this conversation, because this conversation meant feeling something, it meant thinking about Max and doubting Adriane, and it meant pain. More of it. I was too tired.

Adriane was waiting for me, and my only priority was finding her, making sure she was safe, and taking her home.

"Look, I'm sorry," he said. "Maybe you're right, and it's nothing. Either way, I'm coming with you. And I'm staying with you until we get you out of here."

I didn't argue. As long as he was with me, I could be sure of what he was doing, if not why.

It had nothing to do with wanting his protection.

It had nothing to do with wanting him around.

"I have one more question," I said as we walked.

"Ask."

"What happens now? I mean, to you? After what you did?"

"What do you care?" he asked, in a low voice.

"You said anything I wanted to know. That's what I want to know."

The bridge loomed before us, a crush of people. I pulled Max's coat tighter around myself, digging my fingers into the rough wool. A blast of cold wind gusted from the east.

"I broke my oath," Eli said softly. "It's not a sin they forgive. My parents were always very clear on that."

"But they're your family."

He nodded, but not in agreement. It was more like he'd lost the will to hold his head up. "Yeah. They were."

21

He had, after all, saved my life. So I humored him. Adriane was expecting to meet me at nine; we arrived at eight. The empty plaza that bordered the restaurant offered few places to hide, but Eli deemed a couple large Dumpsters tucked beneath a stone archway good enough, and so, feeling like an idiot, I crouched with him behind the brown plastic bins and waited. The perch afforded us a clear view of the plaza and the mouth of the alley leading down to the restaurant, and faint snatches of conversation floated toward us as the occasional diners made their way toward the scent of food. But at this hour, there weren't many of them. And there was, unsurprisingly, no sign of Adriane, who had never been early in her life.

"This is stupid," I whispered eventually, my legs cramping up.

"So go inside. I'll wait here."

"Right. I'm trusting you to lie in wait for her."

"You know I wouldn't—"

"Forget it. We'll wait together. Just so I can be here to say I told you so when nothing happens."

She showed up as the bells were chiming eight-thirty. Half an hour early, but she raced into the plaza, ruddy-cheeked and out of breath, spinning in a slow circle, her gaze a lighthouse beam scanning the area—for us, I thought, though there was no reason for us to be there. Seeing her, knowing I hadn't lost the last person I had left, knowing that Eli had been wrong, that despite everyone else's lies and hidden agendas, Adriane was still simply Adriane, I could finally breathe again. Then I saw my mistake.

Actually, first I heard it, recognizing the irritated inflection of the words almost before I recognized the voice, so many times had I heard it directed at her. "You're late."

Eli's hand was over my mouth before I could gasp. Or scream. Or whatever the appropriate response would be to your dead boyfriend taking your best friend in his arms and slipping his tongue into her mouth.

Eli grabbed my shoulders, holding me in place, or maybe just holding me up. He didn't know me as well as he thought, if he thought I would fall.

It shouldn't have been a surprise, I thought, for the second time that day, as they came together, Adriane's calisthenically honed body twisting around his, lithe arms caressing, Adriane up against a wall, perched on his narrow hips, Max's greedy tongue roaming her lips, the nape of her neck, beyond, below.

It shouldn't have been a surprise, I thought, because Eli was right about the signs—Eli had seen them, Eli had read them, Eli wasn't blinded by his desperation not to know. What else had I decided not to know? What other rock-solid facts of my life were a lie, and how many rocks could crack before the foundation gave way, and I fell through to whatever emptiness lay below?

It shouldn't have been a surprise. But it was.

Wait for me, the note in the pocket had read, the pocket of the jacket that Max had slung over Adriane's shoulders, though I was the one he claimed to love and I was the one who'd been cold.

"I was worried," Adriane murmured.

"I told you I'd be fine," Max said. "Did you do it?"

"She'll be here."

"Alone?"

Adriane nodded, then kissed him again. I forced myself not to close my eyes. We were so close, and dangerously obvious, peering around a corner like cartoon detectives; all they had to do was decide to look—but their eyes were locked on each other. We were invisible.

"I'll be by the service entrance," Max said. "Don't wait too long."

"I got it. But I still don't see why we have to—"

"I told you, it's safer if you don't know. Safer for her, too. I promised you I could fix all of this if you just trusted me, didn't I?"

"Yes."

"And you believe me, don't you?"

"Yes."

"So we're good?"

She kissed him.

"I'll take that as a yes," he said.

"Once this is all over, we'll tell her about us, right?"

"Definitely. As soon as we're all safe and this is over. We've waited long enough."

"She'll understand." Adriane sounded unsure. That was a lie even she couldn't pull off.

"We'll make her," Max said. There was no uncertainty in his voice.

The worst part wasn't seeing his hands on her, or imagining the things I hadn't seen, the things they'd done together, the things they'd said about me—or worse, not bothered to say. It may have been the straw that broke the camel's heart, but it wasn't the worst part.

The worst part was knowing what this meant. It was all true. Max had faked his own death. Which meant Eli was right, and

Max was aligned with the *Hledači*. Which meant Max had done their bidding, had drawn me to Prague, had acted the victim, had manipulated us into tracking down the *Lumen Dei*, had cared only about the clues, the letters, the map. Which meant Max had been using me from the beginning, for my special *vyvolená*-ness and my stolen letter. Which meant Max, who had lied about who he was and what he wanted with us, had wanted only the *Lumen Dei;* the same Max who had stammered poetry and blushed at my touch and declared his love in a Wal-Mart parking lot, had killed Chris.

I wondered what Adriane had for him to take.

Some infinite time later, Eli grabbed my elbow and jerked me away from the sight of the two of them devouring each other.

"The service entrance," he whispered, and I nodded, mutely obedient, happy to follow anyone who had a suggestion for where to aim myself, for how I was supposed to get through the next several seconds, and the next after that.

He circled the restaurant, and I followed him.

He slid into a narrow gap between two large, whirring metal machines: cooling units or freezers or backup generators, I didn't know. I knew only that the entire area stank of fish and rotting fruit, and that I followed him there, too, squeezing in beside him. "'What fresh hell is this?'" I murmured, but Eli only looked at me in confusion. I wondered whether Max recited poetry to Adriane, too, or whether he saved that technique exclusively for the pathetic lovesick girls he wooed on *Hledači* command.

"Did you know?" I panned my gaze back and forth between the service entrance, the parking lot, and the river that curled around it, avoiding Eli, who had seen me see them, which was too much.

"I didn't know he was alive."

"Not that."

"I suspected something. I told you."

"But did you *know*?"

Silence.

"You didn't want to hear it from me."

I felt the bile rise again, tangy and sour. Eli touched my shoulder.

"Don't."

"Nora."

"*Don't.*"

Max's arrival shut us both up. He leaned against a truck with bright, cartoonish potatoes painted on its side that was idling by the service door and checked his watch. Then he checked it again, thirty seconds later, and thirty seconds after that.

My muscles were screaming for release: to leap out of the hiding spot and tackle him, pin him to the ground, interrogate him, my knee pressing down on his chest, or maybe his balls, forcing him to tell me who he was, how he'd survived the fall, why Adriane, why me. Whether any of it had meant anything. Or maybe I would just bear down on his trachea until time ran out.

These were not the kinds of things people did in the real world.

But then, we had left the real world behind. It was busy touring the Louvre and breaking curfew and sleeping through lectures on the French Revolution. In this brave new world, my world, there were clearly no restrictions on the kinds of things people did to each other.

Eli's hand clamped down on my wrist. I left it there. Max watched the door, which, after fifteen minutes, thirty minutes, an hour, never opened. And somewhere beyond it, presumably, Adriane sat at an empty table set for two, sipping her drink, waiting for her clueless best friend.

I could kill her, too, I thought. Smother her in her sleep, Max's coat pressed over her nose and mouth, but not her eyes, because that would deny me the pleasure of watching them fill with surprise, then confusion, understanding, guilt, and terror, before glassing over into a final emptiness.

A gaze blank and pitiless as the sun, I thought. Yeats.

Max would have been proud.

There was obviously something wrong with me.

By ten, darkness had descended over the back lot, the single lamp overhanging the doorway casting Max in orange. Adriane stepped out, her black hair glowing purple under the light.

"She never showed up."

How sweet, I thought. She sounded almost like she cared. Of course, probably she did—for Max's sake.

They argued. He told her that she had promised, that she had ruined everything. He accused her of warning me, or telling me too much of the truth too soon. Then she cried, and he held her, looping an arm around her waist, pulling her to his side, and walking her, head on his shoulder, toward the back of the truck, murmuring what I could only assume were sweet nothings, and I steeled myself for the inevitable end to the foreplay.

Eli had relaxed his grip on my wrist, and his fingers were only a gentle pressure against my skin, less a warning than a reminder.

When it happened, we weren't ready.

"I'm sorry," I heard Max say. "I'm out of options."

The truck doors swung open, and the *Hledači* swarmed. She disappeared into the horde, and it flowed back into the truck as swiftly as it had emerged. The doors slammed. The tires squealed. The truck sped away, Max at the wheel. That fast, she was gone.

22

One moment. That was all.

One thought—no, not even a thought, an impulse. Instinctive and inchoate.

Leave her.

I could turn my back. Go inside, sit down to a quiet dinner, board a plane, leave it all behind.

I could spin a tale for the cops; sell the letters on eBay, rare and certainly valuable pieces of the past that could pay for college somewhere far away, where I could major in something practical and meaningless that would bear no baggage and require no long, silent afternoons in a musty library, alone with my thoughts. Something like accounting or biology or graphic design that would guarantee a safe, uneventful life that had nothing to do with the past.

She had gotten herself into this, whatever it was. Let her take care of herself.

One moment, that was all, and then it passed. One moment, one impulse, wiped away almost as soon as it appeared.

But if nothing is ever erased, how can anything be forgiven?

23

There would be a ransom note waiting for us at the Golden Lion, Eli guessed, and there was, though not the madmen's message of cutout magazine letters Hollywood had led me to expect. Eli—forbidding me to go back there and, when I pointed out what would happen the next time he tried to forbid me to do something, reminding me that the *Hledači*, and most likely the *Fidei*, would be waiting—retrieved it while I waited at the cemetery, telling myself that it was me they wanted, not Adriane, and once they got me, maybe they would just let her go.

Sure. Because up till now they had certainly demonstrated themselves to be on the generous, merciful end of the psychokiller spectrum.

"Anything?" I asked as soon as Eli came into sight.

Only when I saw him did I realize how terrified I'd been that he wouldn't come back.

He nodded. "But first can I remind you of what you saw behind the restaurant?"

Like I would ever forget. "Give it to me."

"You don't know how long this has been going on," he said. "Max killed Chris. You know that now."

It was the first time either of us had said it out loud.

"For all you know, Adriane was a part of it."

"Not possible."

"How can you still be that naive, *now*?"

He couldn't understand, because we were all strangers to him. But Max and Adriane weren't the same. Max was an unknown quantity, a stranger who'd passed into our lives and been too good at being too good to be true. Adriane I'd known for years. I'd had dinner with her parents and stayed up until three a.m. listening to her rants about their meddling; I'd given her pedicures when she'd sprained her wrist and couldn't do it herself; I'd rubbed her back when she'd puked up a night's worth of vodka. I knew her locker combination and her favorite deodorant and the name of her first pet, a turtle who'd died when she was seven because she forgot it had to be fed. I didn't know everything, that was clear. But I knew enough.

"There's still such a thing as impossible," I said. "She's not a killer."

"You're in denial."

"I wish."

"Fine. Let's say she's not in on it. It could still be a trap."

"Of course, it's a trap. Let me see the note."

"I mean, it could be her trap. You could be saving someone who doesn't need to be saved."

But he gave me the note.

Vyvolená. We have your friend. Bring the map to
Letohrádek Hvězda, sundown tomorrow, and we
will give you the girl.

"It's obviously a lie," Eli said.

"Not necessarily."

"Have you lost it? They don't want the map, they want you."

"They probably want both," I said. "And if they get them, maybe they'll let Adriane go."

"They won't. They'll kill her. As soon as they have you. That's who they are."

"You're not exactly an unbiased observer."

"Chris was."

"You don't get to use him again," I said. "Don't even say his name."

"Even if they're telling the truth about letting her go, so what? Are you really willing to trade your life for hers?"

Even I was surprised to find the answer so simple. Adriane wasn't a part of this, not really, and no amount of screwing Max would change that. It wasn't about her, and it wasn't even about Chris, not anymore. It was about Elizabeth, and it was about me: If I didn't go to them, they would keep coming after the people I loved, or thought I did. They wouldn't stop until I stopped them, or until they got what they wanted.

Either way, it ended tonight.

"No," Eli said. "You don't know what they'll do to you."

"They'll use me to get the *Lumen Dei* to work, right? Isn't that the deal with the *vyvolená*? Is that what you're really worried about here? Keeping humanity pure and ignorant, holding off the apocalypse?"

"I'm worried about you," he said.

"You don't get to do that, either."

404

He sighed. "If we're going to do this, we'll need help."

"The cops?" I said, though I knew that wasn't it.

"If you think they'd believe your story and come rushing to the rescue. We do have the ransom note. . . ."

"We also have a warrant out for our arrest and some kind of Interpol most-wanted alert. So not the cops. You want me to team up against these nutcases with the other nutcases. Who, not incidentally, also want me dead."

"Let me take care of the *Fidei*," he said.

"I feel better already." I allowed myself a faint smile. "Adriane was right, you know. Seems like someone like you, who does this kind of thing on a regular basis, really ought to have a gun."

"Funny you should mention that." He reached into his pocket and pulled out a palm-sized black revolver I recognized, as a few hours earlier I'd been staring into its muzzle, waiting for a bullet. "Now I do."

24

"I don't see them," I said, more nervous than I thought I'd be. We'd gotten off the metro at a stop a couple miles from the Letohrádek Hvězda and were taking a circuitous route toward the hornet's nest. *This is me being brave*, I thought, watching my traitorous feet carry me, one step after another, toward whatever was going to happen next.

"Because they're good at what they do," Eli said. "But they're watching. As soon as we find Adriane, they'll move in."

"You hope."

"We can trust them."

"You broke your oath," I reminded him. And then there was Father Hájek, whom I still hadn't asked about. But Eli had his gun. "They're not exactly your biggest fans. Or mine."

"This isn't about us. They'll never let the *Hledači* activate the *Lumen Dei*. They'd burn the place to the ground first."

"With us inside," I muttered, but I kept going. The map was tucked into its money belt again, wedged safely between my hip and my jeans. Not because I believed the *Hledači* had any interest in Elizabeth's cipher now that they had what they wanted, and not that I believed it would bring me luck—if anything, the letter had proven itself a Typhoid Mary, gifting everyone it touched with a fine helping of plague—but because the letter had been the beginning, and it felt only right that it should be present for what promised to be the end.

A block later, we hit a wall of people, lining the wide boulevard shoulder to shoulder as they munched on fried dough, slugged back beer, and roared with excitement as a pageant processed down the street, radiant Amazons in medieval warrior garb firing rubber arrows at a barbarian horde. Wheeling majestically through the battle was a massive float whose speakers blasted some kind of Czech fight song at the eager crowd. Atop the float, a Bohemian queen waved from her golden throne, Libuše herself, watching her faithful maidens spill the blood that had marked the birth of Prague. This was no tourist spectacle—those were Czech toddlers on their Czech fathers' shoulders, waving tiny Czech flags and shouting lisping Czech encouragements to the passing Czech warriors. But, except for the lack of cotton candy and Yankees bashing, it could have been any New England parade on any dreary, cold New England day. Headache-inducing under the best of circumstances. Nearly murder-inducing under these. Especially when the crowd surged into the gap between me and Eli, and he disappeared into the sweaty, sugar-buzzed sea of people.

I caught sight of his head bobbing through the crowd, a few

feet ahead. "Eli, wait up!" I called, trying to muscle my way through the crowd, one jabbing elbow at a time.

Somehow, he heard me over the trumpets and war cries, and turned back—just as a steel baton slashed down toward his head.

"Eli!"

The baton made contact. His eyes widened, his mouth twisted in what almost looked like a smile, as if, a connoisseur of such things, he couldn't help but appreciate the efficiency of the attack, and then he dropped out of sight. "Help!" I screamed, my voice pitiful and small in the din of the crowd, and I pushed forward, saw Eli on the ground, a circle of concern forming around him, saw the hand that held the baton attached to a man in a police uniform, a man who spotted me and knew I saw his costume for what it was. There was a sharp pain at the back of my head, and I saw, though I had always believed that was just a story, spots, bright and fiery, dancing before my blurry eyes, and then I saw nothing.

25

Bones glowed white in the candlelight. Curtains of leg bones swaying in a chill breeze, finger bones and vertebrae ribbing a vaulted ceiling, four pyramidal pillars of skulls, each with a stout white candle lodged in its jaw, dull yellow light flickering in its hollow eye sockets. Bones, jumbled, jagged, stacked from floor to ceiling, a wall of bones, the cracked shards serving as mortar, layers and layers of skulls as bricks. A candelabra of bones dangling above me. A mosaic of bones at my head, an altar of bones at my feet. A church of death, and surrounding me, at five points, death's harbingers, one at each outstretched arm and leg, and—though I couldn't see him with my neck strapped down,

407

I could feel his cold hand on my cheek—one at my head. Their hoods were drawn back to reveal faces with hollow eyes and flesh pulled taut over their skulls, as if they were dead, too, as if they were no more than blood and bones.

My head hurt.

Leather straps bound my ankles, wrists, and neck, pinning me flat to a hard wooden board, suspended a few feet above the ground. I could hear my heart beat. The straps had little give, but I could twist my head to the left and right, make out the men who surrounded me and the gathered crowd just beyond them, Max and Adriane at the fore. Two robed men held her in place; it took me a second to remember where I'd seen her frozen expression before, and then I got it: the night of the murder. And afterward. In the mental institution. A column of bones stood on either side of me. The one on the left towered over a strange contraption of wood and gold, with gears like clockwork, circled by golden orbs like planetary epicycles. Around them wound tubes of spiraling waterwheels, awaiting the fluid that would give them life. It was larger than I'd imagined, with space for a man to slip his head between the orbs and carefully align his gaze with the transparent central sphere, which held a pocket of sacred earth. So this was it, the *Lumen Dei*, paid for in Chris's blood. And that was by design, wasn't it? The machine bound together the four elements: It took blood to make it run. Which explained the small card table on my right, bearing two far simpler objects. A glass vial, and a knife.

A voice by my head spoke in Czech. I caught only one word: *vyvolená*.

The man at my feet responded sharply. His robe was white and banded at the waist by a gold braid. I'd seen him before, on an altar; up close, his eyes were even emptier.

"No!" Max cried, alarmed. Then he said something in Czech, and though it made perfect sense that this was yet another secret

408

he'd been keeping, the smallest and least harmful of all, I started in surprise to hear the familiar voice curl itself clumsily around the foreign words. Somehow, it meant this was all real; Max was a stranger.

"Your Czech hurts my ears," the *Hledači* leader complained, in mellifluous English. "Your mother taught you poorly."

Max bared his teeth, then visibly caught himself. He bobbed at the knee, a ludicrous curtsy-like gesture. "*Má slova neumí vyjádřit moji věrnost.*"

"*Ne!* English!"

"Apologies, my master. She trained me as well as she could. If my language is weak, my loyalties are strong."

Max had never told me much about his mother. I wondered if he'd grown up like Eli, raised in a house of traditions and secrets, bred for lies.

"It is not the strength of your loyalty that concerns me, but its subject." He flicked a hand, lazily, at the men beside Max. "*Zabij ji.*"

"You swore you'd spare her," Max said in alarm, and it took me a moment to realize it wasn't my life he was defending. Adriane didn't react. The man beside her slipped a hand into the recesses of his robe and drew out a gun.

"Only you are to blame for setting these events in motion."

"I was doing what I was told!" His whine made him sound like a terrified child, but not the kind you feel sorry for—the kind who sets his sister's hair on fire, again, then feigns tears when the punishment gets handed down.

"You were told to retrieve the map. Not to kill the boy—"

At this, Adriane wheeled on Max, her eyes wide. A hand clamped down on her arm, but she seemed not to notice. "You said you didn't." It was a church voice, hushed and afraid.

"I swear, I didn't. . . ." Max hesitated, eyes bouncing back and

409

forth between his mistress and his master. "I didn't mean to. It was all an accident. I couldn't help it!"

"Yet you left this one alive," the leader said.

"I made sure she wouldn't remember what happened."

"You? It was *you*!" Adriane screamed. "Nora, I didn't know, I promise, he lied to me, he told me he didn't—and I didn't know they were going to do this to you, I'm sorry!" She lunged toward me, but they held her back, kicking and struggling—and it was ugly, as Adriane was never ugly, ungraceful and clumsy and brutal. "Please!" she screamed as a hand clamped over her mouth and a gun dug into her side. And then there were only soft whimpers and tears.

The leader continued as if nothing had happened. "The toxin is unreliable. You know this. And yet." He shook his head. "You have brought us what you promised, and I am truly sorry you will not witness our final glory. *Zabij je oba*."

As robed figures moved in on both sides of Max, the meaning of the command was unmistakable.

"Stop!" I shouted.

The slap came so hard I nearly blacked out again. There was an iron tang of blood on my lips. The room went absolutely still. A sharp report cut through the silence, and behind me, a groan and a thud. The *Hledači* leader slipped a small revolver back into his robe. "You are *vyvolená*," he said. "You are not to be touched." He turned to face the small crowd assembled for the ceremony. "*Je to jasný?*"

They nodded quickly. Understood. So I had more value to him than his own people. That had to be worth something.

"You can't kill them," I said.

He moved toward me with a liquid grace, his face looming over mine, every wart and wrinkle cast in sharp relief by the candles that ringed my body. He had shot one of his own men

410

for striking me, but I couldn't forget the knife. Or the straps that would hold me in place if he chose to slide its blade across my throat. "You are *vyvolená*, but I am the master. You do not give me orders."

"Yes. I am *vyvolená*," I said, hoping my voice didn't shake. "Elizabeth Weston's blood runs through my veins. Which means the *Lumen Dei* is part of me. That's what you believe, isn't it?"

The leader's face betrayed no surprise at my words. It betrayed nothing.

"Something went wrong, the first time they tried to use it, right?" I was talking fast, thinking faster, but it was a race to nowhere, because all I could see at the end was death. "The blood sacrifice wasn't given willingly."

"A willing sacrifice is not required."

Steady. "Are you sure? Because Elizabeth Weston herself says differently. That's the secret of her father's creation—only one with a spiritual connection to the machine can judge one worthy to use it."

"These are lies." But he didn't look certain.

"Without spiritual purification, there can be no ascendance. God has his standards."

"What would you know of God?"

"You know I stole the map—didn't it occur to you there were more letters? Maybe some that I didn't tell your little lackey about? You said yourself, he's incompetent. He missed some things. Big things." It was a lie; it was also, somehow, the truth. I knew more than I should have, more than he did—because I knew Elizabeth. And they were right about one thing. The *Lumen Dei* was a part of her.

The leader shook his head. But: "What do you propose?"

"I'm willing," I said. "I'm honored to take on my birthright. You think you were playing me—but don't you think this is

411

exactly where I want to be? This place, this moment, with the *Lumen Dei*." He would want to believe it, I hoped, because surely he would prefer a *vyvolená* who accepted the mantle with pride. "And we will face eternity together, but only if she lives."

"What the hell are you doing?" Adriane screamed.

"Shut up, Adriane." But it was unnecessary. They'd already muzzled her again.

This was crazy; this was right. My words felt true. I was strapped to a table in a church of bones. He held the knife. But—I could feel it—I held the power.

"Your friend." The leader nodded. "The girl, yes? And what of the boy?"

I twisted my head toward Max. Max, who had brought me to this place, and watched them tie me down. Who had kissed me softly under starlight, my face cradled in his hands, bathed in his whispered promises. Who had slid a blade into Chris's chest and torn what couldn't be fixed.

"Him too," I said. Not for him, for me. "He lives."

26

It didn't hurt as much as I'd expected. And then, as the knife cut deeper, it hurt more. The leader held my right arm in a gentle grip, and I didn't struggle. Together, we watched the blood from the shallow cut drip, drip, drip into the glass vial. He frowned, and carved a deeper slash. The drip turned to a flow. I should have eaten more today, I thought, with only a tinge of hysteria. This didn't seem like the kind of blood donation that would be rewarded by a sugar cookie.

The glass filled with red. "Enough," he said, and tied a dirty rag around my arm. Good thing long-term risks of infection seemed like something else I probably didn't need to worry about anymore. He turned to the *Hledači* and said something in Czech. They dropped to their knees, heads lowered. Then he, too, knelt before the *Lumen Dei*, the vial of my blood in his hand.

"*Děkuji, vyvolená.* We and our ancestors have waited centuries for this day. We have fought many battles. Weathered many storms."

Slaughtered many innocents.

"And now it is time."

It was, and I was ready. "I have given you my blood willingly," I said. "Now I give you my judgment. And I judge you . . . not worthy."

There was a chill gust of air, as if the room itself had gasped.

"I am *vyvolená*," I said. "And I cannot lie. You are not worthy of the *Lumen Dei*."

"Only the Lord can judge me."

"Maybe," I said. "Maybe not. But who knows, one of your friends might be worthier. . . ."

"*Ne!*" he snapped, as I knew he would. "It will be me. And it will be now."

He tipped the vial of blood into the funnel-shaped opening at the top of the device. It trickled through the tube, setting the wheels in motion.

It wouldn't work, I told myself. Of course it wouldn't. And when it failed, they would believe it was because of me. They would believe my will had been made manifest.

It wasn't much of a plan.

The *Hledači* leader wrapped his hand around a small lever on the side of the machine, and drew in a deep breath. "*Pater noster, qui es in caelis, sanctificetur nomen tuum. Adveniat regnum tuum. Fiat voluntas tua.*"

Our Father, who art in heaven, hallowed be Thy name. Thy kingdom come; Thy will be done.

413

He pulled the lever.

For a moment, nothing happened. Then the gears ground to life, and the golden orbs began to spin. Slowly, at first, then with breathtaking speed. I couldn't understand what was powering the device—there was no battery, no engine, nothing but the gears, the alchemical liquid that coated them, the dust at its center, the blood. It was impossible. And suddenly, I was afraid. Not of the knife, not of the crazed cultists, not of what would happen when the *Hledači* discovered the machine didn't work.

I was afraid of what would happen if it did.

The *Lumen Dei* began to glow. The *Hledači* murmured softly, as one, their raised faces reflecting the eerie light, *"Fiat volunta tua, fiat volunta tua."*

Their leader unleashed an orgasmic groan, and suddenly the machine went dark and he was the one glowing, as if he'd sucked the light into his body. It shined through every orifice, his face a sun, lit nearly translucent from within.

Then he began to melt.

At first, I thought it was a trick of the light. But he staggered backward and grabbed my wrist, his fingers warm and sticky. In a sudden spurt, blood gushed from his eyes and ears and nose, a fountain of red that spattered against me like a warm rain. Screams filled the chamber, then footsteps and the rattling of bones as the *Hledači* dissolved into panic. But I was trapped beneath his looming body, its limbs flailing as if detached from his nervous system and eager to make a break for it. His face had gone hollow, cheeks and nose and forehead collapsing in on themselves, and for a moment, his mouth a perfect O of horror, his face unnaturally long, flesh stretching like taffy over his bones, he looked like a work of gruesome art, the inhuman embodiment of fear in shapes and colors that could only exist in a nightmare imagination—and then the mouth caved in, and with it, the rest of him. There wasn't even a thud as he dropped to the floor, more like a liquid thump, like a pile of sodden rags.

"He wasn't worthy," I said loudly. "Who's next?"

There was an explosion. I craned my head back as far as it would go. The door to the church had been blown off its hinges. The *Fidei Defensor* surged into the chamber, Eli at their fore. The *Hledači* swarmed. Shouts echoed as they raged at each other, the *Hledači* massing before the *Lumen Dei,* a united front to keep the *Fidei* from poaching their treasure. Gunshots rang out. Candles toppled. Flames licked bones. Robes billowed, tore; holy men wrestled one another to the floor, and somehow, over the din, Max's voice. "Run!"

His fingers fought with the leather straps, struggling to unbind them as his brothers-in-lunacy were preoccupied. The restraint at my neck, first, then my arms, so I could hoist myself up and free my own legs, hardly able to believe that, whatever happened next, I wasn't going to die on that table, by that knife.

"I said run!" Max shouted angrily, but his grip on my arm was suddenly painful, and he had a gun in his hand, digging into my stomach. Adriane stood before us, tears streaking her cheeks, arms out, palms up in supplication, head shaking back and forth in a fierce and persistent no. And I understood: He wasn't shouting at me.

"Follow us and I'll kill her," he told Adriane. "Get out of here."

She didn't run. She didn't follow.

Max scooped up the *Lumen Dei* and jammed the gun into the small of my back. "There's a door to the left of the entrance," he growled, his lips at my ear. "We'll stay along the wall. Be smart."

No sudden moves, he meant. *Don't do anything stupid,* he meant. *This isn't an action movie,* he meant, and I shouldn't make the mistake of believing that I had it in me to save the day. We moved quickly, crablike, our backs to the wall, the gun never straying from its target, any *Hledači* that spotted us taken down by the *Fidei*, and vice versa. I saw Eli, standing over a toppled pillar of bones, fending off a *Hledači* knife. I saw him see me, and the understanding that passed over his face when he realized that wherever Max was taking me, he couldn't follow.

"Don't do this," I said, over and over again. "It's me, Max. Please."

He pushed me through a low door behind the nave, then up a narrow stairwell into another chapel, where we didn't even pause. "There," he said, shoving me toward a dingy door that creaked open to reveal a ladder.

"Max, come on, you're not going to shoot me." But it wasn't Max behind me. It was Chris's murderer, the person who'd stabbed him six times and left him to die in a pool of congealing blood. I climbed.

"I didn't mean to kill him," he said from behind me. It was the whine of a child who hadn't gotten his way. "He just had to give me the letter. But he wouldn't. If he'd just done what I told him to do, everything would be different. We would've done this the right way. It wasn't supposed to be like this. It was supposed to be beautiful."

We reached a crumbling turret, its uneven parapet like a mouthful of broken teeth. A sparse graveyard spread across the church grounds, several stories beneath us. Dawn was breaking over brown countryside that stretched to the horizon. Small towns crawled up rolling hills, and in the distance, Gothic spires poked through the fog. "Down," Max said, and, in case I didn't get it, shoved me to the ground, kicking the wooden door shut behind us. It was a tight space, room for little more than him, me, the *Lumen Dei*, and the gun. The latter of which I could have lunged for and, with luck, capitalized on the element of surprise to turn it on him and pull the trigger without hesitation or ricochet. But the flip side of that bright idea was a bullet in my head, or a long, fast trip down.

I couldn't shoot him.

"I gave up everything for this. I did everything they told me to do. I found the *vyvolená*! Don't I deserve this?"

"Max, listen to me. There is no 'this.' You saw what happened down there. The *Lumen Dei* is a joke. Or a weapon. Whatever. It's not what you think it is."

He raised the gun to my temple. "Tell me I'm worthy," he said.

Why couldn't I just let him die?

"He didn't use enough," Max said. "That was his mistake."

"Enough what?"

In response, Max yanked me toward the *Lumen Dei* and, producing a knife out of nowhere, slashed my wrist, a single, deep cut running lengthwise up my forearm. Somewhere far away, there was pain. But I was transfixed by the blood seeping from the wound, a river of it, pouring out of me and into the machine.

The door thudded and shook with the force of pummeled fists.

Behind it, Eli shouted my name.

Adriane screamed.

The door held.

The blood flowed.

"You're killing us both," I told him. "For a fantasy."

The spots were back in front of my eyes, though this time they were more like stars, bright pinpricks dancing across Max's face.

"Tell me I'm worthy," he said again.

"What the hell do you care? It was a lie, Max. It's all a lie." Except it couldn't *all* be a lie, because the man had melted, right in front of me, burned from within by some kind of unholy fire. Because I had withheld my blessing? The machine was no joke. The idea that I could control it, that I had any power at all—that

417

was the joke. I had no power over Max. "Please, Max. This isn't you."

"You don't know me. Haven't you figured that out by now?"

"No one is that good a liar," I said. "You don't have to do what they say anymore. You can choose for yourself."

"Nora." He brushed his knuckles against my cheek, so gentle, so familiar, and despite everything, against my will, my body relaxed to his touch, for one brief second fooled all over again. Elizabeth would forgive him, I thought. She believed in God, in love, in penance and redemption. But he wasn't seeking redemption. "I have chosen. I chose a long time ago. You say you know me. So then you know—I'm worthy. Tell me."

"If I do, will you let me go?"

He cupped my chin and tipped my face toward his. "I need your blood. All of it, if that's what it takes. God will love you for your sacrifice. I will love you."

I spit in his face.

His knuckles reared back and his next touch was far from gentle. My head slammed hard against the stone ledge. "Tell me," he roared.

Sirens in the distance. The battered door shaking on its hinges. Adriane, still screaming, screaming. Blood, pumped by a heart that betrayed me with every beat, spurting from the wound. And Max, who I'd mourned twice, who I'd given too much, Max, the cockroach, who still lived when Chris was dead, asking me for the one thing he truly deserved.

I could feel the blood leaking out of me, bones and muscles desiccating in its wake, my head heavy on my shoulders, my free arm weak, the arm he held pulsing with draining life and at the same time dead, a pale, fleshy stick that might as well have belonged to someone else. I had waited too long to grab for the gun. But I didn't need it.

418

I was not the *vyvolená*. I was not Elizabeth. Some things I could not forgive.

"You're worthy," I told Max as Eli threw himself through the door and Adriane tumbled after him.

"I love you," Max said, to someone.

He pulled the lever.

27

He was right about the blood.

More blood, more power.

As the *Lumen Dei* whirred into action, the light gushed into him, and he released a small sigh. I might have imagined the words he breathed out, the whispered thank-you, before the flames burst from his body and the world caught fire.

Heat seared my throat as I sucked in lungfuls of black smoke. Tears streamed from my burning eyes. Adriane's hair was a conflagration of dancing orange flames. The smoke carried a cloyingly sweet, rotting stench that could only be burning flesh. Eli shouted my name, and then his arms were around me and I reached for Adriane, who held fast to a blistering, burning creature that once had been Max, that somehow still breathed and stood and howled though he was nothing now but flame, a golem of fire that lived only because he'd forgotten how to die.

Blood still flowed from my wrist, but there was enough strength left in me for Adriane, and I broke the human chain, pulled her away from him, as Eli tore off his shirt and smothered the flames swirling around her head.

"Run," he said, and this time she obeyed, flying through the doorway and down the ladder. I was halfway down when my legs gave way.

Eli caught me.

"That's two you owe me," he said as we reached the upper chapel. Coughs racked his body. Smoke billowed from the turret. He wrapped his singed shirt around my wrist, tight, and we both watched a stain of blood bloom across the white cotton. "We have to get out of here."

"I'm just waiting for you," I said, or tried to say, then sank to the floor.

He carried me down the stairwell, my legs hanging over his arm, my head lolling on his chest, and as we raced the flames past pyres of bones and fallen soldiers of God, *Hledači* and *Fidei* blood smeared together across the floor, he whispered to me, a litany of comfort, but it wasn't his voice I heard. It was Max's. It was his hoarse, whispered screams as he burned from within. It was his final goodbye. It was gratitude; it was accusation.

It was soundless, when it happened, when we emerged from the church and were rushed by cops and paramedics, and, as Eli reluctantly handed me off to them, as hands laid me flat on a stretcher, strapped me down, the end returning to the beginning, I could only look up at the tower that had become a column of fire, at the Max-shaped flames that launched themselves over the stone ledge and tumbled down and down, fire streaming behind him like the tail of a comet. There was no final scream. Just the blazing fall, and the spreading flames.

28

When we returned to the church two days later, the cops insisted on escorting us. I was surprised they'd let us go at all, but then, they had been remarkably accommodating from the start, agreeing to wait before alerting the international authorities until they'd put us on a plane back to the States. The cops wouldn't trouble us much there, either, Eli claimed, and I was experimenting with trusting him, at least a little. The *Fidei Defensor* had a long reach, and they owed us one.

With the *Lumen Dei* destroyed once and for all, I posed no further threat to the *Fidei Defensor*, or the soul of the world, and Eli had convinced them that both Adriane and I knew better than to think anyone would believe our story. The cops would get a different story, neatly packaged with a perfect fall guy. The *Hledači*—who, along with most of the *Fidei*, had escaped as soon as the cops had shown up, none of them ever expecting that one of their own would resort to secular authorities—were broken and purposeless, and presumably I was the least of their concerns. It was over. We would go back to the States, back to our families and our lives, and we would . . .

Well, that was a problem the *Fidei* couldn't solve.

I needed to see it one last time. The crumbling remains of the church, its plague bones laid bare to the elements, its graveyard heaped with ashes. It was the bones that had saved us. The bones, and Elizabeth. She'd written of the *Hledači*—or whatever came before it—taking her to a church that smelled of decaying skulls, a church by the Vrchlice River. Somehow, bleary and concussed and nearly trampled by a crowd in patriotic frenzy, Eli had put the pieces together and persuaded the *Fidei Defensor* to join him at Sedlec Ossuary, outside the town of Kutná Hora, by the banks of the Vrchlice River—Sedlec Ossuary, repository of the bones of seventy thousand plague victims, six hundred years old, and now a heap of rubble. It had only been a guess, he said. We had been lucky.

It didn't feel that way.

"How did you know what would happen?" Adriane asked softly. Other than the yes and no answers she'd given to the police, it was the first thing she'd said since the fire. Mostly, she cried. I didn't try to comfort her; I didn't want to know if she was crying for Max.

"I didn't." The three of us stood before the police tape, safe distance between us. Our police escort waited in the car. "Elizabeth said the *Lumen Dei* had the power to end the world. I think she meant her world. I think she meant Thomas."

Tears welled again, but she managed the ghost of a smile. "Dead-girl letters save the day." She cradled her bandaged hand, then played her fingers idly across her shorn scalp. It was disconcerting to see Adriane without her perfect hair. It would grow back, but she wouldn't be the same. "I thought I loved him," she said, staring rigidly at the remains of the church, away from me. "He wasn't like anyone I've ever met. And he treated me like . . ." Whatever it was, she swallowed it.

"Just tell me when. Before Chris died, or . . ."

"Before. Does that make it better? Or worse?"

I didn't owe her an answer; I didn't have one.

"Why?" I said, because it was all I could.

"Chris was yours. He was always yours. I thought . . ."

"You thought what?"

"I thought that made it okay. That Max was mine. I thought in the end I was doing us all a favor."

"Chris loved you," I said, and the truth of it was almost a physical pain.

She wouldn't look at me. "No, he didn't. And he would have figured it out eventually. So would you. Then where would I have been?"

"Not here."

"I wanted to tell you."

"But you didn't."

"Max said we should wait."

422

"Max said a lot of things."

"Honestly? I didn't think you'd be surprised," she said. "I know what you think of me."

"I thought you were my friend," I said.

"No, you didn't."

Adriane noticed everything, I reminded myself, even when she was pretending not to. I'd thought she was spoiled and selfish and an excellent liar; she'd lived down to my expectations.

She wrapped her arms around herself, trembling. "I didn't know," she whispered. "He promised me he could save us. I believed him."

She wasn't the only one, I could have reminded her. I could have held her, and given her permission to cry.

I couldn't touch her.

"I'm glad he's dead," she added. "I wish I'd killed him myself."

"No," I said. "You don't."

She turned away. Her shoulders shook.

"We should go," Eli said. "It's a couple hours back to the city. We don't want to miss the plane."

"You don't have to come with us," I told him. "You said the *Fidei* would take care of the cops."

"It's not like I have somewhere else to be."

My parents would be waiting for me at the airport. Like a firing squad, maybe, stiff and cold and—I could only imagine, had imagined too vividly—accusing me of breaking them, when they had been held together with little but Scotch tape and scotch on the rocks for so long. Or they would be warm, as warm as they allowed themselves to be, and I would let myself believe I'd underestimated them, that they were back and wouldn't disappear again, but then there would be awkward hugs and hovering and that glassy look in my mother's eyes, and the stench of desperation hovering around my father as he yearned to go back into hiding. They would fade away—and I would be left alone to face the people at school, and the reporters, and Adriane, and all the places where Max had taken my hand or breathed in my ear or told me he loved me, and the emptiness that used to be Chris.

But at least my parents would be waiting.

"I never really thanked you," I said.

"I'm waiting."

He smiled.

"Right. Thank you."

"You're welcome."

"Are you sorry?" I asked.

"About saving your life? Twice?"

"About"—I swept my hand across the wreckage—"this. All of it."

"I wonder about it," he said. "The *Lumen Dei*. What it could really do."

"I told you what it could do. You should be glad you didn't see it."

"But maybe you were right. Maybe they weren't worthy. And if—"

"No," I said. "No. It's gone. It's over."

"Someone will try to rebuild it," he said, and there was something in his voice, some hint of curiosity, that made me afraid. *Kdo je moc zvědavý, bude brzo starý.* "Knowing God, touching the ultimate . . . that's not easy to walk away from."

"That's not your problem anymore," I said, and willed it to be true, for both of us. "You're free. To live a normal life, remember? Kickboxing. Laundry. Whatever."

"It was never about being normal," he said. "Not really. I just wanted it to be my life. I wanted to choose."

"And you did."

424

"I did," he said.

Then he took my hand. His fingers were callused; his palm was warm. He squeezed, once, a question. I tightened my grip, only for a second, only slightly, but enough for an answer. A yes.

Adriane watched us, her eyes red. Two of us, one of her: Nothing was the way it was supposed to be.

Maybe nothing ever is.

"We should go," Eli said again.

Adriane's face went pale with panic. Her good hand was wrapped tight around the police tape, as if it were a security blanket. "I can't do this," she said, in a small voice. "Nora, what am I supposed to do now?"

"You go home," I said, Eli's hand warm in mine. I couldn't give her my other hand. I still couldn't touch her. I couldn't smile. Not here, where the smell of grass and leaves was tinged with an acrid edge of smoke, where skulls watched us from piles of toppled brick and stone, where a small red flag marked the scorched earth where Max's body had burned to nothing. She had taken too much away, and even if she hadn't meant to, if she hadn't wanted to, she was still the only one left to bear the blame.

But she was the only one left, and I couldn't leave her, too. "We go home."

29

No trace of the *Lumen Dei* was ever found. No mourners came forward to claim Max as their own. No one was arrested for the destruction of Sedlec Ossuary, which was written off in the Czech press as, officially, a tragic accident that claimed one innocent life.

It had claimed both more and less than that.

We tried not to talk about what the *Lumen Dei* had done, and why. Whether it had been supernatural, demonic, divine, or just the combustive force of four-hundred-year-old chemicals, I didn't want to know. Trying to find the answer would be too much like trying again.

Amid the ashes and the bones, investigators found a letter, miraculously unharmed, which was eventually donated to the libraries at the Strahov Monastery.

Eli tracked it down for me. I was too afraid to ask him whether he still cared, or why. I was almost too afraid to read the letter. But I had to know.

I had to know, brother. I had to see. The machine was a part of our Father, and so a part of me. And after all I had done to bring it into this world, I had to know what would be done with it. Václav had me deliver the Lumen Dei *to a crumbling house not far from where our Father once lived in Nové Město, and it was there I returned, day and night, watching and waiting, until it was time. My reward, his men said, would arrive once they had activated the machine and had proof that I had delivered it intact. Until then, I dared not face Groot, dared not face our Mother or Thomas, and so I became a ghost, haunting my own life, and haunting the thieves who had helped steal it away. Through a small grate at the base of the western wall I peered into their dark lair and saw all.*

Václav was not their leader, I understood this at once. He had betrayed Groot only to fall at the feet of another master, a man with eyes as silvery as his hair, whose face I recognized from those long-ago séances our Father performed, and thus yet another of our Father's maxims was borne true: A man has no greater enemy than his greatest friend. Floating through my memory was an image of him leaning over a smoking cauldron,

426

his face illuminated by the glowing metals within—his face, and the faces of Groot and our Father—but as I reached for it, the image burst, delicate as a soap bubble, gone forever. His name escaped me, but it did not matter then, and it matters less now.

The workings of the machine baffled them, even Václav, who had been so instrumental in its creation, but they swiftly found the cure for that ail, in Groot himself. I saw the great man brought to his knees, bound and gagged, cursing Václav and Prague and the Emperor and God, and then silent, as, infuriated by his refusals, his loyal servant slit his throat. With his final breath, he cursed them, and me.

—The girl. She will save you. Or destroy you.

Death took him, and I will never know his meaning. But I do not doubt my powers of destruction.

The silver-haired man spoke, and beckoned into the darkness.

—We know enough to begin. Ready the source.

I had to see, but I would do anything to unsee this. Thomas, bound. Thomas, quaking. Thomas, dragged out of the shadows and placed before the Lumen Dei. He did not struggle. Not even when he saw the knife.

The sound that ripped open the night was the sound of my heart, screaming his name. They say life is an endless circle, the snake that devours its own tail, and it must be true, for here I was back again, cowardly and hidden, as dark forces menaced the one I loved the most. I failed our Father. I would not fail Thomas. It was not a thought but a need that

drove me to my feet and into the house, flying at the silver-
haired man, at Václav, at Thomas, my arms outstretched in
useless supplication, my lungs bursting with the pathetic cry.
No. No.

No.

I had no weapon. I had no power. I had nothing but the
will to save him. And that was not enough.

—Take her out and dispose of her.

It was the silvery man, who had no doubt patted my
shoulder or stroked my head when I was a child, who spoke.
But it was Václav who gathered me up with his clawlike
fingers and dragged me away. Thomas looked at me only once
through this nightmare, and that was the moment the knife
plunged into his heart.

The knife, wielded by the silver-haired man. In his other
hand, he held a silver goblet to catch the gush of blood.

The screams left me. It felt as if life itself left me, draining
out as quickly as it drained out of Thomas, an endless river
of red.

As the goblet of blood tipped into the Lumen Dei, *Václav*
dragged me from the building. I imagined I could hear the
gears whirring to life, filling the silence left by Thomas's
heartbeat.

I will never know what Václav would have done with me
that night, nor can I help but wonder whether escaping with
my life was a gift or a curse.

I could not cry for Thomas. Thomas, I knew, was gone.
And yet, as if the universe mourned his absence as fiercely as I,
the night filled with screams.

Flames burst from within the stone walls. Flames that danced with a white heat like nothing I have ever known.

Behind them, from the men who had murdered Thomas, came howls of agony as the fire consumed them.

Václav released me and ran into the night, screaming that I was a sorceress, that I had destroyed his master and destroyed all. As I had. I could not run. I could do nothing but watch the fire and listen to the screams. I imagined, in that hellish chorus, I could hear Thomas's voice, and when I close my eyes, that is how I cannot help but remember him. Bloody and tormented, as his body burned and the one he loved did nothing to save him.

The building burned through the night. Screams and panic coursed through the streets. Families fled, their belongings bundled in their arms, expecting the fire to burn through the district. But the flames never spread. Nor were they weakened by water, as a brigade of brave men dashed them with bucket after bucket. The fire was impervious, and soon even the most courageous had fled in the face of its might.

I stayed, waiting for it to consume me, waiting for something to which I could put no name, until the flames burned themselves out, and I faced the rubble. There were no corpses. Nothing recognizably human, nothing alive. Nothing but the Lumen Dei. It was intact. Waiting for me.

I could not rescue Thomas. I could only rescue the machine that killed him.

You see now, dearest brother, why I thought to dash it to pieces. Why I still long to do so.

Why I am afraid to try.

Only Václav survived that night. I know this because I have seen him, stalking me from dark corners and narrow alleys. Now he is the ghost, and I am the haunted. But I fear him not. What can he take from me? What remains?

Only you, and only this.

I bury its final remains here.

I confess, my brother, I have yet to decide whether I will ever guide you to this letter. It is our Father's legacy, yes. But it is a legacy of death. Was that its ultimate purpose from the start? Perhaps my Father's gift for Rudolf was not so different from the one I would have desired. Perhaps, had I trusted him, and followed his final wishes, Thomas would be with me now, and all would be different.

But the principles behind the device are sound, and I must believe that our Father, whatever his intentions toward the Emperor, pursued a higher purpose. The mind of God is knowable, and the Lumen Dei *is the path to knowledge. So perhaps it was not the device. Perhaps it was the blood. Thomas's blood, taken by force, taken with rage. I know of no God that would accept such an offering, and reward it with His grace. No God, that is, that I would choose to believe in.*

I do not know what to believe.

I made my choice, and I chose poorly.

Now the choice will be yours, and I tell you my story so you understand what this Lumen Dei *can do. Not just to stone walls, but to bodies, to minds, to loyalty, and to love. Today I lay the beast to rest, and I trust that you will resurrect it only if you can tame it, as I fear I cannot. I trust you more than I trust myself.*

I have lost so much, and yet every day I draw breath.
Every day I greet a new sunrise. I eat and speak and perhaps
someday I will even laugh once again. I have lost so much, and
still I live, because I have no other choice, and only because I
know one thing to be true, and I cling to that truth with my
life. This monster will never consume another soul. No other
will lose what I have lost. The Lumen Dei *has turned Thomas*
to ash. It has turned me to stone. But it will consume no more.
I end it now.

I end it here.

15 November 1600.

If she had broken the machine, rather than preserving it as her brother's birthright; if she had trusted her own choices, rather than leaving the choice to him; if she had understood that creating had given her the permission and responsibility to destroy; if she hadn't believed the *Lumen Dei* was safely hidden underground; if she hadn't left it there even when her brother was dead, even when there was no reason not to smash it to pieces, unless, secretly, she suspected one day she would want to try again; if she hadn't screwed everything up so very badly; if we hadn't; if I hadn't.

These were things I didn't let myself think about.

The *Lumen Dei* had survived one fire; I would not let myself think it might have survived another. I had seen the rubble myself; arson experts had been through it with shovels and magnifying glasses; there was nothing left.

Elizabeth had probably died believing she had ended it, believing it was over. She'd put the monster in the ground and told herself she was safe, to marry a man she didn't love and pretend the life she still had left was enough. It was like she said, she did what she needed to survive, and maybe even forget. She had lied to herself.

This time, it was the truth. The fire had done its job. The monster had been vanquished, never to rise again.

We were safe, I told myself. This time, it really was over.

And I chose to believe it.

AFTERWORD

It's said that Prague was founded by a witch—a fitting legend for a city that was, for decades, the center of Renaissance alchemy, astrology, mysticism, and natural magic. Sixteenth-century Prague was a strange and wondrous place, equal parts philosophical enlightenment and bloody destruction.

Its secretive leader, Emperor Rudolf II, collected paintings, relics, freaks, curiosities—but most of all, people. The alchemist Edward Kelley and his stepdaughter, Elizabeth Jane Weston, were among them. When Kelley landed in prison, where he died under mysterious circumstances, Elizabeth and her mother were thrown into poverty. Little is known about Elizabeth's youth, or how she surmounted her circumstances to become one of the most famous female poets of her age—I hope she wouldn't mind me using my imagination to fill in some of the blanks.

The letters and events in this book are wholly imagined, but informed as much as possible by the real people, places, and ideas that shaped Elizabeth's world. Rudolf's *Kunstkammer* was infamous, his illegitimate and sociopathic son, Don Giulio, equally so. Rabbi Judah Loew ben Bezalel's golem is apocryphal, but his stewardship of Prague's Jewish community through a golden age is very real. Cornelius Groot, though fictional, is based on Cornelius Drebbel, an eccentric Dutch inventor who became Renaissance Prague's master of mechanical and clockwork curiosities.

The Voynich manuscript, too, is real, its code still waiting to be cracked. Many have called it the most mysterious book in the world, and while decades of historians, cryptographers, and amateur enthusiasts have taken it on, the book guards its secrets to this day.

Only the *Lumen Dei* and its allies and enemies—the *Hledači* and *Fidei Defensor*—are pure fiction. But I'd like to think that in this age—with its golems and its magicians, its wild-eyed alchemists chasing the philosopher's stone, its scientists and philosophers reshaping human knowledge, its religious fundamentalists throwing one another out of windows and slaughtering heretics in the streets, its conquest of the New World and recovery of antiquity, its unicorns and dragons, its angels and demons—there might have been those who sought to combine nature and artifice in pursuit of an ultimate goal, and those willing to do anything to stop them.

Find out more about the people behind the characters and the truth behind the story at bookofbloodandshadow.com.

ACKNOWLEDGMENTS

I couldn't have written this book without my well-worn library card and the towering stacks of books it allowed me to cram into my apartment, including the particularly helpful *Elizabeth Jane Weston: Collected Writings* (edited by Donald Cheney and Brenda Hosington), *Prague in Black and Gold* (Peter Demetz), *The Magic Circle of Rudolf II* (Peter Marshall), *The Code Book* (Simon Singh), *Codebreaker* (Stephen Pincock), *The Problem of Unbelief in the Sixteenth Century* (Lucien Febvre), *Rudolf II and Prague: The Court and the City* (Eliška Fučiková et al.), *Rudolf II and His World* (R. J. W. Evans), *The Alchemy Reader* (Stanton Linden), *Alchemy Tried in the Fire* (William R. Newman and Lawrence M. Principe), and *The History of Scepticism from Erasmus to Descartes* (Richard Popkin).

These books informed the story; Arthur Koestler's *The Sleepwalkers* inspired it. Fifteen years ago, this book changed my life, and in a way, *The Book of Blood and Shadow* is a story I've been trying to tell ever since.

Unlike Elizabeth, I am not a poet, or anything close, and the Latin poem-cum-treasure map in Elizabeth's letter was written by Robert Groves. The fragment of an alchemical formula that Elizabeth buried was drawn from a real seventeenth-century text, *The Booke of John Sawtre a Monke;* the part titles are of more recent vintage, each borrowed from William Butler Yeats.

I'm also indebted to Marta Bartoskova and Jacob Collins for their respective translations of Czech and German, and again to Rob Groves, who supplied all the Latin and patiently answered my many annoying questions about the logistics of translation.

A huge thank-you to my editor, Erin Clarke, whose fierce belief in this book forced me to believe in it, too, and to Nancy Hinkel, Kate Gartner, and the rest of the team at Knopf. I also owe plenty of gratitude, and certainly a few cupcakes, to Holly Black, Libba Bray, Sarah Rees Brennan, Cassandra Clare, Erin Downing, Maureen Johnson, Jo Knowles, and Justine Larbalestier for reading early drafts of the book, and to my agent, Barry Goldblatt, for convincing me I could write it.

Finally, and most of all, I want to thank my history teachers, especially Steve Stewart, Jim Gavaghan, Joan Gallagher, Owen Gingerich, David Kaiser, Margaret Jacob, and Norton Wise—and all the others, from the high school teachers who put up with me when I found the whole endeavor to be a waste of time (and explained this loudly, at every opportunity) to the college professors who showed me my mistake and the graduate school mentors who taught me what really happened and indulged my tendency to wonder, *But what if?*

Most of them, I'm sure, don't remember me. But I remember everything.

ABOUT THE AUTHOR

Robin Wasserman is the author of the Cold Awakening trilogy, the Chasing Yesterday trilogy, and *Hacking Harvard*. She once studied to be a historian of science and, like her characters, is still reaching for answers in the past. She lives and writes in Brooklyn, New York. Visit her at robinwasserman.com.